The Aziola's Cry

A Novel of the Shelleys

Ezra Harker Shaw

ISBNs: 979-8-9873191-8-5 (pb);
979-8-9873191-7-8 (hc);
979-8-9873191-9-2 (eBook)

Book Cover Design: The Book Cover Whisperer, OpenBookDesign.biz
Interior Book Design: Inanna Arthen, inannaarthen.com

Library of Congress Control Number: 2023946223

First Printing: 2024

Names: Harker Shaw, Ezra, author.
Title: The Aziola's Cry: a Novel of the Shelleys / by Ezra Harker Shaw.
Description: [Roseville, Minnesota] : [History Through Fiction], [2024]
Identifiers: ISBN 979-8-9873191-8-5 (paperback) | 979-8-9873191-7-8 (hardcover) | 979-8-9873191-9-2 (ebook) | LCCN: 2023946223
Subjects: LCSH: Shelley, Mary Wollstonecraft, 1797-1851~Relations with men~Fiction. | Shelley, Percy Bysshe,1792-1822~Relations with women~Fiction. | Byron, George Gordon Byron, Baron, 1788-1824~Fiction. | Authors, English~ 19th century~Travel~Italy~Fiction. | Man-woman relationships~Fiction. | Open marriage~Fiction. | LCGFT: Historical fiction. | Domestic fiction. | BISAC: FICTION / Historical / General. | FICTION / Literary. | FICTION / World Literature / England / 19th Century.
Classification: LCC: PR6058.A684 A95 2024 | DDC: 823/.92~dc23

Printed in the United States of America

Part 1

'Do you not hear the Aziola cry?
Methinks she must be nigh,'
Said Mary, as we sate
In dusk, ere stars were lit, or candles brought;
And I, who thought
This Aziola was some tedious woman,
Asked, 'Who is Aziola?' How elate
I felt to know that it was nothing human,
No mockery of myself to fear or hate:
And Mary saw my soul,
And laughed, and said, 'Disquiet yourself not;

'Tis nothing but a little downy owl.'
Sad Aziola! many an eventide
Thy music I had heard
By wood and stream, meadow and mountain-side,
And fields and marshes wide,—
Such as nor voice, nor lute, nor wind, nor bird,
The soul ever stirred;
Unlike and far sweeter than them all.
Sad Aziola! from that moment I
Loved thee and thy sad cry.

Percy Bysshe Shelley

Prologue
July, 1822

*T*he seagull on the wing and the tumbling waves are all that see the lonely white house, *La Casa Magni*, staring out at the bay of *La Spezia*. No other buildings are in sight, and no people pass by.

It was supposed to be a secluded piece of heaven, but to twenty-five year old Mary Wollstonecraft Shelley, lying upstairs on a divan, it has become a prison. Outside the sun beats high and hot, as it does every day here, and the air above the stony beach will be dancing with the heat. But she has not been outside for days; she has been lying here, waiting to die.

Mary inhales, and she is the sound of a wave drifting out, and then, exhaling, rushing back in. Her body hurts so much even breathing quickly makes her wince. She has no idea how long she has been lying here, but she ought to try to get up; she really ought to say goodbye to Shelley. Afterall, she might not last until his return.

The tide is on its way out. She knows because this house stands too close to the sea, built for housing boats, rather than people. At high tide the sea crosses the threshold and claims dominion of the ground floor, forcing the human inhabitants to retreat to the upper levels where they are captive until the waters sweep away, leaving behind sand and shells and seaweed. Only Shelley could have fallen in love with a place as desperate as this, and now he will leave her here alone.

Has he already gone? She can hear, distantly, shouts out on the beach, perhaps her sister, her son, her friends, calling out to one another, perhaps farewell cries to the departing boat, but sounds reach her only faintly, as if she were already half in some other place.

Her eyes flutter open.

Sunlight pours through the open doorway of her sickroom, casting a living, ever-shifting mosaic of sea-reflections upon the walls and the simple white furnishings. A shadow blocks the light, passes through it, returns, and Mary looks up to see the silhouette of her husband in the doorway. With the light behind him, she cannot make out his features, only the shape of him.

"Mary! There you are," he says.

"Here I am, Shelley," she whispers, and she can hardly hear her own voice. "I was afraid you'd already gone."

"In a moment. The ship's ready. I wished to say goodbye."

"And I wish you wouldn't." She closes her eyes.

"Mary," he says, her name a reprimand in his voice. His footsteps cross the room to her; when his voice resumes, it is so very, very close. "If I could leave it another day I would, but our friends will be waiting."

She knows this. And she, she should have been beside him at the boat's prow, as they had planned; she should be well and strong, large with their unborn child, and her friends who have travelled across the ocean to see them again after so long should be overjoyed to see her in that condition of new life.

But instead, Mary is empty and scarred. The child that was to be has been torn from her, taking half her life force with it, and all that is left of her is fading away. Yet the world beyond *La Spezia* inconceivably continues, and her friends will be waiting at the harbour, oblivious to the tragedy. She knows this.

And yet, here she is, dying, and she cannot bear for him to leave.

Poor Mary! Shelley sees with concern that her face is paler than before, the shadows beneath her cheeks and eyes deeper, and yet just this morning she had looked brighter; how quickly change comes upon a person. There is no real fear though. He trusts the doctor's words that she will live, and is certain that even she, with all her fatalistic words, does not believe that this will be her end.

"I don't want you to go," she says.

He notices that she does not ask him to stay, but merely states the fact. He gently strokes her thick auburn hair, its colour rich in this light as loose strands catch the sun's golden flame and burn fiercely.

"You'll be alright," he whispers.

"I might not be."

"You will be," he reassures her. He thinks, but does not say, that they have weathered tragedies more terrible than this.

One might expect grief to lessen with experience, as a body that has sustained a blow and recovered better learns both how to dodge the worst and how to heal. But that is not the case. She will grieve this unborn child a long time, grieve it with the still and silent misery he knows too well.

That kind of grief is alien to his heart. His passions do not run quietly, but shout and scream, and run as far and as fast as they can.

And they are so close now, so close to achieving all that they have worked for. The journey he must make is for their success, and isn't there any part of her that still craves that?

"I'm afraid the tide won't wait for me, my Mary. Ned is already on board. But we'll be back soon, and I'll bring you Leigh Hunt and Maryanne, and all their noisy brood, and you'll be so happy to see them all. It'll be very good for you. Good for us all, I'd say."

There is a coldness in the looks she gives him then, an expression in her eyes regarding him as if from a great distance, as if nothing he does could possibly affect her now.

"Goodbye then," she says. "Take care."

He kisses her forehead, and stands up to leave.

Bright waves are beckoning on the waiting boat;

I should be gone, and yet I hesitate,
Still yearning one kind word from you, my Mary.

Oh, why can't you, great conjuror of demons,
Utilise your vast imagination
To understand the darkness where I dwell?

I cannot know that which you do not tell;
You show yourself to me so seldom now.
It wasn't always so. For once we were
Twin stars shining as one.

How long ago
that seems, and yet the years are not so many,
Since you and I were young, and thought nothing
More powerful in all this world than love.

I think that still; please say you do as well.

My Shelley, you were everything to me.
How did we come to this bleak place?

Chapter One: Shelley and Mary
London, 21st May 1814

A young person in love is a beautiful and reckless thing, like a flimsy boat dancing on dangerous waves. Percy Bysshe Shelley, who has been nurtured more by poetry than by family, is in love again, and it is driving him to distraction.

As he stands by the cold stone wall that keeps Londoners from the Thames, he sees the shadow of his ghost upon the water. A restless wind rushes upon both man and shade, fracturing the shadow, and urging Shelley on from this friendless moment. There is an appointment to keep, and a chance to see Mary, and the wind, like his spirit, wants to run. But, he consults his pocket watch, it is only a quarter to eleven, and he is not expected for over an hour. He must be good and wait.

The morning is grey, chilled, threatening rain. As ever, the river is a swaying forest of masts: boats throng the highway, navigating one another with frustrated patience, regardless of the restlessness of the weather. But Shelley feels it. His ghost upon the water feels it, and has come to warn him, or to welcome him to the storm.

To distract himself he takes from his breast pocket the only objects he has upon his person: a pair of books. Gifts, perhaps.

The first, at least, is easy. Charlotte Smith's poetry for Fanny Godwin on the occasion of her twenty-first birthday. If any friendship owes a token of gratitude, he muses, it is surely the friendship she has given him these past, difficult months. But the other book, that is less simple.

This gift has caused him much worry; it has worn down his fingernails until they bleed, because it is for Fanny's younger sister, Mary.

And therein lies the problem. For it is Mary who has become his first thought on waking, Mary whose words ring through his mind as he goes about his life, Mary whose image even now drifts along beside him, auburn-haired, slender, and bright.

Mary Wollstonecraft Godwin.

Under his breath he whispers her name, and the wind catches it with delight and hurries it off into the clouds.

It is not Mary's birthday. There is no reason to give her a gift. And yet, here it is. If he could give her the world, he would. But all he has is himself. The slight little book bears his own name upon the front page, and above it the title *Queen Mab*.

The copy has been specially bound and, upon a very reckless whim, he has scribbled her an inscription.

He cannot give her it, he suddenly realises, and he strides away from the river in agitation, stuffing the books angrily back into his pocket as he sets off into the heart of London, the wind leaping up around him, delighted to be on the move once more.

The binding, the inscription—both were foolish excess. They make the book special. Had he merely tossed her a worn copy and said 'have a look if you like,' that might be permissible. Fool that he is, he wanted it to be a gift for cherishing. But how can a married man of twenty-one give such an intelligent, beautiful girl of sixteen a gift like this in all decency? Does it not say—*Here, take this token, and know that I love you?*

Amid his anger with himself it occurs to him that, as there are three Godwin sisters he could easily have bought them all gifts on this occasion, and hidden Mary's alongside Fanny's and Jane's. No, no, he shakes his head as a distant thunder rumbles overhead, he must give up all idea of giving Mary gifts. His feelings for her are too strong, and he is bound—legally—to his wife, and must content himself with cultivating a philosophical friendship with this young genius.

His pace along the cobbled streets shortens his breath, and he pauses, bringing a hand to his ribs just as a fierce slap of rain slices across his face, startling him.

Above, the clouds have lowered and deepened their hue, the whole sky trembling with the weight of an imminent storm, one that shall be as brutal as it shall be beautiful, and much worth witnessing. Still, cover is wise and Shelley retreats to the lee of the buildings as the rain begins, but though he slinks along the periphery of a looming grey church he finds no ledge to offer shelter and the first advance of raindrops seeps through his clothes. Pulling his collar up and pressing the books deep inside his jacket—so especially afraid for the ink on Mary's dedication—he runs on, throwing himself at last into the doorway of an unbrightened shop, a coffin-maker's it appears.

No great traffic passes there, and he waits a while. On either side of him dusty, darkened windows are curtained within by respectful black velvet.

The street empties fast, and only a few walkers strive on, belligerent beside the hackneys and chaises; they are mostly servants, their heads low and their burdens high, other people's business more important than their own. All around the rain rushes down.

Shelley becomes aware, out the corner of his eye, of someone watching him from inside. He stills himself, and without turning his head from the scene on the road, concentrates intently, for he is convinced the face is looking at him. Slowly, cautiously, he turns only his eyes to look and, for the briefest second, there is someone else staring back, a strange, girlish face with boys' hair and boys' clothing, staring right at him through the glass and black velvet with absolute curiosity. He spins about to face the image fully, to confront the stranger, suspecting perhaps someone within, but no! How foolish he suddenly feels, it is only his reflection after all. The rain has dampened his hair and worry shadowed his face. He is only half himself. As suddenly as it started, the rain stops. Shelley steps away from the ghost of himself in glass and, hugging the books to his chest, hurries towards his Mary.

Mary Wollstonecraft Godwin sits in the window of her father's study with head bent to a book she has read many times before while ribbons of rain roll down the glass pane. A quiet inhabits the room, beyond which she can hear her family through the house. Her sister Jane sings a popular theatre song a floor or so below, her volume rising and falling in the intermittent way that suggests simultaneous employment in some other task, for Jane in full song is a marvellous thing. In Jane's quieter moments Mary catches the cadences of her father's voice, complaining some long story to his wife who expresses appropriate noises of astonishment and outrage as necessary. There is no noise in the house attributable to her sister Fanny, which is not surprising, for Mary can't think what noise she'd make. She must be minding the bookshop. Their little brother is surely still out at his tutor's, and Jane's elder brother, Charles, is not at home for he too has been sent away to Scotland, as Mary lately was herself.

All of which tells Mary she has some time for herself, and for her book.

The walls of the study are lined with books once neatly ordered, now slumped and slanted, pressed in and piled up in her father's disorder that no one dares disturb, but over time Mary has learned to slide out one volume at a time and return it exactly as left. This particular book has been retrieved and returned more than most.

It is a novel told by a woman in pain, a woman imprisoned by the man she loved, suffering all the wrongs that have been levelled at her sex, and addressed to the daughter she feared would never know her.

The novel is called *Maria* and was written by her late mother.

Its pages know Mary well and open obligingly to her favourite passage.

From my narrative, my dear girl, you may gather instruction, the counsel, which is meant rather to exercise than to influence your mind. − Death may snatch me from you, before you can weigh my advice ... Gain experience − ah! gain it − while experience is worth having, and acquire sufficient fortitude to pursue your own happiness.

Such a pained and tragic life poor Maria lived, much like her author's, and yet, even in the midst of it all, she did not counsel caution, but passion. These lines Mary knows so well, but she seeks them now in need of counsel, and of reassurance in her resolution.

Her attention is drawn away.

Something in the tone of the house has changed. A new timbre has entered the harmony and altered the entire effect. A voice rises through the house, like a skylark on the wing, bringing her joy as it speaks her name.

"Mary?"

She leaps from her seat, pulse racing, and sweeps back her thick auburn hair.

His voice grows closer. The stairs creak beneath his ascent. Silence. And then—

"Mary?"

"Shelley!" The cry peals out of her, and she pulls open the door to find him upon the landing, tall and thin like the silver birch, his flop of brown hair a little damp and wind-dishevelled, his eyes turned heavenwards, listening.

The expression on his face before he sees her is fragile hope and deep concern, a thousand doubts dragging down his lightness, but then he sees her, and an extraordinary change possesses him as happiness bursts across his countenance.

"Mary!"

She runs the short space between them and clasps his hand.

"I didn't know you were coming today!" she says.

"Yes, I've been in with your father. I'm leaving now. I wanted to see you before I go."

His eyes looking down at her seem fascinated, darting back and forth as they take her in, and she is glad she wore her purple tartan dress today, for he has mentioned that he likes it. Again, she recollects her mother's words.

Gain experience! — ah! gain it — while experience is worth having, and acquire sufficient fortitude to pursue your own happiness.

"No," she says, "you can't go just yet. Don't you have a little time to sit with me?"

The flesh of his hand lies beneath her fingertips, as warm and soft as if it were her own skin.

"For you, Mary," he says, his eyes still fixed upon her. "For you I have time."

As they enter the study, he looks up at the portrait of her mother with reverence, a gesture that does not escape her. Mary returns to her window seat, and Shelley draws up a chair from the desk to sit by her.

"So, you've been talking with my father?" she asks.

"I have," he says. "He's been giving me some very severe advice on my writings."

"Papa will not soften his words for anyone, I'm afraid. He can be harsh, but his advice is worth listening to."

Shelley nods. He does not look chastised; he looks happy.

"Tell me," Mary continues, "for I'm afraid I don't know, is your father a literary man?"

The laugh that bursts out of Shelley almost startles her. It is high pitched and loud, so unlike his gentleness, and she is afraid someone will come to scold them.

"He is not!" he says, recovering himself. "He most certainly is not. He is a parliamentarian, a philistine, hypocrite and petty tyrant. He does not approve of my life, and refuses to speak to me, which suits me quite well, for I do not approve of his life and have no desire to speak with him. My mother and sisters, I regret. But I am not welcome home." He shrugs away the matter, as if he really did not care, but Mary pities him, and feels he must be lonely.

"Then I think you all the more remarkable," she says. "To have become the person that you are without kind influence, that shows a true nobility of spirit."

He stares at her intently, something behind his eyes stirring in contemplation.

"I have a gift for you, Mary," he says after a moment.

"A gift?"

"Yes." From the breast pocket of his thin coat he takes a slim book. "You enquired about my poetry, and I thought you might like the opportunity to measure it for yourself. This is *Queen Mab*, it's probably my best work, published work, so far anyway, that is, it has many flaws, I see that already. And it is not a popular style, but..." He stumbles across his words—she has never seen him flustered before. To think of Shelley is to think of him earnest, excited and alert.

"Thank you, Shelley." She accepts the book from him. "I have very much been wanting to read your work, so it is a gift that gives me great joy." She turns the book around, demonstrating her appreciation. "And in such fine binding too! But I don't wish to cause you any expense; I am sure my father has a copy somewhere."

"This copy is for you," he says with a softness to his reassurance. "Do read it, when you have time."

"I have time now." She hands the book back to him. "Why don't you read it to me?"

She leans forward, her chin in her hands and her elbows on her knees so she is very close to Shelley. He turns the pages carefully, glances briefly up at her and a smile curls across his face, and he begins to read.

How wonderful is Death,
Death, and his brother Sleep!
One, pale as yonder waning moon
With lips of lurid blue;
The other, rosy as the morn
When throned on ocean's wave
It blushes o'er the world;
Yet both so passing wonderful!

This way she can watch him as he reads, the feminine beauty of his slender face and heavy eyelids, the peculiar tilt to his chin, the rise and fall of his brows following the emotions of his words.

In speech sometimes his voice rises shrilly and loses dignity in its exuberance, but when he reads the tone modulates tenderly, carrying meaning on a gentle current.

When first she met him, only weeks ago, she read his political pamphlets that pursued the cause of liberty, campaigned for the rights of the Catholics of Ireland, and beseeched the lords of England to reconsider laws that oppress the poor. And in such pamphlets she read a conscientious purity of heart.

Now, listening to his poetry, she is overwhelmed by beauty, and also, by the recognition of his genius. The heroine—the girl child Ianthe—sleeps, and in dreams is summoned by the fairy queen and shown the truth of all that has been and will be in this world.

"That is enough for today," he says at length, and returns the book to her.

"It's beautiful, Shelley."

"Thank you."

"Truly." She wants a stronger way to express her appreciation, but her mind still buzzes with the poem itself. "Ianthe is your daughter's name, isn't it?"

"Yes."

"How old is she?"

"Only a year of age."

"How lovely. I'm sure she is a beautiful child. One day she will hear you read this and she will know the great talent of her father."

The easy peace that had fallen upon them shudders and begins to dissipate around him.

"Perhaps," he says. "I hope so."

"Why would she not?"

He heaves a sigh and his shoulders drop with great weight.

"Ianthe lives with her mother, and for now, with her mother's sister. The sister does not care very much for me, or for my writings and my beliefs. I fear what she and Harriet will fill the child's mind with."

Mary frowns at this information, and tries to fit it in with what she has already gathered about Shelley.

"I have never met Harriet," she says, carefully.

"No. I suppose you were in Scotland when she used to come here with me. It seems a long time ago now." His expression is distant, sad.

"Is she not like you?

"Like me, no. It seems she no longer concurs with my philosophies." He picks at the skin around his nails, his contorted face testifying to an inner struggle. "If she did once that was apparently only a youthful enthusiasm which has faded. She has shown herself to be a person who is easily led and has little real conviction of her own. I thought I had met my soul's double, but she was a little more than a mirror for my own heart." The expression he offers Mary then seems to her almost apologetic.

"I would be interested to meet her."

"Harriet?"

"Yes," she looks at him seriously, "Harriet."

As she watches him, his gaze roams, his mouth opens once and then and closes impotently. He winces, summons a deep breath.

"I don't know."

What is this uncertainty? It is like pain, all across his face and in the fumbling of his hands.

"She hasn't been to London for a while," he says.

Any law of decorum would certainly advise discretion and retreat at such a moment, but over the previous weeks she has come to know Shelley, and to know he does not care for what is proper, so she strides ahead.

"I hope that we are friends, Shelley," she says. "You told me lately that we cannot be wise if we are not honest with each other. Please, trust me with your honesty."

Again, that look of apology, but this time he shakes his head and rolls it into a laugh.

"How right you are, most excellent Mary! Excuse me, I laugh at myself. I laugh that I need to be told my own principles. It seems I have been trying to be someone else for a while."

"I hope not. I like this Shelley very much." She edges forward, trying to further draw him out.

"And I am glad of that. In honesty, as that is what you ask, I have not seen Harriet for some months."

He returns her gaze, and this time, holds it. "We are... cordially estranged. I assure you there is no bitterness, no discord between us. The fact is that I was very ill when I married her. If I had known I would live so long... Perhaps I would have been more cautious."

Mary's heart beats heavy in her chest.

"So, do not be surprised at not seeing her," he goes on, "I dare say the day will come."

"Jane and Fanny certainly speak well of her."

"As well they might. In many ways she is a kind and excellent woman."

"But you do not love her?"

"No. No I do not."

He loves Mary. As they descend the staircase side by side Shelley confesses his heart to himself. How does she know what he feels? Are the passions of his heart written so clearly in his face that anyone who looks might read them there? Or is there a sympathy sacred between them, an understanding shared only by twin souls?

His foot and hers meet each step at the same moment. She is so close in the narrow stairwell that, although they are not touching, his arm tingles with the warmth of her presence, and he remembers the spot where her fingers held his.

What could such a love be? Surely, nothing could ever pass between them. Perhaps she can look upon him with pity, even with affection, as Goethe's Charlotte, in her way, loved Werther, though they could never belong to each other.

And yet, and yet, something whispers in the back of his mind, he does not believe himself.

Having bade farewell to Jane and Fanny and little William, he shakes Godwin's hand, apologising if he has not quite been himself this evening, excusing himself with tiredness.

Stumbling out the house he finds that night has fallen upon Skinner Street, and all the vendors have gone home. The rain has exhausted itself, leaving the cobbles wet and the sky naked. He pauses on the empty street, hardly able to remember which way he ought to go, and considers whether to walk or try to find a cab.

The cool night air smells of wood smoke, and the moon shines high and full.

The street is silent, the market ruins home to nothing but a solitary scavenger cat, and even the thoroughfare bodes no danger, for such is the silence that any approaching carriage would announce its proximity from some distance. A wandering breeze drifts by and he closes his eyes the better to feel its refreshing sigh. Mary held his hand. She was glad to see him. The certainty of that fact eddies through the rivers of his mind, and the thought of her rushes over everything else.

Yes, he should walk. Walk and clear his mind.

He gazes speculatively upon the house he has just left; the doors and windows are already shabby, the houses on either side empty and unwanted, the sign above the door—*M.J. Godwin, Booksellers*—the only thing in sight with dignity.

Yet this is London's Olympus, where sleep the gods forgotten and yet unknown. How terrible that Godwin, whose name was once a paragon, is a joke amongst the elite. And Mary... what will her name one day mean? *Mary Wollstonecraft Godwin*, the wind brings it back to him in a whisper, having kept it safe all day. Perhaps one day she will be a Corinne, processing through adoring multitudes with her head crowned in laurels, a queen of philosophy and the arts. But only if the world is just.

As he looks back at the house, his eyes climb heavenwards to a high window where a pale face behind the glass looks placidly down. Is it only a reflection of the moon? No, it is a round, white face, and one that is certainly watching him. For a moment he stands beneath the silver moonlight, blissful in the silent benediction, until a cloud comes and Mary withdraws.

Shelley waits a moment more, willingly bewitched, and then, with a silver secret in his heart, begins his way back to the empty apartment.

Chapter Two: Three Sisters
Skinner Street, London, 21ˢᵗ May 1814

*M*ary watches him leave, her pulse pounding in her temples. She feels like a novice enchanter who has cast a spell by accident. But no, not by accident.

The rest of the house clatters with tidying and preparations for bed, but Mary is alone in her father's study, the door closed for her privacy. Putting her mother's book to one side she brings Shelley's gift to the windowsill and lights a single taper. The thin golden flame and the moon's white-wash reveal the words he has given her, and she, in turn, allows herself to be enchanted: his words curl into her mind, shaping her thoughts. Oh, how wonderful is the poet, the poet and the poetry he makes! His voice is unworldly, as if he sees what others cannot. What a gift to receive from such a man. She turns the pages without reading, thrilling for all the stories yet to come.

But it is not only poetry. There are several notes to the poem: moral and philosophical digression that reveal her poet.

Law pretends even to govern the indisciplinable wanderings of passion, to put fetters on the clearest deductions of reason, and, by appeals to the will, to subdue the involuntary affects of our nature. Love is inevitably consequent upon the perception of loveliness. Love withers under constraint: its very essence is liberty.

She lets her hand lie upon these words. The message is familiar from her father's writing: a declaration of the importance of free love, a rejection of the laws of marriage. Once again, the name of Harriet Shelley rises in her head. He is married. Yet, her father wrote similarly, and he married, married for the sake of their child, herself.

Shelley does not love his wife. The fact sits before her, expectant, demanding.

From the stairwell come footsteps and Mary snaps the book closed and hides it in a skirt pocket.

But as the door creaks slowly, spilling light into the study, it reveals only Fanny with the lamp.

"I thought you must be in here," Fanny says from the threshold. "I hope I didn't startle you?"

"Not at all," Mary replies, trying to still herself.

"I'm going up to bed."

"Good. I'll be there in a minute."

"Were you looking for anything, Mary?"

Mary shakes her head. She extracts their mother's book.

"Just visiting *Maria*."

"Ah!" Fanny now slips into the room, the door drifting closed behind her. As she crosses the room her lamp sends shadows sliding around the books, and when she reaches Mary's side she raises it to light the portrait of their mother that still hangs above the mantelpiece.

"I thought often of you while you were away in Scotland," Fanny says. "I thought you'd be missing her books."

"The Baxters had them," Mary replies. "They were very much our sort."

"Were you happy there?"

"I was. But it's been nice to be home."

"We're glad you're back." As Fanny says this she glances up to the picture, and Mary follows her gaze.

In that moment a hush falls not only upon the two of them but, it seems to Mary, upon the whole house, the street beyond, even the whole city. The world holds its breath for two sisters at their mother's altar. If the ghost of Mary Wollstonecraft ever descends to touch her daughters' heads and bless them silently, she does so in this moment.

Regarding the portrait upon the wall, Mary sees warmth in

that figure, in the mild expression and side-turned gaze, and if she lets her focus drift just a little, she could be looking at a real person. She turns her eyes away, feeling a wetness there that threatens to betray her, and turns to Fanny with the intention of breaking the moment, chattering about some other thing, but is taken aback by the image of her sister in the candlelight, face raised piously to the portrait.

Fanny's long face has earned creases that Mary has not noticed before. Her thin lips raise the smallest smile to her mother, and with the candle held so close, her normally-colourless skin is cast in warmth. Her devotion, her pose, makes her—for once—beautiful, Mary thinks, and is immediately ashamed of the thought.

"Come, Fanny," she says softly. "We should be getting ready for bed."

The bedroom at the top of the house is a clutter: around the three narrow beds are trunks, a dresser, two small tables piled with trinkets, dresses hung from every ledge, and books both neatly stacked and sprawled face-down. Lying across Mary's bed, propped up on her elbows reading, is Jane, undressed to her slip, and around her the debris of daywear has been strewn here and there without care.

Mary is glad that Jane wasn't with them in the study, for though Jane loves Mary Wollstonecraft, reads her avidly and swears by her edicts, yet Jane is not her daughter, but the previous child of the second Mrs Godwin, and any claim Jane makes to kinship grates Mary's nerves, as surely it must grate Fanny's too, though she knows Fanny would never say so. That quiet moment belongs only to the two of them.

"Where have you two been?" Jane asks, without looking up from her book.

"What do you mean where have we been?" Mary replies, swatting at Jane's mass of dark curls and dropping onto the bed beside her. "We've been here, in the house, all day. Where were we supposed to have been?"

"We were in the study," Fanny says peaceably. Mary is immediately irritated with her for saying so, and tries to change the subject.

"What are you reading?"

"Byron. What were you talking about?" Jane asks, now flinging aside the book. "Were you talking about Shelley?"

"No!" Mary replies a little too hastily, guiltily it might seem, for they *weren't* even talking about Shelley, but Jane, sitting up, grins at her as if she knows everything.

"Isn't he wonderful?"

Fanny goes around the room, picking up discarded clothes.

"Would you like some help, Fanny?" Mary asks, looking pointedly at Jane.

"Oh, no," Fanny says, "I can do the tidying. Make myself useful."

Jane shrugs at Mary and continues her interrogation.

"What do you think of Shelley?"

Until now a need for secrecy has possessed Mary, but, steeled by the events of the past few hours, she consciously elects honesty.

"I think he is a marvellous person."

"He says the most excellent things!"

"Jane," this from Fanny, trying to pass the narrow space between the beds across which Jane's legs now extend. "Would you mind?"

Jane rolls her eyes and swings her legs out of the way. "I hate the name Jane," she declares, easily distracted as ever.

"Poor Jane," Mary says in mock sympathy, and begins to remove her own stockings which she lays beside her.

"Last I heard you wanted to change your name to Emily," Fanny says, picking up the dress that Jane—or Emily—has left on the floor and shaking out the creases.

"No, I can't. That's too much. I was thinking of Claire. And I want my own surname. I'm not going to be a Godwin just because my mother married a Godwin. I was born a Clairmont, I shall be a Clairmont."

"Very well, dear," Fanny says peaceably, and shares a knowing look with Mary. This is an old tune, and no name ever sticks.

"Are you enjoying school?" Mary asks.

"I am! I'm doing singing and French, and I'm doing very well, and I hate the other girls who all think there's nothing so important in the world as getting a good husband and talk silliness about *connections.*"

"You can't blame them for that," Fanny says, her back to them as she folds Jane's stockings into the chest of drawers.

There is a moment of quiet in which Mary wonders if Fanny would have liked school. For herself, her father scoffed at the idea, saying there was no girls' school that could further the education Mary already possessed.

Her reflection is cut off by Jane who has sidled up to her.

"I heard something about you," she says.

"Oh? Can you get off my bed please?"

"About you and a certain Mr Baxter from Dundee," Jane continues, not getting off the bed.

Mary scowls at Jane. She knows this insinuating tone.

"I've heard," Jane says, "he wants to marry you."

Before Mary can retaliate, Fanny interrupts, her voice thin and startled.

"You aren't going to, are you?" Her face is concern; the clothes slip from her grasp and she fumbles to catch them.

Mary is rendered dumb. She sees Jane's eagerness, Fanny's shock, and in her mind the image of Robert Baxter as she saw him last on the shore, freckle-faced and windswept, wresting with something he wanted to say. All he had managed was 'I will write to you.'

And has he written?

She anticipates her own excitement at the possibility, but it does not come. Instead, she hears Percy Bysshe Shelley's voice quietly reading her the most exquisite poetry.

Blood rushes to her face and she shakes her head in confusion.

"What gave you that idea?" she asks, giving herself time to formulate a reply.

"Mama said," Jane says, somewhat proudly. "She said she's heard from the Baxters and they're keen to see it happen, and Robert's going to come visit us and it's practically all settled."

The surprise in Mary solidifies into a precise anger.

"Your Mama," she says tartly, "ought not to gossip."

Fanny, still holding Jane's discarded stocking in one hand, comes to join them on Mary's bed, sitting lightly by them.

"But is it true, Mary?" she asks. "Do you love him? Will you marry him? And if you did... you'd go with him to Scotland forever, and we wouldn't see you anymore."

"What? No. I—I don't know. Robert was very kind to me when I was in Dundee." She cannot look at her sisters, and instead fixates on her own hands. "And I did feel very warmly towards him. He's a good man, and interesting. Intellectual, conscientious. And he'll soon be working in the publishers in Edinburgh I hear." She straightens up. Honesty. The courage to pursue one's happiness. "I might have felt differently about it before I met Shelley."

"Oh, Mary," Fanny says, in little more than a whisper. A kind, regretful whisper.

"But Shelley's married," Jane puts in, very childishly.

"I know that," Mary replies, "but I do love him." A rush within her. It is spoken. "And I'm coming to the opinion he loves me too."

"Oh, Mary!" Fanny echoes herself.

"You are earnest!" Jane whispers, aghast, if a little delighted.

Mary meets her eyes.

"Of course I am."

Jane breaks into the biggest smile, her eyes sparkling with delight. "It's true," she whispers. "One would not say he is *happily* married..."

Fanny cuts them off abruptly.

"You're still so young, Mary," she mutters. "And you don't have a mother to guide you. I think..." She looks up, not to Mary but beyond, to some scene in her imagination. "If I were in a position to advise you... I would tell you to be careful of Percy Bysshe Shelley."

A tension balls up inside Mary. She had spoken frankly with her sisters in anticipation of support but she should perhaps have anticipated this resistance.

"I understand it," Fanny goes on, "and believe me, Mary, I do know. And I know why." She swallows, takes a moment, resumes. "He's a marvellous person. Unlike any other. And yet..." She is so firm, using her eldest-sister voice. "He hasn't been married even two years, and he brushes her off for you. His heart, I think, may be fickle. And I wouldn't want to see you ruin yourself and find his affections change."

"I don't think you know him as I do," Mary whispers, just as seriously and almost coldly.

"I have known him significantly longer than you have, Mary." Fanny counters. "Take time, don't be rash. He is kind, but he's terribly wild, and he has the strangest notions sometimes. About a year ago he wanted me to go and live with him and Harriet in Wales. This was merely when he and Papa were corresponding; he'd never even met me." Fanny looks down at the garments in her hands and smooths them once more.

"And don't you wish you'd gone?" Mary asks, her jaw firmset. Even Fanny with her quiet ways, her timidity, must long for adventure. But seeing her now, twenty-one and still wearing padded corsets, in their mother's dress some thirty years out of fashion... has she no hopes for herself, Mary wonders?

A colour rises in Fanny's cheek and she turns away. "I don't think it would have been right."

"And just because he's nice," Jane interjects, "doesn't mean he loves you. He's nice to all of us. He's nice to me. He's even been out to my school to see me. So that's probably just the way he is with everyone." Mary notes a wistful thinness in Jane's voice, something like disappointment.

Fanny stands up, her hands now pulling absentmindedly at the pale-yellow ribbons on her dress, straightening their creases and winding them around her bony fingers.

"Think about Robert Baxter," she counsels, and braves a smile at Mary. "It would be such a good thing for you to marry well. And Jane, you shouldn't mock such concerns. Believe me, whatever happens, you don't want to get to twenty-one and still be a burden on your family."

With this she tucks in the last paired sock and closes the drawer. She keeps herself turned away, rearranging stray items upon the dresser top.

"You know you're not a burden, Fanny," Mary says softly, her irritation loosening a little.

"I think we three all know that I am," Fanny says. "I've been meaning to tell you. They want to send me away to Ireland to live with our aunts. Perhaps there I can make a living for myself. Become a governess, perhaps."

And what can Mary say now? That great density of anger melts into compunction, and all of herself and her love for Shelley is washed away in care for her sister.

"Are you really going to Ireland?" Jane whispers.

"It sounds that way." Fanny turns towards them, but cannot quite look at them. "And soon, I think. I'm not marriageable, and I'm far too dull to earn my living."

Mary rises from the bed and, picking her way through the cluttered floor, embraces Fanny. Although Mary clasps her tight, the thin cold hands Fanny brings to her back lie lighter than windblown leaves.

They come together back at Mary's bed where Jane curls into them and Fanny, with uncharacteristic strength, puts her arms around both Jane and Mary to comfort them, as if it were their misfortune and not her own.

But silence and misery do not last long, and Jane soon recollects 'something to cheer you up,' leaving the comfort of the group to bound after her discarded book.

"Look, Mary, you haven't seen this yet, have you?"

"It's Lord Byron's latest publication," Fanny says to Mary, with her eyebrows raised and a fond smile at Jane. "She must almost have it memorised by now."

"*The Corsair,*" Mary reads. "I have not seen it. Go on, then."

The candle burns low as they read aloud sections of the daring escapades of the renegade corsair Conrad, of his one man fight against the world, and of Gulnare, the beautiful slave girl who rescues him from peril. As each retires to their own bed they pretend that they have quite shaken off the earlier melancholy, and bid each other 'goodnight' in merry tones. Nevertheless, Mary lies awake a long time, her eyes watching the candle splutter on her bedside table, and her mind tying itself in knots of children and writers and governesses and Robert Baxter.

At last the gentle breath of sleep sighs first from Jane and then from Fanny. But Mary, wakeful, turns her thoughts to a story she began writing in Scotland. It was about a girl on a windswept moor with a choice before her: to go to sea and pursue adventures, or to be good and dutiful. The momentum she had while in Dundee failed amid the excitement of her return to London, but she still has the unfinished chapters. If she could revive it, could it be a story worthwhile, could it be something worth sharing with those who matter most?

And if there is an opportunity to share with those who matter most, will she have the strength to take it? To share work, and to share life?

She snakes her arm out of the duvet to the bedside table where she has secreted Shelley's *Queen Mab*. She curls her fingers around it, and draws it into the warmth of the covers, not to read, but to clasp to her chest.

When the opportunity comes, she will seize it.

Chapter Three: A Declaration
London, 27th May 1814

Dawn comes, but Shelley has not slept. Yesterday's clothes are still upon him, though jacket and cravat were pulled off and thrown aside many hours ago. Pages of abandoned scribblings lie a little way from him. The days—the nights—they're all like this now; his mind fails him, thoughts of Mary Godwin disturb his attempts at philosophy, and strange, horrible visions trouble his dreams.

He sits cross-legged on the rug, a glass of water and a bowl of sugar before him, absentmindedly dipping his finger into one and then the other. An ache is advancing through his head; he feels heavy, slow, desiccated. How long has it been since he had a good night's sleep? Though he searches back through the days he cannot find one. The headache reminds him of having drunk too much, though he hasn't tasted alcohol for years.

Days are pointless.

What is he doing with his time? If he could write, that would be something... Write something that might help this wretched world. For a moment his heart lifts with an inspiration as fragile as a glint of light on a wave; a moment later he crashes back into gloom. Even if he could write something, who would read it? He channelled everything he had into *Queen Mab*, made it a great testament to philosophical and poetical thought, and yet, who bought it? No one. Who read it? No one. His words are powerless if unread.

But Mary heard them. That is something. He remembers her dedicated attention while he read to her. And perhaps she is even now reading his book.

What a remarkable young woman she is.

A knock interrupts his thoughts. The landlady of this pokey room he is renting lets herself in at his word.

"Letters for you, sir."

She is about the age of his mother, and similarly slim, but in a sinuous, tough way quite different from Mrs. Shelley's softness. The landlady's demeanour reminds him of a determined mouse, scurrying about brazenly but always ready to run.

She scowls at him as she hands him the letters and looks around at the mess of the apartment, and at the bowls on the floor. He ignores her as best he can and rips open the letters. The first is from his old university friend, Thomas Jefferson Hogg.

"Will you be wanting any breakfast?" the landlady asks.

"No, no!" He waves her away, and she moves behind him to make the bed.

Hogg is currently off in Edinburgh on his lawyerly business. If Hogg were here, Shelley thinks, he'd have someone he could unburden himself to. He would pour forth all the disturbances of his heart and Hogg would sympathise and sigh and no doubt fall half in love with Mary just from Shelley's description of her. But Hogg is beyond his reach, and, with his family still resolutely rejecting him, there is no one for him to talk to.

The second is from his wife.

It bares only flimsy news. Harriet has bought a dress and seen her sister a lot and asks if he can acquire in London the specific tea that she likes as she cannot find anyone in Bath to get it for her. Ianthe sends her love to Papa and hopes he will see her soon, for, like a clever little girl, she can now say 'bye bye' and 'thank you.'

Poor Ianthe. The hand that holds the letter drifts down. Must his daughter grow up under the governance of a petty, shallow-minded aunt? Harriet alone would school her tolerably well, but the sister, always the sister. Must the child's untainted mind be filled with prejudice and society's frivolities? She is, as yet, so pure; all the world of possibility before her... and yet here he stands, a father, impotent in the education of his own child. He feels her die is already cast, and that Harriet's family will shape her absolutely to their own image.

He knows that he is cut off from Harriet and Ianthe already. There have been no words so harsh they couldn't be soothed, but he sees the hatred Harriet's family has for him, sees how Harriet is swayed by their pettiness, and knows she is not the girl he thought she was.

Stooping to collect the sugar bowl he remembers that he is supposed to have sworn off sugar in support of the abolition movement. They use slaves in the sugar plantations, and for a moment a horrible image rises in his mind, a young dark-skinned man, with all a man's ambition, hope, and pride, shackled, picking sugar for the convenience of Europeans in silk and lace.

In a sudden rush of fury Shelley hurls the sugar bowl across the room where it shatters with a crash.

The landlady screams. He had quite forgotten she was there, and spinning around sees her cowering with her brittle arms raised over her face.

He is as startled by the noise as by the unexpected presence.

"The sugar!" he cries out. He is half aware that that is not an explanation, but he is too agitated to immediately say more.

"That's my china!" she shrilly shouts back at him.

"It's the sugar," he tries to explain. "You mustn't buy sugar!"

She stares at him with a horrified, baffled expression, and any anger morphs into irritation.

"That was my grandmother's bowl before it was mine," she says.

"Oh, don't be ridiculous," he says. "Look, I'm sorry about your bowl. I'll buy you a new one. But do you know about sugar? Do you know of the torturous human suffering required for its manufacture?"

Her shrewish face twitches, and she darts past him, and begins picking up the shards of pink and white china. "All I know," she says, her tone short now, "is that I buy it from Mr Jones by the market."

"They use slaves in the sugar plantations."

"Mr Jones doesn't. He's got a boy right enough, but I'm sure he pays him as well as anyone."

"Your Mr Jones doesn't make it, he just sells it. Sugar is grown in the West Indies."

"Well, I don't know about all that."

"I'm telling you!" He follows her, trying to make at least this one woman listen. "They capture people and enslave them. People who are afforded no rights, no liberties, no opportunities! This is the cruelty of man we are contending with. And although I try to believe mankind perfectible, that morals can be learned, that the human condition can improve... the enormity of misery seems overwhelming." He paces away from her turned back.

"And what can we do? Does it really make much difference if the fashionable people in London decline sugar in their tea? Very little. It shalln't significantly hurt the plantation owners."

He tries to recall if he has noticed the Godwins boycotting too; he resolves to ask Mary about it—and quietly hopes that her recent absence will have kept the news of it from her, so that she might be interested by his concern.

"What we need," he returns to his monologue, "is a revolution of ideas. All that is in my power is to write."

The landlady turns about, shakes her skirts and pushes past him.

"That is my calling," he says, somewhat weakly. "I am a philosopher, and, to an extent, a poet."

"Good for you." The crockery and sugar gathered up in her dust pan, she has gone back to the abandoned work of making the bed. Shelley wonders where she got the dust pan from, and if she actually left the room at some point.

"It is not good for me." He throws himself into an armchair. "And it is not good for anyone else. What is the point of dedicating my life to writing when no one will read what I have written?"

"I'm sure a fine gentleman like yourself has plenty of connections," she mutters. He isn't sure if she is patronising him, or trying to be reassuring. There is a bluntness about this lady he rather likes.

"I don't. I'm a pariah."

"Are you?" She looks him over uncertainly.

"Certainly. You don't want the likes of me staying at your establishment."

She gives a non-committal "Hm" and carries on.

"I have tried, you know. I met Leigh Hunt once. You know, editor of *The Examiner*?"

"I've heard of him. Didn't he end up in prison?"

"I tried to call on Wordsworth and Coleridge but they were away. I met Southey though. He and I aren't on best terms anymore."

"Did you go about smashing things in his house?" the woman asks.

"Certainly not."

"How uncommonly civil of you."

He grins at her. She tuts, gives the sheets a last twitching tug, and takes herself to the hearth.

"They're not always what you expect, these great men," he says. "I am acquainted with a great philosopher... I shall not name him out of respect for his once elevated state, and I pray, should you divine of whom it is I speak, you not divulge my opinions of him to any other."

The landlady gives him an amused look, makes as if to speak but thinks the better of it, and continues her work laying the fire. Shelley realises she probably could not name too many philosophers, and pities her for it. She will not understand him. Who better to unburden oneself to?

"I read him in younger days, and was deeply moved by the enlightened thought, the insightful sentiments I there discovered. I confess, I thought the great man no longer among those numbering this earth, and upon discovering my error made every speed to contact him.

"I am truly grateful for my acquaintance with him. He has shown me into his house, and introduced me to his wonderful daughters, each of whom delights me. However, this philosopher, he is fallen from public grace, and cannot help me find the community I so desperately seek. Furthermore, the more I speak with him, the more I feel he has reneged on his once brilliant ideals. He has become conservative in age. When he was young he spoke with fire, determination; he wished to see the world change."

"Yes, well, the French wanted the world changed and look how well that turned out for them," his interlocutor remarks. She pushes herself up to standing with a grunt and hesitates, regarding him.

Amid her open irritation and disapproval is something of a

mother's fondness. Shelley wonders if she has a son his age, if that fellow is as reprobate in her eyes as he is to his family.

"I am sorry life is not going quite as you would wish it, sir. I'm sure things will come about in the end."

She gives him an encouraging nod, and shuffles out past him.

For a moment he sits in the silence, and then a strange mirth comes over him, and he laughs, loud and heedless, rocking back so he is lying on the floor and simply laughs in a directionless giddiness.

He bounds into the bookshop on Skinner Street, invigorated at last. As he swings on the door's momentum, the bell above clangs and rattles, as if irritated with his haste.

The first thing he sees is Fanny at the counter, surreptitiously stowing away her book, and smoothing the front of her dress to meet an anticipated customer.

"I caught you!" he cries, just as she looks up. For a moment her face flinches in anxiety before collapsing into relief.

"Shelley!" she says warmly.

He crosses the shop in a leap and launches himself up onto the counter, making Fanny give a small squeal and then a giggle as she leans back out of his way. He twists himself to sit perched upon the countertop and swing his feet merrily as he reaches for Fanny's hidden book, which he examines with mock scrutiny. "What is this you are reading? My goodness, Elegiac Sonnets? Don't you know that nonsense will depress you? Terribly melancholy. Not the sort of thing impressionable young ladies ought to read at all. Have you considered a conduct book instead?"

Fanny swipes the book back off him and bats him very softly on the arm with it.

"Get down!" she says in a gentle reprimand.

He is about to tease her more, but they both turn their heads at the sound of a heavy tread in the passage, accompanied by a muttering; Shelley swings himself off the counter, and instantly adopts a posture of indifferent browsing. A moment later Mrs Godwin appears carrying a stack of new books, uncut and unbound.

"Mr Shelley," she says as she walks towards them. "I hope you aren't distracting Frances from her work."

"Not in the least."

She gives a raised eyebrow, but says nothing, taking the books to the counter.

"We didn't expect you so early."

"You didn't?" he expresses surprise as sincerely as he can. "And yet, here I am. My dear Mrs Godwin, how can one delay on a day like today? The sun is out and the air is fine."

She shakes her head at him with a familiar air of motherly scepticism.

"But there must be some mistake," Shelley goes on, a thought occurring to him. "You see, your fine daughters have engaged me."

She looks warily at Fanny. "Have they?"

"Yes. It was Mary's idea. They are going to take me to her late mother's grave to permit me to pay my respects." She nods as she separates the books into two piles.

"No one thought to consult me," she says once her task is finished, and quite archly, still eyeing the books. "Well, you stay here, Mr Shelley. I shall fetch the girls. I don't want you going upstairs and causing cacophony. My husband is working and most particularly does not want to be disturbed. Fanny, these arrived this morning, could you enter them in the ledger?"

As she turns into the house Shelley leans in to Fanny. "I hope they play along," he confides in Fanny. "There was no such plan. Shh."

"You shouldn't encourage them. Jane's mind is already enamoured with any plan of subterfuge."

She bows her head, some far away thought occupying her, and then turns her attention back to him.

"You look tired, Shelley," she says.

"On the contrary, I am full of energy!"

"There are shadows on your face. Did you sleep well last night?"

"Last night? No, to be truthful. How good you are, Fanny. I barely lay down. My head is much too full."

"You are worrying?" she asks. She fiddles with the corners of the galleys Mrs Godwin just brought in, but she shows no sign of attending to them.

"Sometimes I never stop worrying," Shelley admits. "It seems I have reached a premature old age, and all my life is spent, and I have nothing more to give, and weariness overcomes me."

"If you don't sleep, you will certainly feel weary." She reaches out a hand and gently pats his arm.

He laughs then. "Fanny, will you come and look after me and tell me when I need to go to sleep? I simply can't be relied upon to do it myself."

"Surely Harriet can do that."

"I'm afraid Harriet is in Bath. With her sister. She does not think of me."

"I believe there is discord between you."

"We are not in harmony, it is true."

"I am sorry to hear it. I am very fond of you both. I wish there were something I could do."

This, this is the kindness of Fanny, and he is about to say something to her, something of his gratitude, when in rushes Jane, still adjusting her cap, beaming at him.

"Shelley!" She giggles. "I hear we have an arrangement."

"Oh yes we do," he says, very seriously. "We definitely all agreed to it yesterday. I'm surprised your mother doesn't remember."

Mary is close behind her. Her face contains the most wonderful contentment, and he thrills to think he is some part of that happiness.

"Shall we go?" she asks meekly.

He opens the door and steps aside for them. Jane dances through, and Mary glides past.

"Come along, Fanny," he says, holding out his arm to encourage her.

"I can't," she says, still behind the counter. "I have to mind the shop."

Shelley stops short, and frowns in disappointment. "Can't Mrs G.?"

"She has asked me to."

"But we're going on an adventure," he pleas. "Close the shop!"

"We can't do that." There is now in her tone genuine exasperation.

"But... Fanny..." He leans forward as if he were communicating a great secret. "No one's here."

Jane bursts out laughing from the doorway. Fanny frowns at them, and the corners of her mouth draw tight, and Shelley realises he has misstepped.

"Someone may come," she says. She turns her back to them and attends to the pile of books her step-mother left her. "Have a nice walk."

Jane runs back in from outside, grabs his arm and tugs. "Come along, Shelley!"

"Fanny's not coming," he informs her. Jane barely notices, and applies her strength to dragging him. Shelley keeps his eyes on Fanny, wanting a look for forgiveness, wanting to see in her face that is not truly upset, but she does not turn.

"Well you'd better come next time," he calls back, for Jane has made some progress, and the pair of them stumble down the steps, the bell clanging behind them.

Mary stands quite patient, waiting for them.

The day has brightened, and become hot. Mary leads the way with a straight-back posture that suggests the importance of their journey. Jane beside him is in white, and fidgets with her cap.

"Ouch!" she says, "my shoes are pinching."

"Are they?"

"May I lean on you, Shelley?"

"Of course." He offers her his arm, and notes the smallest irritation from Mary, glancing back at Jane with a withering look. Of all of them, it is Mary's favour he wants, and so reaches out for it.

"Do you remember your mother at all?"

"Can't forget her," Jane mumbles.

"Alas, I do not," Mary says, allowing her step to slow so she is almost in line with them. "She died bringing me into this world. She lived only ten days after my birth."

"I am sorry to hear that."

"Fanny does," Jane says.

"Yes she does," Mary replies, very quickly. "Perhaps you can ask her for her recollections."

Shelley had considered the oppressive effect the ghost of Wollstonecraft might have upon her successor, the second Mrs Godwin, but he had not fully considered the hierarchy knowing her might place upon the three girls of the household—Fanny, the only one who knew her, Mary, the one to bear her name, and Jane, who is not a blood relative and has no claim whatsoever.

"My feet hurt," Jane whines.

Mary ignores her. "I know my mother only through her writings. But I feel that is sufficient to know her intimately."

"I agree," Shelley reassures her. "When a mind so great has left such bountiful testimony of its glory, that is a great boon."

"And no one knows her writings as well as I."

"I believe it." He has no doubt this precocious girl can not only read and comprehend all of Wollstonecraft's writings, but discourse eloquently upon the ideas therein and even advance them.

"Oh goodness, it's hot," Jane says.

"We were having a conversation, Jane, please don't interrupt," Mary says curtly.

"I'm sorry, I thought you had said all there was to say."

Observing the tensions between them, and how likely it is that Jane in this mood will disturb his conversation with Mary, Shelley lights upon a plan.

"Poor Jane, are your feet still hurting?"

"They are." She beams at him, and lifts her dress to show him her dainty shoes. "I really shouldn't have worn these, they nip terribly, but they are so sweet."

"Come, take a seat, there is a low wall here where you can rest."

He guides her to a shaded spot, where she gladly sits and takes out a fan.

"Thank you, Shelley, you are so thoughtful."

"Well, I must take care of you. I think the heat may be a little much, and you ought to rest here a while. It is only a few minutes to St Pancras from here, so Mary and I shall walk on, see the grave and pay our respects, and return to you swiftly."

If Jane's expression before had a hint of smugness, that is gone as soon as she realises she is to be left behind. She tries to protest, but Shelley is firm, assuring her they will be within calling distance and that the rest will do her good.

After they have walked a little way from Jane and spoken very little, Mary takes his arm. When it had been Jane beside him, the contact was meaningless, but Mary's hand resting upon his forearm and the closeness of her body are as intoxicating as a heady draught.

"I have enjoyed reading *Queen Mab*," Mary says. "Thank you for the gift."

"You are very welcome to it. I wrote it because I desired to share my thoughts with the world."

"The world needs to hear them." She speaks slowly and meaningfully, and while he recognises something a little naïve, a little romantic in the tone, nonetheless it flatters him, and the charred remains of his self-esteem flicker with a gentle flame.

"Ah, here is the church."

A vast copper beech stands in the graveyard, at this time of year its plume is a funereal dark-plum purple. It is a darkness on this summer day that seems to draw all shade to it, and shames the leafy greens that celebrate their vitality amid the graves. They slip through the gate, and walk the narrow grassy paths. He follows only a step or two behind her.

"This is beautiful," he says.

"Yes," she says. "This is my favourite place. Do you think that macabre of me?" Mary asks.

"No," he replies, "I do not see why the spirits of the dead should not keep us better company than the living. My father will not see me—but Milton never fails me."

"In your work, I admired that you spoke out against the tyranny of marriage."

"I did."

"I am surprised, given your avowed conviction, that you have undertaken the wretched matrimonial ceremony, marrying Harriet not once, but twice." There is something scolding in her tone, and the look she gives him is of a teacher disappointed in a once-promising pupil. Shelley feels ashamed.

But this should be a magical moment, and he is irritated to find her cross-examining him like this, picking discrepancy between philosophy and deed. Does she not know his heart is pure?

"Do not believe I recant what I have written." He is aware of something complaining in his tone, and endeavours to master it, to be reasoned in his defence. "The legal ceremony is a regrettable necessity in contemporary society to ensure the safety of spouse and offspring. Harriet's family did not initially take kindly to our relationship—indeed, they still do not, but they are now willing to talk to Harriet where once they did not—and knowing they might not provide for her in the event of my death, I wanted to ensure she would have security from my inheritance. The second marriage, as you may be aware, was undertaken for the sake of your own father: I am attempting to secure a loan for him, for your whole family." Again the irritation rises in him. Ahead is a beautiful patch of willows, their branches swaying in the lightest breeze, the sunlight illuminating their leaves to a verdant glow. They should not be talking of loans in this beautiful natural environment, in this precious moment alone. "I am borrowing against my future inheritance, and the lenders required we marry in England, for our first marriage was conducted in Scotland, to ensure no complications."

She does not reply, but leads him on to the willows, and ducks beneath the trailing boughs, holding them up behind her for him to follow. How little does she think of him? Why will she not reply?

A nervous energy has infused Mary, her breath is short and she can feel her blood thumping everywhere, her head, her hands, her lower back, her knees, places she has never before noticed a heart beat. She does not want to look afraid—indeed, she isn't afraid. She feels empowered. This is the opportunity. He is alone with her, and she knows above all else that she loves this man, this marvellous man with his large eyes and delicate gestures and strange, wild laugh.

"Here," she says.

Trees grow around the tomb, not pressing, but present to screen the outside world. There the heavy beech with all her silence, there the silver birch diffusing sunlight with her leaves, and here the willow drawing her whispering veil across the scene. A raised tomb, six feet long in sombre grey stone bears the legend: *Mary Wollstonecraft Godwin, Author of a Vindication of Women.*

Shelley kneels before the tomb reverently.

"I often bring her books here to read them by her side," Mary says. "Or else I just come to be with her. To seek her council."

She sits in the long grass beside him.

"What does she say?" he asks.

"That I must live in my own way. That I must be slave to no man. That I must seize opportunity."

"That is sound advice."

She knows this, and will not let opportunity pass.

"So you do not feel yourself bound by the legal ties between yourself and Harriet?"

"Marriage is nothing to do with love. Marriage is a contract of law that allows one human control of another. Where there is bondage there cannot be freedom. Love is precious. It may change with time, for all things in life are mutable; to promise to love when love has faded is insanity. It knows nothing of human nature. But the union of souls who love purely is a profound and beautiful thing. It is the greatest feeling."

Within her, her spirit seems to be rising on sacred winds.

She rests her fingers on the stone to feel anchored to the earth. Lichen has returned, despite how often she cleans it away. Some things cannot be dissuaded.

"I appreciate the candour with which you have shown yourself to me," she begins. She pauses to still the tremor which threatens her lip. *Be confident,* she tells herself. *Be wise!* "Allow me to speak equally with full sincerity. For lately I have been concealing a deep and powerful emotion that moves me greatly. To conceal such a truth is not merely regretful, but wrong."

She swallows.

"You tell me you are unaffected by the standards of society. That the legality of your marriage is irrelevant. That you believe in the principle of free love. All your philosophies and writings point to an enlightened mind. And yet, you do not tell me you love me. Why not?"

He stares at her in astonishment, but surely there is happiness there. He shakes his head and the sunlight sparkles around him like a gem. "I know that you love me, I see it in your countenance every day. And I love you, my dearest Shelley."

Breathless, he almost laughs, never breaking ... and in one moment his arms are around her, and he is lifting her off the ground.

"Mary Wollstonecraft Godwin!" he says. "What an extraordinary young woman you are."

She clutches to him, giddy as he sets her back on the earth, and the words that have filled her mind overflow at last!

"I love you, Shelley. The ardour that beats in my breast is no passing whim, but a deep and profound connection. I know there are many who would condemn me for even speaking such a desire, but I have no concern for the petty opinion of society. I will always be your friend, but I would also be your lover. I give myself to you, body and soul, if you will have me."

There are tears upon his face as his fingers grasp for hers; one arm still encircles her, and she presses herself into his chest, thrilling at the closeness, the warmth of his touch.

He draws back, lifts her chin and studies her face. "Oh dearest Mary!" His voice is barely more than a whisper. "You know the life I lead... I have nothing to offer you..."

"You have yourself, and I ask nothing more."

He is doubting, thinking, calculating, she can tell. She knows what he is thinking, she is sure, for it has been running through her mind these past weeks. She has weighed it all, and knows that love is stronger. She lays a finger upon his lips, and smiles up at him, lifting her face to his, and with a sudden ecstasy of joy he clasps her to a kiss.

Chapter Four: Repercussions
London, 1ˢᵗ June 1814

*M*ary is summoned to her father's study. He stands at the window with his back to her, and commands her to sit without looking around.

She takes the seat drawn in front of his desk and tries not to look up at her mother's ever-placid face.

"As I am sure you know Percy Bysshe Shelley—a man whom until this day I considered my friend—has been here this morning saying the most unimaginable things; namely that you and he have conceived a ludicrous childish attachment to one another and that you propose to live as his mistress in disregard of church, state, and society."

He does not pause to allow her to speak, nor does he turn to address her, and Mary fixes her subdued gaze upon the edge of the desk, and recalls sitting there for a lecture some years before when she had said some hurtful things to her stepmother, though what they were now she cannot recall. How ashamed she was then, how devastated by her father's reprimand. Now, though, she finds she does not fear his wrath. She knows she has acted well.

"Shelley," her father continues, "is gripped by his delusion and lamentably unmovable, but he is a wayward young man with wild, often dangerous ideas, and currently without the guidance of his family. My hope is that you, my daughter, will be more reasonable."

Now at last he turns to face her, hands clasped behind his back, his stooped posture emphasised from her seat.

"You are not to see him anymore. You will not leave this house without our supervision, and he will no longer visit. One thing only is in your power, and that is for you to write to him, to break off this..." he searches for the word, and lands, hard, on, "infatuation." He clears his throat. "It may be that you have the ability to cool his ardour by renouncing him yourself. Such an action would go some way to atoning for your rash actions and restoring my and your mother's good opinion of you."

A silence. Mary grits her teeth.

"I cannot promise that, father," she says. "I will not. I love him, and love is—"

"Enough!" he shouts, and the word echoes off the bookcases. She stops short.

"Of all the children in this house I had the highest hopes of you, Mary," her father says. His praise is sufficiently rare that even though he says this with a saddened tone and a shake of the head, she still feels a little pride.

"I concede that a susceptibility to youthful infatuation is not uncommon of your age and sex but that you would not curb a desire which promises not only to yourself more misery than happiness, but to your family only shame opprobrium, that astonishes me. I had thought your sensibility and intellect sufficiently advanced to elevate you above your peers.

"Young Shelley is an idealist. He has a philosophy about the world that is yet immature and dangerous in its misconceptions. Just because there may be a better way of living does not mean one can act as if the laws that currently bind our society do not exist. He is a most exceptional young man, I grant, but bizarre. To march in here with all his principles and tell me that he is in love with you..." He shakes his head. "It is extraordinary behaviour.

"I suppose you have some romantic notion of emulating her. But you are sixteen years old, you're not a child anymore," her father continues. "You know how the world works. Shelley is married. Much as Fanny's father Imlay was married all the time he was your mother's lover. I don't suppose you have read the recollections I wrote of her. It is time you did. She was miserable, Mary. Imlay brought her nothing but misery. She, the finest and best of women, made attempts upon her own life. She should have been revered!"

He stops abruptly, dismisses what he has been saying with a wave of his hand.

"I do not wish to see you suffer in that way. I do not wish to see you ruined by scandal. Be prudent. Let this childish passion cool and in time find a suitable match." His voice is softer now, heavy with tiredness.

A timid knock interrupts them.

"Come," Godwin says.

Only a narrow gap opens and Fanny slips herself half through.

"Papa, Harriet Shelley is downstairs."

"I am expecting her. Please show her up."

Mary feels the sudden shock of ambush; as the door closes her father turns a beady glare on her, as if challenging her, or worse, savouring a victory over her.

"Now, Mary," her father draws up a chair beside her own, and himself takes his usual seat at the other side of the desk. "I have summoned Harriet to speak with you. I am aware that your time in Scotland has meant you are less well acquainted with her than the rest of us are. She is a good friend to this family. It is important that you confront those who would be hurt by your behaviour. Listen to her. Think of her situation, and that of her daughter."

The nausea Mary feels is part dread of the impending confrontation, but more the horror of finding her father pitted against her. Is there any chance Harriet will come with an enlightened solution? Will she explain to Godwin that all involved believe in and practise the principles of free love, the very principles he once espoused, and he will come to understand their philosophy? Harriet was Shelley's choice, after all.

The knock comes again, and Fanny opens it for Harriet who smiles gratefully back at Fanny and lightly touches her arm as she departs. She is very pretty. A little taller than Mary with a face thinner and more refined. Her hair is like Mary's but more golden, and tied up in a great many artful loops. She has not removed her cape which gives her a commanding presence, and the reticule she clutches is made of such intricate beadwork it must have been expensive.

She smiles sweetly at both Godwin and Mary as if nothing in the world were wrong.

"Mrs Shelley," Godwin says. "Thank you for accepting my invitation. I am sorry it came upon such unfortunate circumstances."

If Harriet is embarrassed by the mention of 'unfortunate circumstances' she doesn't show it, but nods eagerly.

"My daughter, Mary."

Harriet turns a forgiving look upon Mary and holds out her hands for her as she takes a seat.

Really, Mary has no choice but to offer her reluctant hands in return. Harriet's hands are soft, like everything about her. "I am glad to have this opportunity to talk with you, and am grateful to your father for his invitation." She gives Godwin a nod, and he sits back, apparently taking the note that the conversation is to be between the two young women. He does not leave, though. "I imagine you might prefer not to see me under these circumstances," Harriet continues to address Mary. "However, the situation compels me to act with a most lively urgency."

She seems perfectly proportioned; her hair is neat, her dress pristine, and her speech is immaculate, without the Scottish quirks of language Mary's father keeps reprimanding her for.

"As I believe you well know, my husband has conceived an attachment for you. Do not be embarrassed. It is no uncommon thing—he is not the first husband to be struck with an infatuation outside of his marriage, nor shall he be the last, I am sure." A shy, sorrowful laugh with an affectionate look of understanding at Godwin. "And believe me sweet girl, I do not blame you—how could I resent you for loving as I do? However, you are young and perhaps want a little schooling in the ways of the world. We must act carefully, or it could be ruinous for us all. Do you understand?"

To all this Mary can say nothing.

Harriet squeezes her hand.

"I'm here to ask you Mary, to beg you, for as women we share a common trial that Bysshe for all his understanding will never truly grasp..." Her face is very close now, and Mary can see it is powdered, and that there are lines of care beneath the powder. "Please, Mary, do all you can to calm him, let him subdue his passion. For all our sakes."

A hot, tearful shame overcomes Mary, and, unable to control her emotion anymore, she finds tears spilling down her face. Her father walks away, and it is Harriet who strokes Mary's shoulder, saying gently, "It's alright. It's alright."

In her bedroom, Mary sinks down on the floor with her back to her bed in the smallest nook the room provides. Her fingernails press into the tired wood of the old floorboards and she stares, fiercely, at her trunk, on which are balanced a pile of books, a blanket, an old fan. Her eyes run over these things: the paper spine on the topmost book that is peeling at the base, the thick weave of the blanket, the faded yellow of the paper fan, scarcely grey, scarcely brown. They are nothings. They are stupid, stupid nothings, and ought to be burned.

Except—she reaches up under her pillow where she hid the magnificent book that Shelley gave her. *Queen Mab*, by Percy Bysshe Shelley. She whispers his name, and opens to the page where he had written in his own hand to her.

Can they really separate her from him?

In the silence of solitude she writes in flyleaf: '*I am thine, exclusively thine. I have pledged myself to thee and sacred is the gift.*' As she writes she sinks lower over the book, as if it were him, as if she could draw closer to him through its pages. '*This book is sacred to me and as no other creature shall ever look into it, I may write what I please. Yet what shall I write? That I love the author beyond all power of expression and that I am parted from him. Dearest and only love, by that love we have promised to each other although I may not be yours I may never be another's.*'

She hears footsteps on the stairs and she snaps the book shut, hides it among the fabric of her dress.

"Mary?"

Mary glances, only briefly, and sees Fanny standing in the doorway and a few steps behind her, Jane. She cannot stand to look at them; she does not hear what they have to say.

"I'm so sorry, Mary." The bed sinks as Fanny sits down by her. "You know Papa's only acting as he feels best. I'm sure that was unpleasant for you. But Harriet wasn't cross with you, was she?"

"No."

"She's really very nice. If you knew her better..."

"I don't need to know anything about her." Mary scrabbles to her feet, catching Shelley's book and clutching to her chest. "She can be the nicest person in the world but the fact remains that Shelley doesn't love her."

"It's more complicated than that, Mary," Fanny says. "She's his wife."

Mary turns to her sister, sees her sad, apologetic face, and knows she will accept whatever the world throws at her, and never fight for what she could have. She has always suspected this of Fanny, but now she sees her sister expects the same compliance from her.

"You don't understand it at all, do you?" she asks. "All you see is the rules and what society has deemed proper with no care for what might actually be right." Fanny frowns but Mary does not let her interrupt. "You would condemn Shelley to a life of misery because the law states it ought to be so. As humans we are blessed with choice and shifting inclination, and yet we are enchained by custom. I won't live that way. And neither will Shelley." Her voice rises in pitch, scraping close to something quite unlike herself, but Fanny is unabashed.

At the door, her back to the wall, Jane is unusually silent. Mary watches her as Fanny speaks, longing for an ally, but suspecting Jane will not pipe up on this matter. She has clearly been given a dressing down herself. She was after all the chaperone who left them alone.

"You can't behave like this, Mary; you're upsetting Papa and Mama. I'm sure you think it is unfair, but you must acknowledge you are not the only person in this household to make sacrifices. A union between yourself and Shelley simply cannot be." Mary edges away from her sister, wishing she could run, run from it all and block out the gloom of this whole family.

"I don't in any way dispute his feelings," Fanny says, "but I've known him longer than you, I've seen him... There was a time... When he first came here, he was so kind, so attentive... But that isn't it." She shakes her head, stealing whatever she was about to say from Mary's knowledge. "I do not think Shelley is the path to your happiness," she says after a brief consideration. "And I love you, Mary, you're my only real relative in this world. I want your happiness. I just do not believe Shelley is it."

Fanny heaves a sigh, and rises.

"I'm going to get ready for bed." She passes Jane at the door and affectionately brushes her chin, as if she were a naughty child, forgiven. "Papa wants to talk to me first thing in the morning about my trip to Ireland." Mary notes the weak smile, but can't stir herself from her own heart to share.

There is a stillness to both Mary and Jane as Fanny washes her face at the basin, as she brushes her hair. Mary begins to do likewise, but Jane does not seem to know what to do with herself, and continues standing by the wall, shuffling a few steps this way and that.

"I'm going to read for a while," Jane says at last. She sits on her own bed with a book in hand, but Mary notices she barely turns the pages.

Only once Fanny is in bed and her candle snuffed does Jane raise her eyes to meet Mary's. There is fire there; Jane is brimming with an unfathomable meaning and seriousness. Suddenly Mary suspects, and her heart leaps.

She leans forward, unable to speak.

Everything in Jane's face is alight, bubbling with such high emotion Mary is astonished she is keeping it in.

With the swiftest glance back over her shoulder to ensure Fanny is turned away, Jane reaches out her clenched fist, dropping onto Mary's coverlet a piece of paper, folded small and crumpled into the shape of her palm. Mary grabs at it. It is damp from sweat, and her trembling hands are too afraid to open it.

Jane leans across the gap between their beds and her mouth moves almost soundlessly.

"You write a reply. I can get it to him. Tomorrow morning."

Mary wants to kiss her. Dear, magnificent Jane!

They share a radiant expression of mutual delight before Jane lifts her book to her face. Mary picks up the volume of Walter Scott by her bed, just in case Fanny should stir, for she clearly cannot be trusted with this secret, and unfolds the little note. Mary's heart quickens as she sees the familiar, wonderful scrawl, writing fast and urgent, passionate and sincere.

Shelley!

Chapter Five: One Shared Path
London, 27ᵗʰ July 1814

*T*he union of true love may be inevitable. That is how it feels to lovers. In Shelley's mind there was never any other option but to be with Mary. And whatever the world will say, Fate forgives a midnight tryst. Though as Shelley waits in a parked carriage on an empty street, it is long past midnight. Holding up his pocket watch to the dim lamp he reads the time as half-past-three. He snaps it shut, and opens it again, as if his fervour could untie the hours and bring Mary to him. He is time's prisoner.

It is only time keeping him from her now. He closes his eyes and rests back against the seat, trying to envision her as she is at this second. She too will be awake and watchful, already packed and dressed, ready to fly into the night.

He sits up sharply as unease slinks around him and into his thoughts. This night has been long for him, as full of doubt as of hope, and he has nothing to lose. Meanwhile, Mary waits in the house where her beloved father sleeps; she must write a note of farewell and leave it upon the mantelpiece. How easy for her to reject the escapade, to climb back into the safety, the comfort of her girlhood bed, and let sleep keep her from her Shelley.

Ah, but Jane is with her.

Jane will keep Mary strong.

The bells! The hour descends, and Shelley is released. He gives the word to the driver and the horse pulls them down the street, around the corner, and as the fourth toll sounds, Shelley can see the

Skinner Street house. They stop opposite it, and Shelley scrambles out. All is silent. The house looms dark and impassive. No light betrays life.

The minutes stretch. Nothing. Would they not come and leave him here? What would there be for him then? Percy Bysshe Shelley disintegrates into the night.

He stares so long at the edifice that shadows drift about his vision, and he does not realise at once that two of them have solid form. Two cloaked figures fussing with the door, each carrying a large travelling case. The breath that rushes upon him is almost a sob, and he lurches from the cab and takes two half-scuttling steps in their direction.

Away from the door, from the house, from their home, they run, and Jane is first to him, embracing him warmly and breathlessly. He hands her box to the driver and lifts her into the carriage. And there, there is his Mary. Concern lightly veils her face, but as she puts her hands upon her shoulders, he sees his joy reflected in her expression. For one indulgent moment he kisses her in the dark street, before urging haste to all.

"Come, we must be swift. They may pursue us when they wake. This coach will bring us to Dover where we can take a boat to Calais. Once in France, we are free."

Calais, 29ᵗʰ July, 1814

The sun rises over France. It rises on a day Shelley could scarce have dared to hope would dawn. He lies with Mary, their bodies so entwined that limb from limb is indistinguishable. Their bodies are become communal, just as their lives, their cares, their fates, are now united.

And she is extraordinary. The *manner* in which she gave herself to him, and simultaneously claimed him as her own astonishes him, even now in the quiet morning. Through the gaps in the shutters come the rays of sun already waxing full and the lazy call of a seagull. In the simple *auberge* room, with bed and washstand and little else, Shelley sits up, pillows at his back, and Mary, with her head against his chest, doses, her beauty bliss, her abundance of hair let loose to fall all around them in accents of red and gold and brown. He lets his fingers snake through it, and marvels silently at her.

A journal lies in wait upon the bedside table, and, holding her gingerly, he reaches over, cautious not to disturb her. She has need of rest. Poor Mary. As happy as she swears she is to be with him, he can't forget the look she cast back to the house she fled under cover of darkness, where slept the father she still loves, oblivious to his imminent loss.

He reads over what the journal holds so far.

July 28th
We engaged a small boat to convey us to Calais.

We were proceeding slowly against the wind when suddenly a thunder squall struck the sail & the waves rushed into the boat. Even the sailors perceived that our situation was perilous, they succeeded in reefing the sail – the wind had now changed & we drove before a wind that came in violent gusts directly to Calais.

Mary did not know our danger. She was resting on my knees that were unable to support her. She did not speak or look. But I felt that she was there. I had time in that moment to reflect & even reason upon death. It was rather a thing of discomfort & disappointment than terror to me. We could never be separated, but in death we might not know & feel our union as now.

The morning broke, the lightning died away, the violence of the wind abated. We arrived at Calais whilst Mary still slept. We drove upon the sands. Suddenly the broad sun rose over France.

"What is that?" Her voice vibrates through his chest. She stretches her hand up to his neck, and where it lies a pulse flickers; he cannot say from which heart it beats.

"Something I wanted to show you. But I don't want to disturb you now."

She turns her face up to him, her eyes docile and sleep-heavy, her cheeks a rosy pink.

He lays a kiss upon her pure forehead, and opens the book up to its first page to show her. He has written a title: *Mary and Shelley's Journal.* She chuckles and her laugh echoes through the skin that lies against his torso.

She reads all that he has written.

"I like this," she says.

"Good."

He leans awkwardly across her with some amusement, inks his pen, and begins to write while she watches.

France. Friday 29.

I said – Mary look. The sun rises over France. We walked over the sands to the sea. We were shown into an apartment that answered the purpose both of sitting and sleeping room.

Mary was there. Shelley was

"If this is our story," Mary murmurs, "then I ought to write it too."

"Of course you must," he says, and stops at once the line he has begun.

She curls the pen from his hand, teasing his fingers with soft touch as she does, and, despite her angle to the page, completes the line.

Mary was there. Shelley was also with me.

"And what shall we write in this story of ours?" she asks.

"We shall write our lives, our stories, all the great deeds we shall do."

"Great deeds," she echoes, "and so much more."

With that, Mary draws a firm line under the entry, and closes the book in favour of other things.

Chapter Six: Adventurers Abroad
Neuchâtel, 20th August 1814

*S*helley gazes upon the magnificent shapes of the alps for the first time; it is a horizon higher than any he has ever seen before. He and Mary and Jane have journeyed, mostly on foot, through France, Holland, Germany, and Switzerland. They rest now in Lucerne. There is no haste, nowhere to be. Perhaps they will settle here.

"I have an idea for a story," he announces. Mary sits by his side in the hotel garden that is thick with bright flowers. A little further down the garden, close enough she could hear if called, but not so close that she is part of their conversation, her head bent over a book of Greek, is Jane.

"I'm happy to hear that," Mary says. "What is your story to be about?"

"Well, I've been reading this history of the society of the Assassins in Lebanon, and the more I think of their religious idealism, the more I think they would make an excellent subject for a tale. But I should want their tale to be a Christian one, the ideas are similar, to show the true consequences of the Christian religion."

"It would be interesting to write of the fall of Jerusalem, that is their point of origin, isn't it?"

"Yes. But I want to talk of their isolated community in the mountains, in a pure environment unadulterated by the tyrannies of men. Then," here he jumps up and sits upon the table before Mary, causing her laughter, so that he may be close, sincere with her. "What happens," he pushes aside the empty tea things, "is that a stranger comes into their midst. I am not quite sure who he is yet, half Christ, half wandering Jew, a man in the grip of revolutionary fervour, and he sees the peace of this community and wants to be part of it, and this is the appeal of all the ideas of pantisocracy, but—here's the rub—he cannot. Because he knows the suffering of the world, and once they all know the suffering of the world, they cannot accept their peace. They must wage war, in whatever way they can."

"It sounds like a very important work," Mary says.

He hears the voice in his head that says, *only if people read it.* And what chance of that now? The loan Shelley acquired for Godwin— which he now wishes he had kept more of, for he is begging off everyone he knows—has reached the disreputable quarters of the British press, and the conclusion they have reached is that the disgraced atheist son of Timothy Shelley, gentleman of Surrey and heir to a baronetcy, has *bought* the two daughters of the decrepit philosopher William Godwin.

As fast as it kindled enthusiasm is snuffed.

To Mary he only says, "I must write as best I can, and trust that the world will understand me."

"May I help?"

"You wish to help?" He plants his feet upon her chair, either side of her legs, and leans forward, a Shelley cage for her loveliness.

"I want to help," she affirms, unruffled by her imprisonment. "I can write it with you. I can scribe for you."

"I thought you were writing a novel."

"I am somewhat disillusioned with it. I am not sure I am on the right track. But let me help you; I am sure I could do both."

"I don't doubt you can. Well, yes, I would appreciate your opinions." He throws himself back, freeing her, but she only leans forward, and, with her arms, traps him in kind.

"I've been thinking... Did you give Harriet the address of the post office here or in Brunnen?"

"Here, I think."

"I wonder if there will be a letter from her. I would so like her to join us."

"How good you are, my dear Mary. That does remind me, I

had better go to the post office today, my money is all but spent. Do you have any left?"

"Me? No." Mary suddenly looks concerned.

"Oh, don't worry. My solicitor's supposed to have sent me some, as indeed is Hogg."

He strokes her pretty face, and she seems reassured.

"Do you think Harriet will come?"

Shelley frowns. Only a week ago he sent her a letter, urging her to friendship, sisterhood, and not anger. There is no reply as yet, and their last conversations return in his heart. "I doubt it. I wish she would though. We could really do well for her. And I swear I do still have the strongest regard for her." He takes a seat beside Mary.

He binds his arms through hers, and they are tangled, irrevocably, it feels in that moment, as if they are Baucis and Philemon turned to living wood, branches intertwined for all eternity.

But he must shake his head and return to the necessities of life.

"But money, my love, is growing short, and the day is slipping by. I must go on to the post office, where, I hope, there shall be some money for us. Or else we are very much in trouble." And she lifts her face for the kiss as he leaves.

"Then you had best go, my elfin knight," she says, "and hurry back to me."

Walking through the small town, his head is full of story, of the images of innocence—a child playing with a serpent, for the serpent has always seemed a peaceful beast to him, and to play with the Edenic image is pleasant. And Mary will help him, which is almost as buoying as the story itself. To write with her beside him. To have a companion in creation is exhilarating. Enthusiasm accompanies him as he strides through the town. The French language flutters around him with its charming half-familiarity and screens him from whatever vulgarities or pettiness might be enacting all around. He is only himself, veiled in ignorance, with Mary in his mind.

He enters the Poste Restante and gives his name and waits while the clerk goes to check, drumming out a rhythm with his fingers as he glances blankly around. And although his assassins would be attached through principle to peace, upon learning of the tyranny and suffering extant in the wider world they must leave their bliss and seek change. Of course they must! How can one live in comfort while others suffer? That is the same mistake his forefathers have made. But he will have Mary to guide him.

The man returns, empty handed.

"*Desolle monsuir. Rien.*"

"*Rien?* Nothing at all? Are you sure?"

"*Oui. Rien. Peut-être demain.*"

And he looks past Shelley with all politeness to the next customer.

Rien. Nothing. Shelley's throat is suddenly tight. The time it has taken them to travel has been plenty for the remittance to arrive. Nothing from Hookham. Nothing from the family solicitors. He had even asked both Harriet and Godwin for a little to tide them over, though he hadn't really expected much from either. But nothing at all... His father is to blame for this. He must have stopped even the limited amount he allowed; that is the only conclusion. But this is more than his father's wrath. This luck dried up everywhere; credit defunct; good will gone. He has nothing.

Shelley is suddenly very aware how far from safety he is, and how far from safety he has brought Mary and Jane.

As he leaves the post office he checks every pocket, finds two napoleons, a pocket watch, a pen. His waistcoat is embroidered silk, beautifully made, and he can do without it. The waistcoat and the watch will get them something, but not enough to get home. To the bank then, to do whatever it takes. He straightens his back, smooths the dust of the road from his coat, and strides confidently towards the bank.

He still has a rich man's ability to make demands and force flustered clerks to pay out a small amount without guarantee.

He gets just enough.

Within a few days they dismiss their plans to stay in Switzerland and set about a river voyage to take them up to Rotterdam where they can board a boat back to England, to speak with those who do not help them now, and more, to hide in the safety of one's own country.

Shelley, as we begin our life together,
I give myself to you entirely,
twinning our destinies, and find it sweet
At last to call you mine. Our lives unfold
Before us now, not two, but one shared path.

I sought in every place a sympathy,
Expecting those who seemed like me to share
The inner workings of my heart; alas,
Too rarely have I found a kindred soul.
Except in you, oh child of light and love.

Our journey now shall be illustrious
And greatness is foretold within our stars.
Leaving my childhood home I look towards
A destiny of travel, love, and work,
For I would shame my parents and myself
if I did not contribute to the quest
for understanding and perfection of
mankind.

I caution you with much regret
To turn not from your purpose, but this know:
Too few today will listen to the truth;
In darkness – I confess– I do despair,
For poetry unread is wasted ink.
Still, a written word may slumber long:
I hope that future eyes awake my songs.

The world is disillusioned with its youth;
So many are like us, each malcontent
At what the powers of king and law proclaim.
I envied once my brothers' education;
However, now I find my thoughts more free,
than many finely taught and know my schooling
much better serves a free, enquiring mind.
My father gave me books without restraint,
Quizzing me on my conclusions, and when
my naïve deductions were imperfect,
His corrections took form of questioning.
I've come to the belief that, rather than
Learning by rote philosophies of men
Determined wise and good, we thinkers should
Answer instead to our own morality,
Learning by witness and contemplation.
We do not need some abstract creed which says
'This is the one true way the world should be'
But to each situation weigh anew
Discov'ring there a single moral truth.

If witnessing meant understanding, ah!
Our task would be so simple. But, alas,
In corrupt times we cannot guarantee
The good and candid nature of mankind.
Hence parliament – that nest of vipers – sits
In state, decreeing death upon the poor,
Ruin upon the good. And so we must
Awaken minds with words as best we can.
The offspring of my mind shall grow anew
Within a sympathetic stranger's thoughts
And so a bold idea may people earth.

Part Two

Chapter One: A Cold Reality
London, 22nd October 1814

A rich man may have debts unchecked, but anyone known to be in desperate circumstances will soon hear his creditors calling, and so Shelley, abruptly finding himself cut off from family money, meets not with compassion, but demand from those whose debts, mere months ago, he could easily have satisfied. Now he must hastily pack a bag with half an eye to the window in fear of the debt collectors who, he has word, are coming to arrest him.

As he grabs his razor, his shirts, his Shakespeare and presses them into a portmanteau, Shelley mutters fiercely to himself, his body quivering in anger. Someone has betrayed him. Godwin? Harriet? There is a pettiness to it that matches his father's cutting him off. His father, who had condemned his marriage to Harriet, now apparently condemns the dissolution of that marriage. That is hypocrisy.

He pats the pockets of his waistcoat, automatically reaching for his pocket-watch, but, of course, it is gone. Sold on the journey back to England. He has already taken his microscopes to the pawnshop this morning, and feels the dizzying lightness of having little left to sell.

The apartment door clatters and Shelley scuttles backwards, dragging the table with him and keeping it between himself and the intruder. This was what he hoped to avoid! Someone is already within the rooms, and there is no way of escape. He frantically considers the windows once more, but his shoulders surely would not fit. It is jail, it is the end!

And then, Mary's voice.

"Shelley?" She bursts into the bedroom where he stands, her cloak still upon her, and runs to him with arms outstretched. "You're still here!" she declares, pressing into him.

He clutches his lover with a relief he cannot quite believe. "I'm still here," he whispers back. "You've been to your father's?"

"He would not see me."

"And Jane?"

"She is with them now."

An extra flare spikes his already heightened panic. He cannot leave Mary alone. "She is staying with them?"

"No, she's coming back here."

"Good. Good." One thing to be grateful for. "You must look after each other. These will be difficult days. But they'll be short. I will find a way to clear my debts and come back to you, I promise."

"Where will you go?" she whispers.

He does not know, and he can hear the fear in her voice, so rather than the truth, he says, "It is better you do not know, for your own sake."

Her eyes are narrow, scrutinising him. "Let me come with you. We can hide together, leave this place."

"No, my dear, wonderful Mary." He tries to put his own pounding heart aside, to subdue his anxiety and show her calm. He strokes her cheek. "I want nothing more than you by my side but we must be cautious. One may fly faster and hide better than two. Three, indeed. No, you must stay, and look after Jane."

A solid, cold look comes over her face then. Something he cannot quite read. His attention is drawn from it by the sight of a cufflink lying on the floorboard. He snatches it up, catching a splinter in his knuckles from the floorboards as he does. He swears and sucks at the graze. But where is the other cufflink? Two will fetch more than twice one at the pawn shop. There is no more time to be sentimental, to remember that his mother gave him them when he went up to university. There is only now, and the need for money, for food, and for fuel for the fire.

He glances back to Mary, wondering how much of their peril she perceives. She is very still, her brow stern and eyes watchful.

A shout outside makes him jump, but it is met by another, and the voices settle. Some minor disagreement on the street, it seems, and nothing to do with him. "I should not stay here any longer," he says. "It isn't safe." And he clamps shut his portmanteau, whatever he has must be enough. He kisses Mary on the cheek, but she is rigid against his affection. He has no time. Without another word, he leaves.

Outside, London is submerged in darkness. Lamps are lit, but their light is blinkered, kept from those who don't deserve it, and withheld from darkest corners, from the lowest forms of life who cannot let light touch their skin.

In this darkness Shelley creeps, his collar turned up against the rain and the eyes of others. Each muscle in his body weighs heavy, as if the skin and sinews that hold him together are straining, and may well snap if real rest does not come. Propelled into the night by his fear, his oppressors, he is haunted by the firm set of Mary's jaw, her following eyes, and in his haste he cannot shake the suspicion he has disappointed her—that she has seen who he truly is and has found him less than she imagined.

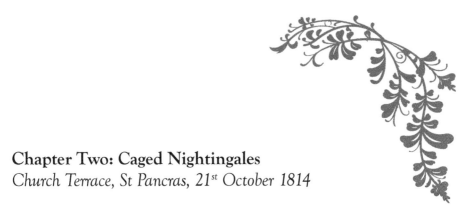

Chapter Two: Caged Nightingales
Church Terrace, St Pancras, 21ˢᵗ October 1814

'Soul of Ianthe!
Awake! arise!'
Sudden arose
Ianthe's Soul; it stood
All beautiful in naked purity,
The perfect semblance of its bodily frame;
Instinct with inexpressible beauty and grace –
Each stain of earthliness
Had passed away – it reassumed
Its native dignity and stood
Immortal amid ruin.

Upon the couch the body lay,
Wrapt in the depth of slumber;
Its features were fixed and meaningless,
Yet animal life was there,
And every organ yet performed
Its natural functions; 'twas a sight
Of wonder to behold the body and the soul.

Could Mary's soul now rise from the body curled tight against the cold, it would flee through London's heartless streets and embrace him. But she is stuck in this shabby apartment, waiting for news of Shelley.

She hates the apartment, and tries to block it out as she stares at the pages of Shelley's book before her. The walls are a repugnant green, an exceedingly old paper that is torn away at places, revealing stone much the same colour, which makes Mary suspect it is mould that is green, and that the paper may have originally been any colour at all. But it has to do. This is the kind of place where questions are not asked, where a girl who might be pregnant with her married lover's child can stay while he hides from the law.

Her chill fingers slip through the pages of poetry, and her fancy struggles to transcend the lodgings and soar with his imagination. The late-morning sun, though winter-weak, leaks through the thin curtain, and the pages are half translucent like the autumn seed-cases of honesty flowers. Her fingertips caress the words, feeling the minute ridges of ink as if they were the residue of him, as if absorbing it could bring her closer to him. But the page is only rough beneath her fingers and her hand wilts.

A distant church bell tolls the hour. She counts eleven knells. Still three hours until she meets Shelley. She is Psyche waiting for darkness.

Despite the sun, a shudder creeps through her and she draws the blankets closer, for she still lies in bed, propped up on one elbow, the book beside her on the pillow. The day is wearing away, but no matter. She has arranged to meet Shelley at two, if it is safe for him to get away. She will wait for him, even though yesterday he did not come. But two o'clock is still a long way away, and there is no purpose in rising before she needs to. She will only get cold and hungry. If he were here they would spend the day in bed together in the loveliest way, but since he is not, she must make do with words.

There is no one she wishes to spend time with that she can reach, and those she would like to spend time with have left her their testaments. On the pillow, her lover; on the bedside table, her mother. She tugs her nightgown sleeves down her arm, for the blanket is scratchy against her bare skin. Leaving Shelley open, she reaches out for her mother's book and holds it close to her.

"Mother," she whispers.

She wants to offer some heathen prayer, some request for help, but there is nothing she can ask, and no faith with which to ask it. Closing the book, she tucks her head and pulls the blanket fully over her so she is curled up, round and foetal, her own warmth around her. Curled like this her hands rest on either side of her belly, and she wonders... She has been his lover some weeks now. Surely the inevitable will follow. Does something already grow within her? Is she different?

Her reverie is shattered by the punch of a strong fist pounding upon the apartment door. She sits bolt upright, for a moment paralysed and listening, hoping she is wrong. But the pounding comes again, and into the green bedroom rushes Jane with round, wild eyes.

"It's bailiffs, Mary!" Jane squeaks.

The pounding is accompanied by a rough voice hollering, "Open up in there!"

Determination snatches Mary and she leaps out of bed, sweeping her dress around her as fast as she can, her fingers grasping at the fastens until she is just decent enough. Then she straightens her shoulders and strides to the front door, hauling it open with a quickness intended to surprise.

"Yes?" she demands, with what she hopes is imperiousness.

The apartment door opens onto a narrow, grubby stairwell where two men in black are standing shoulder to shoulder staring in at her.

The gentleman who was knocking, the man, rather, is surprisingly handsome, with thick brown hair and prominent cheekbones, but there is a peculiar quirk to the side of his mouth that disturbs her, a perpetual sneer, even as he lowers his fist and rights himself.

"We want Mr Percy Bysshe Shelley," he says, not rudely, but certainly not kindly. There is another at his elbow, more the sort one expects of a bailiff: broad built, unshaven and narrow-eyed. But the first is too well-spoken, as if he has chosen this occupation from a desire to do it, rather than from necessity.

They have considerable advantage in height, but all the same she draws herself up as straight as she can and, glad they cannot see the tremor in her leg, matches his smooth tone.

"I'm afraid Mr Percy Bysshe Shelley is not currently in residence here." She makes to close the door, but his foot is already fast in the frame. Mary stares pointedly at it. Behind her Jane is whimpering, but Mary keeps her gaze steely cool, though a tremble runs through her.

"Where might I find Mr Percy Bysshe Shelley, then?" the first bailiff asks, affecting a smile. He says Shelley's name with such a mocking lilt, as if it were an insult.

"I'm afraid I don't know."

"You're obliged to tell us," the first man goes on, his second remaining mute and smug beside him. "Mr Shelley owes a considerable amount of money. To a considerable number of people, I hear. And we've come to arrest him, do you understand?"

"I believe I do," Mary says, still even and composed, "but that doesn't change the fact I have already stated to you, that I simply do not know where he is."

"Can you tell us when he will return?"

"He does not live here."

"The landlady says he does."

"He does not. Mr Shelley kindly arranged this apartment for myself and my sister."

"I think we might have to come in and have a look."

"You shall do no such thing!" Mary declares. The voice she uses is certainly not her own; it has something of Shelley in it, but more, she notes with irritation, of her step-mother, who is always playing the fine lady. In such a moment one grasps whatever weapons one has. "My sister and I are alone here. I am afraid I cannot permit you to come in."

The man at the door chuckles to himself; a chuckle of enjoyment. His stubble-faced companion remains expressionless.

Without further words the men simply step into the house, pushing her aside with a firm movement. Mary is utterly powerless to stop them. She retreats to the edge of her bedroom where Jane is still stood and clasps her sister's hand in her own. The apartment is sufficiently small that in a few paces one can see into every room and the bailiffs are quickly satisfied that their quarry has not concealed himself.

"Miss Godwin," says the first, and then checks himself, "it is Miss Godwin, isn't it?"

Very reluctantly, Mary nods. They know all about her it seems.

"Please tell Mr Shelley we were looking for him, and advise him to make himself known to us with all haste. Good day, Miss

Godwin." He nods to them and makes his way out, his mute accomplice pausing to give the girls a long, lecherous stare, before following suit. The door snaps shut behind them, sealing Mary and Jane into their silence.

"That was horrible," Jane whispers into the quiet as tears begin to roll down her face. "Poor Shelley! God, don't let those terrible men catch him."

"He'll be fine," Mary says, stroking Jane's dark hair reassuringly, "I'm sure of it." But she is not at all sure of it. They weren't so terrible, they were almost courteous. But their threat lingers in the flat, and the only comfort Mary can take from this intrusion is that Shelley is not yet caught.

And here they are, Mary alone in the world except for Jane. Jane of all people!

And Shelley, somewhere out there, with no one at all.

Please let him keep the appointment today, she prays, so she can tell him, warn him they are looking for him. And also, she hopes, feeling a pang of hunger, so he can give her some money, for they are running out.

At half past one Mary steps out of the lodging-house and onto the street. She takes her mother's book with her, tucked into the breast pocket of her jacket. The street is narrow, with scarcely room for two carriages to pass, yet it is crammed full. People gust about with the wind, their own business propelling them on.

Taking her first step into the masses Mary feels a weakness that is only partly her lack of food.

Above, grey clouds sail through a deep, shifting sky.

She will be early to meet Shelley and will just have to stand about where people may stare, but she will not risk missing him. And besides, Jane has been making serious hints that she doesn't want to be left alone in case of the bailiff's return, and Mary certainly will not let her come and spoil the precious Shelley time.

Scarcely has Mary gone three paces from the door when her eye is caught by familiarity. Shivering in a corner, in a long grey dress and black cloak is Fanny, waiting.

Tears flood Mary's eyes and without a word she stumbles towards her sister, clasps her hands.

"Fanny! You're here! I'm so, so glad to see you." Her voice chokes.

Fanny nods, and smiles with tight lips, drawing her wordlessly to the side of the street and out of the thoroughfare.

"You're back from Ireland!" Mary says. "How wonderful. Please, please come in. I don't have long now, but Jane is here and I'll be back soon."

She tries to lead Fanny towards the lodging house, but Fanny, glancing both ways, stays rooted.

"I'm afraid I can't," she says.

"You can't?"

"No, Mary. I'm not allowed to come in."

Mary stares at her sister. Fanny keeps her eyes lowered.

"Father's absolutely forbidden me to step foot inside." She coughs, and pulls her cloak a little tighter. Her face is white but pinched with pink at the nose. She looks so cold. How long has she been waiting?

"But you'll talk to me here?" Mary asks, trying to keep incredulity from her voice. She doubts her father would be remotely sympathetic to this circumvention of his edict, but she has no desire to chase Fanny away. "You can just come in, he won't hear of it from me."

But Fanny is resolute, and so Mary walks with her down a side-lane, where there is comparative silence, and the mud gathers thick between the cobbles.

"Papa is very angry," Mary says.

"He's not happy with you."

"He is well, though?"

"They're all well, just worried. You can imagine how grieved Mama is."

"Wailing over her lost little Jane, I'm sure."

For the first time Fanny offers something like a smile, and Mary laughs with relief.

"Thank you for coming, Fanny. Were you waiting long?"

"A little while. Don't think of it."

"I am so grateful. It's been ghastly since we got back to London. Shelley's in debt, and there's a warrant out for him. He could go to prison. And we have so little money left; if he doesn't come soon... It's just been awful."

Fanny regards her evenly. "Why did you do it, Mary?"

The question hangs between them, and Mary cannot find an answer. If Fanny doesn't know, how can Mary explain her own heart to her? How to tell her that it was inevitable, that *not* to act so would have been the impossible thing.

"I know why you love him, I do. But, Mary! To throw away everything. His wife! His child! His children—surely you know Harriet is expecting? And didn't you think about us? Do you know what people are saying about our family?" There is a ring now to Fanny's voice, an exasperation, even an anger. "They are saying that Papa sold you to him."

"People will always talk," Mary says, but very quietly.

"Yes, they will. We know that. We know what they said about our mother. So, you know what talk like that will do to our business." Fanny stops herself abruptly, and shakes her head. "But do not worry about us. My poor sister, didn't you think of yourself?"

In Mary's hands she feels Fanny's fingers cold and heavy. She swallows deeply.

"I had to, Fanny."

Fanny closes her eyes for a second, presses her lips together as if fighting something back, keeping something inside. Whatever it is, she overcomes it and sighs.

"And Jane?" she asks, conciliatory.

"Jane is well."

"She is?"

"Yes."

"Good. And does she... I mean... is Shelley..." Fanny looks to the clouded sky, as if searching for the right words, but apparently they do not come, for she shakes her head. Still, Mary guesses. She knows what they must all be wondering. Is Jane Shelley's mistress too?

How to say that Jane is sister to them both, that she climbs into their bed and shares their warmth, and that Mary's trust in him is absolute. And if love were to be shared, that would be well. She and

Shelley have talked of free love, of the foolishness of jealousy. But just as Fanny cannot ask, Mary cannot explain.

"I'm glad you took her with you," Fanny says brightly. "You oughtn't to be alone. Shelley isn't living with you now, is he?"

Mary does not want to answer this; it is too like being wrong. But there is something else as well, a nagging guilt. She took only one of her sisters.

"Jane orchestrated it all," she says. It is an explanation, if not a defence.

"I'm sure she did," Fanny says, not meeting Mary's eye. "It all sounds so much like Jane. I'll be honest though, it doesn't sound much like you. I do wish you'd spoken to me."

"You were away."

"I know."

"Would you have come with us?"

Fanny swallows something down and raises her eyes to the heavens, and the reflection of the clear blue utterly overwhelms her grey-brown irises.

"I must go," she says.

"Wait," Mary pleads, and casts out her arm to detain her sister. "You, Fanny, are you well?"

"I am well enough. The house is sadly quiet. Worse now than before when you were away. Charles is in Edinburgh. William's at school most of the time. Just me left. But I've got my chores."

"I'm sure you're a great comfort to father."

"I try to be. I'm not sure though. More than ever I'm in the way now. But the aunts didn't want me." Fanny smiles as she talks, though her forehead is creased and her eyebrows contract. Mary winces. However much Fanny did not want to go to Ireland, to be sent back must still hurt. "So," Fanny continues with a shrug, "it's just a case of making myself useful and hoping I can earn a place in the family. There's a lot more to do in the shop with you two gone."

"Don't let them boss you about, though."

"No. They're both so cross at the moment. Well, never mind. I hope I see you soon, Mary. But I really ought to go home now. I'll try to come again, if I can. Jane is invited home, as I'm sure she knows. They do want her to come back."

"But not me."

Fanny shakes out the hood on her cloak and raises it gingerly over her head. Although the day is grey and cold, the moisture in the air is light.

"You can't blame them, Mary. They have to protect themselves."

As she turns away, Mary lets go her arm.

"Fanny?"

"Yes?" She looks back.

One last thing to say. One last thing her sister must know.

"I think... I think that I shall have a child soon."

Fanny is perfectly still, but across her eyes tears rise. She only looks at Mary, and Mary, biting her own lip, looks back. Fanny brings a hand to dab her eyes.

"Remember that I love you, and Shelley. I am always your sister." Fanny leans in and kisses her sister's cheek. For a moment Mary smells her: wax paper, candle smoke, and old linen. Against her face the wool of Fanny's cloak leaves a greater impression than the light kiss. Fanny withdraws, and with a small, sad smile, leaves Mary alone in the side street with the scent of home dissipating in the misty rain.

Percy Bysshe Shelley to Mary Wollstonecraft Godwin
24th October 1814

This separation is a calamity not to be endured patiently; I cannot support your absence. I thought that it would be less painful to me; but I feel a solitariness and a desolation of heart where you have been accustomed to be. But, my beloved, this will not last; prudence and self-denial will discomfort our enemies. I shall meet you soon; You may meet me with perfect safety at No. 60 Fleet Street.

Mary Wollstonecraft Godwin to Percy Bysshe Shelley
25th October 1814

For what a minute did I see you yesterday – is this the way, my beloved, that we are to live? When I awake I turn to look on you – dearest Shelley you are solitary and uncomfortable, why cannot I be with you, to cheer you and press you to my heart? Oh, my love, you have no friends, why then should you be torn from the only one who has affection for you? But I shall see you tonight and that is the hope that I shall live on through the day – be happy dear Shelley and think of me. I will meet you this evening – will you be at the door of the coffee house at five o'clock? I send you Diogenes as you have no books.

Percy Bysshe Shelley to Mary Wollstonecraft Godwin
27th October 1814

Oh! my dearest love, why are our pleasures so short and so interrupted? How long is this to last?

Praise my forbearance – oh! beloved one – that I do not rashly fly to you, and at least secure a moment's bliss. Wherefore should I delay; do you not long to meet me? All that is exalted and buoyant in my nature urges me towards you, reproaches me with the cold delay, laughs at all fear and spurns to dream of prudence. Why am I not with you? Alas! we must not meet.

How hard and stubborn must be the spirit that does not confess you to be the subtlest and most exquisitely fashioned intelligence; that among women there is no mind equal to yours! And I possess this treasure! How beyond all estimate is my felicity! Yes; I am encouraged – I care not what happens; I am most happy.

Meet me to-morrow at three o'clock in St. Paul's, if you do not hear before.

Adieu; remember love at vespers before sleep. I do not omit my prayers.

Chapter Three: An Ideal Community
Hampstead Heath, London, 11ᵗʰ November 1814

*A*s swiftly as it was withdrawn, liberty is restored. Through all the pecuniary trials of the Godwin family no moneylender in the city was ever wont to offer Mary's father a loan. But the name of 'Shelley' with its attendant baronetcy, squires, sirs, and members of parliament is, at last, well met, and Shelley secures a small loan against the inheritance that will inevitably one day be his. Enough to stave off the debtors, enough to reunite them.

And so Mary and Shelley have packed a winter picnic, and carried it, along with a great many blankets, out onto Hampstead Heath where they sit now, her head on his shoulder, his arm on her waist, and begin the life they have longed for.

Mary cannot quite believe their situation so suddenly resolved; she clings to liberty with astonishment and gratitude, and listens with joy to Shelley's talk of a free community unhampered by the restraints of modern society. All the theories they talked of he now seeks to put into practice, and Jane especially chatters about the prospect of free love, of a community without property, of intellectual development and equality between the sexes.

Into their group Shelley brings many friends, and the most important joins them on this chilled afternoon: Thomas Jefferson Hogg, Shelley's university fellow with whom he was expelled for writing atheistical pamphlets. Mary likes Hogg. He is amusing, affectionate, and his admiration for Shelley is unbounded.

Watching them together brings her a particular pleasure;

sparks fly as they debate and discuss and burst into laughter. There is no doubt Shelley is the brighter star, but Hogg shines beside him in the cosmos, has written books, and what is not to be dismissed, has secured a living for himself as a lawyer. He is handsome enough, and well dressed, and quite in love with Mary.

She wasn't surprised when she received the epistle declaring his love, and nor was Shelley.

"Do you love him back?" Shelley had asked, all curiosity and excitement.

She had hesitated, realising his own excitement, his desire to share those he loves with each other.

"That is not the word I would use," she'd said diplomatically. "I like him. Very much."

"What will your reply be?" he asks.

"My reply... That I do not yet love him, but that I think I might, with time."

In her reply she had shared that sentiment, but insisted there was no question of his sharing her bed until the baby she is now definitely expecting is born.

And now she can sit on the blanket watching these two excellent young men and feel a quiet satisfaction in the knowledge that she has kissed them both.

"Come, let us eat!" Shelley cries, "and let us eat well, for we have much to celebrate." He had taken it upon himself to procure the goods of the picnic, and Mary now notices he has provided them, almost exclusively, with sweets. There is an abundance of Chelsea buns from a street vendor, a plain loaf from a baker, and a box of marzipan fruits from a confectioner who had apparently looked at the scuffs and stains on Shelley's jacket with distaste.

"He would have loved to send me away, but, alas! I had money."

Shelley cackles to himself, and leans his back against the trunk of the willow tree they have laid their blanket beneath.

The spot is peaceful, sufficiently far from the paths that they have privacy, but afforded an expanse of light by the stretching pond beside them.

"I say, I certainly am glad you're out of danger now, Shelley," Hogg says, taking his seat beside Mary on the picnic blanket. With an affected toss of the head, he shakes his hair from his eyes. It grows long, as Shelley's does, but it is tufty and stubborn, while Shelley's follows the wind and light like a wild plant.

"Safe for now. It's not going to do for long, but it's something." Without specifying what he wants, Shelley reaches out, and Hogg, with the intuition of a good servant, hands him a bun. Hogg offers Mary one, and she takes it, though she hasn't the stomach for sweets today.

"I'm sorry I wasn't in London to help you in your hour of need," Hogg says. "You know I would have, anything you required!"

Whatever Shelley might say about his love for Hogg, Mary thinks, Hogg's love for Shelley is as absolute as a dog's for its master.

"And your father won't give you anything?" Hogg asks, his eyebrows raised with canine curiosity.

Shelley runs his fingers through the grass. He always shows reluctance to discuss his family. "He certainly won't. And I'm not going to ask him."

"It's a terrible shame." Hogg tuts to himself, and picks up another pastry, examines it suspiciously before stuffing the whole thing into his mouth in one motion. "A man like your father..." he says through a full mouth, crumbs tumbling, "he must know. He'll know what you've to go through. Do you think he hopes you'll relent and come home repentant?"

"Ha!" Shelley's laugh is an unfeigned bark, a contemptuous delight. "Even he must realise that will never happen."

"But he must know. The interest you'll have to pay on that loan... I dread to think of it. Surely it's exorbitant?"

"Is it?" Mary asks, her sharp concern cutting through their talk.

"One needn't worry about it," Shelley says lightly. He tears up a fistful of grass and scatters it into the still air. "The loan is against my inheritance. It shan't be called in until my father dies, and then it shan't be a problem."

"When your father dies..." Mary echoes. This world is alien to her—futures full of money, negotiations she cannot comprehend. And Shelley, despite his recent brush with poverty, does not really understand what it is to live precariously. He always believed something would come, and it did. She tears a small scrap off her cake and tastes it gingerly.

"And do you know," Hogg asks, swallowing down his cake, "just how much will you get on that sad, sad day?"

Shelley only shrugs.

"Must we talk money?" he sighs. "It is the spring from which so much evil flows. A mechanism of cruelty only."

"I accuse you of equivocation." Hogg points a long finger at Shelley and arches an eyebrow. "A number, Master Bysshe."

Shelley rolls his eyes. "I believe, if the estate is entailed, about one hundred thousand pounds."

Mary cannot believe it.

"One-hundred-thousand!" she cries, drawing out the phrase.

Hogg tilts his head appreciatively. "That's not a bad sum."

"Something like that."

"It's an extraordinary sum!" Mary says. She does not want to show her astonishment, but even Hogg is impressed. "My goodness," she mutters. "I suppose I knew people owned such sums but I never really thought about it before. What on earth would any one person, one family, do with such an amount?"

"Hold on to it, mostly." Shelley shakes his head. "It's jealousy and greed and nothing else. I'm quite aware no one in the family wants me to inherit because they know I'll disperse the fortune. I'll give it where it's needed."

"Can they keep you from inheriting?" Hogg asks.

"Not really. I'm the only son. The only legitimate son. There's a bastard as I understand, but no real claim. Still, it will be useful if Harriet's baby is a boy. An heir never hurts."

Mary's heart suddenly chills. Whatever they may say amongst themselves, she is only a mistress, and Shelley's wife will soon have her second child that may rightly bear the Shelley name. She wonders once more about Shelley's obscure family. It is still many months until her own child will be born, but when it is, will they hear of the birth? Will they care? Even if they cannot recognise it as their own, won't his mother put her hand to her heart, and think with kindness on a grandchild? But now she thinks of it, will her own father forgive her enough to come and see the child? Surely so, surely.

Emotion chokes her, and she forces it away with a pleasant expression.

"That's the way they think, Mary," Shelley says very softly. "Please don't let their prejudices cloud your happiness."

She is not so alone in the world, she tells herself. She has Shelley, she even has Hogg, and that is so much more than poor Harriet has. A pang of guilt shoots through her, but she cannot hold it, and so lets it go.

"Here, Mary, let's open the marzipan fruits!" Hogg says cheerfully. "I haven't had these for years."

"They're never quite what you expect," Shelley remarks. "They look so refreshing, but taste, well, quite dry."

"Thank you." She takes the proffered dainty. She has never had one and is astonished at the craftsmanship of it. In her hand it looks just like a tiny apple, but it is soft to the touch. She stares at it a while. "What a lot of money that is," she says, still staring. "I don't think my father had that much money in his whole life."

"And when I inherit, I will ensure that your father is comfortable," Shelley reaches out and touches her knee, "I promise you that."

She takes comfort. Shelley is her family now. She bites into the fruit and finds it grainy and sickeningly sweet.

"Really," Shelley goes on, "all wealth is shameful. If one has more than one needs, and another has less than they need, well... There's only one rightful thing to do."

"Hear, hear!" Hogg cries.

Hogg takes out the latest copy of liberal literary magazine, *The Examiner*, and points out a few interesting articles, before calling upon Shelley to recount the time he met its editor, Leigh Hunt. "A fine man, one of the few willing to publish the truth in this damnable world," Shelley declares. "A West Indian apparently, though you wouldn't know it. We had breakfast and talked about the horrors of Christianity."

Hogg cheers this and proposes a toast to Hunt. With a little prompting from Shelley, Hogg launches into an explanation of Godwin's principles of the hypocrisy of property and the slavery of marriage, and how these ideas should be expanded today.

Mary recognises his arguments as feeble copies of Shelley's and knows that, despite all their university scholarship, she knows her father's philosophies better than either of them, but all the same she sits back in modest silence to listen. When Hogg leans in close to her, she does not move away. The evening is beautiful, and Mary is with two fine, intelligent young men; she has plenty reason to be happy.

The afternoon is rich with winter's peculiar sunlight; the sullen sky fades from the purest blue at its height down to a dusky lavender at its depths. The mists drift low from the city.

Shelley knows some things must be celebrated. For though there's a little colour back in Mary's cheeks, storm-grey shadows have settled beneath her eyes, and her face has grown thinner. When he saw her last night, revealed entirely to him in a new bedroom to be made their own, her ribs were visible at her breast, and around the taut dome of expectancy her white body was wiry, weak.

In this late afternoon light her fair face has an ethereal quality, and with her abundant hair bound in pinned-up braids and her slender frame bound in her purple tartan dress she looks like an ancient Celtic goddess. How extraordinary that she should be his! It is time, at last, for them to begin their life together. He cannot demand ownership of her, of course not. This is a moment to prove they will truly live by the laws of liberty. After all, he spends so much of his days with Jane now, he thinks it quite probable that he could kiss Jane and still love Mary. The one would not end the other. And while she may love him, may she too not kiss, not even love elsewhere?

Hogg's flirtations are clumsy, but his demeanour is noble and his enthusiasm is clear. Mary laughs prettily at him and holds his hand, and Shelley feels only happiness. This is how their lives should be!

Shifting his weight onto one elbow, Shelley reaches into his breast pocket and finds, as suspected, a carefully folded sheet of blank paper, hastily stowed earlier—or yesterday? He forgets its intended purpose. As he flattens it out he listens to Hogg.

"Your laughter does me the greatest good in the world, dear Mary," Hogg is saying. "I have been quite woebegone of late."

Glancing up, Shelley grins at Mary who, though her ear is leant to Hogg, has turned her eyes to back to him. There is a heavy loveliness in those lids, a knowingness in the smile as she follows his hands at work. Firmly he folds the page in half, pressing the crease before deftly sliding down the corners.

"My heart has been broken, perhaps Shelley told you?"

Mary's eyes roll round to Hogg. "He did not," she says.

"Yes, there was a lady I loved, some time ago. Hers was the loveliest spirit I ever met. But she died, very young, poor thing."

Shelley tucks the two corners in and spins the paper in his hand.

"I am so sorry."

"Yes, that in itself was awful, but not as awful as what came afterwards..."

Shelley can feel Mary's gaze upon his hands as silent benediction upon his creation.

With one last motion Shelley fattens out the paper boat he has constructed. Mary chuckles and he balances it on his first finger, like a magnificent hat.

"He used to make those out of bank notes," Hogg says wryly.

"You objected," Shelley admits.

"I certainly did!" Hogg appeals to Mary with a look of horror that makes her laugh.

Beyond Hogg and Mary, the sky has darkened. Out across the moorland the grasses absorb the nightness, and their fellow men are only phantoms drifting slowly homewards. It is time for a little light. Shelley scrambles over to Hogg, and familiarly reaches into his breast pocket, causing his friend no small bewilderment and another bloom of baffled laughter. Shelley finds the matches he seeks, and striking one, applies it to the topsail of his little boat. The flame is bright, stunning in the darkness.

Across the moor, phantom shapes drift and dissipate. But one stays solid, as if it were searching rather than straying. Shelley squints, willing the figure into focus, and standing up, he holds the burning boat aloft, a beacon in the twilight. The shade resolves itself roundly, an arm of greeting raises, waves enthusiastically.

"There you are!" Jane's voice cries out. Her pale dress is stark white in the fading light.

Shelley lays his boat upon the pond where it bobs uncertainly a moment, the flame now possessing the sail entirely, before finding its current and dancing away.

Into the evening Jane erupts, shaking out her hair and throwing herself down upon the blanket.

"Setting things on fire, are we?" she asks with enthusiasm. The flame swells and subsides, and Shelley turns his thoughts to finding more paper.

"Shelley is," Hogg says, agreeably.

"How was your afternoon?" Shelley asks, steadying himself against the willow as he stands up.

"Well! It was hilarious!" she cries, and then, looking serious, "But first—have you heard the news?"

"Certainly the latest gossip on Lord Byron's divorce," Mary says conspiratorially to Hogg.

"No, not that, although that is fascinating. Apparently, he *murdered* someone."

"Lord Byron murdered someone?" Mary echoes with a frown.

"No, probably not, but that's what people are saying. Anyway! Not the news I wanted to talk about." She turns to Shelley and composes her face into solemnity.

"I read in the papers something... About Sir Bysshe Shelley. He's your relative, isn't he?"

Shelley is startled at the turn.

"Yes," he says, "He's my grandfather."

"Yes, I thought he might be. Oh, Shelley, he's dead."

The image of his grandfather rises in his mind. A looming patriarch with a wicked laugh. It is old Bysshe who gave him his name, and that is perhaps the only fact that made the old man indulgent towards him.

"I'm sorry to hear that," he says. It is what one says, but the memory is so misty it might not even be his.

"Are you upset?" Jane asks, her face sad enough to make him so.

"Not really. He was kind enough to me when I was young but we weren't close. I don't think we'd have liked each other as men. He certainly hasn't offered me any support in recent years."

There is a moment of respectful quiet, before Hogg very discreetly mutters.

"I should say there'll be some money in it for you, Shelley."

There certainly should be. Shelley nods.

"But, come, Jane, you were going to tell us about your afternoon."

"I've been at Skinner Street," she says, "and weren't they all foolish! What are these?" Jane steps across the blanket to inspect the goodies and takes a marzipan fruit, biting into it and expressing a high noise of delight as she stands back up. "Yes, Mama was fawning and sobbing and in all high histrionics. She's had the slightest cold and is convinced she will die soon and do so separated from her beloved daughter. She's not remotely sick, I swear to you. And Papa is all cross, and Fanny just sits in the corner too timid to say a word." Jane grins at them all. "It was so funny, I wish you'd been there, Shelley. They had the audacity to lay out for me my 'options'!" She throws the rest of her marzipan at Mary who catches it with some surprise. "I can come home if I promise to behave and not to have further communication with that scoundrel Shelley, or I can go to Bath or Bristol and be a governess or a companion, can you imagine!"

"And what did you say to them?" Shelley asks, rather wishing he'd been there to see her give fight.

"I told them I am an independent woman!" Her voice rises heroically. "I am the latest in a new genus!"

"Jane!" he cries, clapping his hands, for he recognises quite well her echo of Wollstonecraft's words. He looks to Mary to share this triumph, but she only smiles weakly and brushes the crumbs from her dress. Apparently, she has no time for Jane's moment of victory. But Shelley feels a high, bright joy. Around him are the people he loves, asserting themselves against an indifferent world; here, at last, is a community of intellectuals, of radicals, of those who dare to defy convention... here is none of his father's aristoc-racy, corruption, restriction, none of Harriet's prudishness, par-ticularity, false philosophy. Here the chains are off, and there is a chance to step towards true liberty.

That same enthusiasm is in Jane's flushed face. She tosses her hair, and her plump lips press together in a pleased pout.

"I tell you," she says, "Mama kept saying 'but Jane, but Jane, you can't!'" She modulates her voice, mimicking her mother very well. "As if I couldn't! I shall make my future." Breathless, she looks at him, waiting, wanting something. His approval? His delight? "Shelley?"

He steps across the blanket, coming towards her and her fiery eyes. "Wonderful Jane!" he says, full of happiness.

"I don't think I want to be Jane anymore," she says to him. He can feel Mary and Hogg watching, and is aware of something strange and powerful flowing between them all. "And I certainly don't want the name Godwin," Jane goes on. "He's not my father. I shall bear my mother's name, thank you, I will be a Clairmont, and I think I should like to be Claire Clairmont!"

Shelley snatches at her hands and holds them tight, a tremble passing between them.

"Then you, Claire Clairmont, are magnificent!" he whis-pers, and then throws back his head and shouts. "Magnificent! Magnificent Claire Clairmont! Magnificent Mary! Magnificent Hogg! We are the free and we shall choose our own names!"

His voice reverberates out across the water, and Claire shrieks with laughter, Hogg gasps, and even Mary exclaims at the spectacle.

Night sets in. There is mauve in the sky and darkest navy in the water. With a flurry of inspiration, Shelley demands that they all search their bags and pockets for every scrap of paper they have. End pages are torn from Voltaire's *Candide*, from his own notebook come sheets of half sketched poetry, and setting to work, Shelley makes a fleet of boats. The others join in, trying to follow the deft movements of his hands. Once they have a small fleet, Shelley crouches on the bank, setting flame to the tip of each boat, while Claire—for Claire she must now be called—launches each little vessel, the sparkling threads in her shawl reflecting the fire upon the water, and her face glows bright and happy. From his seat beneath the willow Hogg calls encouragement and cheer to the ships, while Mary's wise dark eyes weave her silent spell of blessing upon the vessels.

The flaming armada drifts slowly out across the water. As Shelley watches them from the shore silence comes, hand-in-hand with twilight, over them all. The quiet is the quiet of death, of sleep and solemnity. How still the wind must be, or else some charm in the stray strands of Mary's long hair resists even its most persuasive whisper. Mary is so still and serene; marble-fair and robed in amethyst, she is the colour of the night. Shelley sits beside her, lays his head against her shoulder while the newly-christened Claire stands upon the bank, gilt with firelight. This is the hour of their life.

Chapter Four: Of Family
Horsham, Sussex, 7th January 1815

Shelley marches back to the family seat in Sussex, a captious energy sparking within him. Determined to catch everyone unprepared, he hops a ditch, climbs a wall with the help of an apple tree, lands on the leaf-soft earth, and is upon his father's property once more.

He only faintly remembers his grandfather—a capricious old man with a sparkling eye and deep voice. Bysshe senior had a wild youth, eloping with a sixteen-year-old and without consent, much to the family's chagrin, but ultimately was forgiven and became the family patriarch. Shelley goes now, not to pay respects, but to claim what is his.

The sinews of his body are strung tight as he strides through a dense web of rhododendrons, breathing in their sticky leaves and heady scent. There is no version of today he can conceive that is not a fight, and he is ready.

Through the dark web of branches and leaves, long lawns gradually emerge until he pushes out of the woods, and there is Field Place itself, squat and sprawling, a clutter of windows in regimented neatness, exactly as it has always been. The vision, and all the years of memories it invokes, is cloying, and though Shelley scowls and hunches up his shoulders, he does not break the pace of his approach.

Up ahead the door opens and a slim, pale-faced figure in a wide black dress steps hesitantly out, gaze fully upon Shelley. Her face is his own—the large blue eyes, the slender nose—but marked by a peacefulness he has never attained. His sister Elizabeth. Now behind her comes Margaret who has grown from childishness and wears long dresses like a lady though she is only thirteen. He quickens his pace to something like a run, and Elizabeth too is running now across the lawn, and Margaret cries: "Bysshe! Bysshe!"

And for one moment Shelley is overjoyed, running to embrace his sisters, until between them falls a vast, heavy command.

"Elizabeth! Get back into the house."

She freezes at their father's voice, and only so short a way from Bysshe. Their eyes meet, and hers are sorrowful as she lightly shakes her head. Margaret has already retreated, and, turning down her gaze, Elizabeth goes back into the house, slipping past their father at the door.

Sir Timothy Shelley, Baronet, glares out of the black doorway.

"Bysshe," he booms, and despite the distance Shelley is cowed. He is Bysshe again, the wayward child, and though he attempts to draw himself up tall before the furious gaze of his father, he cannot convince himself he is a man. He tries to step forward.

"By your actions," his father shouts, "you have made it clear that you do not desire to be a part of this family; by my words I have made it clear that you are not welcome in this house."

Shelley quickens his step, and draws in breath to reply to his father, but the door is already closing, his father slipping into the darkness within, and by the time Shelley has his feet upon the steps the house is locked to him.

The anger that has lain waiting begins to seethe and to bubble and in one swift, catlike movement he leaps the stairs and pounds upon the door.

"Father!" he shouts, his voice high and scratchy after that low baritone. "I would speak with you!"

He hammers his fist, and the old door trembles beneath his anger. Will it release its ancient hinges? Will it sense the injustice committed and seek to right the Shelley family wrong? "Mother? Father!"

Nothing.

"Father! Do not think you can forget me! I shall command the wind to cry 'Bysshe! Bysshe! Bysshe!' as it tears around the house. The rivers shall remember me and wherever you go you shall hear my name upon the waves!"

But the house is silent. Were it not for the three people he has just seen, and his certainty of many more—his mother, his other siblings, the governess, the tutor, the myriad servants—there could be no one there. Just a great wall of silence.

Are they all in there, listening until he goes away? He thumps once more upon the door and in despair drops down onto the step.

Very well, if they are not going to greet him, he shall wait. He shall play their game and remain quiet until they think he is gone and open the door and then he shall catch them and demand, demand they notice him.

In his pocket is the Milton Mary has lent him, so he stretches out his legs upon the balustrade and makes himself as comfortable as he can to sit and read.

Milton calms him; the necromancer Comus is attempting to subdue a fair lady and compel her to his wicked will, but she resists, and argues eloquently for self-restraint and chastity.

It is some time before the door behind him creaks, and he does not deign to look up.

"Well, well. You've returned have you, Bysshe?"

The family doctor comes down the steps, positioning himself where Bysshe cannot help but see him over the top of the book.

"I desire to speak with my father," he replies, coolly.

"I don't at all think that's a good idea." The doctor shakes his head. "You're quite upsetting the family as it is. Your mother is crying in her bedroom, Bysshe. Don't you feel any compunction?"

"She would have no cause to cry if my father would let me in."

The doctor tuts to himself.

"What are you reading?"

Bysshe does not reply, and the doctor snatches the book out his hands. Registering the cover, he snorts, and he flicks the pages disparagingly until he comes to rest on the fly leaf.

"The daughter of Wollstonecraft and Godwin," he reads, for there is Mary's neat hand declaring her property. "So I'd heard. Honestly, Bysshe, why are you here? What is it that you want?"

Shelley looks then fully upon the doctor, his head tilted to one side, and is suddenly aware that the gesture is a Maryish one.

"I have come to speak to my father, and to hear the contents of my grandfather's will."

"Then for heaven's sake, speak to the lawyers!" the doctor cries. "You know no good can come from your being here. Bysshe, you are the heir to all of this. Will you please be sensible? I speak harshly to you, but I swear there is nothing I'd rather see than a reconciliation between yourself and your father. And that will require some compliance on your behalf. Mend your ways, stop gadding about with the child of William Godwin of all people." He throws the book back. "And if you cannot do that, at least be respectful of your family."

"I would like to see my sisters."

"Definitely not." The doctor shakes his head.

"The thought of them locked in this place puts me ill at ease. I do not approve of this curtailing of their liberties."

"No, I dare say you don't, and your father precisely suspects you will snatch them away at the first opportunity, and that is why he keeps them so very close. Please, Bysshe, you've already broken your mother's heart, don't make it any worse."

Shelley folds the book shut, but says nothing.

"Listen, there's something for you in the will, of course there is. And we're not going to stand in the way of you getting it, though I think there are... some negotiations your father would like to make. Return to wherever it is you've come from, and wait for communication from the solicitors."

"Very well." Shelley stands.

"Thank you." The doctor offers his hand and Shelley, after a pause, shakes it.

"I shall write to the solicitors, then. I thank you for the courtesy you have extended to me, doctor."

"Perhaps we shall meet here again in better circumstances, Master Bysshe. I have every hope of your return to this family."

"That is kind of you to say, but I have none," Shelley says, and with a smart nod, leaves his family home, and the thought occurs to him as he leaves by the drive that he may never return.

20ᵗʰ March, 1815

At the end of November Shelley received a letter saying that Harriet had been delivered of a healthy baby boy. He sent her his best wishes, and once more offered his friendship, to no response.

They expect Mary's child in April, but she is born in February, lives two weeks, and then dies.

The delicacy, the tininess of it. The heat of her, and then the cold and stiffness she had on that morning. Mary falls mute.

It would have been easier for her had the child been still-born, Shelley thinks. Then they would not have chosen a name: *Clara* for her aunt. Nor would the other aunt, Fanny, have come to coo and to tell Mary how lucky she is. Mrs Godwin would not have sent blankets for the little thing, blankets with a tantalising promise of parental forgiveness.

And when now he wants to go to Mary and wrap her in his arms, and hear her grief, she will not speak to him, but makes a reassuring smile and says that she is tired.

"Come, Mary, shall I read to you?" he asks as they sit by the fireside.

"No. I don't want any stories just now."

"Anything you like."

"No, thank you."

They sit in silence a while. Claire is off to bed. Hogg calls every day, and sits with Mary while she nets little trinkets for him, and then goes home in the evening. Shelley does not know how to approach this silence. It is something new. He waits. The fire crackles in the grate. The darkness whispers in the corners of the room.

At last, she speaks.

"I had a dream last night," she says. "I dreamt our baby was still alive. That she was not really dead, only cold and we were able to warm her and bring her back to life."

He wants to reach out to her, but the fragility of her worries him. What if he should touch her, and she recoil?

"Have you been to see your son?" she asks. She does not look at him.

"No," his reply is no more than a whisper. "No. I would have told you if I had."

She nods.

"Charles," she says. That is the name Harriet has given the boy. "I suppose he was never so small as ours was. What about Ianthe? Was she that small?"

He rises from his seat, and kneels before her, taking her passive hands in his own.

"No. Ianthe was never that small. I don't think any child living was ever that small. It's extraordinary that our Clara lived even as long as she did."

Again, Mary smiles that thin, wan smile. As she stares at him the firelight reflects upon the surface of her eyes, hiding the emotion within.

"I want to make you happy again, Mary," he says.

She shakes her head as she replies.

"I am not ready to be happy."

Chapter Five: The Exchange
London, 8ᵗʰ April 1815

*M*ary lets Thomas Jefferson Hogg hold her hand as they walk down the Strand, quite aware of the pleasure it gives him. A few paces ahead, Shelley and Claire are arm in arm, giggling to each other with gleeful mischief.

"Let us have an adventure!" Shelley had cried out over breakfast, with such sudden fervour Mary dropped her bread, prompting a spurt of laughter from Claire, and Shelley offered atonement on his knees. They summoned Hogg, of course, because they always do now; his presence has become as inevitable as Claire's.

The adventure is to the London Exchange, where, as well as shops and curiosities, a menagerie of exotic animals is housed.

She likes Hogg's presence. She has taken to calling him Jefferson, which he likes. He is easy, gentle, and with his encouragement she has joined the outings more frequently of late. The misery has lessened, though her sense of self is shaken. She was briefly a mother, but is one no more. She is not mother, she is not wife. She is the seventeen-year-old mistress of a married man. She tries to distract herself.

"Have you been before?" Mary asks Hogg as they press their way along the broad street. The pavement width permits only three pedestrians at a time, so whenever they meet another couple arm in arm, Hogg steps down and onto the road, loosening his hold on Mary, if not quite relinquishing it, only to hop back up once they have passed. "We can just walk on the road, there's plenty space," she says.

"Certainly not! I can't permit Miss Godwin to walk in the road." Hogg shakes his head vigorously. "And to answer your question, no, I have not been, but I have spoken to those who have and I hear it really is excellent. I hope particularly to see some of the big cats, which I think I might write about in my next novel."

"Are you writing another novel?"

He grins with enthusiasm, but at once his face falls as he considers the matter. "Not quite. That is, Shelley thinks I should. So, for him, I shall come up with something. Something oriental and exotic I think. With big cats in it."

"I look forward to that."

"I don't really know what to do next, though." Hogg shrugs and gazes ahead at Shelley and Claire. Mary knows full well that Hogg's Prince Alexey is based, with little imagination, upon Shelley, a fact which makes her love Hogg more.

With a shake of his head, Hogg dismisses the topic.

"Claire seems to have cheered up," he says.

"She has," Mary concedes.

Up in her bed last night Mary heard Shelley and Claire telling each other ghost stories right into the small hours, and then, what a surprise, Claire had nightmares and spent the rest of the night crying, with Shelley alternately reprimanding her folly and soothing her. The excursion is suggested, no doubt, to cheer the sulking face and petulant pout that haunted breakfast.

Up ahead, Claire is now squealing childishly.

"I think I might be frightened of the lions, Shelley!" she cries, casting a rosy grin back towards Mary.

"Nonsense!" Shelley replies. "Anything so much as growls at you, I shall growl back twice as loud!"

And never mind the people on the street, Shelley throws back his head, shaking out his mane of hair and makes a great roar. Claire shrieks with delight and feigned embarrassment, circling back and wrapping her arm through Mary's, leaving Shelley quite alone.

Shelley takes his abandonment good-naturedly, and strides across the road to where the Exchange advertises itself in bright colours.

As they approach, Claire leans in to Mary and whispers, "Lord

Byron came here recently." Hogg, on Mary's other arm, probably can't hear them, and adopts an air of agreeable disinterest, as if he does not care.

"You have already told me that," Mary replies in the same hush.

"I must have read all the reports about it. Apparently he was most taken with the elephant."

"I'm sure he was."

"He might well come back." Claire's attention scans the crowds, as if she expects the celebrated poet to step towards them at any second. "Can you imagine? What would you do?"

"I would do absolutely nothing," Mary chuckles, "but you, my dear, I dread to think what you would do!"

"Everything they're saying about the divorce... It really is quite brutal."

"Yes," Mary sighs. It would be hard enough to avoid the subject simply in the papers, never mind how often Claire brings it up. "I feel very sorry for both of them."

"I just mean to say, he's in London. We should find a way of making his acquaintance." They have come to the entrance, and press eagerly in. "For Shelley, you know," Claire says. "It would be good for him to know Byron. He needs some connection. For his writing."

"Perhaps it would," Mary replies, and she squeezes her sister's hand.

The Exchange is packed. The lower floors are crammed with shops and into those shops press rich and poor alike, all there to ogle and to rummage. Shouts from vendors rise in every direction, crying the prices and the qualities of their wares. But above these sound the strange rumblings and screechings of animals upstairs. Without pausing to consider the trinkets, though Claire looks longingly at the stalls, Shelley leads them up to the menagerie at a run, and as they proceed the heavy perfumes of the stalls give way to a hot, sweaty smell of beasts.

"If you get at all nervous," Jefferson says, close by Mary's ear, "just let me know and I'll take you outside. It's quite cramped."

Mary thanks him with as little condescension as she can muster.

At first all she can see is a sweep of bonnets and hats. She is not tall, even for her sex, and Jefferson does little better, but craning she can spot Shelley's uncovered brown hair rising through the multitude of hats and bonnets. She tries to wriggle through the crowd after him, but almost at once she finds herself separated from all her companions. This does not trouble her. She shakes her arm to relieve the pressure of Jefferson's recent grip and presses on as best she can.

Quite suddenly she breaks through the crowd and into the long room of the menagerie. Cages are raked all along the walls, often stacked two or more on top of each other, and in these cages the most extraordinary creatures, creatures Mary has never seen in her life. Some she recognises from drawings, but some utterly alien to her. Monkeys, a great beautiful sloth, all kinds of big cats, a lion, a tigress, glorious creatures all, pacing their enclosures and staring back at the dense crowd of people with only mild, tired curiosity.

The people, however, are delighted, and cry out shrilly to one another. Somehow, Mary feels they ought to observe the respectful silence of the church or gallery before such exquisite beings, and she keeps her distance.

It is the people who seem strange. They all look so foolish, in their frills and bonnets, gaping at the animals. Yet, she reflects, are there not frills on her dress, a bonnet upon her head? Is she not also there to stare at the creatures behind bars? As her gaze roves the crowd it falls upon something that makes her heart stop.

A balding head of close white hair, and familiar hunch in a heavy black jacket. Strangers obscure the view and she steps hurriedly forward to secure it once more: yes, there is her father, and with him Claire's brother Charles. She did not even know Charles was back in London, he's been away in Edinburgh, apprenticed to Turner's publishers, and working alongside Robert Baxter, the boy she could have married. Will that always be the phrase she recollects when she thinks of Robert? But, after all, she has not thought of him so very much lately. What would he say to know she has two lovers now? But, more pressingly, what would her father say? She glances about, but can see no sign of Shelley, Hogg, or Claire, and is glad.

She wants to be alone to watch her father. Charles Clairmont says something the old man frowns at. But he frowns at everything, it is not necessarily unwelcome information. They move off together, perhaps to look at something else. How strange to see these two grown men at the menagerie, without even little William to justify the excursion. Charles walks a step or two behind his step-father, hands clasped respectfully behind his back.

But hasn't her father aged in these months? He looks so much smaller, his hair thinner, his skin looser. Is this her fault? Has he had sleepless nights on her account? She hasn't even seen him since she was, so briefly, a mother. Her teeth clench and her chest rattles with the threat of emotion but she hauls in a single big breath and moves back.

There is another Mary in her mind, one who cries 'Papa!' and moves gladly to her father, who makes his wrinkled brow rise and brings light to his face, who gets a kiss on her cheek and a pat on her hand and hears 'My daughter. What a wonderful surprise!'

The Mary who is here now will not let her father see her. As long as he has not seen her he cannot turn from her. He cannot shake his head and say 'That is no child of mine.' With a sudden urgency she turns about and presses back into the crowd, pushes her way through, away, away where she will not be seen.

"Mary!" Shelley cries, and raises his long arm above the crowd.

They have gathered before the elephant cage and look upon it with awe. One of the guards is telling them all about the creature.

"Came from India," he says. "His name's Chunee, and although he's meek today, don't be fooled, he's a wicked temper this one. Sometimes he stamps and rages! He's injured good men. But don't you worry. As long as he's on this side and you're on that side, you're perfectly safe."

The elephant is enormous, far, far bigger than she'd imagined a creature could be. Where most of the animals are stacked in two-tier cages, his cage stretches right up to the ceiling. It is broader than any other too, but yet it does not look nearly broad enough. He could pace perhaps a single rotation, but no more. Obligingly, the elephant stands at the thick wooden struts of his cage, and reaches his trunk through to the humans on the other side. He lifts Jefferson's hat right off his head with a long trunk and tosses it up into the air, and all Jefferson can do is gasp and clap along with the rest.

It is not really surprising, Mary thinks, that such a creature would turn on those who enslave it. Days may pass when he will accept his lot, but surely, at some point, he'll dream of a greater freedom.

A laugh goes up from the crowd, apparently she has missed something amusing in her reverie, but she cannot tell what it was. She glances over her shoulder for her father, but there is no sign of him. It will take him a long time to reach this end of the room. She looks to Shelley; he leans against a pillar, his large eyes roving, his lips slightly open. It is a look she has come to know, a faraway thought, a consideration and deduction. Her gloved hands reach out to him, and he pulls her towards him, turning his attention down from the heavens to her.

"Are you alright?" he asks. She bites her lip and attempts a smile, but the question sets off an emotion in her she is not ready to release. At once concern becomes him. "What's wrong, Mary?"

She shakes her head.

"It's a little hot in here, I think. Somewhat crowded. Perhaps I'm not quite well."

He nods, a serious nod of understanding, though he still studies her face in search of a truth she does not speak.

"Claire, Hogg," he says, not loudly, but his voice cuts through any sound, "I'm taking Mary outside. We'll see you down there when you're ready." He wraps one arm around her waist, and supports her down the stairs. She clings to him, hurrying him on, away from the strange and the beautiful, to the safety of their shared quiet.

Chapter Six: Dissatisfaction
London, 8th April 1815

*B*ack at their apartment the afternoon passes quietly, and at last the night sweeps in, ushering Hogg back to his home. Shelley, following suit, sends Claire to bed without any ghost stories, and enters the bedroom where Mary sits up reading Brockden Brown's *Wieland*. By her side a single candle burns, its tall flame shuddering at a breeze too light for him to feel. He lies on the bed, propping himself up on his elbows, and waits until she folds the book closed around her finger.

"How's your book?" he asks.

"Marvellous. They've just heard a ghostly voice, and it can't possibly be the person it sounds like because she's far away. I'm very much enjoying it."

"Perhaps you could read it to me one day?"

"I should like that. I like it when you read to me."

"Claire was asking if we could all read something together."

"I'm sure she was," Mary says, and the sentiment comes out as a complaint.

"You don't want that?"

"No, it's fine. She's just around all the time." Her teeth are gritted, her eyes avoid his. She laughs to herself. "You know," she says, a little brighter, "she's determined to find Lord Byron. She thinks she can orchestrate a chance encounter."

"With Lord Byron?" He chuckles gently. "The way the world's gone crazy over him, I should think there would be a long line of young women at every chance encounter."

"Well, indeed!"

"How strange his life must be."

"I don't think I would like it," Mary mutters. "To be celebrated to a point where I was recognised wherever I went, and to have such pressure put upon whatever I wrote. I should imagine that would make writing difficult."

"I think it would be wonderful to have people wanting more of what one had created."

"I suppose," she muses. "A sense of purpose."

"Exactly."

"What are you writing at the moment?"

For a moment he cannot answer. Here is a line of conversation he cannot quite meet.

"Nothing much," he replies.

"I enjoyed the story we wrote before," she says, and lays her book aside. "Do you remember? When we were in Switzerland, and you decided to write a romance? That was such a good story; I'd love to see it finished."

Shelley tries to give her a fond smile, but the story was insufficient. He will not return to it.

"But really I think what I would like to write is histories, like our mysterious author of *Waverly*," she goes on. "But I was thinking, in those historical novels the fiction is somewhat divorced from history, and I do not see that ought to be necessary. If one wishes to write Napoleon, why must one to do so allegorically?"

He tilts his head, intrigued.

"What if one could write Napoleon as a character in a novel? And so expose the processes of his mind? Wouldn't that be an interesting thing to read?"

The focus of his mind catches onto her idea and flies after it, following where it leads.

"It would be more than interesting," he whispers, and the candle flame ducks back at his breath, "it would be important."

"We already represent historical figures in plays," she says eagerly, "but think how much better we could show them in a novel."

"The service you would be doing our society by such a creation... with such a tool one could expose the errors of the tyrant, demonstrate how they fall into false reasoning... and lay a warning for those who may follow in his footsteps." He leans his chin in his hands, contemplating what they have said. To truly show the mind of a tyrant would be an incredible thing. But could one do it? Could a creature as undeniably good as Mary access so dark a mind? Probably, yes.

"I do believe, Mary Wollstonecraft Godwin, that you will one day present the world with a work that exceeds Shakespeare's genius."

He raises his eyes to her and sees she is taken aback by this declaration; for a moment she tries to speak, but finds no words.

"You can't be surprised."

A soft, sweet look comes across her. "I would like to write by your side," she says.

"Is that so?"

"Yes. I think you will do marvellous things, and I would like to be there with you."

"Mary, may I ask something?"

"Yes?"

"What happened at The Exchange today?"

"I think I got frightened," she says, her eyes fixed on the cover of her book.

"Frightened? Not by the animals?"

"No."

"No. I didn't think you would be. Please, Mary, tell me." And as he reaches for her hand he finds a tremor there, and holds it tight between his own.

"I don't quite know. I saw us all... and I'd been so excited to go out and see the menagerie. But once we were there... it was like it wasn't us, Shelley. We were other people." She shakes her head, dissatisfied.

"Go on," he urges.

"I don't like this life, Shelley. Here in London, worrying about who we might see, or who won't see us. And..." she bites her lip, "right now, it isn't worth it. I never see you these days, you're always off with Jane, with Claire, whatever she's calling herself now. And—" She breaks off abruptly.

"But Hogg's always here with you."

"He is. Yes, he is. And he's wonderful, Shelley. But he's not the one I want with me. I want you with me."

He clasps her hand all the tighter, and kisses her fingers. So this is what made her sad, this life they have built, this attempt at a free community. He cannot deny a disappointment, and yet he knows it has not been everything he hoped. Their community is too small, too anxious.

"It is not my principle that wavers," she says hastily, "but my heart. We have agreed we ought to be free to love who we wish. I wish to love you, and I want to be every day with you, and without Claire."

"Without Claire," he echoes, nodding to himself. He would miss Claire, he knows.

"Couldn't we go away?" she whispers. "Just the two of us? Now that we've a little money we could find a proper house somewhere? Out in the country... Windsor, perhaps. You said how much you like it there. Then we wouldn't be so far from London when we wanted to come in. A little house, just the two of us."

"What about Claire?"

"At some point Claire will have to find something to do with herself, she can't simply cling to our coattails wherever we go. She could be a governess or a companion. Her French is good, she's a fine singer, there are plenty of things she can do. She must."

Shelley watches his beloved Mary and knows that if this is her will, then so it must be.

"She won't like it," he warns.

"No. But then, life is not ideal."

"Sadly, it isn't."

"If we could have built the community we'd dreamed of..." He sighs. "I really think Harriet could have come with us, and been a friend to her. Goodness, Fanny should have come!"

"I think all of us in one house would not have lived well."

"We might have. It might have been wonderful. Alright. Alright then, we'll find a way. We can talk to her in the morning. Do you want to talk to her alone? Should I be there?"

"You, definitely you. She likes you."

"She loves you, you're her sister!"

"I'm her step sister, and that's very different from liking."

"Not really. But I know what you mean. You and me then. We shall get out of London."

"And we'll write!" Mary says, pulling herself up, and sweeping her cascade of hair to one side, so it makes a veil that blocks the darkness of the room. "Tell me Shelley, what are you thinking of writing?"

The sigh he releases is vast.

"I'm not going to get any rest tonight without telling you, am I?"

"Almost certainly not."

"Very well. I've something in mind."

"I'm quite aware of that. What is it?"

"I've not quite plotted it all out. Something like *Queen Mab*, but more immediate. A reflection of sorts on the revolution, upon the revolutionary spirit at least. Of a fighter. Two fighters. Twin spirits. Idea lovers, both of them warriors."

"It sounds wonderful."

"I hope it will be. I have so many things I want to express. Everyone's so muddled about everything, and I really feel I could help, if I could only find the right way to do so."

"You will, my elfin knight," she says.

She lays *Wieland* upon the table and blows out the candle, slipping their bedroom into darkness.

The apartment in London is exchanged with some negotiations for a house in Windsor, a house for two only, while Claire goes to Bath.

Mary soon recognises a second pregnancy, and determines to take her term as carefully as she can. She lies late in the mornings, reading in bed while the birds sing outside, only rising at lunch time, when she strolls out to meet Shelley returning from the woods where he spends the days writing. Always his eyes sparkle after these days of writing, and he meets her joyfully, babbling his thoughts and his new words to her. Two creations, growing apace.

Wieland is long finished by the time they arrive, and it goes directly to the shelves. *The Sorrows of Young Werther, The Mysteries of Udolpho* and *Waverley* all take their turn upon the bedside table. Mary reads the great Madame De Staël; *Corinne* is a novel without equal. It tells of a renowned Italian poetess, and the man painfully in love with her, conflicted between his desire for Corinne and his duty to his family obligations. Corinne herself is celebrated by her countrymen, adored by the multitudes, so beautiful, so gifted in the arts, so enchanting to the male sex.

Nonetheless, Mary finds the author more interesting than the heroine. De Staël fought with Napoleon once, not with sword of course, but with her cunning tongue, telling him not to play with her as if she were a doll, but talk with her as if she were a man. Mary loves the idea of this woman mocking Napoleon, belittling him in the salons of Paris. She must be a formidable woman, a woman to aspire to.

As summer succumbs to autumn, Shelley lays his manuscript before her: *Laon and Cythna: or the Revolution of the Golden City*, an epic poem in twelve cantos.

"There," he says, "my summer task is ended. I have written something of which I can be proud."

Their quiet home curls itself close and quiet for the winter, and at the turn of the new year, a child is born; they name him William for his grandfather.

This earth is made of more than flesh and stone;
I feel with utter certainty a power
Within the universe uniting all,
Swift flowing through our bodies and our thoughts.

Is not this power the thing many call God?

In doing so they bow to aeons of
Oppression and persecution. The word
'God' has become a tool by which a man
Murders his brother.

'Tis true, and yet I know
In many simple houses 'God' provides
A watchword for this nameless power you feel.

Though I deny that vision of a tyrant,
I'm certain of a force beyond what we
May see in this poor realm of dark shadows.
That force I name as universal love;
Compassion could, if given chance, assuage
All human ill.

Would fiend or murderer
Or arbiter of woe proceed if they
Did truly comprehend the harm they caused?
What man would persevere towards an ill
Did he not have a pain within to feel?

Such is the great importance of our task
For if the world can see its wrongs perhaps
A revolution can at last begin.

Part Three

Chapter One: Claire's Conquest
Windsor, 1st May 1816

"*I* have some further news on my acquaintance with Lord Byron," Claire announces.

Mary, standing by the fireplace with her baby, shakes her head. "Since making said acquaintance you talk about little else." But she says it quietly, more to William in her arms, than to Claire across the room.

Shelley sits cross-legged atop the dining room table, his head in his hands and a great happy grin across his face, pleased to hear every detail on the great poet. It seems to Mary that Claire's visits delight him just as much as they irritate her.

But despite herself, she is curious for the news. Claire, true to her word, hunted out the notorious poet, declining to state by what means, and after a brief acquaintance even brought Mary to meet him. He was not what she expected. Proud and handsome, yes, and the veneer of the seductive adventurer she'd heard so much of was present, but underneath he seemed like a large, strange boy out of place in the world. He was curly-haired and plump, though athletic, the club foot she had heard of less pronounced than she expected.

"What news has our clever Clara?" Shelley asks.

Shaking her hair over her shoulders self-consciously, Claire leans back on the table.

"May I have some tea?" she asks sweetly.

"You little fiend you shall not!" Shelley cries, clattering his fists upon the table in mock outrage loud enough to make Mary jump and clutch William to her. But Shelley laughs high and leaps from the table to take Mary and William in a reassuring embrace. "Forgive me, Mary. What is your news, Claire? Tell us!"

Irritated by this energy that is always riled when Claire comes, Mary takes herself from his reach to the armchair and sits half turned away from them, soothing the child, who, if she were honest with herself, has no need of soothing.

"Well, it's very exciting news." Claire walks around the table so she can be seen by both Shelley and Mary. "Somewhat complicated. I suppose I ought to start by saying—in case you haven't guessed—I have..." she holds a significant pause, "*befriended* his lordship." The word befriended she speaks so carefully its *double entendre* cannot be missed, and Mary looks sharply up.

"God, Claire, you haven't!" she mutters.

And Shelley straightens up and cries, "Have you really!"

He seems quite as surprised as Mary, if less horrified.

Claire smiles at them both, apparently pleased with the effect produced.

"I have. I am in love with him."

Mary winces. Everything about Claire looks the part of the heroine: her dark curls, the pink satin flowers at her neckline, even the wistful tilt of her chin. And now she has seduced, not the noble hero, but the wicked rogue. Byron's now-divorced wife has sworn that he is mad. She will have her heart broken, Mary thinks. Even if he loves her back.

"And, do you see him very often?" Shelley asks, diplomatically. Mary knows her thoughts are also in his mind.

"Actually," Claire clears her throat, "I have not seen him very lately. He's left England." Her delicate fingers trace the edge of the table, and she does not look at either of them. "Gone to Geneva. And he left so suddenly. I understand there were some court proceedings he wished to avoid..."

Mary has read the papers, she knows. Allegations of incest with his half-sister, and of sodomy with his servants. Punishable crimes. Immense public scandals.

"He left so quickly," Claire continues, "I didn't even have time to tell him my news."

"What news?" Mary asks, full of dread, just as Shelley says, "Oh Claire!" in a voice of surprise and some pity.

"It appears that I am somewhat in the family way," Claire laughs, and though she does so with a charming flutter of lashes, there is falter in her gaiety, and Shelley wraps her in a brotherly embrace.

For a moment everything is still, quiet. Mary meets Shelley's eyes over Claire. He nods.

Sniffing a little, Claire emerges with a neat smile.

"Which is why I wanted to come to you both. You see, at one point, he did talk of taking me to Geneva with him, I think he would have, if he'd had more time. But we could go to him, all of us together. He so wants to meet you Shelley, I gave him your writings. Don't you think?" She looks between them. "Don't you think we could all go on something of an adventure?"

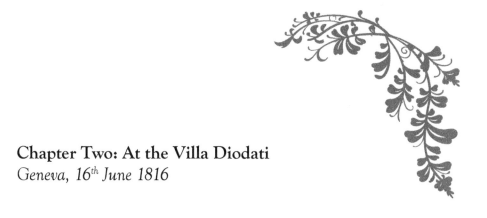

Chapter Two: At the Villa Diodati
Geneva, 16ᵗʰ June 1816

*C*ightning sears across the lake of Geneva, illuminating the attendant mountains and setting the surface of the water white.

The illumination draws all eyes to the window, and consequently to Lord Byron, who stands with his back to the room, gazing out at the storm with a self-satisfied smile, as if he were its architect.

Mary watches him closely. His presence is magnetic, dominating the gathered company in both eloquent discourse and silence. She had not expected him to fall at Claire's knees as her sister had predicted he would, but the oscillation of his behaviour from protracted coldness to sudden passion baffles her. It is clear that Claire adores him, for she follows him everywhere, and sometimes he allows her to stay, but already they are squabbling with one another.

On the journey to Switzerland it became necessary to take on a nurse, as Mary and Shelley realised it would be advantageous to leave William sometimes while they were visiting the infamous poet, and it is with Elise, a stout Swiss woman with kind eyes and emotional cleverness, that they have left William now. Mary, Claire, and Shelley are at Byron's Villa Diodati, less than a mile along the lakefront.

It is a magnificent house, and the drawing room where they are now gathered along with Byron and his young physician, a British-Italian called Dr Polidori, is an opulence Mary has never witnessed. The room is furnished with ornate vases and clocks, picture frames of gold gilt, a grand piano worthy of Versailles, chairs fitted in velvet, and beside the austere bookcases of custom bound books, an impressive bust of Dante, complete with laurel leaves and haughty sneer.

The grandeur is illuminated only by a few candles that encourage depth in the shadows, and shudder their light across the ornaments, enchanting them to something like life. Upon one sofa an enormous black dog sleeps, while another patrols the room uneasily.

A low growl of thunder draws an exclamation from Claire who is reclined upon a purple velvet *chaise longue* with studied elegance. Lord Byron laughs low.

"It certainly isn't safe to go out in that sort of weather," he announces, looking out onto the lake with a death's head grin upon his face. "Yes, you'll definitely have to stay here tonight."

Shelley stands by the fireplace, an arm lent upon the mantelpiece, while at the other side, like a matching bookend, stands Polidori dressed in silky black, his dark Italian eyes turned up towards the storm. They have the same seriousness, but to Mary's eye Polidori has a self-consciousness that Shelley lacks, an awareness of himself and his position that does not let him rest.

"You expect us to believe we are safe here?" Claire says, gesticulating theatrically about them. Byron turns a long hard stare upon her as the lightning strikes again, delineating him with a stark whiteness, but he says nothing. In response to his nothing, Claire shrugs and smiles. This is a new Claire, Mary notes, and a new Claire is always dangerous.

But she does not trouble herself with Claire, for Byron leaves his position by the window, walking slowly with his limp, and sits beside her, though she is a little apart from the company.

"You watch much and say little, Miss Godwin."

"There is much to take in," she says meekly.

The evening so far has been passed in the telling of ghost stories, and the visions conjured in their minds of headless brides, of wandering corpses, have charged the room with a restless jumpiness.

Polidori edges towards them, and asks if Mary would be so kind as to entertain the company with a song, perhaps?

"Claire would do a better job than I," Mary states, without false modesty.

Claire is upon her feet at once, but refrains from approaching the piano, awaiting some signal from Byron that she may. He gives the merest ascent of his eyebrows. It is enough. She takes her position; this is a role she plays well.

"You do not sing, Miss Godwin?" Byron asks Mary.

The first few notes of the piano step sweetly forth. In this dark, oppressive evening they bear a sad beauty, like the memory of happiness beyond reach.

"Not well," she replies. "Certainly not as well as Claire. And you needn't call me 'Miss Godwin,' you know, I think this past week has made us better friends than that."

"I can't very well call you *Mrs Shelley*, though, can I?"

She sees the wicked glimmer in his eye but declines to pay it heed.

"Of course not. You may call me Mary," she says evenly.

She is aware of Shelley joining Claire at the piano, aware too of the quiet muttering between them. Polidori examines the bookshelves, perhaps to disguise that he is shut out. For now, she leaves them all be.

"Very well, *Mary*," Byron says.

A chord closes, and from quarrelsome Claire comes the loveliest sound, a fine, pure note that hovers perfectly in the air and then falls to another.

"*Vorrei spiegarvi, oh Dio!*
Qual è l'affanno mio."

"And what am I to call you?" Mary asks, softly now, so that Claire's song is undisturbed, "Does everybody call you 'Lord Byron?'"

"Yes, they do."

"What do your family call you?"

"Your Lordship."

"What an insufferable sibling you must be."

"You can't imagine."

"And your friends?"

"A damned bastard, I'd imagine."

"Well I'm afraid I refuse to call you either of those. What is your Christian name?"

"George. But I forbid your use of it."

"You forbid me?" she raises her eyebrows in challenge, and he straightens his spine just a little to return it. "Very well. Lord Byron it must be. However, I find it something of a mouthful so I may just abbreviate to L.B. Or Albe. How do you like Albe as a name?"

He chuckles low, and leaning forward, he takes her hand and brings it to his lips for a chaste kiss.

"From Mary Wollstonecraft Godwin, I consider it an honorific."

A scrambling little step is heard just outside of the room, causing both Mary and Byron to turn toward the open doorway. A broad beam of light streams into the room, in which an extraordinary shadow moves, holding Mary's attention. There is something bewitching in the monstrous, unidentifiable shape that steps ever closer. All at once a large bird enters at a run, an immense tail dragging behind it. Claire shrieks, abruptly shattering the music, and Polidori drops the book he is holding. Mary gasps and then laughs. The bird stops short amid all the noise and turns its head about uncertainly, at last fixing its gaze upon her.

"Is that a peacock?" she cries, and Byron chuckles softly at her surprise.

"Yes. I've two of them here. They're beautiful creatures. They wail like banshees in the morning though," he notes.

The bird regards Mary with its round, black eye. She returns the look with respect. Carefully he raises his gorgeous tail, fanning out feathers of a thousand colours, richest shades of blue, green, and gold that glimmer in the candlelight.

"I think he's trying to impress you," Byron whispers.

"Then he'll need more than a fine coat," Mary replies smoothly.

The others exchange a mutter of relief.

The enormous black dog that has slept soundly through the afternoon, raises itself sleepily and stretches its way off the sofa. This sends the peacock stalking off into the shadows, and then, with a heave of glittering wings it flies a few feet up to sit on top of the bookshelves.

"How many animals do you have?" Mary asks, as Claire, still whispering to Shelley, begins to touch the keys again, though this time she does not sing.

"I'm not entirely sure. Quite a lot. I only brought my favourites with me."

"Don't they ever eat each other?"

"None of them has ever been devoured, but they've fallen foul of each other's tempers now and then."

"And have you never feared for your own life?"

One of the huge dogs approaches Mary, sniffs her hands and leans his weight against her legs. He is softer than she had expected, and as she strokes his ears he raises his head happily, great tongue lolling out the side of his smiling mouth.

"Our lives are in danger every day," Byron says, casually, as if the thought does not trouble him, and reaches out to rub the black dog. "I could tomorrow be crushed by a reckless carriage, or shot by a jealous husband, or drowned in an unexpected storm, and it would be no bad thing."

"You value your life lightly."

"On the contrary. I value it very highly, which is why I live so very much of it. But I would not overstay my time. Now what has happened to the music?" He raises his voice, "Come, Miss Claire, do not let a bird scare you; your voice is sweeter than his. Let us hear your song."

Looking past Lord Byron, Mary watches Claire gather herself. Shelley leans in close to whisper something, but she shakes her head and begins to play a new tune, a moment later joining it with her rich and lovely voice. Without looking at the singer, Byron nods his approval.

"Albe." Mary whispers this sufficiently quietly that no one else will hear, and Byron smiles at his new name. "I fancy you don't love our Claire."

"I don't," he replies bluntly, but matches her caution. "And I have never claimed to."

"That will be hard on her. She does love you, I think."

"I have always been honest in my dealings with the girl—it was she who threw herself at me, and she professes to understand my thoughts and feelings." He turns his face away, and to Mary his face in profile is serious, even solemn, with just the smallest flickering of an eyelid suggesting anything less than absolute certainty.

"So she says," Mary admits, "but she does not mean it. She has deep hopes of reforming you, I suspect."

"Then she makes the same mistake my wife made when she married me." He rolls his eyes back round to her. "I think you are very wise, friend Mary," Byron says. She feels a flush of pleasure.

"I'm glad you think so."

"Especially for one so young. How old are you?"

"I am eighteen."

"The same as Claire then. And yet so much the better."

"I think fate has been a little kinder to me," Mary says. "For one thing, the man I love loves me back."

He smiles a small, sad little smile and nods. "That does make life more bearable. Your Shelley is an exceedingly interesting young man."

For a moment Mary is torn, wanting very much to talk of Shelley, to promote him before this greatest of poets, but sensing this rare opportunity to speak frankly on Claire's behalf. She closes her eyes and proceeds.

"Have you ever known that pain of unreturned love? I am fortunate enough to say I have not, but I see it on her now. Can you understand how it hurts her?" she asks, quietly, delicately, just as Claire's sad song rises and falls for its final line. He turns to face her once more, but now he gives her a glimpse of something unguarded, something savagely pained.

"More than I can say," he replies, and sighs heavily. "But it is the human condition to suffer. And I think you have known suffering."

"I have seen hard times," she says carefully.

"I am sure you have. And the life you have chosen... I dare say you will see more."

The awesome power of fine intellect acts as a fire; if the mind that would approach it is open and willing, the radiating heat shall warm the mind until it begins to glow, to spark, to crackle. Years of learning, thinking, reading all combine to ensure that one is ready kindling for evenings such as these.

And yet, Shelley finds he cannot rise to meet the opportunity. His delicate thoughts and the transient words that would share them, catch and snare on invisible thorns.

He sits on the piano stool beside Claire while she plays a simple sonata, conscious that he must look after her in this company. Mechanically, he turns the pages of the music. Before his eyes the lines and dots ripple into the harmony they represent. How strange, that abstract marks communicate such beauty. But the written word is no more direct.

"What are they talking about?" Claire mutters. Her hands continue to find their keys without faltering.

At first Shelley only hears the sounds, the long interrogation of the vowels, the triad of sharp stops that hit the letter 't'. Meaning follows ponderously.

"Who?" he asks, in little more than exhalation.

Claire nods her head towards Byron and Mary.

"Ah," Shelley is drawn back into the present. "Them. Yes. I suppose they have all sorts of things to talk about."

Claire snorts her discontent. Shelley smiles to think that this too is a form of expression. "I'm sure he'll want to ask her about her father and her mother, and she will enquire about his poetry," he says.

To speculate makes him feel strangely lonely.

"I'm sure he'd much rather it was the daughter of Wollstonecraft he'd fallen in love with and not her silly step-sister," Claire mutters bitterly.

"Oh hush, you." Shelley elbows her in the ribs.

"I showed him some of my writing," she says, watching them intently.

"You've never shown me any of your writing."

"He said it wasn't any good."

"What qualifies him to judge?"

"He's the most famous writer in existence."

"Pah!"

She nudges him and he turns a page, trying this time to pay attention to the pattern of notes.

"Actually, I don't think he likes me that much," Claire whispers. Her face is set into a scowl, whether it flits to the music, or glares back at Mary and Byron.

In the corner of his eye Shelley senses Byron turning to them. Such is the power of this man he need not stand nor shout, but only turn his attention, and all will respond.

"Come!" Byron says. "It has been far too long since anyone was scared out of their wits. Let us have another ghost story!"

Claire clicks her tongue but plays on, a little slower and a little softer, for even she is subservient to his will.

"Not more ghost stories!" Polidori says with an uneasy chuckle, edging himself back into the centre of the room and consciousness of all. "They are not high art. I for one propose a discussion of the principles of poetry."

"Bother that." Byron cuts him off. "I grant you plenty of these ghost stories often don't have so much of quality about them, but there is no reason why they shouldn't."

"I'd like to see you write one!" Claire casts out the challenge. Shelley watches her closely; they have sat up late telling each other ghost stories so many nights, he knows how easily she scares, how susceptible she is to mystery. But she is distinctly not herself tonight. A rashness, a wildness, a freak has taken hold of her.

Byron barks his harsh laugh, his eyes fixed upon Polidori, as if utterly oblivious of Claire.

"I didn't realise we had an expert on fine literature amongst us," he sneers, narrowing his eyes at Polidori. Claire laughs with him in a base sycophancy that displeases Shelley, and he feels for the young doctor, whose face has become pinched, though he holds his chin high.

"If I may further Dr Polidori's point of high art..." Shelley intervenes.

"It'll only encourage him," Byron scoffs, but Shelley holds his nerve and continues.

"It is true," he says, carefully. It is important that Byron should hear what he has to say, and he must not phrase it insufficiently. "It is true of most ghost stories that their sole purpose is to frighten, and that their authors care only for fleeting entertainment. That may have its place. But our great writers," he pauses, unsure if he ought directly to include Lord Byron within this, or if it would be implied, "our great writers ought to dedicate themselves to furthering the common good. Do you not agree?" He addresses the room, but none other replies; they all know for whom the question is intended.

But Lord Byron only sighs. "Must *everything* be so high minded nowadays? I'm tired of all these reformers—as if what a writer said ever affected something in the real world, as if there was any real chance of *changing* anything... Let's all just agree that human kind is going to hell and every government that arises will be a little more corrupt than its predecessor."

To that, Shelley can say nothing. Byron speaks recklessly, but with such ease that Shelley feels there can be no artifice to his speech.

But here, here is the man whose works hold perhaps a wider reach than any other living writer's, and what does he care for it, nothing! Why, if Shelley had such a readership he could change the world.

"That you could feel so is terrible!" he hisses, and Byron arches an eyebrow. "Utterly terrible. Haven't you read Godwin?"

Claire groans, but he carries on.

"Yes, we live in troubled times, but saying nothing can change them is criminal. That you of all people should say so! You who have the ability to affect thousands with your words. You have a duty! Are you not changed—every day, in every way—by the writings of Godwin, of Rousseau, of Shakespeare, of Milton?"

The room is silent. No one stirs but the great mastiff, who rolls over in sleep to acquire a more comfortable position.

"I find you fascinating, Shelley," Polidori remarks with a troubled scrutiny. Shelley lowers his eyes, unable to bear their looks. "You call yourself an atheist, and yet the more you say, the more I am convinced you are the most morally-guided person I have met."

This is surely kindly meant, but Shelley's cheeks burn. He has overstepped propriety, he has made himself ridiculous, and the sooner they move on, the better. Into the silence Byron's soft voice purrs.

"Why should morality require Christianity? Plenty of avowed Christians are, after all, thoroughly immoral."

"And consider," Mary says gently, "Christ himself was an infidel."

"Are you our Christ, Shelley?" Byron asks with a laugh. There is a general chuckle, and Shelley tries to join in. "You look quite right for the second coming."

"Perhaps he is Shiloh!" Polidori chimes in with eagerness. "Do you remember the woman Southcott, who claimed an angel came to her and she was to have the second son of God!"

"Yes, yes!" Byron laughs. "Precisely that! He must be Shiloh Shelley!" Everyone laughs again, even Mary, who Shelley sees watching him closely.

"Come, Shiloh!" Byron cries. "Tell us a ghost story from beyond the mortal realm!"

"Yes, tell us of the afterlife, Shelley," Polidori echoes.

Shelley looks at them uncertainly; he is being mocked, he knows, but perhaps not cruelly, and there is a genuine expectation in their expressions.

"I think we should write ghost stories," Mary says softly, darkly, and Byron nods his agreement.

"Yes. Let us each do one. Polidori's shall be awful I am sure, and Shiloh's shall be divine."

Shelley sits up a little straighter, to compose himself. There is yet an argument to be won with Byron.

But Byron now is asking Mary if she will join in the story writing.

"I do not know," Mary replies. "I haven't yet thought of one."

"You don't have to," Byron says, almost dismissively, "not everyone has to be a writer."

The mere suggestion that Mary Wollstonecraft Godwin might not be capable of the challenge stirs Shelley back to animation, and, seeing hesitation upon her face, he springs to his feet.

"Mary is an excellent writer," he informs Byron, "as you may expect. I do not doubt that you will be greatly impressed."

Byron turns to look at him, amusement sparkling his face, and then back at Mary, something unspoken passing between them.

"Very good. Then I look forward to reading your ghost story, Miss Godwin."

Shelley, finding himself standing in the centre of the room, goes to sit by Mary, and takes her hand in his own. Only then does he realise he is lightly trembling. But her hand is cool and confident, and squeezes his fingers with reassurance.

As the night wears on the air within the room grows oppressive, while without the tempest thickens, the bouts of thunder so frequent they form a low growl, and Shelley thinks of the Titans testing their strength upon the earth. He tries to take a steadying breath, but it comes shallow and restricted, making his heart run a little faster. Beyond the unclosed door come the snarls of Byron's wolf-dogs as they set upon one another. Listening to them with growing concern, Shelley fears the people of this house shall soon lose their senses too and turn teeth upon each other, for the flickering lights form faces in his tired eyes—ghoulish masks that laugh and disappear.

"Who shall tell the next ghost story?" Byron asks, and looks at each of them with his wicked grin.

As much as he wants to, Shelley dares not meet Byron's gaze but looks down at his own lap where his white hands are trembling. He must steady himself. What will Byron say if he should faint? Such a scene would be unbearable. It is his health that troubles him, Shelley feels. That and the unusually late hour. There is a small bottle of laudanum in their bedroom—perhaps a few drops would calm this tremor.

"Shelley," Dr Polidori asks, making him jump, "are you quite well?"

Shelley nods, and resolves to wait the night out.

Byron takes his position by the fireplace; the flames stretch and shudder behind him, reaching around his legs and sending sparks up to his darkened face as he begins to recite from memory.

"The lovely lady Christabel,
Whom her father loves so well,
What makes her in the woods so late,
A furlong from the castle gate?"

It is Coleridge's 'Christabel' that Shelley has read so often he could tell it himself—yet never until tonight has he felt the story quite so vividly. In a lovely wood the fair maiden Christabel meets a woman—a beautiful, terrible creature, woman in image alone...

The few slender tapers cast eerie light upon Byron's face, twisting the sinews of brow and cheekbone into a fluid, mercurial thing that is half spirit. His voice, so low and impassioned now, stirs the darkest parts of Shelley's captive soul. A terrible magnetism imbues his words, each one another spell upon his captive audience lays. Shelley is gripped by a fear that the demons painted in words are moments from materialisation. He reaches out for Mary, for her comfort and strength, but his eyes fall instead upon Claire; she is sat near Byron's feet, her knees curled up to her chest, her eyes and her lips open in passionate awe; she exists entirely in the story he is weaving.

And Mary?

There she sits upon her throne, a vision of sibylline wisdom and beauty, a knowing smile upon her placid face. The sight makes him shudder—there is no fear in her expression, only the darkest pleasure. Who could watch the devil's alchemist with such composure but the maker's master, an alchemical architect with powers beyond the comprehension of all around?

As the story's heroine is drawn deeper into the witch's trap Shelley longs to call out, to stop her, but the candles flicker with Byron's intake of breath; he cannot be stopped, he has his tale to tell. The stranger, taken to the inmost sanctuary, the sacred space of Christabel's bed chamber, begins to speak strangely.

"'Off, wandering mother! Peak and pine!
I have the power to bid thee flee.'
Alas, what ails poor Geraldine?
Why stares she with unsettled eye?
Can she the bodiless dead espy?"

Everything is wrong! Shelley cannot bear to listen longer. Mary sits and smiles, her bosom heaves with a sigh of satisfaction.

He puts his hands across his face, and in that darkness Byron's voice resounds even louder in his ears, telling of sweet Christabel's danger, of how she brings the demon woman even into her very bed chamber to slumber by her side.

There let her sleep, poor Shelley prays, but still behind his shuttered eyes he sees Christabel's lovely outline, the figure of her innocence. Against it there, all serpentine, the deadly form of Geraldine. Down her back an aureole of auburn hair flows as she unties her silken robes. A face familiar, with Mary's brow and Mary's eyes, but something dark, not Mary's smile—the robe slides down a body pale and wasted, deformed, consumed, and most awful of all, within those warped distorted breasts, lizard-like and live, two wakeful, glowing serpent eyes!

A scream, a shriek of utmost despair, the terror of what he sees—the demon queen—and he is scrambling, tearing at all things trying to impede him. He runs, far, far from the voice, from the light, through tunnels and corridors of darkness his steps resound, while a cackling laugh bounces wall to wall, and in every shadow the familiars of the witch cower and growl.

A corridor runs short. He finds himself in an unknown part of the house, alone, and out of breath; he lets himself fall heavy against the wall and slide down until he is a heap of man upon the floor, gasping for breath and clinging to the wall's solidity. This passageway is almost entirely unlit, save for a single burning lamp in the stairwell close by.

He listens: all is silence but the pounding of his own blood and the heaving of his own breath.

Leaning on the wall, he draws himself up a little and tries to think. He pulls his hands through and through his hair, as if doing so could drag the thoughts right out of his mind. He is in the Villa Diodati. There is no witch. His friends are upstairs, no doubt laughing at the spectacle he has made. There is no witch, no sorceress here. His own hands grasp his face and feel the sweat there; he tries to cling to this certain physicality, mentally reprimanding himself in his father's voice: "Pull yourself together, Bysshe. Don't disgrace yourself."

It is a sobering bit of ventriloquism.

A slow step echoes down the corridor, and hot shame rises in Shelley, run through with no small fear, as he anticipates Byron's mockery. But it is Polidori's voice that speaks.

"Shelley? Shelley?" A moment later his slim figure appears at the end of the corridor. He holds a light aloft. "Are you alright?"

Bysshe cannot find words; he tries to move his head, but is not sure if he shakes or nods it. The light and Polidori draw nearer, and once he is close he kneels. His long pale hands are trembling before him in the half-light. Shelley cannot explain, his lips are forming words but saying nothing.

Polidori has his bag with him, and from it takes out a little bottle.

"Drink," he says.

Shelley takes the vial, though Polidori guides his shaking hand, and drinks. A sharp shock to his throat, to his mind. He takes in a deep, gasping breath, and feels a little stronger. Before him the doctor is impassive and attentive, his dark brown eyes shining.

"Don't worry," says Polidori. "You're quite safe now. You've had a fright, my friend, but you're alright. We're going to go through to the study, where you can rest."

Shelley nods weakly as the doctor helps him up and half carries him through the study where three candles are waiting, and all the while, Polidori keeps up a steady line of easy chatter. Shelley finds himself upon a study chair, and in it he feels grounded, secure.

"You're shaken, aren't you?"

"Yes."

"Yes, it seems so. Can you tell me what frightened you?"

"I saw..." but he cannot say. *A sight to dream of, not to tell.*

"What did you see?"

Something stirs in the shadows, and Bysshe breaks off, watching for the source of the movement. It is only a breeze stirring some loose papers.

"My Mary, my Maie... that terrible witch..." he murmurs. With a great will he steels himself to look up to Polidori. This close there is a benignity in the slow blink of his thick black lashes, a kind intensity to his attention.

"I heard tell of a woman," Bysshe says, "who had eyes in her breasts. Where her nipples ought to be there were eyes." Polidori's eyebrows raise, but he makes no comment. "Can you imagine such horrors? I reached out for Mary, and in that moment I felt that she was that terrible creature." His breath rattles out of him and leaves him hollow.

"It was only a fleeting vision," the doctor says kindly. "I think you are overwrought, Mr Shelley. And I am sure you are tired."

"I am tired."

"Yes, you ought to eat better. I've seen you eat nothing but sweets and bread since you arrived."

Realising his hands are shaking, Shelley clasps them tight and presses his chin against his paired knuckles.

"I am tired." The bones against his jaw quiver and Shelley lets his eyes close. Somehow, he trusts the silence Polidori offers, and finds it a relief to speak. "I have so many people relying upon me. Mary is wonderful, but her father—who won't even talk to her— keeps writing to me asking for money, and I daren't tell her. I have left my sisters behind to goodness knows what fate. And I'm sure you know that Mary isn't my wife."

"I am aware."

"My wife and children are in England, and what can I give them? My father has cut me off, I have so little at this point, whatever scraps and loans that I can find. I will have nothing secure until my father dies. Meanwhile, I must protect all those who fall under my care, which now includes Claire and her child... I cannot be responsible for them too."

"You need not be responsible for her."

Shelley shakes his head.

"She is Mary's step-sister, and my dear friend. I care very deeply for her. She has fallen to my care and I must protect her, but I cannot control Lord Byron. I cannot see her way well through this."

"Your burden is heavy."

"Understand me, I am not greedy, I do not wish to keep riches for myself, but I give and I give—my money, my attention, my affection, my care... and there is nothing left. I am emptied."

Polidori sits on the stair beside him.

"The world will do that. If I may offer my advice, do not spread yourself too thin. A man must take care of himself."

"No, not alone. One must love one's fellow, wherever and whenever one can. I truly believe love is the guiding principle of the universe."

"Then love yourself. Care for yourself. Your principle is

theoretically good but practically flawed. I have learned that whatever you lay before others—it will never be enough."

Shelley is surprised to hear him speak this way—his youth should not allow for such a pessimistic resolution. "What is your ambition, doctor?"

"Of course. I should like to leave the physician's life, be recognised for my own merits."

"You are a poet?"

"I would say so. I try to write—but you have heard what Byron thinks of my writing."

Shelley nods.

"Then you know. There are certainly things that someone like Lord Byron will never understand. His aristocracy has given him the gift of a life without doubt; whatever he wills comes to be. It is harder for those of who must serve, and work, and strive. He may be supremely talented, but I fear him. I fear he will ruin us all."

Chapter Three: A Letter From Home
Geneva, 22nd June 1816

*B*yron has taken Shelley on a boating trip around the lake; they may be away as much as a week, and Mary, who has thought of the most horrible story, is happy to be left in Diodati to write. Claire, however, is less content, and stomps around in an ill mood, interrupting Mary every half hour, until she puts down her pen, and together they go back to their house along the lakeshore to see William who has been left in the care of Elise.

"Byron is the most difficult man to comprehend," Claire complains. "He is so *attentive* to me when we are alone, but in company he will scarcely acknowledge me."

Mary has her arms full of her son, and is too busy marvelling at him—a whole week she has been parted from him; how can that be!

"We of course have our own *understanding*, but I wish he would share with me a little more," Claire goes on. They are in an unlit parlour, Claire strolling the house and picking up stray objects without interest and setting them down again.

"Men do not have hearts like we women do," Elise says, "and yet we are compelled to love them."

Mary smiles gratefully at Elise; though she doesn't agree with the sentiment, she appreciates the intervention. Her wisdom has been invaluable, for Elise has already raised her own children and when William cries and Mary frets, Elise will stride in and say, "No, no, Madame, it is quite well. My girls would always be so."

She has become a comforting part of their little band.

"There was a letter while you were away." Elise produces an envelope that Mary immediately recognises as her father's. It is addressed to Shelley. Mary takes it from Elise, holding it some distance from her body as if fearing snakes or scorpions might erupt from the unassuming envelope.

"Open it, Claire." She passes it on and holds William a little closer, as he stares in open-mouthed delight at all three of them.

Claire rips it open, scans it quickly, rotates the pages several times and frowns.

"What does he say?"

"Ah..." Claire seems to scan the letter, as if she has not yet read it.

"Papa says exactly what we would expect: money, money, disappointed in us, money. But Fanny also writes. Look at this!" Claire holds the letter open.

In the centre of the page is Godwin's narrative in his certain hand, well-spaced and elegantly sloped. But in every cranny of the margin creeps Fanny's cramped writing, turning the corners and bending at the ends of the lines, apologetic but eager.

"He couldn't just give her a sheet of paper to write upon herself, could he?" Mary mutters. In that tiny writing Mary sees Fanny's urgency to speak, her need to be heard, and more than all, her loneliness.

"It's quite rambling. She met a friend of our mother's recently, she thinks of going to Ireland again, and not to France. Was she going to go to France? But here," Claire sighs, holding her head sideways to read, "she says: 'I understand from Mama that I am your laughing stock—the beacon of your,'" she squints at the writing, winces, "'the beacon of your constant satire.'"

It is Mary's anger that speaks first, fierce and dangerously low.

"What lies has your mother been telling our Fanny?"

"I don't remotely know what she's talking about," Claire replies coolly. "Besides, how exactly would I know?"

"Well you're the only one they still talk to, so I imagine they're getting this from you."

"You take everything too seriously."

Mary snatches the letter from her. "Why don't you go back to Diodati, see if Byron has returned, then you can annoy him for a bit. I would like to spend some time with my son."

She stalks off into the other room, William held in her arms, the letter clutched in her fist. She can hear Claire complaining to Elise behind her and shuts the door fast. She will take a corner and write her story with her child on her lap. There is no Claire in her story, and that makes it a pleasant place to be.

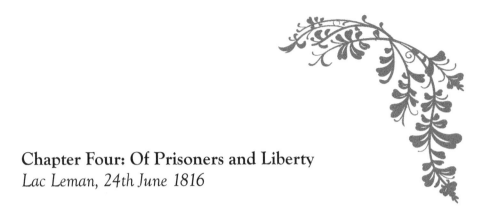

Chapter Four: Of Prisoners and Liberty
Lac Leman, 24th June 1816

*I*nto the darkest cavern Byron has led Shelley; they have sailed the coasts and explored the scenes renowned from book and legend, coming at last to the Chateau de Chillon, a silhouette of a castle perched at the mountains' feet before the great expanse of Lac Leman; now by the light of a torch grown weak in the putrid drafts they stare at the castle's dungeons.

The damp walls are bare ancient rock, rough-hewn many centuries ago, from whose crevices still protrude time-warped chains and shackles.

"Not even the light of day, nor the breath of wind to offer kind remembrance," Shelley murmurs. It is a ghastly place, and he feels his skin recoil as if it would curl itself inside him, so as to avoid such horrors.

"No, no light," Byron echoes. "We have descended a long way."

"These dungeons," their guide says, "are dug down below the lake."

That is why the air is still and sound is dead, much as when one is submerged below the water's surface.

"Many were imprisoned here," their guide goes on, addressing the crowd of *Inglese*. "One was a monk named Bonnivard who was chained to his two brothers, and though they died, he lived on, imprisoned here for six long years."

Shelley imagines the man bound at wrists and feet to those of his deceased kinsman, to see those beloved bodies rot, the flesh slow-worn away, and to live every day without the hope or possibility of change.

He wants to cry, to prostrate himself upon the flagstones and water with tears the sufferer's memory. And all obeisance done he wants to climb out of this cavern and breathe the air with new gratitude and hasten back to Mary, to run all the way and inhale her youth and loveliness, to kiss the child of sunlight they have made.

In Byron's company he may do neither. His lordship, for his part, has taken to chiselling his name into one of the vast stone pillars.

To cry before Lord Byron would be to lose face, especially after the night of ghost stories; women may weep where men must have fortitude. But it does not seem right to him to have to suppress such emotion in such a place.

Every minute is an agony, and Shelley begins to fear that when they try the heavy door through which they came they will find it unyielding, its ancient locks enlivened by a ghostly gaoler.

But when the time comes Byron easily draws back the door and they ascend through the castle and back out at last into the crisp air.

"I'm very glad to have seen the place, as horrible as it was," Byron says, as they head back to the boat. Rounding the corner of the castle, the lake is abruptly revealed before them. Ahead Lac Leman lies, dark and serpentine, its once sparkling surface now dulled to a storm-cloud grey, chastened by the savage peaks that ascend sharply on all sides.

"Can you imagine Rousseau coming down here on such a day?" Byron says gazing about himself as if the magnificent scenery were naught had it not been first viewed by that finest of writers.

"I do. I imagine him everywhere. It is Rousseau that taught me of this heavenly place," Shelley says, placing a hand on his breast where his copy of *Julie* is tucked into a pocket, aware Byron too has one upon his person. They have been haunting the scenes of those stories. "I think even Rousseau must have been humbled by such a scene."

"Do you think," Byron says, "that we shall write better poetry having inhaled the air of Rousseau's garden?"

Shelley laughs at the idea. As he strolls on the thought slinks into his mind that one day future travellers may trace their footsteps in pursuit of Byron's own greatness.

And what shall those future pilgrims recall of the great man's peculiar companion? The thought sweeps over his mind like a dark cloud obscuring a summer's day. Shelley fixes his eyes upon the boat up ahead of them and walks as naturally as he can.

"The power of the writer!" Byron exclaims, catching up with Shelley. "I'd swear I had been here before, and with people I love so dearly. Isn't that the great skill?"

"It is a rare gift," Shelley murmurs, trying to smile, "to create characters from nothing and give them life."

"To make them real!" Byron exclaims.

They approach the boat where the Swiss crew is already preparing for departure. Shelley steals a glance back at the terrible castle of Chillon, rising out of the lake, steep-sided and many-turreted, taught boldness by the mountains.

"Damn me, but I love Julie almost as well as I've ever loved any woman," Byron says. "I tell you I'd dash my brains out for her. Do you know that feeling, Shelley?"

"Yes," Shelley says quietly.

Byron swipes at the air dismissively.

"There's no point discussing love with a man like you, Shelley."

"There isn't?"

"No. You believe in it too whole-heartedly," Byron laughs mirthlessly. "I never like to discuss a subject with anyone who believes in it. Besides, it would be too terrible for two poets to sail together and talk of what love might be."

Shelley, exceedingly interested in the conversation of what love might be, is tempted to ignore Byron's dismissal.

"And besides," Byron cuts in before he can talk, "you have Mary, and that is different."

"You are impressed by Mary, aren't you?"

"Immensely so," Byron says with a shake of his head. "She has a keen understanding." They have reached the boat, and, pausing before they board, Byron turns to Shelley. "Do you intend to keep her?"

The question stops Shelley in his tracks.

"I love her," he says. "She is my dearest friend and my greatest joy."

"Yes, I thought so. You see, different." Byron shrugs his shoulders light-heartedly and boards the boat.

Shelley follows slowly, his mind disturbed. Is this a man who does not know how to love? His genius is clear, but what is genius if principle is missing? If he cannot love romantically, can he love his fellow man at all? Can he feel true friendship? Can he truly care for the people who read his works? And if he does not, he is profoundly dangerous.

They do not talk as they sail out into the lake. The afternoon has brought an eerie light to the sky, and only a slip of evening sun seeps through a small aperture of dark, heavy clouds, turning the lake a murky green.

As they drift homewards along the lake, Byron scratches in a notebook with passion, his breath following the flow of the lead upon the page. There is no other sound, besides the regular to and fro of the water upon the hull and the weary sigh of the winds in the trees. All else is a strange, empty, quiet.

Shelley tries not to look at Byron, whose pencil moves ceaselessly, losing scarcely a moment to the usual considerations of a writer's mind. But the ease and speed are distracting.

Shelley wonders if it is some letter in which he mocks the peculiar gangly boy who has become his companion, and at once reprimands himself. More likely it is some memorandum of a pressing matter. He cranes his neck slightly, just lifting himself up in his seat, so that he has a fleeting glimpse of the page.

It is poetry.

Poetry! With lines cancelled and corrections marked just as he flows along. This, this is what makes a master! An innate ability so effortless it shows mortals from gods. Shelley bites down hard on his lip and pulls his jacket tighter to him. The wind is stronger now, and it tugs at the pages of Byron's book and sends an undulation through the lake that rocks the whole boat. Byron pins down his notebook and looks up, meeting Shelley's eyes. On impulse Shelley turns away, embarrassed to have been caught watching, and then, as he looks out across the lake, is angry at his own embarrassment.

"I think I have offended you, my friend," Byron says softly, taking Shelley by surprise.

"Not at all."

"I have upset you, though. Forgive me. I spoke flippantly of a thing you consider sacred." He closes the book and folds it back into his jacket. The muse is forsaken at his whim, and she shall surely be ready and waiting as soon as he desires her.

"Believe me that I envy the joy you possess, and regret that I do not experience it too." Byron stretches himself out and stares full at him. "You are in a pit of happiness, Shelley. Do not be surprised if you cannot fathom those outside of it."

"The pit of happiness?"

"It's like that dungeon. You're shackled and you don't see it. You're delirious."

There is a mischievous smile that lurks at the edge of Byron's mouth, and Shelley allows him to continue.

"Sometimes I think we were as well to stay away from love altogether. You know in Rousseau's *Julie*, St Preux, at the very first letter to Julie, he says she must not let him kiss her. He says, '*We must give up such games which can have fatal consequences.*' I quote it exactly, you can trust my memory. Fatal consequences. He knows even then. Some part of him knows. The best loves, I often think, must be doomed to death. Death does not permit the inevitable decay of affection."

"You talk of narrative, and not life."

"I talk of life," Byron says, his dark eyes fixed and serious.

Leaning back in his seat, Shelley gazes up at the grey sky and tries to formulate a response.

"It saddens me that you should feel this way," he says after a moment. "I feel that there is a truth you are close to—but you are looking at it entirely backwards, as if you looked at the matter the wrong way through a telescope. Love is the great restorative power of the universe. The romantic love a man feels for a woman is part of that, and it is akin to the love man feels for fellow man, or for the earth, or liberty."

"The love men feel for men?" Byron cocks an eyebrow at Shelley, and then shakes his head. "I suspect your girl knows something about that. But never mind. What I want to say is this: You are an idealist. And love simply isn't that fulfilling."

From Shelley's reclined position he is, for once, looking up at Byron; from this vantage the proud silhouette rises above the horizon. Despite the gloomy sentiment he professes, Byron seems to be perfectly at peace, looking ahead with cold sharp eyes, facing into a wind that lifts his hair and tugs at his jacket, at his cravat— even, Shelley fancies, at his heart, as if that wistful wind would carry him away with it. But Byron himself is solid, immovable.

Shelley shifts his gaze back to the vast sky, a solid tapestry of endless undulating white that makes the ceiling to his world, as he drifts by beneath.

"I would have died without Mary," he murmurs, mostly to himself, unsure if Byron is still listening. "When I was told I couldn't see her anymore, when she was still with Godwin, I took a quantity of laudanum in the hope of death... It was very foolish, all I got was a heady sickness for a day or two. I must confess I felt quite humiliated."

"There is no real use in that sort of thing, Shiloh." Byron's voice seems to come from the clouds that drift above. "One must live on. A new love always comes along. And if it doesn't, then we write. Love is not a thing we ever attain. It is the ideal we chase, and we chase it in our lives and we chase it with our words. You have found one love, but you will always seek another. And I wouldn't change that in you, Shelley. I would never have you forget the ideal. But look at you, I don't believe you ever could."

The boat lurches on an unusually large wave and they both reach out to steady themselves.

"Don't you want to stop searching some day?" Shelley asks.

"Then I'd have nothing left to write about, would I?" Byron sways, staggers, grips tight to the side of the boat, and scowls out at the horizon. "Life is so much more satisfying when it's put into words."

"Yes," Shelley mutters. "Words, words, words."

"Now you sound as if you were out of love with poetry, which

I shall never believe. I've heard you harp on about Wordsworth too much for that!"

The wind rushes at them, carrying a thousand tiny droplets. Shelley tilts his head to catch it, closing his eyes against the things he doesn't want to say.

"The great worry," he manages, with something of a laugh, "is to find readers. I shall never be out of love with poetry, but to write without hope of anyone ever reading is a sad thing. And honestly, I am beginning to despair I shall never have an audience. Perhaps my work simply isn't of a popular bent." As the sway of the boat threatens to dislodge him Shelley grasps the side of his seat and draws himself up.

"I've read..." Byron pauses at the cry of some huge bird above and cranes his neck to watch it soar before continuing. "I've read one of your works," he resumes, gratifying Shelley's trembling spirit. "Someone sent me it some time ago, although I can't for the life of me remember who... but when your Claire first came to me in London, she brought a copy with her, and I knew it already; *Queen Mab* this is. It was partly her acquaintance with you that struck my interest in her. It is a very good poem, Shelley. Very good. You're an extraordinary poet, and if the fellows over at the *Quarterly* don't recognise that, well, I don't esteem anything they call noteworthy, so I'd take their criticism as a compliment."

To reply 'thank you' seems perfunctory, both too much and too little at once, and Shelley bows his head to acknowledge his appreciation. But Byron's face has settled into a frown. Not about the work, but about something else, something far away, Shelley imagines. But it is a concern growing closer.

"I think we might be heading into a little trouble, Shelley," he says. Shelley draws his attention from Byron to the lake, to the sky, and takes in the full implications of the rough weather.

A growing wall of thick black cloud has swallowed up the mountains, and the rain is tearing the lake into a tumultuous swarm of fierce, restless waves. It is only then Shelley realises the crew are agitated, moving about the boat with pace and purpose. A crackle of panic shivers through the air from one to the other like electricity. Someone shouts something that Shelley doesn't catch, but Byron at once rips off his own coat and pulls off his boots, just before the largest wave yet hits the keel and sends them both staggering. Once Shelley is up once more he is struggling his own jacket off, trying to look as prepared as Byron is to swim for his life.

"We should sit down and hold onto something secure; we're only going to get in their way," Byron says to him, and pulls him down before the next swell of the waves. All at once a new ferocity of rain is upon them, battering down upon their heads, drenching their clothes in moments, and amidst the pounding of the water and the roar of the waves, all Shelley can hear is his own breath dragging through his body. In this moment of peril, he is paralysed by fear, not for his life, but of the humiliation he will feel if Byron tries to save him. There is a large heavy trunk by his feet, and when he sways in the ship's pitch he winds his hands around its handles and swears to himself if they capsize he will hold fast to the trunk and let it take him directly to the bottom.

They lurch side to side as the rain thickens, drenching them in a horizontal sweep, obscuring from Shelley's eyes everything except his tight grip on the trunk, and his determination to die.

All at once the squall passes as suddenly as it came. Shelley lifts his head, sees Byron before him, grinning. In the distance a grey veil of rain still pounds the lake further up, but fleeing away. The waves still rock, and he is soaked through with water trickling down his face, but the danger is passed.

"That was exciting!" Byron cries out as he jumps to his feet, shaking the water from his head as a dog would.

"I thought we would all die," Shelley whispers, too stunned for artifice.

Byron laughs heartily and slaps him on the shoulder. "Not a thing of it. Nothing we couldn't have waited out, even if we had been pitched into the water."

"I can't swim," Shelley says helplessly and shrugs up at Byron.

"Well that's rather stupid for someone who spends as much time in boats as you do. Come on, get yourself up or you shall catch a cold, and poor Mary will have to play nursemaid for the rest of your time here. This is what we live for, isn't it? The fear of death! Dry yourself off, there's no harm done. But the next sunny day we must both of us into the lake, and I shall teach you to swim."

Chapter Five: The Story of Frankenstein
Geneva, 10ᵗʰ July 1816

*M*ary announces to the company that her story is finished.
"Then you must read it to us," Byron says simply.

It is the final opportunity, for some friends of Byron's have arrived, boisterous young men who like their drink, and Shelley has quietly suggested it might be time for their own party to move on, perhaps travel a little further into the mountains before returning to England for the autumn.

Energy grips her as they take their seats around her. She is not nervous, but ready.

At first the story eluded her. Day after day she'd examined various ideas, much as a stable master might examine horses before purchasing one, looking each over for strength or defect, but nothing her rational mind offered held any promise, and one by one each was dismissed.

In the twilight land between waking and sleep her imagination took dark paths, and it was in this wilderness she saw a student of unhallowed arts, fierce and young and passionate, and compelled by determination defying reason to enact the work of the gods. The picture was complete and extraordinarily vivid: the scholar knelt over the lifeless clay of a creature he had made, and through his subtle art imbued it with life. Only when the creature first stirred, first beat open its jaundiced eye, would the student realise, too late, the horror of what he had created, and recoil from the beast of his own making.

She had sat up in bed, breathing fast, chilled to her heart's core by the wild fancy her own mind had summoned, and though instinct had urged her to waken Shelley, to take succour in companionship, a thought sliced through that urge.

I could write this.

And at once she grew calm. *I could write this and scare them all as thoroughly as I have scared myself.* She even resisted telling Shelley the story, saving it for the recital.

All the week she wrote as if possessed, shunning adventure and companionship in favour of her work, and now the story is complete.

One last evening then of ghost stories, though how different this from that night of the storm. Clouds line the heavens, but now that the sun is sinking it can slant its rays about them and shine on the glossy coats of the black dogs. Byron and his fellows leave their sport and sit nicely to listen. Polidori joins them. Shelley and Claire sit side by side, close and eager.

Mary opens up her notebook as silence falls, and all eyes turn towards her.

"It isn't quite a ghost story," she says without apology, "but it is, I believe, a story of terror."

A polite murmur. The settling of anticipation. She clears her throat, holds them a moment in silence.

"*It was a dark night in November that I first beheld the subject of my toils.*" Everyone is listening. "*With an anxiety that almost amounted to agony, I collected the instruments of life around me that I might infuse a spark of being into the lifeless thing that lay at my feet...*"

She describes that body, fabricated of death and flesh, laid out upon the floor. Claire squirms and shares her disgust with Shelley in an upturned expression—the enjoyment of terror.

And then, to that cold material object Mary's scientist gives life, the spark flares and takes, and the yellow eye opens.

"*How can I describe my emotions at this catastrophe?*" she asks in the voice of her scientist, and Polidori, his eyes wide, his breath suspended, lightly shakes his head. "*I had desired this with an ardour that far exceeded moderation; but now that I had finished, the beauty of the dream vanished, and breathless horror and disgust filled my heart. Unable to endure the aspect of the being I had created, I rushed out of the room.*"

She tells them of her scientist, describes carefully his good family and fine connections, making the young Cantabrigians shift uncomfortably. She extols his diligent study and prodigious intelligence, nodding to Polidori and to Shelley. With her eyes upon both the famous Lord Byron and her wild and reckless sister, she remarks his profound passion in pursuit, his great and terrible pride.

And where now is the creature he has created? This man, so like them all, has made something he cannot control, and in his fear has cast it out, and so made an enemy of it. An enemy who will pursue him the rest of his days.

My heart palpitated in the sickness of fear; and I hurried on with irregular steps, not daring to look about me:

'Like one who, on a lonely road,
Doth walk in fear and dread,
And, having once turn'd round, walks on,
And turns no more his head;
Because he knows a frightful fiend
Doth close behind him tread.'

And with these words she closes her book, and all is still and silent.

For a moment a cold ominous silence hangs above them all, before Byron claps his hands and swears heartily, bringing laughter from his fellows and a respectful applause. It is there in their pale faces, their blinking eyes, their longing for merriment: she has disturbed them all. Yes, she is pleased.

She sits amongst them once more, as talk turns to the imminent departure and the tour they will take before turning home, but Claire still grins at her wildly, and Shelley squeezes her hand ecstatically. As the others talk, Byron catches her eye, and merely gives a nod, as of a master craftsman acknowledging an equal.

That evening they leave Diodati.

The sun is low, just hovering above the distant mountains which cast their long shadows blue over the lake, but the grass about their feet is kissed with warm orange light for a few minutes more. The waters are blissfully still, and all is quiet as the world reflects this tranquil hour.

Mary goes ahead with Claire while Shelley stays behind to talk to Byron. Now, when it can no longer be put off any further, they must deal with the matter for which they came: the future of the child that Claire is carrying.

"I really ought to be in there," Claire mutters. She strides along the narrow track, giving fierce little kicks at any debris that gets in her way.

"No, you ought to let Shelley handle it," Mary replies smoothly. The unexpected sunset after so many storms and the look of respect that Byron gave her story has lifted her spirits and made her light.

"It's my life they're deciding on."

"And Shelley knows what you want, and will negotiate for you without yelling at Byron."

"Perhaps he deserves to be yelled at." Claire turns away from Mary, and glares out at the dark lake as if it has offended her. "Maybe I don't want him bringing up my child. Maybe I'll return to England alone and bring her up by myself."

"Don't be ridiculous, Claire." Mary says. Claire pauses on the path to let Mary catch up.

"I'm not. Once again, it is my life."

"It is your life," Mary hisses. "It's your life Shelley has come all this way to fix. If you barge in there, you hot-headed child, you will probably be very rude to Albe and he will not be disposed to help you in your exceedingly vulnerable position. You have behaved recklessly, and now we are all adjusting our lives to try to save you."

"*I* have behaved recklessly?" Claire spins about, her dark eyebrows high in astonishment as she stares back. "And how has my behaviour been any different from yours?"

"Infinitely!" Mary cries.

"No, not infinitely. Slightly. You took a married man for a lover. Mine is divorced."

"I gauged the character of the man," Mary says hotly. "I loved a man whom I could trust. You threw yourself at a man because he was celebrated, with no care for consequences."

"You were lucky, and no more," Claire replies with fierce self-importance.

Mary can feel a sharp retort on her tongue, but is prevented from unleashing it by the cry behind them of Shelley, running along to catch them up. Claire narrows her eyes at Mary, letting her know their fight is not over.

Shelley looks tired, but pleased, and he gasps out his reassurance as he draws level.

"Albe has agreed to recognise the child as his own," he says. "As long as Claire stays with us, and keeps courteous, he is happy to take the child into his care, and give it every luxury he can afford. So, as long as we can keep the pregnancy a secret, Claire will not be tarnished by the affair at all."

"That's good of him," Mary says sternly, keen to set the tone for Claire.

"It's the least he can do," Claire mutters. She returns her gaze to the lake, to the mountains beyond.

"Yes, it's good, it's good." Shelley runs his hand through his hair, and catches his breath. "And we must take care to keep all circumstances of this pregnancy and birth a secret."

"Of course," Mary says in Claire's place, and, taking Shelley's arm, recommences the walk towards their home.

"I mean actually secret," Shelley goes on. "I think that should include your family."

"Why would I tell them?" Claire snaps. She lifts her shoulders in a shrug, and strides off ahead. Mary can feel the tug from Shelley's arm that would want to keep up with her, but she deliberately slows him, and gives Claire some distance.

Every moment the sun gets lower and the evening more beautiful.

"Thank you," she whispers. "Claire will thank you too, one day."

"I think it is the right thing," he says with a frown, watching Claire go.

He is all concern these days; she sees his watching and his worrying about where they will live, about their children, about their future... and she loves him all the more for it. Rising up on tiptoes, she plants a kiss on his cheek, surprising him out of his thoughts.

"Hullo, my pecksie," he says, as if he had only just seen her.

"Hello, my elfin knight," she replies, smiling up at him. They chuckle at themselves, at the old names, and proceed a while in silence.

Up ahead Claire's outline is fringed with gold. She has put some distance between them, and wanders now at her own pace. She looks quite beautiful.

Mary looks at Shelley, and notices that every strand of his lovely messy hair is clear and bright. She leans herself into him, so that there will be no outline between them to any wild thing watching.

"So, back to England then?" she asks.

"Yes. Back to England."

"You know, I've been thinking, Shelley, we ought to be selling our works."

His expression is instantly pained and regretful.

"I'm quite convinced we could," she goes on. He may take some convincing, but she is confident. "Done properly I believe we could actually make enough money to keep ourselves without too much worry."

"It isn't the most lucrative venture, and besides, my name is somewhat controversial."

"Then we don't use our names," she says patiently. "Do you think half the customers of our bookshop would come if they knew that their children's books were being written for them by the radical philosopher William Godwin? Of course they wouldn't. That's why the books we sell are written by 'Edward Baldwin.'"

His expression is set; he does not believe her.

"I don't think there's anything I could write that the reading public would actually want to read."

"I'm not talking about philosophy or poetry. We could start with a travelogue. I was lately looking over the diary we wrote when we first left England together, and I couldn't help thinking that other people would certainly like to read it, once we have taken out the personal details, and it wouldn't be so hard for us to put together a little book; it's just the sort of thing that would sell. And I'm sure we've more to add now—we could edit the letters we've been writing home. Perhaps a few poems that describe the landscape. It could be something of which we could still be proud."

Shelley shakes his head in fond admiration.

"What a clever little pecksie it is," he says. "She just might save us all." He wraps his hand around hers. "I hope you know, your story was extraordinary," he says, quite quietly, as if not wishing to disturb the evening.

"Thank you, my darling."

"I really mean that."

"I have made the best I can of it."

"But is it finished?" he asks. Ahead, Claire is nearly at the house and is calling to little William, who, held aloft in his nurse's arms, has spotted them.

"I think so. I might edit it a little more, but not too much." Mary sweeps her own hair back to see him better.

"I think it should be more than it is." He speaks low and earnestly, with that anxious urgency he acquires when he speaks important things. "You have created something marvellous. It should not be so small a thing. Were you to make a novel of it..." he leaves the thought there for her.

"I shall think on it," she says, and in a buzz of happiness runs the last of the way to her child, kissing him in the glow of sunset.

Chapter Six: The Tribute of Human Thought
Vale of Chamonix, 25th July 1816

*T*he mountains are less magnificent than the ravine that cleaves through them, plummeting down through centuries of rock as if it sought the underworld, and the thundering waters of Arve speak to Shelley in voices older than any language he has learned, telling him over and over their purpose in words he cannot understand.

And yet, he listens, standing on a thin wooden bridge with gaps between his feet revealing the torrents close beneath, and feels content.

He stares down between his stocking feet (shoes discarded somewhere in the long grasses) and watches the ceaseless motion of the waters, at once dizzying and inspiring. And when from this tumult he raises his gaze, along the gentle verdant slopes to the distant savage peaks, the blood rushes through his head and all certainty of person and of body dissolves.

He feels his soul borne along on the wave crest—ever and anon more waves come on while he is transfixed upon this narrow bridge. He is almost nothing before the power of the water, the looming presence of the mountains—and yet, he is more than both, for he contains them both in his mind, a mind that hums with a thousand busy thoughts too fast to catch, flying like leaves upon the winds of experience.

"Shelley!"

A call reins him back from his height and reminds him that, like the kite which ascends the heavens, he too is tethered. There is something comforting in the thought. He looks around him. On the meadow bank sits Mary, shaded by an ancient pine, writing book in her lap, awaiting him.

He goes to her, sits by her side in the long grass.

"Are you alright?" Mary says, her voice low and quiet. "Isn't this beautiful?"

"It's extraordinary," he agrees. "I never knew I had not imagined what mountains were before."

Mary rests her head on his shoulder.

Further up the valley Claire sits sketching and humming to herself. Claire of Diodati has withdrawn, and the old familiar one has taken her place. They must look after her.

"She's definitely happier away from Byron," Shelley comments. "Much more herself."

"As are you," Mary replies.

An initial surprise is swept by, for she is right. As marvellous as the company was, he was restrained by it. Here in the clear air he can exhale more easily.

"Maybe. What have you been writing?" he asks.

"I've been thinking about my Frankenstein story. How I could expand it."

Shelley grins. "Good. Yes, that is very good."

He lays his hand upon her knee and for a while they sit like that without speaking. The rich air throbs with melody of bird song and cricket chirp decorating the rushing drone of the Arve.

A certainty settles upon him here, a feeling, rather than a knowing, of power greater, wiser than himself. It is perhaps the presence of the mountain, which seems to declare itself a testament to the extraordinary. Yet, that snowy peak is distant, even as it looms close, and it is not in the earth but in his mind he feels it.

The mountain, his worries, even Mary and Claire, they are there, inside his mind, startling clear, whole, but ever shifting.

He fumbles in their bags for a book in which to express this sudden vision. Without a word Mary hands him her pencil and leans back against the pine trunk to read over what she has written. He presses her hand in swift gratitude, but he is only half aware of her, for his mind is already occupied with the phrases he is turning over and over—*in day the eternal stream of various thoughts*—but he can feel her there. His breath lies high, his hands trip too eagerly and stumble over the words they try to shape. Each line exists a moment in his mind, hovers there to shift and stretch until he fixes it on paper. And then, how few lines, once made solid, must be struck and reformed. The progress is slow, but exhilarating, for he is writing, writing properly for the first time in far too long, something that is entirely true.

> *The everlasting universe of things*
> *Flows through the mind, and rolls its rapid waves,*
> *Now dark – now glittering – now reflecting gloom –*
> *Now lending splendour, where from secret springs*
> *The source of human thought its tribute brings*
> *Of waters – with a sound but half its own,*
> *Such as a feeble brook will oft assume,*
> *In the wild woods, among the mountains lone,*
> *Where waterfalls around it leap for ever,*
> *Where woods and winds contend, and a vast river*
> *Over its rocks ceaselessly bursts and raves.*

He writes and writes with words existing more than anything around him, and when at last he emerges he finds that the day's light has dimmed, that Claire has returned, and she and Mary are talking down by the stream. He folds the book closed and presses it into his breast pocket. This poem is good, he knows. A better work than he has written in some time, and he thrills with the knowledge that he will return to it, work upon and shape it to his vision. This is the exhilaration of creation, and it is not merely poetry, but being, deciding, much as he chooses now to lift himself, to cross the field on shaky legs, and embrace the girls, much as he chooses this moment to live, to be.

Shelley, what is it like when you are writing?

It feels much like a woodland glade that grows
With daedal intricacy as I watch.
Each vine curls with purpose amid chaos,
Creating a heavenly harmony
In revolution of birth, life and death
And life once more. It is quite magical.
For everything I see enchants me so
I pour an unpremeditated song
Upon the waiting page, although some words
Are slow in budding. I sing more with heart
Than with my mind.

That is extraordinary.
Yours is the poet's gift and I admire
It utterly. However, your description
Has little resonance to my own craft.
My novels are a garden whose rough soil
Is ploughed long months before the first flower blooms.
Planting, pruning, watering all take much time.
Uncultivated are my early thoughts
How glad I am my task is not solitary,
As everything I tend grows stronger for
Your ministrations.

If I can aid your growth
My art has done a greater good than I
Ever humbly imagined that it could.
Although my wild unchallenged mind can show
Elysian beauties wondrous to behold
This is not what I want the world to know.
The corruptors of the sacred forces of
Justice, liberty and sweet human hope,
Insidious error, casuistry,
And wanton malice are my wicked muses,
Breeding a raging fury in my breast
Whose only remedy could be revolution
Of mankind's wicked churches, laws and thoughts.

Such noble cause you have and yet you choose
To write in language of sumptuous beauty.

To clothe one's thoughts in fine array must be
The highest principle of all poesie.

What if the richness of your language clouds
Your very meaning from a humble reader?

'Tis true to say I write for the select
Of cultivated sensibility.

When you could write for all who care to read.
Your message now may have a shorter reach.
Could you not address your sentiments
In the simpler, common language of plain men?

I know not how, and can't be what I'm not.

One can always adapt as is required.
An idea may many garments wear,
Attire is secondary to high purpose.
With stories we can show the world such scenes
Its cruelties and kindnesses to mirror.

A vision is far better than a mirror.
To show the world not as it is but dream
Of what this wretched place could one day be.
Your choice of Prometheus is most apt
For this hour of injustice and disgrace.
Yet your Frankenstein is an enchained
Prometheus. I would break his shackles.
Could we not envision a Prometheus
Unbound?

Part Four

Chapter One: The Other Sister
Bath, 25th September 1816

*A*lthough it is a lazy autumnal afternoon in Bath, and the comfortable apartment is peaceful and warmed by the crackling fire in the grate, Mary's thoughts are in an alpine blizzard. She recollects Mont Blanc as they saw it so lately, but adds to the scene a towering figure striding down the mountain with unnatural speed and agility, bearing down upon poor Victor Frankenstein.

She lays aside her pen and looks up from the page. Through the open window comes the delicate chirp and chatter of the town about its stroll in and out of the Pump Room. Shelley lies stretched out on the Turkish rug in a patch of late-afternoon sunlight, eyes closed, mouth twitching with sleepful thoughts, and William unceremoniously spread-eagled upon his chest, blissfully unconscious. All afternoon Shelley has been running around the town square with William on his shoulders, chasing after leaves and dogs and goodness knows what else, never mind the looks they received from fine ladies. And now, much as Mary predicted, they have hit happy exhaustion.

Father and son seem to take in the sun's rich rays and exude them back out, as if their bodies were made of only light; the least breath of wind could disperse them, leaving nothing, and she could not be surprised.

On the sofa with feet elevated is Claire, reading Livy and eating madeleines off a china plate that is balanced precariously on her baby-mountain stomach. She has her own apartment a few streets away so that Bath society will not talk and will not think the imminent arrival Shelley's. It was all arranged with great trouble and expense, and yet, Mary cannot help noting once again, here Claire is, today just as yesterday and the day before and the day before.

A crick winds its way along Mary's spine and she rises to stretch it out. Removed from her work, she decides to get some water, and, leaving the desk, tiptoes around Shelley's slumber.

"Mary, dearest?" Claire asks.

"What?" Mary whispers.

"Could you be a darling and bring me my wrapper? I am quite concerned I shall take a chill. It would be a terrible thing, for the baby, you know?"

Mary stalks out, irritated, though she knows the request will not take her out of her way. A saccharine 'thank you, dearest' follows her out.

Claire's wrapper is quickly found in the hall, left flung upon the banister, but as she gathers it something catches her eye. A letter, lying on the table by the door; the handwriting her father's, as familiar to her as her own. Without hesitation she picks it up. It is addressed to Shelley and already opened. Yet he has not mentioned it to her. She opens the letter and reads a few words. They are enough. It is only her father demanding money once more. A quick skim affirms that he is still not asking after her. She grips the letter too tightly, sending deep crevices through his words. There is home in this paper, in this writing; there is Skinner Street, and the evidence that it goes on existing without her. She frowns as she lays the letter back down and straightens it out. When she returns to the drawing room she drops the wrapper on Claire without a word and sits back at her desk.

She is ruminating on what new tragedy ought to befall Victor, when a neat tattoo of knocks upon the door startles them all; Shelley wakes with a start, clutches William, who only stirs, and looks about blearily.

"I'll go," Mary says, keeping her voice mellow and reassuring.

Shelley rests his head back down onto the carpet, though his eyes stay half open as he regards little William, and as she walks past he bats softly at her foot, smiling sleepily up at her.

Mary blows him a kiss, but closes the sitting room door on the three of them, for not one of them is any use to her right now. In the hall she dusts down her skirt and goes to the front door with a polite, assumed smile.

But it is Fanny.

Mary throws the door wide in her astonishment.

"Fanny!" she cries, and wants for a moment to sweep her in, to hug her, to welcome her. But in a split second she realises the fragility of the situation. Bath has been chosen to keep Claire's secret, a deception that includes their family, and Fanny, Fanny cannot know. In a moment of panic she says, quite loudly so the others may hear, "Fanny, what a surprise to see you!"

Her sister beams at her; she stands tall, her cheeks flushed by the autumn air.

"What brings you to Bath?" Mary asks, and, hating herself, places her arm across the doorway.

"I..." Fanny falters after that first word, scans the hallway behind Mary, then Mary's face. "I was visiting friends," she says, her voice diminishing even as she speaks, "I thought I'd call on you."

"Well, how lovely!" Mary laughs. "Come, I was just about to take a walk, let us walk together."

If she can keep Fanny away hopefully Shelley will realise and have the sense to send Claire home. At this late stage there is no mistaking her condition. Claire out of the way, Mary could invite Fanny in properly.

The door opens onto a cul-de-sac of a mews, and Mary brusquely links her arm through Fanny's and leads her away from the house, out to Abbey square, where Shelley and Claire will be able to see them through the windows, allowing Claire to slink out the back unnoticed.

"I hope you don't mind us coming out," Mary says, brightly, "but Shelley has some company. A difficult sort of fellow, and I was making my escape anyway."

There is the smallest shred of truth in Mary's words, and that shred gives her conviction.

Fanny follows with reluctant step, but without protest. There had been courage in her stance at the door. And now that the panic has passed Mary notices the new blue coat—the fabric distantly fa-miliar, perhaps some old forgotten thing that has lived in the chests for years, reclaimed and refashioned at last. And not only a new coat, but a new style to her hair. The strands left loose around the temple are curled into four ringlets, probably neat this morning but now wilting. The tail of an off-yellow ribbon at the back of her head drags listlessly.

"You look lovely," Mary says, guiding Fanny towards the bench in the square where they may sit a while before the Abbey.

"Thank you," Fanny replies, with regret rather than pleasure.

The day is wearing on, but there are still plenty of visitors to the square, to the Abbey, and to the tea rooms and gift shops around it. Below their apartment is a bookshop, and next door a perfumier. Women move slowly in pairs, a gentleman hurries by at a run, a small gaggle of poor children are ushered away from the windows they'd been peering in.

"Did you have a nice time with your friends?" No sooner does Mary ask that, she realises that there probably are no other friends in Bath, that Fanny has come all this way just for them. Her sister nods, without making eye contact.

The sunlight slants down across the rooftops to them, and does its best to warm them against the autumnal chill. Summer has gone, and will not return for a long time. Dried leaves whisper in the corners of the buildings as the wind stirs, and Mary watches a single orange leaf catch a breeze and fly single-mindedly up to the window of their apartment.

"Yes," Fanny says. "I had someone to visit here." Her gaze flits back and forth across the cobble-stones, as if she is searching for answers in the gathering dust. "Yes, and I've visited them already. And I thought, since I was in Bath, I should come and see you and Shelley. I thought that would be nice. I do miss you both. How is Shelley? I worry for his health."

"He is well," Mary replies, grateful for the pretence they are both carrying on. "I think I told you in my letter that he had some trouble with a cold, but he's quite better now. It wasn't anything to worry about. You look well. This is a lovely coat. Is it new?"

"In part."

"You should get some new ribbons to go with it." Mary delicately touches the loose ribbon. "A nice vivid colour. There's a lovely haberdasher here in Bath."

But Fanny recoils back from Mary's reach, her hands flying up as if to protect the decoration.

"This was mother's."

"Ah," Mary says, "of course, I didn't recognise it. It's lost a bit of colour over the years."

"Perhaps." Fanny reluctantly releases the ribbon and clasps her hands in her lap. "How is my nephew?"

"Growing strong and beautiful," Mary replies. Within her rises a longing to show off her child, to watch sister and child together, to hear his praises sung. Perhaps Claire will be gone by now.

"Dear William," Fanny says, and her eyes flicker back to the front of the house with its blank windows. She makes an attempt at a smile. "And Jane?"

Mary does not correct her.

"She is fine."

"You told me you'd got her a piano forte," Fanny says, fumbling in the long slim bag she carries, and brings out a folio of sheet music. "These were left at the house, I thought she might like them. I know no one else uses them, and Jane is always happiest in her music, don't you think?"

"She'll be very grateful," Mary says, and then, because firmness and clarity are going to be necessary, she adds, "I'll pass them along."

"You aren't wearing a shawl, Mary. Aren't you cold?"

"No!" Mary laughs, "not at all. It's really quite warm. And for September too! Far too warm inside with the sun coming through the windows. Besides, it's quite the fashion here!" Mary tries to laugh and waves her hand at all the ladies making their way in and out of the Pump Room and the Abbey, gossiping beneath their parasols and behind their gloves. Not one of them is without a jacket or shawl. The wind gathers dead leaves at their feet. Mary withholds a shiver.

A silence falls between the two sisters. Across the way, a child in a too-big coat is running in circles with unrestrained delight, tottering unsteadily on short legs. For a moment it seems the child too will fall, but kind arms reach down, support it and carry it on.

The two young women watch the family wordlessly.

"Did you have a nice time in Geneva?" Fanny asks at last.

"Yes. It was wonderful."

"With Lord Byron?"

"Yes."

Fanny picks at her cuff. "Is he everything we thought he'd be?"

"Yes. And no. He is just a man. But quite unlike any other."

"I'm sure." Fanny bites her lip. "I'd love to meet him one day."

Mary nods, but says nothing, for she cannot imagine such an interaction going at all well.

"He did ask after you—after the child in Mother's book."

A little warmth enters Fanny's cheeks. And in the smile that takes Fanny then, Mary understands something: Fanny has no greater desire than to be Wollstonecraft's child. In itself that is an honorific greater than any ambition within her.

Through their childhood whenever Mary tried to push her mind, to improve herself, Fanny was content, and for the first time Mary sees that quietude not as insufficiency to regret, but as a choice.

For a moment Fanny sits tall and the natural sun lights her profile more beautifully than any stage spotlight could. She is certainly plain, but so lit there is a strength to her jaw, an elegance in the curve of her nose, and she looks like a portrait of some noble lady with all the world before her.

But a wandering thought brings a shadow to her eyes. Though her back remains rigid, something within her slumps.

"I wish I'd known you were leaving," she says. Her voice is heavy and regretful, but still not accusatory. "You're the only family I have, Mary. You and little William."

"Oh Fanny, we couldn't have told you... Think what Papa would have done to prevent us going if he'd heard—"

"You think too little of me," Fanny cuts her off. "I would not have told him. When you ran away from home with Shelley—it hurt, being left behind, but I understood. I probably would have told Papa; I didn't think you should do it. I'm glad to be proven wrong.

But you were a child then, Mary. And without a mother. I felt I had to look out for you. We're women now, both of us. You're all I have in the world, I'd keep a secret for you. I might have been able to help you—goodness—perhaps I might—" she stops short, holding back a thought from words. The weight of that unspoken thought hangs upon them, but Mary cannot detect its shape. She reaches out for her sister's hand.

"We had cause to leave abruptly, Fanny. We did not tell anyone," Mary mutters. "There were reasons, believe me. We were in a difficult position, and I can't explain it, even now. We are still in a difficult position. But I never meant to hurt you. You know that. I am so, so sorry if we did. It was never our intention."

"I know that," Fanny nods sharply. "But Papa said Shelley had written that you might not come back."

"He didn't mean that," Mary says, knowing it was true. She strokes her sister's unresponsive hand.

"That you could leave so easily . . ." Fanny murmurs. Her eyes are cast down, her eyelashes ghostly pale in the evening sun. She speaks without looking up.

"You know, Mary, I think you quite remarkable. All that you have done—yes, we know how many would criticise it—but I do believe our mother would be proud. I should like to make her proud too. I have come to a determination recently." She sits up a little straight. "I shall never live to be a disgrace to her. I do believe that if I endeavour to overcome my faults I shall find beings to love and esteem me."

This is such a strange speech Mary does not quite know what to say to it, but just then she spies Shelley slipping out of the apartment and gliding through the crowd towards them, beaming at Fanny and holding out his arms. There. His coming is a relief to her, and to Fanny who embraces Shelley like a brother, and holds tight to him. He has always had a way with her, and now Mary sees her sister melt into agreement with him. He manages to tell her that she must come and visit them soon and make it seem an invitation for the future, rather than a rejection in the present.

"Come, what time is your coach? How about I walk you back?" And linking his arm in hers, with a serious nod to Mary, he escorts Fanny away.

Mary goes back into the house, relieved at its warmth. Claire does not seem to have shifted, but her plate has been refilled.

"Was that Fanny?" she asks with her mouth half-full.

"Yes, it was," Mary says grimly. "Where's Will?"

"Asleep upstairs. What on earth is she doing in Bath?"

"I think she came to see us," Mary says.

"Well she can't see *me*," Claire scoffs.

"Yes, that is rather the problem, *Claire*," Mary snaps, suddenly angry. The afternoon has slipped away and left a cold, shadowy evening with a void where a visitor ought to be. "She can't see you, so we've had to send her away. Honestly, why are you here? You have your own apartment now. I ought to be able to invite my own sister into my house."

Claire is unruffled. This pregnancy has brought a certain levity to her, and she does not rise to temper as often as usual. She picks biscuit crumbs off her bosom, leaving Mary standing there, impotent in her anger.

"There's no point being cross with me," Claire says. "Fanny should have written first. I don't know what she means by turning up uninvited. It's damned peculiar of her. As far as my being here, Shelley says I shouldn't be alone so much. So you ought to go chide him."

Mary snaps up her writing book and goes out. She could hit Jane. She could just slap her across the face. They are only in Bath to help her, to protect her child. All of this is for her.

Why is it, Mary asks herself, that she found herself bound to Claire, with whom she is not related, and with whom she has always fought, and yet almost estranged from her blood sister, who has never done her ill? How different life might have been if Claire had been sent to Ireland, and it had been Fanny at home when Shelley asked her to elope...

But that would not have happened. For Claire was their go-between, Claire urged her on. Fanny would not have run away. Not then at twenty-one, not even if a man as wonderful as Shelley had declared love for her when she was sixteen. She has always been good. And now Mary has, in helping one sister, probably wounded the other.

What Fanny said sticks in her mind. Only Mary and now William are her family. She lives with two parents who are not her kin and their son who is not her brother.

And Mary remembers the rain, the dingy apartment with mould-green walls, and her loneliest misery in London, stepping out when she thought the world had forgotten her, and seeing Fanny standing there in her grey cloak, waiting for her.

As she goes to her writing desk she is unhappy with their behaviour. Perhaps, she thinks, she will write something for Fanny, a story to show her how much she matters.

Chapter Two: A World Too Wide
Bath, 9th October 1816

*S*helley is carrying little Will down the hallway when he spies two newly delivered letters.

"Now, what have we here?" Bending to collect them, he braces Will to his chest, for the child grows almost too heavy to carry.

"A letter from Byron. We'd better not tell your Aunt Claire about this," he whispers to the boy, "at least until we've read it and ensured he hasn't said anything too terrible about her, eh?"

"Asanasa," Will pronounces, with an infant's certainty that he speaks perfectly.

"Exactly," Shelley concurs.

"Inabad?" Will seems to ask.

"This?" Shelley turns the other letter over. "This is from your Aunt Fanny. That's good."

"Ina boda now now."

"Yes indeed," Shelley says, tucking the letters into his pocket and hoisting Will up to a more comfortable position on his hip. "We shall have to see her soon. I'm sure she's desperate to see you." Will chuckles appreciatively as if he agrees. "Yes," Shelley goes on, dropping his voice as they enter the drawing room where Mary is working away, "for you are her little favourite, aren't you? You're her precious Willmouse."

Mary looks up at them, her eyes tired; she leans back in her chair.

"We don't want to interrupt," he says.

She shakes her head.

"You're not. I was reading back over this morning's work. I'm pleased with it."

"I imagine it is excellent," Shelley says.

William adds an enthusiastic babble, and Mary rises to kiss them both.

"I am ready to read the next section, whenever it is ready to be read. Now, where's Claire?"

"Upstairs. Taking a nap she said. Though why she is napping here I don't know."

"A letter just came from Byron," Shelley says, and at once he sees her attention sharpen.

"What does it say?"

"I haven't read it yet." He nods to his pocket and Mary, allowing no delay, takes William from him to free his hands. "There's one from Fanny as well," he says as he fumbles for the letters. He scans Byron's letter as swiftly as he can—correspondence between Albe and Claire has become bitter and fierce of late, so whenever they can intercept, they do. Claire will post her epistles without their knowledge though, and set the blaze raging once again.

"It's fine," he says, a little worry slipping away, and a little pleasure rising as he sees his friend's enquiries.

"Good," Mary says. He gives her the letter, which she reads over William's head, keeping it out of his reach, and he opens Fanny's letter, noticing at once that it is unusually neat. He reads.

Dear Mary, Dear Shelley, Dear Jane,

This is the last you will hear from me. I depart immediately to the spot from which I hope never to remove. I write to share with you all my love and my kindness. I beg you to love and cherish each other. To care for yourselves. Perhaps to hear of my death will give you pain, but you have each other, and you will soon have the blessing of forgetting that such a creature as myself ever existed. I have long determined that the best thing I could do was to put an end to the existence of a being whose birth was unfortunate, and whose life has only been a series of pain to those persons who have hurt their health in endeavouring to promote her welfare.

Yours,

Fanny Godwin.

He stares at the words, one part of him trying to compel understanding on the part that refuses to acknowledge what the paper is telling him.

The panic falls upon him like an axe slicing the cords that keep his peace of mind. He looks up and finds Mary staring at him, and realises she has been saying his name. There is concern in her face—the mildest worry. She has not even the smallest suspicion of the catastrophe.

"Fanny," he gasps, and in releasing her name energy runs in and he leaps to his feet, pressing the letter into Mary's hands. "She has resolved to take her own life."

He turns the letter over: Bristol postmark. Why didn't he notice? Bristol. Not twelve hours ago.

"She writes from Bristol, but 'I depart...', she is travelling still. I can catch her."

From the letter he looks again to Mary and she is now all shock. He clasps her by the shoulders and kisses her. "I must go."

He shouts for Claire as he begins to tear around the apartment, frantically trying to think of what he will need. He gathers money, papers, a coat... what else? He cannot delay! But a pause may save much time. Claire emerges into his whirl-wind sleepy-headed and startled; Mary goes to her, explains in a low urgent voice, the letter clasped in her shaking hand.

"You shall have to stay," he says to them, cutting over their low talk, his mind racing over a hundred possibilities at once. "I'll be faster alone, and Claire's in no condition to travel. If you both stay here you can be ready to receive news. Write to your father, see what he knows. I'm going to Bristol, and if fate is with me I may overtake her before it is too late. Send word to me at the inn there."

Mary nods one brave, serious nod. Claire stares round-eyed and bewildered. He kisses them both and flies out into the city, running through Bath faster than he has ever run in his life. Running for the coach, for speed, for dear Fanny, and despite his deepest held beliefs he makes a prayer that it will not be too late.

It takes three hectic days for him to find her, and when he does he is eighteen hours too late.

The pursuit sent him buffeting from town to town, cajoling reminiscences out of coachmen and innkeepers, sliding coins across tables for information and discretion. Sleepless nights in anxious wait for the next leg of the journey. He arrives at last in Swansea, at the Macworth Arms, and hears at once of the suicide there the night before of a young English lady leaving only the initials 'F.G.'

Exhausted by his failure, he takes a room in the hotel where she passed her last night. It is then, finally, that he collapses in grief and fatigue, and weeps for the neglected girl he would have called sister.

When last they parted there had been something unspoken in her mouth. As he escorted her to the coach that day she came to Bath she had held his arm with the grip of a drowning man clinging to driftwood.

"You have always been very kind to me, Shelley," she had said. And what had he replied? That his kindness was born not of charity but of the pleasure he took from her company, that he loved her as family, that her soul was a rare and magnificent one, all the lovelier for not knowing its own worth? No, surely nothing so sincere.

Because he cannot speak he sits at the table in the empty room and tries to write, but only a few lines struggle free, pained and urgent.

> *Her voice did quiver as we parted*
> *Yet knew I not that heart was broken*
> *From which it came, and I departed*
> *Heeding not the words then spoken.*
>
> *Misery – O Misery*
> *This world is all too wide for thee.*

A knock at the door breaks his silence. The room has grown dark while he has sat staring at nothing, and now he can scarcely make out the unfamiliar room. The knock repeats. A small voice with a soft Welsh accent speaks his name.

"Excuse me, sir? Mr Shelley?"

"Yes. Come in," he calls, for the energy required to get up and open the door is more than he can summon. A maid peeps her head in and peers about the gloom, letting out a small exclamation when she spies the room's occupant.

"A letter come for you, sir. Shall I light the fire for you?"

She brings him the letter, and wordlessly lights the candle for him to read it by. For a while he only stares at it, too tired to work out how anyone knew to address him here, but slowly he realises the letter is from Godwin. With stiff, heavy hands, he eases it open.

Shelley,

We received a letter from Fanny telling us of her intent. We received one from Jane yesterday telling us of your pursuit. You will not be in time to prevent the course she has chosen.

You will wish me sympathy, but sympathy is of no use to me. Your actions at this time, however, can be.

My advice, & earnest prayer, is that you would avoid any thing that leads to publicity. Disturb not the silent dead. Do nothing to destroy the obscurity she so much desired. It was her last wish.

Think of the situation of my wife and myself, now deprived of all our children but the youngest.

We are at this moment in doubt whether during the first shock we shall not say that she is gone to Ireland to her aunt, a thing that had been in contemplation. Do not take from us the power to exercise our own discretion... What I have most of all in horror is the public papers. We have so conducted ourselves that not one person in our house has the smallest apprehension of the truth. Our feelings are less tumultuous than deep: God only knows what they may become.

The following is one expression in her letter to us, written from Bristol on Tuesday. 'I depart immediately to the spot from which I hope never to be removed.'

Thus the letter ends. Bysshe stares at the final line. Fanny's voice speaking hesitantly at him through her step-father's hand. And is even the great Godwin so overcome that he cannot sign himself at the end of his letter? Perhaps he now knows the treasure he has lost.

So there is nothing to be done. Her body shall lie in an unmarked grave, without a tomb to bear her name.

The maid is still in the room, busy with lighting a fire in the grate. Shelley finds himself staring at her in some wonder. This young girl knows nothing of tragedy. She carries on her business, oblivious. She even taps her feet to some tune in her head while she waits to see if the flames will take.

"Thank you," he says with some difficulty, and she waves a dismissive hand.

She is friendly, and in a good mood it seems, despite the news she must have heard. She lifts herself to her feet and heads out. Did she set a fire in Fanny's room at this time yesterday? Or was Fanny here, in this same room, watching her, knowing in a few hours all pain would be over.

Just as she closes the door behind her Shelley staggers to his feet and follows her. She is half way down the short corridor, and turned back to him in surprise and perhaps some small alarm.

"Forgive me," he says, and leans on the door frame, trying to master his emotions. "But I heard a lady died here. Do you know about that?"

She bites her lip. She is only a little younger than him, probably Mary's age, but her face has a childish roundness, and her emotions play there as plainly as fish in a clear pond.

"That's true," she says with a cautious, proscribed seriousness.

He remembers Godwin's injunction—Fanny's last wish—and tries to seem disinterested.

"That's a sad thing, isn't it?"

"A very sad thing," the girl says eagerly.

"What was she like?"

"Oh I saw her!" The words burst from the girl. "And I'll tell you what, you wouldn't have thought it! I certainly wouldn't. She looked so ordinary, if you know what I mean. Just like anybody you might see. She was so polite!" She shakes her head in some wonder. "I don't think I'd be so polite if I were going to do a thing like that. She told me she didn't want any dinner and she didn't want to be disturbed, but oh so nicely, like she was just a bit tired, and very grateful for whatever we might offer. And she didn't give her name, which I suppose might have been strange, but it wasn't really at the time. Plenty reason a lady wouldn't give her name. I sort of thought she might have been someone important, you know? I suppose she might've been."

"I am sure she was important to someone."

"Of course. I'll say a prayer for her on Sunday. She seemed so nice. But perhaps that's wicked of me to pray for a suicide..." She frowns.

"I don't think it's wicked," Shelley says hastily. "I think it's very good of you." And Bysshe, despite his long-avowed atheism cannot help but think of that great unknown; he feels only one thing with certainty—if there is a beneficent God, they cannot deny Fanny Wollstonecraft Godwin admission into the highest sanctuary of heaven.

The girl has so thoroughly discarded her duties that he senses she would like to go on talking, and that to ask her more might simply seem like humouring her.

"Did she stay in this room?"

"Goodness! Can you imagine? No, she stayed down the hall. To be candid, I shall feel peculiar going in there now."

"Is she... still there?"

"Heavens, no. They took her off somewhere. I wasn't here while she was... well you know. I wouldn't have liked that at all. I do know the fellow who found her, though. He knocked and went in when she didn't come out and he said he saw her all still and pale. He had to wait there by her while they went to fetch someone. I suppose someone'll have to give it a really good clean soon. You'd want to, wouldn't you?"

"I suppose so."

She falls into a pensive silence.

"Can I see the room?" Shelley asks.

The girl looks at him slowly, distrustfully; she must be suspicious of such a strange gentleman. He reaches into his pocket for a coin to ease her conscience, and at once she is on her way, nodding obligingly as she leads him down the hall.

"It's right this way, sir," she says.

The room is only two doors down, and though she opens the

door, she will not step inside, allowing him a privacy he couldn't have requested. It is much the same as Shelley's room. Small. Practical. Minimally decorated. A second-rate painting of bluebells and forget-me-nots in a cheap frame above the bed. She might never have been there.

He stands there a while, perfectly still, as tears inundate his eyes, filling the room with water. In the drowned room he can imagine her, hanging up her coat, glancing out the window, and yes, admiring the painting; however rudimentary its execution, she would have appreciated it. The maid is sufficiently far away that with a shuddering sigh he lets the water drain away, carrying Fanny's ghost with it, and leaving the room as dry as a picture. But there is something on the bedside table now. A small neatly wound coil of faded yellow ribbon. His hand reaches instinctively out for it—he glances back but the maid is examining her shoes and does not see him—his fingers close upon the soft silk and it disappears into the skin of a closed fist.

He leaves sharply, thanks the girl and with one hand makes offering of another coin for discretion, while in the other he holds all that remains of Fanny Wollstonecraft Godwin.

Chapter Three: An Ally
Bath, 2nd December 1816

*M*r and Mrs Godwin do indeed tell their friends that Fanny has simply returned to her aunt's in Ireland.

"How can they say such a thing?" Mary says to Claire through gritted teeth. Claire is sitting in Mary's drawing room, as usual. "That's your mother's pettiness," Mary continues. "It's a barbaric lie to tell. That level of cowardice, that inducement to humiliate the dead to avoid the inconvenience of the gossips' scandal. She pretends she is such a respectable woman. Who does she wish to impress? I could tell them a few stories about Mary Jane Clairmont that would shock."

Claire flicks through the pages of her book with a dangerous quiet, her chin raised and lips pouted.

"I'm sure you'd be delighted to bring my mother down," she says, with calm indignance. "But do you honestly think your beloved father isn't a party to this lie, if not, as I suspect, its orchestrator?" She stands up, wrapping her shawl around her with the flourish she loves to make when winning an argument. "Your father is no angel."

Mary rounds on her, blocking her path and staring into her round, surprised face.

"He was once," she says. "Before you and your mother came into our lives. I remember." She spits these last words, and Claire looks shocked for once. Between them is a crackling silence, alive with all the cutting things they could say to one another.

A shudder runs through Mary, and she has to get away. She rushes from the room and up the stairs, bursting in on Shelley at his desk.

"I don't want her here!" she almost screams.

Shelley is startled and sets down his pen at once.

"I don't want her here!" Mary repeats. "She needs her own life, her own home; she needs to stop ruining our lives!"

"Alright," Shelley starts. But she does not want to listen to what he has to say.

"We need control of our own lives, our own choices. If she hadn't been here when—" That half thought bursts out of Mary, and she cannot finish it. She has been careful not to say it, because even to think it is awful.

Shelley rises to his feet and opens his arm to her, but she pushes him back.

"We got her her own rooms, and it isn't enough. You said you would look for a house for us. Please! We talked about Windsor, Surrey, somewhere not far from London, I don't care! Give me my own house for the two of us and Will, with a garden and an absence of Claire."

His expression is resigned, tolerant; they have been over this before, most often when Mary is this angry, and he will certainly try to pacify her, which will only make her angrier.

It is something else that irks her though; Claire's voice rising through the house.

"Shelley! Shelley!" Her tone is high delight, and followed by scampering footsteps (still moving like a child, Mary notes, despite being eight months due).

She bursts into the room, waving a magazine at them.

"Look! Shelley! The Examiner! Leigh Hunt! A notice—"

"Please, Claire," Mary says angrily. She wants to push her sister out, but it is too late: Claire's high spirits have already infected Shelley.

"You!" Claire says to him. "He's talking about *you*, Shelley! Leigh Hunt!"

Shelley grabs the article from her, crumpling the paper in his haste, and now even Mary is interested. Claire points at a certain paragraph, causing more delay in pawing at the pages.

"*The object of the present article*," Shelley reads, "*is merely to notice three young writers, who appear to us to promise a considerable addition of strength to the new school. Of the first who came before us, we have, it is true, yet seen only one or two specimens... but we shall procure what he has published, and if the rest answer to what we have seen, we shall have no hesitation in announcing him for a very striking and original thinker. His name is Percy Bysshe Shelley,*" as he reads his own name a childish smile dimples his face, and Mary feels a rush of affection for him, "*and he is the author of a poetical work entitled* Alastor, or the Spirit of Solitude!"

Claire gives out a squeal of joy and claps her hands.

"Isn't it wonderful, Shelley? Aren't you delighted?"

"It is incredible," Shelley says, a little breathlessly. He doesn't seem to quite be able to believe it, and skims the rest of the page as if looking for some clue to unlock the mystery.

"It said three young poets, who are the others?" Mary asks.

Shelley stares short-sightedly at the page, struggling to focus his mind as much as his eyes. "Reynolds... and Keats. I don't know John Keats." He lets out a slow exhalation and then looks up at Mary with shining eyes. "Mary! This is something! Claire! Do you realise what this is? This is *The Examiner*. People read *The Examiner*. This is exactly what I have sought for so long... It's..." He runs out of words and simply waves his arms about.

Mary finds herself grinning at his happiness, her earlier ill mood stowed away in this moment of good news. Shelley is right. Everyone knows the Hunt brothers and their work. Everyone Mary and Shelley would want to know respects the Hunts. Leigh Hunt's good opinion could unite Shelley with the readership he so desperately craves.

In her positive attitude she even shares a look with Claire, but Claire is brimming with something else, a smugness that infuriates Mary.

"What?" she demands.

"This was Byron," Claire says.

Shelley lifts his attention from the newspaper and tilts his head quizzically.

"It must have been Byron. Don't you remember? Byron told

you that you ought to be acquainted with Leigh Hunt. He's put in a good word for you. You mustn't waste it. Write to Hunt today. And all of this," she looks specifically at Mary now, "would not have happened if I hadn't befriended his Lordship."

She is so pleased with herself she bounces on her toes as she makes her way back to the door. "I'll leave you two to think on that. *I* am going to treat myself."

Mary scowls at her: what Claire in her obnoxious self-congratulation does not see, but Mary does, is the single crease in Shelley's brow that indicates an uncertainty.

"However Hunt heard of you, he would only have written about you if he genuinely admired your work."

"Of course," Shelley says. "One doesn't want to be beholden."

She clasps his hands.

"This is a reason to celebrate, my love."

"You are right," he says, and beams at her. "I shall write to him. I shall visit him as soon as possible. This could be truly invaluable. If Hunt thinks this well of me, he may assist me to some remarkable new opportunity to change things in this corrupt country. He is no petty-minded social climber, he is a proponent of truth and justice!"

He grasps her in his arms and kisses her, and Mary is overjoyed to see this happiness on her Shelley's face once more.

"This is good news at last!" he cries.

"It is indeed," she laughs. "And I think we deserve some good news after all we've been through."

Dear Shelley,

While I was yet endeavouring to discover Mrs. Shelley's address, information was brought to me that she was dead — that she had destroyed herself. You will believe I did not credit the report. I called at the house of a friend of Mr. Westbrook; my doubt led to conviction. I was informed that she was taken from the Serpentine river on Tuesday last. Little or not information was laid before the jury which sat on the body. She was called Harriet Smith, and the verdict was found drowned.

Your servant,
Thomas Hookham

Chapter Four: Mrs Shelley
London, 30ᵗʰ December 1816

*T*he desolation of winter speaks with more honesty than the beauty of autumn. All those fanfares of red and yellow have sunk to black, revealing the annihilation they presaged: a dull, dead world of stone and thick ice, once white now dirtied by a thousand filthy feet. The sun has not been seen for weeks.

Mary stands alone in the colourless churchyard. It is the end of 1816, a year of such heights and such terrible depths. And now, the final day of the year, she is to be married.

In her boots her feet are freezing cold; her hands she keeps tucked under her jacket, clutching her ribcage.

Today she will marry the man she loves, and it will be no small relief to her to have that legal contract. Yet the least appreciation of the circumstance chokes her with regret. How dare she take pleasure in this moment?

She stares at the cold ground, at the gravestones aged and fresh. Inside they will all be waiting for her. She had promised to be only a moment. Her moment is gone.

Mary heaves the cold air into her body and longs for it to freeze the mechanisms within her that keep her from action. The breath gusts out of her, fresh and white in the grey air, rushing from her and then drifting slowly amongst the graves. Shaking off the clumps of snow that have clung to her black skirts, Mary makes her way into the church.

In all the secrecy of Fanny's death, her father tried to forbid the public show of mourning clothes. Anonymous in Bath, Mary ignored him. But now Harriet Shelley too has chosen death and London knows of it, so why should Mary not wear black. A black dress, a black shawl, a black veil for her wedding day.

Mrs Shelley is dead, and a new woman must take her place, and be mother to her orphaned children.

Two suicides in a matter of months. Two people they are supposed to have loved, two people they are supposed to have taken care of, left so miserable that life held no charm.

So, Mary Wollstonecraft Godwin will be a bride in mourning, and the great skeleton of Death shall materialise to escort her down the church aisle. Death has haunted all her waking hours of late, and many of her dreaming ones. His hand rests upon her shoulder as she writes.

"Perhaps you should stop killing all the characters in your novel," Shelley recently suggested, with that mask of pained concern he wears these days.

She has killed the little boy; she has resolved to kill Victor Frankenstein's best friend Clerval; she has killed Justine, that kind-hearted orphan who was never really part of the family. A servant, beloved, but never appreciated. So guiltless, and yet so cruelly treated. She knows the character is too abruptly inserted into the story, but Fanny was too abruptly taken from the world. Mary could have written a kind story about Fanny, an atonement, but she has written a condemnation of herself. It is her life and her deeds that have brought so much death: Harriet, Fanny, the still little baby. And so Victor Frankenstein will lose all that he loves.

She will not kill him, though. She will leave one person alive to feel the guilt and the pain of being left behind.

Pulling open the heavy oak door to the church Mary almost expects to see that phantom reaper of her fantasy waiting for her. Instead she finds Shelley in the antechamber, leaning against the wall, his eyes fixed on his feet. He too is all in black, and it makes his face all the paler, pretty widower that he is. He pushes himself up at her entrance. She can feel him seek her gaze, but she is reluctant to give it, all of her energy goes on holding everything in—were she to make eye contact, something might slip. But as she brushes by him, she pauses a moment, lets him lightly kiss her forehead, and nods for him to lead the way. She walks the aisle a step behind him, without ceremony.

A wedding she thought she would never see. By the altar her father and his wife, ready to forgive now that they know how utterly they can lose their children. Claire has stayed in Bath, looking after William, for her pregnancy is still a secret, even from her mother. It would seem an unbearable dishonesty, but Godwin has lied to even their closest friends about Fanny going to Ireland, so apparently no one cares for honesty or decency anymore. Mary stares at her father. He looks smaller than he once did. Less magnificent.

A parson with hollow eyes and bony hands presides. Clarifications are made. Small talk is dismissed. It begins. His voice is low and monotonous. He speaks carefully and enunciates each word particularly. She cannot hear what he is saying. Mrs Godwin smiles warningly at Mary and nods towards the parson. She catches the meaning: *pay attention, Mary.*

Godwin signs his consent for the marriage of his underage daughter and the pale widower.

Shelley holds her hands in his as the prescribed verse is read. His face is grim. There is no pleasure in this ceremony, no spark of joy from bride nor groom.

Shelley steps out of the church into a fresh fall of snow that tries to hide the filthy ice with a thin layer of momentary white. Beyond the church gates flow the unforsaken, busying about their lives oblivious to the marriage that has taken place.

He hates that he is here again, performing the detested ritual, feigning belief in god and law.

Behind him comes Mary, who wordlessly puts her arm through his. A gentle pressure of her hand tells him she wants to speak, but they are followed close by the Godwins who, to Shelley's chagrin, pause by them.

"Will you come dine with us?" Godwin asks, and actually *smiles* at them—as if he had never renounced his eldest child, as if the past years had never happened.

"Perhaps in a while," Mary says. Shelley can hear the heaviness and strain in her voice. "I think Shelley and I would like to take some time."

"Quite understandable, you happy newlyweds!" Mrs Godwin says.

Shelley hates them both quite profoundly in that instant, and is too tired to keep the emotion from his face.

"It is a good thing that has happened here today," Godwin says pointedly. He pushes his top hat securely onto his head and with a shiver settles fully into his coat. His cheeks are ruddy with the cold but he wears a look of contentment. "A decent, honourable thing." Then, to his wife, "Let us be going. I shall have a great many letters to write this afternoon. Good news must be sent abroad. Good day, Mr and Mrs Shelley."

As they walk away Shelley hears a snatch of their conversation, and the words 'son of a baronet' reach him. Who has this once brilliant man become?

Within the churchyard the snow drifts down slow and hazy. It lays upon the bodies of the dead a mute, forgiving blanket.

He wants to express his anger, to rail against the Godwins, and marriage, and law, and all of it, but he knows Mary does not share his venom. Indeed, as they begin to walk around the churchyard, he senses that some part of her is glad; that she feels things changed between them, and that the day's events have formalised their tie in a way that the past years—even their child!—have not.

Claire has a healthy hatred of the law, and he decides he will write to her once they return. She is still in Bath, of course, and he misses her. Her liveliness is the sunlight of their days, bright and playful, and quite easy to take for granted until gone.

But it is Mary who is with him now, and he brings his mind back to the present as they stop in the lee of the church. Mary takes off her bonnet to adjust its ties. In the echoing snow-light her gauzy auburn hair is magnificent and her pale skin almost luminous. Holding the bonnet at her breast she is completely unaffected, completely natural, and Shelley feels a rush of love for her. As awful as these past months have been, at least he has always been with his Mary.

"Well," Mary says with a sigh. "Hopefully this marriage will help."

"Yes," he says. "It is for the children."

"For poor, dear Harriet," Mary says softly, an anxiety troubling her face.

Shelley puts his arm around her shoulders and kisses her forehead. It had seemed to him inevitable, but very wrong, that on this day no one should say Harriet's name, but Mary, his beloved Mary, has spoken.

They begin to walk again, side by side among the tombs. The white-touched graves no longer glare but sigh into the earth with resignation. And the living, who have so little time, must be glad to be alive.

If there was once a path here, it is now obscured by ice and snow. Theirs is the way to make themselves.

"What now, my love?"

"Now? Home, I suppose."

The snow quietens the city and their voices, their sinking steps, are loud to only them.

"Home, indeed."

But what can home be in this world?

The tightening of hand on sleeve says much, and head on shoulder momentarily rests.

"Have we done wrong?"

"We have always tried to do right. Perhaps we have erred."

"Others surely will say we were wrong."

"They shall say all sorts of terrible things."

Their pace is slow, their footfalls matching, providing now the softest crunch. Their shoulders are speckled with white dust.

"They will never love us."

"We have love enough for each other."

"And for our children."

"We will be more of a family than before."

"Indeed."

"We have love."

"We are lucky."

They are twin stars in perfect alignment, two single lights that seem, for a moment, to one, shining out amid the tempests.

Bath – 13th Jan 1817.

Dear Lord Byron

*Shelley being in London upon business I take upon myself the task &
pleasure to inform you that Claire was safely delivered of a little girl yesterday morning at four. She sends her affectionate love to you and begs me
to say that she is in excellent spirits and as good health as can be expected.
That is to say that she has had a very favourable time and has now no other
illness than the weakness incidental to her case.*

*A letter ought not be sent so far without a little more news. The people
at present are very quiet waiting anxiously for the meeting of parliament –
when in the Month of March, as Cobbett boldly prophesies a reform will
certainly take place.*

*For private news if you feel interest in it, Shelley has become intimate
with Leigh Hunt and his family. I have seen them & like Hunt extremely.
We have also taken a house in Marlow to which we intend to remove in
about two months – and where we dare hope to have the pleasure of your
society on your return to England. The town of Marlow is about thirty miles
from London.*

*My little boy is very well and is a very lively child. It is a long time
since Shelley has heard from you and I am sure nothing would give him
greater pleasure than to hear news of your motions & enjoyments. Another
incident has also occurred which will surprise you, perhaps; it is a little piece
of egoism in me to mention it – but it allows me to sign myself – in assuring
you of my esteem & sincere friendship*

Mary W. Shelley

Chapter Five: The Hunts
London, 4th February 1817

*A*s they cross Hampstead Heath a light sleety rain falls, casing the tufts of grass in a sleety grey. Mary is glad to be with Shelley, glad to be going to see the Hunts with him once more; while Shelley is required so much in London they have been staying at Skinner Street, but that house with all its memories and all its little tensions has become suffocating, and kind Leigh Hunt has invited them to stay a while.

Across from her in the cab, Shelley looks tired. The last few months have aged him and a grey pallor haunts his troubled face.

The Heath is bleak today and offers no comforting beauty.

"Do you remember that summer we used to come for picnics here?" Mary asks.

Shelley is slow to stir from his thoughts, but then he brightens at the memory. "Oh yes. With Hogg and Claire. We sailed burning boats on the pond. Those were jolly times, weren't they?"

Mary nods, and looks back out. She would not quite call those days 'jolly,' but in all the years she has known him she has learned they remember things differently. That is probably inevitable between two people, however close they may be. Something about the recollection of those days disturbs her.

They pull up at a row of picturesque cottages with trees and flowers rambling all around them and a sheltering swell of land blocking off the open heath. The cab has barely stopped before a sea of children floods out to meet it. As they step down, Mary lifts

William gingerly up out of their reach, but Shelley is at once on the ground at their level, listening to all their rambled greetings and stories.

These are the Hunt children. The eldest, Thornton, is about six, and everyone's favourite. Horatio and Florimel are at Shelley's pockets, either putting things in or taking things out, Mary doesn't know. There is another in their midst that Mary might not have met before, and she wonders if this is a Hunt that she has missed, or perhaps a friend or servant's child that has slipped seamlessly into the group.

"Have they capsized Shelley already?"

Mary looks up to see Maryanne Hunt at the door, visibly pregnant and carrying in her arms little Swinburne, who is a year old, just like William.

"I'm afraid so. He's lost to us." Mary comes to her, they embrace, and let the two little boys stare at one another in delight.

As they step towards the house the front door is thrown fully open, and Leigh Hunt himself is there, arms spread wide to greet them.

"Shelleys!" he cries. "Welcome to Casa Hunt! Forgive our foibles, our chaos, and our enthusiasms; our home is yours as long as you will it."

He is more charming than handsome, and incredibly likeable. His skin has a dusky hue, and his face has pleasant, pronounced features, framed by dark hair to his chin.

He kisses Mary's hand, and with a 'look at the little precious' kisses William too.

"The children have overcome Shelley," Maryanne says ironically, with a nod to where Shelley is now sitting cross legged in the dusty road surrounded by little Hunts, the cab driver hovering behind them all with some uncertainty.

"I presume that fellow is wanting to offload your bags," Hunt says. "Allow me."

As Hunt makes himself useful, Shelley gets to his feet, bringing up with him one of the small children on his shoulders.

Deprived of their playmate, the older children run to Mary and tug at her skirts.

"Now Thornton," Hunt calls, as he lifts Mary's travelling case. "Don't try and topple Mrs Shelley, she's much too good for that."

The cases are dispatched to an upstairs room, and Mary is ushered to a cosy sitting room with a warm fire, and sat in an old, cracked leather chair, worn into comfort by years of use; tea is brought, and Maryanne sits by her, while Shelley remains on the floor amongst the children.

"So!" Hunt cries, collapsing himself into the armchair by the fire. "My fine young friends, what news? Most especially, what news of your little children, Shelley?"

"The Chancery case continues, and I am still fighting for custody, but a great many forces seem to be fighting against me."

"I don't understand why they haven't just given them to you at once. It's a disgrace. I don't understand it at all," Maryanne says. "Their mother is dead, God rest her poor soul. Where else should they be than with their father?"

"Harriet's family are trying to slander me. They have always hated me."

"They have behaved despicably," Mary says seriously.

Shelley smiles at Florimel who has dropped herself into his lap, and he speaks with a smile and soft tone so his words don't disturb her. "I know I have not been a good father to my children, and I regret that now. But I left them in the safe care of their mother. Harriet's family hate me so passionately, and were so often cruel to her, I do not know how they will treat these poor darlings. I should hate them to be brought up in a family where they felt they did not entirely belong."

Mary notices him swallow something down, and it occurs to her he may be thinking of Fanny. Is that what he feels he must save his own children from?

"You let us know what we can do," Hunt says. "As I've said before, if at any point it's useful to bring them to us, if your house isn't quite ready, or you can't travel, or whatever the reason, they will be loved and cared for here. And if there is anything I can publish in *The Examiner* that would help to promote your case, I will of course do so."

A rush of affection for this man sweeps over Mary.

"You are very generous, Hunt," she says.

"You are." Shelley looks up at him earnestly. "I warned you when we met that my name is poison. The proceedings of this trial may give you a sense of the extent to which I am execrated. It is unwise to link your name with mine. I do not understand it, for all I desire is to improve the state of mankind, and everything I have ever written, everything I have ever published has that as its sole aim."

Leigh Hunt is shakes his head as Shelley speaks.

"I am aware of that from your writings," he says, assuring them with a fatherly calm. "I care for what I care for and shall not be put off it. We have a review of the 'Hymn to Intellectual Beauty' and one of *Alastor*. Send us everything you publish and we shall review it fairly. If you have small things you have written we would be honoured to publish them. And, listen, you are welcome here, as long as it pleases you to stay. We shall have plenty society; we have guests to dine more nights than not, so you shan't be bored. I want you to meet Keats, a young poet like yourself, and Hazlitt for that matter. The Novellos as well I think will entertain you. I honestly think you have the striking poetic voice of the time, and that, as you have said, you are misunderstood by the world. Today's society is not kind to those who think for themselves. But let us not dwell on the forces of evil. Once your children are returned to you—and I have no doubt they will be—what are your plans?"

"We shall settle for a while," Mary says. "The house at Marlow, you know, we have taken."

"Marlow?" Hunt frowns to himself, "Where is that Mrs H.?"

"Buckinghamshire," Maryanne replies promptly. "Out past Windsor."

"Delightful!" He grins at Mary. "I rely on her for everything."

"Once our house is ready, then you must come and stay with us, and allow us to repay your hospitality."

Hunt nods at her, but seems distracted, and rises from his chair.

"You must excuse me—I think the children are up to mischief."

There are indeed noises of some juvenile squabble from an adjacent room, the children having apparently become bored of adult conversation.

"You mustn't be offended if he doesn't take up your invitation," Maryanne says to them in a hushed tone once her husband is gone. "Since his release from prison he has never been comfortable far from home."

Shelley tilts his head. "I'd have thought the opposite would be the case, that he would be hungry for the wide world."

"We are all delicate creatures."

"Indeed," Shelley says thoughtfully. His brow is troubled and his breath comes heavier than usual. "How terrible that enslavement can actually fetter the mind, until the very soul of a person is conditioned to the state of wretchedness."

Mary knows this manner of his, and knows he is faraway in other thoughts, with little awareness of what he speaks or who he speaks it to.

"Of course, Leigh is not wretched," she says to Maryanne, so as not to offend their host. "He has great society and a lovely home. Had I such a home, I am sure I would not wish to leave it."

"Maryanne, could you?" Hunt's voice comes from the next room, preceding his arrival. Maryanne heaves herself and baby up at once, and the two Hunt parents momentarily converse in the doorway.

Shelley is still lost in thought, and Mary takes the respite to lean back in her chair and appreciate this life of the Hunts. She can see herself in a home like this, full of arts and kindness, and busy with life.

"Mary," Maryanne says, drawing her out of her thoughtfulness.

"Yes?"

"Would you like to come and see my sculptures?"

"I should love to!" Mary says.

"Well then, come!" Maryanne says. Mary rises, careful not to wake sleeping William, just as Hunt settles himself in an armchair. "We can leave the babies with their fathers. Here!"

Hunt takes little Swinburne with much fuss. "This is a terrible idea; I don't know what to do with him," but settles the baby familiarly against his chest.

Mary dispatches William to Shelley with a little reluctance as the baby stirs in transition, and the older Hunt children crowd around.

"You have such a marvellous face, Mary," Maryanne goes on, leading her out of the room. "Such a high and broad forehead; they say that's a sign of intelligence, don't they?"

"My father did consult a physiognomist at birth."

"What did he pronounce?"

"Much what you suggest." Mary tries to keep her voice modest.

"I would love to sculpt you one day," Maryanne says, calculating as she stares at Mary with an artist's eye.

"That would be a great honour."

"And me!" one of the children shouts from the doorway. "I want to be a sculpture."

"I've already done a bust of you," Maryanne says mildly.

"The house is overflowing with busts of the children," Hunt remarks, *sotto voce*.

"Luckily they break half of them," his wife rejoins merrily. "Right, we shall leave you men to it."

Mary follows Maryanne out the room with a mild misgiving that she may be missing out on good conversation, and they go through the kitchen, around to what may once have been a parlour. Clay busts and figurines are crowded along the shelves, without category or order.

"These are wonderful!" Mary says, and forsakes her concern.

It is the effect of them all that is most satisfying. Individually the imperfections are visible, though a couple of Maryanne's children stand out as being particularly characterful and instantly recognisable.

"Ah, there's Hunt!" Mary spots his familiar face behind an unfinished dancer. "That's a good likeness."

"It's not bad," Maryanne says, rubbing her stomach thoughtfully. "He's a little older than that now. I did that while we were in Surrey County Gaol."

"It must have been awful," Mary says, hushed.

"It was. But we have managed; we must make sacrifices. This is what it is to live on the outskirts, to object to society's cruelties, to try to bring about change. We have married great men, you and I. The world shall be cruel to them, and we must do what we can to ease that pain."

Maryanne smiles kindly at Mary, and Mary, from politeness, returns it, but feels uneasy.

"It is not only men who can be great," she says cautiously. "Do you not have ambition in your art?" She gestures to the sculptures.

"Yes, yes, of course. But I am not so gifted as my husband. He is special; yours is too."

"He is," Mary agrees, but at the same time feels herself belittled. Is there some unspoken assumption that a woman may not be married to a great man and be great herself?

In her travelling case is her first full novel and she is very nearly finished her revisions. It is, she is sure, quite good. But she doesn't say this to Maryanne. She simply keeps quiet.

Chapter Six: The Wards of Chancery
Marlow, 4ᵗʰ March 1817

*I*t is ten o'clock in the evening by the time the coach from London arrives in Marlow. Shelley staggers off it, only too glad to at last be out of its turbulence and have his feet on solid ground. As the carriage rattles westward, he is left alone to breathe in the night. The air of the dusky grey sky is damp, the ground dewy, a few birds still chirp and rustle in the hedges. And the great black mass of the river Thames whispers as it slinks by.

Only the windows of the small town glow, and behind them distant chatter, laughter, clinking of crockery. In one of those houses, only just out of his sight, Mary waits. But Shelley is not ready to go to her, not ready to say to her what needs to be said. He walks away from the lights and towards the river.

All day he was energetic, passionate, arguing with the highest court in the land before witness and jury. Fighting with every word and skill in his arsenal.

All the journey home he shook with anger at his defeat, at the duplicity and cruelty, at his own failure. Only now does his energy leave him; and he sinks upon the muddy bank and watches the water.

Looking upon the Thames, he recalls the moment in Switzerland when he held the Arve in his mind and marvelled. How different these waters look: powerful, threatening, strong enough to sweep life away.

This river carries the dead.

Questions come to him that in his strength he has been shutting out. Harriet has been much in his mind today, and he must look now at her final moments.

Death by the river. Did she jump from a bridge? That seems uncharacteristic. More likely she would have eased herself in from the bank, getting dirt upon her hands, moving to wipe it away, and then realising there is no need. Could she have laughed, however wryly, at that instinct? Or were the tears flowing, she already more water than woman, a meagre tribute to the waters of the Thames.

Bearing herself and her unborn child into the river. For, they told him she was with child, the origin of which he cannot guess. Was it love or desperation?

Poor Harriet. Whatever her flaws, she did not deserve this fate.

Out in the water there is something pale. It could almost be his reflection, but it is too far away. He squints his heavy eyes, but finds he cannot focus. In that uncertainty he sees a child out on the water, a girl, golden haired and robed in white. He knows her. He has known her a long time.

Ianthe. She was the invention of his fiction and the namesake of his daughter. A creature of absolute innocence, unaffected by the hypocrisy of this world, a divine possibility for the future.

Her cheeks are rounded, like Harriet's, her hair falls as Harriet's did. But her expression is miserable, a contorted, pleading agony. Her mouth moves in a desperate, wordless cry, as Lavinia's helpless lips called out silently when she was reunited with her father.

"I cannot save you," he whispers. Tears roll down the girl's face as the waters sweep around her. "They will not let me near."

And with a surging of the waters, the child disappears.

Night is fully upon the market town by the time he approaches home. Lights glow from within, and as soon as he opens the door Mary is chattering to him.

"How late you are! I'm glad you found a coach at this hour. You should sit. Look, look what Mama has sent!" And how rarely does Mary call her step-mother 'mama'? She must be happy. "Some of my brothers' clothes. I imagine they'll be too big even for Charles when he gets here; though he may be a tall boy like his Papa." She looks Shelley over foot to head with a calculating eye. "But he will grow into them soon enough!" She smooths the piles of neatly folded clothes as she talks. "And if he doesn't, William will. Two boys! They'll have to share at some point. And this! This!"

Mary holds up a child's pinafore in pale yellow, embroidered in bright colours, though whether they form a butterfly or bird or dragonfly, Shelley couldn't say. "Isn't it beautiful? It was Fanny's, and then mine. It's a little thin, but very good for summer. A little discoloured here and there, but I can add some lace to it, make it nice for Ianthe."

Shelley takes the dress from her and runs his fingers over the embroidery. It is very badly done. Probably a child's work. He imagines Fanny, grown too big for the dress, embroidering it for her little sister.

He holds the collar in one hand and with the other stretches the skirt out to its full length. About three feet. The baby he left with Harriet will now be walking unaided. She will be able to reason and to argue. She will have stories of her own. But she will never wear this dress.

"Don't you like it?" Mary asks. He draws his attention back to her, and sees the pursed lips, the close brows. "I know it isn't the nicest dress, and I'm sure she'll have some very fine things from the Westbrooks, but I thought it was a very nice gesture from Mama to send these things over, and goodness knows what has happened to their belongings in all the turmoil of the past months."

She is reaching now for the dress, withdrawing it from his grasp. He grabs impulsively for her hands, dress and all bound up with them, and looking clear into her eyes, speaks.

"It is a beautiful dress, Mary. And I wish I could see my daughter in it." That alone is too much to say and his throat closes around the rest of the necessary words, caging them inside him, trying to prevent the pain they will certainly cause if they escape. But there is no avoiding it now.

"They will not give me custody," he says.

He feels her fingers beneath his loosen.

"You are their father," she says, and shakes her head as if to knock away the thought.

"It is unprecedented," he murmurs, and, keeping one hand holding tight, he raises the other to her head and gently strokes her hair. "Nevertheless, that is the decision. The court has decreed that I am unfit to be a parent. They say that I am an atheist, and a revolutionist, and they believe I could not give my children an appropriate moral education." She does not look at him, her eyes fixed on some distant thought. "They refuse to grant me any visitation rights, though I will continue to fight that. They are not to be left with Harriet's family either, though. They are currently in the custody of the court. They are wards of chancery. A foster home is to be found for them."

Those are the words, and having escaped him they expand to fill up this little house, polluting its air. Shelley finds he is suddenly exhausted, and pressing Mary's hand once more, he crosses the room and collapses onto the sofa by the fireplace.

Mary remains standing.

"You told them we were married?"

Her voice is thin and small. He does not have the energy to turn to her, and only manages a quiet 'yes.'

"Did you tell them about this house?" She hurries around the sofa and kneels before him. "Did you tell them about the lease? Twenty years! We are stable. We are secure. Did you tell them about William? That he is so strong and healthy and beautiful... No one could look upon him and think we were not good parents. They should come here, come and see all that we have done!" She holds up her arms, gesturing to the house she has furnished with care and consideration, as if the very drapes could be taken to Chancery as testimony.

Shelley shakes his head dolefully.

"Harriet's family brought my poetry into the court. They read from *Queen Mab*." He bites his lip until the taste of blood washes through his mouth. "They brought my book in and they stood there and read passages from it, and Lord Eldon himself decreed it an immoral work."

Only as he says this does the fight go from her eyes. She sits on the sofa beside him, her face downcast.

Shelley reaches out a hand, and she lays hers in his open palm.

"You're all muddy," she whispers.

Shelley looks at his black clothes, and indeed, there is mud all over his trousers, and now it is smearing itself onto the new upholstery.

"So I am. I should change."

She waves a hand, gesturing him to stay.

"Sometimes I make the mistake of thinking things have changed in this country." Her voice is heavy with bitterness.

He squeezes her hand. There is nothing to do, nothing to say.

"Shelley," she says.

"Hmm?"

"Did they mention William?"

"They cited that I had illegitimate children, but were not interested in hearing about him."

He is dismissive, but Mary sits straight, taut.

"He's not in any danger, is he? I mean, they wouldn't take him from us, would they?"

If misery is lethargic, fear electrifies. To have lost so much, and realise there is yet more to lose. Shelley stands up. "Where is he?"

"Upstairs. Asleep. They couldn't, could they?"

"They probably could. All law is disregarded in the face of Eldon's prejudice." He speaks softly, but his mind is racing. He wants to run now to William, to clasp him close, to hold in his arms his only remaining child. "We will not let them," he whispers. He is calculating, planning.

Mary is looking up at him, her jaw is firmly set, and though her eyes are glassy, she is strong. Shelley clasps her arms.

"They will tell themselves they can do anything they want, but I swear to you I shall not let them. If it comes to it," he says, trying to reassure her with all the confidence his voice can muster, "we flee in the night. We go to the continent. We fly beyond their reach. We can live out our days in Italy, in Greece... So long as we are together, what is there to keep us here?"

And though Mary looks around the house they have made, and the quiet life they have built, she draws the back of her hand across her eyes and nods.

In the small hours of the night, Shelley sits awake and writes.
The billows on the beach are leaping...
The bark is weak and frail,
The sea looks black, and the clouds that bound it
Darkly strew the gale.
Come with me, thou delightful child,
Come with me, though the wave is wild,
And the winds are loose, we must not stay,
Or the slaves of law may rend thee away.

They have brought William to their bed, as if thieves might creep in and catch him from his cot. No, it would not be like that, but through the tedium of court. He glances down at his son. William's open mouth curves in a lovely cupid bow and his thumb rests upon his lower lip.

"I will not let them take you," he whispers once more.

What of Charles and Ianthe? Orphaned by the law, wards of chancery without a home. And he exiled from his homeland, forever? It is no pain to leave England, but painful to flee it. And the cost.

He strokes his son's blond hair.

There is another child to think of: Allegra, Claire's daughter. Allegra who belongs to her father, and who must join him in Italy. Well, then, Italy may be a good place to start. Italy may be their future, and a turn for their fortunes.

Our lives are brief and ever fraught with woe.
The thought that any deed of mine has made
The task of life more grievous to a soul,
Has burdened down with pain the pure of heart
Tortures me through my night's long waking hours.

Do not believe that guilt is bound to fault;
It is a fair response to natural grief.

But how does one continue on?
We must.
What would you? Cease human action in fear?
And in your grief decree, as Ceres did,
That nothing on this blighted earth will grow
While her beloved child is taken from her?

Ceres was right to act just as she did.
She had a tyrant with whom to reason,
And then a punishment to deliver.

None here deserves a punishment, unless
It were the universe and circumstance.

A universe with far too little love.
And have we always been as generous
In dispensing love as we could have been?

We all have done the best we could, my love.
We have done the best we could.

Part Five

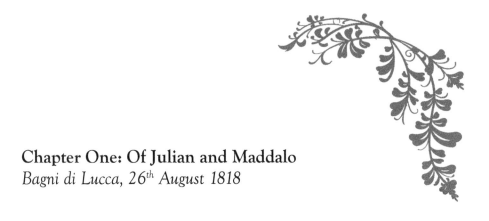

Chapter One: Of Julian and Maddalo
Bagni di Lucca, 26th August 1818

*T*hey have a small house in a spa town in the Tuscan hills. In the meadow that slopes downwards to the river Mary sits, while the sun gets low and the hum of cicadas blends with the river's babble. She is by herself with only the children, for Shelley and Claire have gone to Venice in quest of Byron. William toddles by himself through the long grasses, his steps still wobbling, but rarely failing him. "The quadruped becomes a biped!" Shelley had said, and the memory of it makes Mary smile now. She misses him in his absence. But there was no question of her going to Venice with them. Beside William they have a little girl now, baby Clara, almost a year old, who is dozing on Mary's lap.

With half an eye on William's wanderings, Mary is full of tangled thoughts. Her novel *Frankenstein* is published, and rather than publish at her own expense as Shelley does, she has been paid a modest amount for it. Even Byron's publisher John Murray was interested, though he could not ultimately be persuaded. Back in England, copies of her book will be sitting on booksellers' shelves, and even now a stranger may be reading her words. It is a wonderful thing.

She has been reading *Corinne* again, and the years have changed it in her mind. Corinne is perfect, intelligent, sensitive, but she withers when the man she loves does not love her back. That grief is a downfall sufficient to entirely destabilise her.

In a world that grants women so few options, a woman cannot

afford to be weak. It takes determination and resourcefulness to survive.

Mary's mother wrote of the dangers of feminine graces, of how sensibility and delicacy only weakened a woman and Mary herself has no desire to be feminine. She prefers to write in the voices of men, because she desires to be treated like a man. But it has started her thinking; could she not write an exemplary woman? An enlightened woman, a lover of liberty, empathetic and kind, but determined in her conviction? A leader of men... Such a woman would hardly be respected. Yet she has considered before a novel of a Napoleonic leader, a demonic Promethean who reaches without regard for those hurt in the wake of his ambition. She'd thought before of taking the Italian prince Castruccio Castracani for her subject, and now that she is in Italy, all the materials are before her. But is there a historical woman who could meet her criteria? If there had been such a person, would history have remembered her?

"Mama!" William cries out, calling her back to the moment. "*Farfalla!*" Around his golden head a white butterfly is bobbing hazily. As it takes its mazy motion away across the field, William runs back to her.

"A butterfly," she tells him as she draws his warmth and weight against her. Standing while she is sitting, his head can loll against her shoulder.

"Butterfly," he echoes.

She puts her arm around him and hugs him close. At the neck of his blue jacket is a yellow ribbon; it hurt her to cut Fanny's ribbons, but now she has a short length for William's jacket, and a bow for Clara's cap, and coil for herself, though she hasn't quite decided what to do with that yet.

"English *butterfly*, Italian *farfalla*," she says quietly, smoothing out the ribbon.

"*Farfalla*," he repeats.

The butterfly is only a speck of white winding above the flower tips, getting ever smaller and further away, but they watch it together.

"It's pretty, isn't it?" Mary whispers. William nods seriously, his little face frowning after the wandering beauty.

But as lovely as the evening is, the shadows are growing long, and Mary must take her children indoors. It is time they were in bed. There are two servants in the house to help her, but the evening will be quiet without Shelley and Claire. Blissfully quiet without Claire, lonely without Shelley. Perhaps, she thinks begrudgingly, as she gets to her feet and hoists up Clara, even Claire is company better than none.

Venice, 27th August 1818.

High above Venice a storm of fierce dark majesty sweeps its broad arc of cloud, and from great height drops down torrents without remorse.

Crossing the lagoon with Claire in a roofed, coffin-black gondola, Shelley watches the storm through the stained glass of many colours. Only the slightest tilt of his head drenches the city in a new hue: through a regal sapphire Venice seems a city of angels, while a wild vermillion drenches the city in sin. They are only at the edge of the squall, a perfect place to view it. The veil of rain is ever-shifting, revealing and then obscuring the distant towers and spires, so Shelley cannot quite hold this mercurial city in his mind.

By his side Claire frets, shifting her weight side to side in a nervous energy the storm only exacerbates. But he cannot attend to her as he ought, cannot turn himself from the scene of awe.

A sudden crack of thunder forces a sharp scream from Claire, and Shelley impulsively clutches her, as the interior of the gondola lights up in a flash of vivid colour. He realises how afraid she is, despite the fact that she shakes her head, as if disapproving of her momentary fear. He keeps his arm around her, and presses her to him, silently chastising himself for his negligence.

"It's alright. Just the storm. We're nearly there."

"I know," she says. The muscles in her neck are drawn taut, and her jaw is set. There are more than storms causing her grief.

To tell her all will be well would be patronising, and possibly untrue, so he only holds her, giving her the comfort of his presence, and promising nothing. She nestles into his shoulder to keep the lightning from her eyes, like a child frightened by a ghost story.

For all the love he bears Claire, for all she has improved her mind these past years, there is still something of the reckless heroine who will rush into adventure, and here at last must extricate herself from it. For they go to Byron to find her daughter, to save her daughter, as she has often said this past week. And to do that they must face Byron, or, Shelley hopes, *he* must face Byron, and Claire with her hot head and harsh words be kept at safe distance.

"She could be starving," Claire mutters, turning her head on Shelley's shoulder. "Neglected. Abandoned."

He makes the same reassuring hushing sound he uses when William is tired but not yet sleepy.

"He *swore* to look after her," she goes on. "He has no right to cast her out. I trusted him with her, fool that I am. But he is the greater fool if he thought I would relinquish her absolutely. She is not his to dispose of, she is his to *care for*. That was our agreement."

"He will have ensured she's well cared for," Shelley says, watching the rain slide down the coloured glass. They are further into the storm now, and the water hitting the roof drums insistently.

The closer they get to Venice and Byron, the more agitated Claire becomes. If only Mary were here. Despite all the bickering, she can calm Claire when it's necessary, while his attempts seem only to distress her further. What would Mary do? She would be blunt and practical. She would remind Claire how much there is to lose. How necessary tact and reserve are to be in the next days. But Shelley cannot bring himself to chide Claire for being a concerned mother.

In thinking of Mary his mind slips, momentarily, to the Tuscan home, to the green valleys between the mountains, of the warm afternoons they take alone together, while Claire is out and the children are cared for. The taste of her.

Ah, but Mary is two hundred miles away, and he has a frightened Claire he must care for.

"It's going to be alright, Claire."

The drumming of rain diminishes, and stops.

They look at one another, as if either of them had the answer. Shelley leans forward to peer through the glass. Outside, the water only undulates with the rhythms of the other boats, and the city grows close.

"Look," he says. "The storm is gone. And there, Venice."

Clutching at his arm, Claire scrambles forward to look.

"What an extraordinary place," he murmurs as they glide into the mouth of a canal, the city rising up on either side of them. "It can't be real. It must be a city of dreams. I don't think it can hurt us, Claire."

As they stare out across the water the clouds stir enough to create an aperture through which light pours, streaming down through the sky and hitting the water where it scatters into a thousand shifting gems upon the wave-crests. Captivated by their motion, Shelley seeks a phrase to describe it, if only for letters home. Then again, perhaps this city will find itself in something more poetic; such a setting is deserving of tragedy.

"Isn't it extraordinary? Look at that water, Claire, look how it shifts and sparkles."

"I'm looking at the water," says the voice at his shoulder, and he turns to share with her a sentiment of wonder, but her nose crinkles and her lip curls in disgust. "It's filthy," she says, staring down his rapture. "I certainly wouldn't want to touch it. It's so murky. I'd bet there's disease here." She slumps back into her seat and sighs out, "Oh, my poor Allegra!"

Claire clasps her hands at her breast, her miserable face gazing at nothing in particular. It is a pose from a tableau, and Shelley understands her need to hold court. He turns the shutters on the windows, hiding the enchanted world from view, and waits attendance upon her, ready to comfort as required.

Claire reiterates her worries in myriad forms as they sail up the canals, until at last the gondolier announces their arrival at the British Consulate, where Allegra lives for now. The streets shine with the recent rain as they disembark. The guardians step out to meet them; introductions and explanations are made, a few tears are shed by Claire, and in the midst of all out comes a little pretty thing dressed all in black, toddling before their old maid, Elise. Claire's hands fly to her mouth, but she hesitates. As Shelley realises her concern he aches for her; she is not certain that this is her daughter. What if, by chance, this were some other child. A full year has gone, the infant babe is now a walking child, the face drawn longer, the hair lightened. How terrible, too, to get it wrong, and in the presence of these strangers.

"Allegra, it's your Mama!" Elise says, and Claire rushes upon the little child with tears and kisses.

After a few polite words, Shelley leaves Claire there, assured of her safety, and promises to return when he can; in the boat, he gives the gondolier Lord Byron's address in Venice. He will go alone, and see what negotiations can be done.

"Look here," Byron says frankly. "I don't care what happens with Allegra. I took her because you all wanted me to. And obviously I'm not going to keep her in my house—I promise you that is *not* the place for a child. But, honestly, if you want to come and take her for a while, fine. My only condition is that I have no intercourse whatsoever—if you will excuse my pun—with that Claremont girl."

"Of course!" Shelley cries, drawing his horse alongside Byron's. "I think that best for all."

"Fine. I want her kept away. The things she's written to me! She's insane. I don't even want her in Venice. I know you'd try to keep a rein on her, but I also know she'd slip it."

"Wouldn't dream of it," Shelley assures him, pushing aside the discomfort of deception and the need for a fast plan to get Claire out of the city.

They ride side by side along a narrow sandy strip of uncultivated island that shelters Venice from the Adriatic, the Venetian Lido. The horses Byron has provided are large, powerful beasts, and Shelley grips the steed with his legs, mildly nervous of this new height. Byron, however, rides with centaurian grace.

Their horses take a regular, easy pace, for there is nowhere to go, but that movement is pleasant. Ahead, the soft sands of the island stretch with only the lightest dunes and occasional scrub to break the monotony. Byron brought him out here almost at once, from the very moment he opened the door he seems to have felt nothing but pleasure at seeing Shelley, a pleasure that brings some compunction to Shelley, for he does not find Byron as he left him. The liveliness behind the expression is the same, but the skin has grown sallow and stretched. The thick black curls recede from the striking brow and have an oiliness Shelley recoils from. His figure too is much changed. He has gained weight, not as a healthy man expands into his later years, but in odd patches here and there, so that it looks as if he hides misshapen packages beneath his clothes. Shelley cannot keep from staring time-to-time, trying to trace the exact differences.

And then they talk, and all change is forgotten.

"She's a pleasant child," Byron says into their comfortable silence. "Very intelligent for her age. She'll do well. On the subject of which, I heard the news about your wife, and your children."

As Shelley forms his answer he looks out across the bay. There is no trace of the recent storm beyond the streaks of cloud that the sun now casts her rays upon. "It was a horrible business," he says at length.

"You can't blame yourself."

"I don't," Shelley says. "I assure you there was no ill will between the two of us. She was a sweet girl with great promise, if, at times, a smallness of mind. I loved her still, not as I once thought I did, but sincerely. She could have come with us when we left, I invited her." Shelley watches a lone straggle of weed drift across the open sands. "I feel nothing but pity for her." The weed is caught up in the wind and carried away. "And then there was the most abominable mockery of a trial for the custody of my children."

"I heard about that. If I had been in England at the time I would have moved heaven and earth to be of service to you. Every power I am capable of wielding would have been at your command... but I suppose that might not have helped your case so much."

"Perhaps not." Shelley smiles weakly.

"What was the final reason they gave against you?"

"That I am immoral, that I am a revolutionist, and that I am an atheist. So my children are kept from me, to be brought up in the most respectable corruption England has to offer."

"As someone who has the charge of immorality levelled against him often enough, I sympathise. I have been deprived in my own way, but not as you have been."

"The whole thing has hurt Mary very deeply. I think she does feel guilt, though she oughtn't. And she looked forward to bringing

Harriet's children into our home. She'd have loved them just as she loves her own."

"Yes, I'm sure she would. Come, this way." Byron points to a sandy track that leads them around the point of the island. "And is Mrs Shelley well?"

They talk of Mary, and Shelley boasts of William and Clara. Learning they have not taken a house in Venice yet, Byron offers his house in Este. "It's only a day away, and then you can both come and see me often."

"We'd love that," Shelley says, again stowing away the implications of the lies he is weaving, and the action he is agreeing too.

"What is Mary working on? Tell her whatever it is, I'm looking forward to reading it. I loved *Frankenstein*. A remarkable work, and all the more so coming from a girl of seventeen. Make sure she knows it."

Shelley glows with pride to hear his Mary praised, far sweeter than any praise for himself, for it carries the promise of future reward of her joy should he tell her of the esteem.

"Do you know that Walter Scott reviewed it? She was so delighted that she had to write to him to claim authorship. Otherwise she is very glad to remain anonymous. For now, she is studying. Lately she translated something interesting, a document on the family Cenci and I am trying to persuade her to write a tragedy on it, but so far she's resisting. Do you know the story?"

Byron confesses he does not.

"A young girl was executed for the murder of her father."

"Sounds just her sort of thing."

"It's a very sad tale. But by all accounts he was a thoroughly heinous man. He raped her. The daughter. Beatrice."

"Oh, excellent! How Gothic! Tell her to write it." Byron grins, "She'll treat it excellently."

"I know she will. But she's a little resistant just now. It would be good: a treatise on passion and violence, their temptations and their consequences."

The wind blows at Shelley, shaking out his long hair and drawing it across his face so that the beach before him seems only half there, and Byron's voice is the strongest anchor he has to this world.

"And you, Shelley? What are you working on?"

"I desire to write a work that would not only speak a profound truth as to the means best to bring about a positive change in this poor world, but would actually incite such a change by its words."

"You would bring about revolution?"

"Not of violence, but of ideas."

"You are an idealist, Shelley. The world does not operate upon such pure principles as you anticipate."

"Almost all of Europe is overshadowed by despotism." Shelley shakes back his hair to see the world clearly once more. "You and I may have left our home country but we cannot be insensible to its plight. Thousands go hungry while the few grow fat. There is a whole class of people born to servitude, whose meagre days will be lived out working for King or Lord, tilling another's fields, filling another's coffers, until the coffin is ready and they may be laid low. We live in a time when men in America proclaim freedom while keeping a tight leash upon their fellow men as slaves. So many born into a state in which they will see no flicker of liberty from birth to death, you cannot tell me you approve of that?"

"Of course I do not approve!" Byron scoffs.

"Well then, what are we to do about it?"

"Buy a powder keg and blow up parliament, I'd say."

"You aren't taking me seriously."

"On the contrary, I take you very seriously. If I speak irreverently it is to show you how others will interpret your well-meaning words."

"Words have power," Shelley insists. "Words can teach a man to live with liberty in his heart, and to resist the shackles when others would put them upon him. Words can teach another man the harm of shackling his brother."

"And what of the man who will not learn?" Byron eyes him critically, "What will you do with the brute? When half the world carries liberty in its heart as you desire, what of those who exploit other men's kindness?"

"I cannot offer an easy solution," Shelley murmurs. "I cannot promise all men will be good."

"Of course you can't, and that is the problem with your

doctrine of nonviolence. Nonviolence will be met with violence. And which of those will win, do you think?"

"Perhaps in time, through ideas and discussion, we can ultimately reach a better way. I propose a peaceful means."

"I would like to think you are right. So when are you putting all your fine ideas into something the public can actually read? What is the work you propose that will change the hearts of men?"

As before, Byron's tone swithers between mockery and earnestness, never alighting long enough on either for recrimination.

"It seems to me there is no figure more required for today's struggle than Prometheus; Mary is entirely right there. It is apparent to me that we are in desperate need of change, and that there is no easy way to bring it about."

He breathes in deeply and the wind ushers him on. He glances at Byron who is still watching, entirely focused.

"I don't need to believe in a Christian God to see Christ's wisdom," Shelley says. "I consider him a revolutionary philosopher, and one I am often inclined to agree with. Prometheus' act is defiance, and his suffering, like Christ's, is exemplary. But where Christ rises after crucifixion, Prometheus remains bound; he remains the prisoner of the ultimate tyrant. I have been thinking a great deal about Aeschylus' lost *Prometheus Unbound...*"

"Don't tell me you're going to write it for him." Byron says, a mischievous glee in his voice that is not unkind. "Do it, Shelley! Never was an act more Promethean!"

"But it isn't enough!" Shelley cries. "To reconcile so great a champion with the tyrant of the world would be abhorrent to me. It would need to be an overthrow. I would have to change the story. Find a way for Prometheus to *forgive*. And that forgiveness, that rejection of violence, would ultimately set him free."

"You sound positively Godwinian."

"Godwin never went far enough."

"All that talk of a perfectible world," Byron sighs at the wind and casts a regretful glance at Shelley. "Mankind will never change. Each age seems to me a little crueller than the last. By all means help those you can while you can; yes, that is doing good. But ultimately all the philosophy in the world will not make any *difference*."

"It might. Ideas travel. They can wait. All they need is the right soil, and they will grow."

"You shall certainly write something magnificent. And for that reason alone I encourage you."

It is remarkable, Shelley thinks, as the sky begins to darken, and they leave their horses and embark on the gondola that brought them, that Byron, who has greater audience than any living writer, has so little faith in the thing he creates.

Byron stands in the prow, unbuttoning his jacket. The air is damp, but mild, and Shelley, leaning back in the stern, is utterly at his ease. The water now is black, reflecting in fragments the orange sky that lies about the silhouette city. The easy lap of the waves upon the hull lulls Shelley into a dreamlike state, and every now and then the occasional strain of an unseen singer reaches his ears distant and mellifluous.

"Have you learned to swim yet, Shelley?" Byron asks.

Without disturbing his calm, Shelley shakes his head.

"Then I declare you're a fool," Byron says, pulling off his shirt to discard it with the jacket, and revealing in the process his broad, pale belly. "You miss one of the greatest pleasures this world offers, and our race back to the palazzo shall not be a fair one. I shall race you all the same."

"You aren't swimming in that?" Shelley laughs—for despite the water's beauty, he recollects Claire's diagnosis.

"Of course!" Byron shouts back. "It's perfectly fine." And with this declaration he leaps into the water, disappearing a moment beneath the murky green, and then surfacing ahead of the boat, casting back a wicked grin. Shelley shakes his head extravagantly, and Byron stretches out a powerful arm and pulls himself into a confident, easy stroke.

"Keep well behind him," Shelley instructs the gondolier. The boat drifts dutifully behind its master, and with a soporific wonder Shelley leans over the side, the very tips of his fingers only daring to dance upon the wavelets, and watches Byron swim ahead. There again is that prowess, that speed and strength. He cleaves through the water effortlessly, as a swan does. Though the canals are thronged with boats there isn't a single other soul swimming.

Shelley grows anxious for his friend as they enter the neck of the canal, but Byron manages the boat traffic with ease, drawing a few glances from the *gondolieri* and pedestrians. One calls out his name, but Byron either cannot or does not wish to hear it, for he continues on, pulling himself forwards with strong arms.

Shelley leans back in the boat. Now that he is left alone, he processes the lies he has told, and the swift actions he must take to cover them. Claire must be got out of Venice, and Mary must be ushered into it so that he may present her soon. Perhaps she will be cross. But it is all done for Allegra, and for Claire. He rummages in his coat pockets and finds paper for a letter. He will tell her everything—but most of all he must urge haste. She will get this letter in perhaps... four days. A day to pack. And then, if she rises early she can get to Lucca and on to Florence in a single day. From Florence it is three days to Este.

My dearest Mary,

He writes with the letter held uneasily upon his knee, the first volume of Madame De Staël's *Corinne* from his pocket the only thing to act as a table, and it is so much smaller than his letter he must adjust the paper every few lines. He sketches his meeting with Byron. He writes instructions, advising her to avoid the hotel he and Claire took in Bologna. He winds it up.

In nine or ten days we shall meet. I have been obliged to decide on all these things without you: I have done for the best—and, my own beloved Mary, you must soon come and scold me if I have done wrong, and kiss me if I have done right—for, I am sure, I do not know which—and it is only the event that can show... Enclosed is an order for fifty pounds. If you knew all that I had to do!—Dearest love, be well, be happy, come to me—confide in your own constant and affectionate
P. B. S.
Kiss the blue-eyed darlings for me, and do not let William forget me. Clara cannot recollect me.

Chapter Two: Music in the Memory
Este, 10th September 1818

*M*ary takes her husband on faith and travels to Este as instruct-ed, passing her twenty-first birthday upon the road, and ar-riving exhausted on the tenth day with a poorly baby Clara and a quarrelsome William.

But the moment the coach draws up at the villa Byron has leant them, Mary knows it is worth it. Shelley is waiting for her, hatless and happy, bursting with smiles. He hands her down from the carriage, and at once a flurry descends upon her. Servants come to take the luggage inside; Claire rushes out to kiss the little ones and babble on to Mary about Allegra, how beautiful she is, how quite like herself; William waves his arms for Papa, and Mary scarce-ly has a moment to orient herself.

It is not until evening, walking slowly round the house arm-in-arm with her husband, that she takes it all in. A palazzo of Italian grandeur surrounded by flowering gardens, larger even than Diodati and stocked with servants and horses and everything they could wish. It does not seem so bad to give up a Tuscan cottage for the life of Venetian royalty. Without the heat of the day, it is lovely to stroll in the gardens with their rows of layered flowers, the heady scents of the jasmine and freesia intoxicating.

"Thank you for arranging all this."

"I hope I did the right thing."

"I shalln't deceive you, I wasn't much pleased to leave you alone like that, and so abruptly, but now that I am here... it is rather wonderful."

He squeezes her arm.

"We have an invitation to see Byron as soon as you are ready," Shelley says into the lazy evening quiet.

"I look forward to seeing him."

"Yes, you'll find him changed."

"For the better, I hope."

"I shall let you decide."

"I presume just us, without Claire?"

"Indeed." Shelley takes a deep breath and glances around, as if worried someone—the servants?—might overhear them. "I have implied that she is not with us. I know it seems preposterous, but it was really the only way to make everyone happy."

"It's a difficult situation. And really, you've been very kind to Claire, which, despite everything, I appreciate. All the same, it's a dangerous game you're playing here, Shelley."

"I know." He winks down at her and she shakes her head, marvelling at his unlimited capabilities. He will go to such great lengths for those he loves.

"How have you been?"

"Me? Well enough. I've finished reading *Corinne*."

"I am much behind, I am afraid."

"I'm not as impressed with it as I was before."

"Why not?"

"As a vision of womanhood, which it purports to be, it is weak. Corinne is the object of Oswald's story; she is beautiful and talented, but ultimately she lets love destroy her."

"And?"

"And I think I could write something better."

He chuckles, "I imagine you could. Something in the vein of your mother's writing?"

"Yes. Do you remember back at Marlow I was researching Castruccio Castracani? I've thought of telling his life alongside some female opponent. A queen to rival him."

"That would be quite a remarkable novel."

"I think so too."

"Then perhaps you had better write it."

The day they have arranged to meet Byron is burning hot. They get off the coach in Padua, and Shelley, finding when the next is due to Venice, cannot decide if the stuffiness of the coach was worth it for the shade it provided. The open air does something to disperse the cries of Clara, who began to bawl some miles back and has not stopped since.

Returning from his enquiries, Shelley joins Mary where she stands by the canal, swaying the screaming baby.

William has retreated to the shade of a statue and clings to its base with his eyes downcast in an earnest frown.

"Shelley, I'm worried about her. I think she's sick."

He holds out his arms to take the baby.

"Do you want me to take her for a while?"

"Please. I can't make her hush."

The transition from parent to parent is enough to confuse Clara a moment, and she looks at them with miserable incomprehension.

"Hush, hush, little Ca," he whispers as she begins her wailing once more, and he wipes away the tear and spittle from her hot skin. "There's a coach in fifteen minutes," he says to Mary, "or an hour and fifteen. I know a rest would be nice, but I think we ought to press on to Venice as fast as we can. If she is troubled by anything more than the heat it would be good to get her to a doctor quickly."

"Why to Venice?" Mary screws up her eyes against the sun, and gazes out along the river, and then hastily over at Will, still in his patch of shade. "We should stop here. Claire saw the medico in Padua, didn't she? We could go to him."

Shelley remembers the *medico*, his anxious hands and sly sneer. Claire had recoiled from his inquisitive touch, and they had walked out abruptly.

"I didn't trust him," he says.

"But..." she heaves a sigh, "how long would the journey be?"

"A few hours I think, maybe more. I know it'll be an unpleasant journey for us and for her, but once there a good medico could make all the difference in the world. We don't want to endanger her."

"No," she says, her reluctance turning to conviction. "Let's go to Venice."

William complains querulously about having to get into the coach again, and wants to sit by the pretty canal and get a sweetie.

"Now, my darling William," Shelley says, kneeling before his son, and bringing the infant down to his level. "We have to go to Venice to get a doctor for poor Ca. She's not feeling well. Look at her." William stares at his infant sister with distrust. When Mary takes his hand he follows sullenly and does not look at them.

As they climb onto another coach Shelley hands Clara in to Mary and lifts William in after them. It is a relief to be free of the heat of the baby.

"I wish Elise were here," Mary murmurs. Yes, Shelley thinks, Elise would be helpful, comforting here. But she is now bound to Allegra, and they must manage on their own.

"You will love Venice you know, Will," Shelley says, and the coach rattles off. The only other passengers are two Italian gentlewomen with the appearance of maiden aunts, and they smile at William's grumpy face. He is aware of them, and looks up at his father with less conviction than before. "Listen to me, little Willmouse. It is a whole city full of canals. There isn't a single road, only rivers, and instead of coaches and chaises we shall take boats everywhere we go."

"And we will see Albe, too," Mary chimes in. "Do you remember Albe?"

"I doubt he does," Shelley says, smiling to himself.

William shrugs his shoulders and buries his face in Shelley's sleeve, peeping out at the Italian women peevishly. That at least is something, and Shelley puts his arm around the boy.

"I am looking forward to seeing Albe," Mary says.

"It was wonderful seeing him... but..."

Clara has wiggled an arm out of her dress and Mary wrangles it back. "I think she might sleep now," she whispers, and turning back to Shelley, asks, "But what?"

"His way of life really is appalling." Shelley stares through the scenery that hurries by outside the window, and keeps his voice low, glancing over at the two ladies, but they aren't listening. "There was a woman," he goes on. "A young woman, who he fancied. And he bartered with her father for her. For the night, you understand."

Mary looks up from the baby, eyebrows raised.

"Apparently it is common enough practice here in Italy," he whispers, "but still—it sickens me. To see a man like him reduced..." He shakes his head. "But I'm sure he'll be well behaved with you around. And he knows we're bringing the children."

"Does he still have all his animals?" Mary asks, perhaps to return the conversation to something more child friendly.

"You'll like his animals, Will," Shelley says. "I saw some cranes... a peacock..."

"I wonder if it's the same peacock..." Mary ponders.

"I *heard* the dogs, but I didn't see them. Oh, there was some kind of... I honestly don't know what it was. A fox-monkey." He grins down at the child whose blue eyes are staring up at him, all attention now.

"Won't you like to see all the animals, William?"

William considers this a moment and then turns his attention out the window.

"Papa?" There is something pleading in his voice, but no question follows.

"Be a good boy, Will," he says.

Poor thing, he is tired of all this travelling. Shelley brushes Will's blond hair back off his forehead. His large blue eyes gaze out searching, scouring the landscape for something beyond their adult perception.

"He looks more like you every day," Mary says quietly.

Shelley leans against her; he likes to hear this, and they hear it often. "He's changing so much lately. I think something new in him has emerged over the past weeks. He's got your mouth, your eyes, your way of looking at the sky."

"Mama," William says, "*Venice è bella?*"

The two ladies laugh.

"*Lui e` un po 'italiano!*" they chuckle to each other.

Mary beams at this, and thanks them in Italian, commenting that William will soon outstrip his parents in his command of the language, while Shelley quietly replies, "*Sì, Venezia è molto bella.*"

Clara splutters out of her short sleep, and for a moment her face distorts in silent pain before the howl starts up. Mary clasps her close, whispers to her. But she will not hush. Shelley tells the Italian ladies as politely as he can that they are on their way to the medico, and apologises for the noise. The ladies are nice, but contort their faces with each renewed cry.

All the long journey, Clara cries. The kindness of the maiden aunts wears out. They scowl and fuss, and once demand that something be done. But there is nothing to be done.

Spittle gathers around Clara's dry mouth, and each cry is hauled up from the depths of exhausted lungs. She cries until she begins to shake with convulsions. Shelley's heart quickens, and he looks out of the window often to see how far they are, as if looking could bring the city closer.

Arriving in Venice they fling themselves out at speed, searching for a boat to take them into the city. But there is a fight at the city borders. They do not have the right papers. Shelley grows angrier and angrier with the officials, while Mary's tears fall freely onto Clara's face, perhaps cooling the fever there.

"My child is sick! She may be dying!" he screams, abandoning his scholarly Italian for his native tongue. He had not meant to say so, and the words bring a cry from Mary. But their adversaries are, at least, intimidated, and let them through, with many cautions.

They clamber into a boat, and Shelley, trembling, draws Mary close. Her pale grey eyes are frightened, but calculating. A silent look sweeps between them, and he nods.

What can they do?

They will do everything they can. Everything.

He puts one arm around her, and one around William, and the little family huddle close in their powerlessness.

When they get near the British consulate, Mary and the children alight, and Shelley goes alone to hunt out the *medico* with greatest speed, pausing only a moment to kiss Clara, and Mary scolds him toward haste.

The second he disappears around the corner Mary is overcome with fear. She is a mother alone with her children in a strange city where she does not know her way, where the faces and the language are unfamiliar to her, and what if he cannot find them again in this labyrinth of narrow streets and murky rivers?

They are in a narrow backwater, a thin channel of dark green water between a narrow cloistered walkway and a sheer, damp wall. Mary retreats under the awning, away from the restless waters, and draws her children close. This must be the back wall of a church that no doubt opens its doors onto a square where the sun still shines.

Embedded in the wall above a bench is a sculpture of the Madonna, eyes sorrowfully bent, hands open downwards, shedding kindness onto those who would seek her shelter. With some tentativeness, Mary brings her sick daughter and frightened son to sit beneath the blessed virgin's benevolence. Clara is quiet in her arms, though her chest leaps arrhythmically and still the open mouth twitches.

"Don't cry, little Clara," she says to the babe, and William climbs onto the seat beside her and clumsily says, "Don cry, Ca."

"No, don't cry. Papa will be back soon," she says. William nods earnestly in agreement to his mother's words. "And he'll bring the doctor who will make you all well."

The baby shivers. Mary hugs her close. The shivers increase in speed and severity, and all Mary can do is stroke the pretty curly hair and bite her own lip. She almost chokes on her own stifled sobs as the child convulses once more and falls still.

"Hush Ca, hush, Papa will be back soon," William says.

Mary holds her breath. Everything in her ceases. A tear drops onto Clara.

"Don cry, don cry," William says, his little fingers stroking Clara's cheek, but her face does not move.

Mary carefully slides one hand out from under Clara, and holds it above her mouth. There is no slight disturbance of the air against her trembling fingers. No gentle exhalation. She takes Clara's tiny hand in her fingers and encounters no resistance. Nothing. There is nothing. A blackness quietly creeps around the edge of Mary's vision, and for a few seconds she is possessed by a dizziness that takes all sensation from her.

William's voice draws her back.

"Mama?"

It is whispery and urgent. Slowly, her sight comes back. Her control of herself. She nods to William, and wraps Clara tightly, presses her close to her breast. But, no, strangely, Mary has no tears.

She says nothing when Shelley arrives in a boat full of strangers, but reveals the still infant to them. At once he is by her side, his arms around her, his words, so melodic and sad, fill her ears, but they do not make it into her mind. She is guided into a boat, and here is someone called Mrs Hoppner; this is the woman who has been looking after Allegra. Mary tries to make a few words to her, but isn't sure if she succeeds. An obscure, extraordinary city speeds by her, ornate and decaying; she is aware, only faintly, that she ought to feel something about it. And then there is a house where she lets herself be led inside. She nods to the kind, sorry things that are said at her.

Somewhere, she realises, Clara has been taken from her, for her arms are empty.

These strangers give her a room to compose herself and say she should join them when she is ready. It is a large, empty guest bedroom with walls a sick sort of yellow, and windows that look only onto other walls. There is a bed and a small desk and a few other little trinkets. She sits upon the end of the bed. Through open windows the constant undulations of indistinct Italian voices, their cadences rising like bubbles and bursting amid the ceaseless splash and patter of the waters.

Although the sound disturbs, her bones are far too heavy to rise and close the window. The light that slips in is low, apologetic: the sun has gone, and life fades from the day. This is all there is left. For a long time she sits and stares at a blue rug beneath her feet. It is frayed at the edges, revealing white threads that criss-cross one another and abruptly snap off. Someone ought to fix it. Or hide it. It would be easy to tuck the rug under the bed, but she does not.

Mary is still. The air, dense and forgiving, settles upon her head, her shoulders, her tired limbs.

The room fades to darkness around her. Shadows slowly slink across the yellow wallpaper.

Then, a noise without disturbs the sepulchral silence. A faint conversation, the shuffle of bodies on the other side of the closed door. Her heartbeat accelerates.

The handle creaks down, and William's little voice asks, "Is Mama in there?"

William. Panic begins to swirl in her chest, and she clenches her fists to anchor some stillness. A sliver of light breaks through the door.

"I think she is," says Shelley's voice, so weary, so pained. "Shall we go to her and give her a kiss?"

They emerge around the door—the fragile child, slipping from the well-lit hall into Mary's dusky gloom, and with him his bent-over father, head hung and greying.

"No," she whispers.

"Mary?" Shelley asks, "May we come in?"

He is asking for William, but the fierce speed of her blood, the pounding in her wrists, her head, stir her.

"No," she says again. "Please. Leave."

The words march forth like a battalion across the room, stopping short before husband and child with weapons raised. She will not look at their eyes, though she feels Shelley's gaze through the gloaming. In her mind she repeats over and over her command. *Please. Leave. Please. Leave.*

"Are you sure?" a voice asks. It is neither one of them completely; it is a boy's. Has her command aged William, or reduced Shelley to childhood? She does not reply.

There is a murmur. A shuffle of feet as they withdraw. As the door closes she hears William say, "But I didn't give Mama my kiss," and a pain strikes into her heart. Had she kissed Clara? She chastised Shelley for wasting time, but he took his last kiss. What was hers? She tries desperately to remember. When was that last moment? Had she kissed her after death? Her lips must touch no one. Involuntarily her fingers rise to her dry lips—is some friendly drop of death upon them still? And as she finds her cheeks slick and wet her shoulders begin to shake.

Chapter Three: Work
Venice, 3rd October 1818

*D*ays pass. The dawns and the twilights come and go like waves—
each very much like the last to Mary's eye. But one morning
brings Byron in a blue velvet coat—fatter than he was, but tall and
strong still—and the Hoppners insist that they all go out and see
Venice, to take the air, and clear the spirits.

So they leave William with Elise and the solemn, black-haired
child of Claire's, and drift out into the city. Somehow Shelley can
go along with them all, dancing across the piazzas, gesticulating at
the architecture, gasping after the paintings and sculptures with
hunger. Mary cannot understand it. There is an assumed sobriety
in the party, it is true, but her sharp eyes see the mourning veil slip
often. The Hoppners are proud of their city, and tell Shelley every
fact they know, pointing out every detail, all of which he consumes,
and at once demands more.

For herself, there is very little she can take in.

At her first slight unsteadiness Albe offers her his arm. They
have exchanged greetings, but spoken little, and this offer of intima-
cy is agreeable to her. They take a slow pace, soon falling behind the
rest of the party.

"I don't suppose you like Venice very much," he says.

Mary stares at this strange, precarious city with its narrow walk-
ways and its bridges of crooked steps.

"I have no intention of giving it a fair hearing," she replies.

He nods his understanding.

"Do you like the house at Este?"

"Yes. It is beautiful, thank you."

"I'm glad. I imagine you will feel better once you return there, recover yourself a bit. Work."

Mary agrees. All this week people have been saying such little things and pretending they are enough, as if the handkerchief of sympathy could absorb the oceans of grief. But Byron does not pretend, and for that she is grateful.

"What are you working on just now, anyway?"

"Shelley wants me to write a tragedy about the Cenci family. My father thinks I should write a history of Charles the first and the English Commonwealth."

"And what do you want to write?"

"I don't know just now." She shakes her head. "I can hardly think of work. What are you writing, Albe?"

"Lots of things really. I've just finished a long poem called *Mazeppa*, about the Ukrainian military hero. Battles, forbidden love... you know, the usual."

For a while they walk along in silence, their eyes passing over the buildings in mock appreciation.

"I don't suppose you'd be interested in doing a little work for me?"

His expression is tentative, his eyebrows raised though his gaze avoids her. Her spine straightens a little and eagerness faintly flushes through her.

"What sort of work?"

"Well," he clears his throat, "if you are unoccupied and... that you feel that some occupation would be of benefit to you... Perhaps you could do me a very great favour?"

"Yes," she encourages him. To wake up in the morning and have something to *do*, to be *needed*, however triflingly, seems a wonderful thing, and she already fears to lose this undisclosed task.

"I have a rather long poem I've written," he says, "and I'm in need of a fair copy to send back to my publishers in England. If it isn't a burden to you—and *only* if it isn't a burden—I know you've good writing, and quite honestly I don't have anyone here that I entirely trust to do it."

She is talking over him even before he can finish.

"If I could be useful to you—I think that would make me very happy. I am honoured you would trust me with such a task."

"Trust you!" He grins broadly, any momentary awkwardness sweeps away. "Mary, it is you who honours me."

"Well, I do not know how much longer we shall stay in this city, but while we are here, I shall work on it whole-heartedly."

"If that is agreeable to you."

"It is."

"Mary," he pauses, watching the others wander ahead. "If you will forgive me I shall speak frankly to you."

"I hope you always do," she replies.

He turns his eyes to her.

"I heard about Shelley's wife. And... I thought, I *feared*, they meant you. I was quite disturbed until I learned the truth. What I wish to say, is that we all need you to be strong." He nods firmly. "You are loved and valued here, and if ever despair encroaches on your life, you must resist it. For our sakes, if not your own."

She presses his hand. His kind words touch upon a fear that circles inside of her—to have to live for someone else, when joy is gone... that might be a painful thing to have to do.

Chapter Four: Moonlight Upon the Ruined Stones
Rome, 9th June 1819

A still, dusky evening sweeps through Rome. Any cry or clatter is distant, echoey, its source hidden from view. Shelley has left Claire at her books and come out in search of Mary who, some hours ago, went out to see the Colosseum one last time before they leave.

Having reached Rome after months moving through Italy, from Venice to Naples and down through the country, now they are fleeing it. They seem doomed to a peripatetic life. He looks on the city with regret. There is so much still here. He pauses his search for Mary to stop in the Protestant cemetery at the edge of the ancient city. He sits awhile on the grass. No occupation takes him, no book nor thought to write. He only sits, his eyes vacant, his thoughts ponderous.

He rose late this morning, which is entirely unlike himself; all the night and half this day were swept away in fitful dreams. They have left him weak and tired. Perhaps he will return to this city in better days, when he can see it fully. Perhaps he will return in some other form.

He ought to write to his friends back in England, he thinks, and tell them of Rome. Leigh Hunt and Marianne have requested letters describing it all—and there is so much to tell. The Medusa of Leonardo, the Minerva, the Baths of Caracalla, the view from Gianicolo Hill... But how to say it?

My Dear Friend,

Rome is yet the capital of the world, its antiques, its beauties are beyond compare. But this week, our little William died.

That is the only thing that is true to him, and the only part of Rome that means anything is this graveyard that lies beyond the old city walls where the Protestants, the heathens, and the outcasts must lie. And with them, he must lay his son.

They have buried two children in less than a year.

A gentle wind sighs around him now, nodding the clematis and honeysuckle that clamber on the graves, immodest of their life. There are beautiful tombs here, and soft pathways that meander between. After this week whose every day has been a year, after this week of watching by his son's sick bed, driven through despair to a madness that almost brought him to prayer, the outside world is fresh, vibrant.

Nearby stands a great pyramid to some long-forgotten general, audacious in its magnitude. How foolish it looks to Shelley. Whoever that man was, he was nothing compared to William. And before Shelley's mind rises the image of his child, golden-haired and ocean-eyed. They brought him here not long ago, to wander the meandering paths between the beautiful graves and the sculptures of bone-white weeping angels. And while Shelley and Mary had talked of Virgil and of Cicero, William had befriended a grey cat with lilac-blue eyes who had led him through the long grass, purring as it went.

The memory brings a shudder of sobs that shake his whole frame.

Because it is all done. The first flush of the fever. The retirement to the sickroom, and there, six long days of powerless watching. Mary hovering at the door, a pale shade who could not bear to stay and see. Six long days of fluctuating hope and fear. Shelley never left; if he ever slept it was only with that small hand held in his own. If there had only been something he could do... If he could have marched down to the shores of the Styx, and dragged the bark readied for his beloved child out of the water, and far, far up along the shore, he would have shown a strength unknown to man. If by wealth or words he could have bought that little life, there would be no cause for death. Two deaths in a year, and they are no longer parents.

Very suddenly, and very certainly, he needs to see Mary, and he stumbles to his feet, pushing the misery from his eyes, and sets himself up after her.

The sun is getting low as he arrives at the Colosseum; this ancient amphitheatre, once a glorious testament to the strength and power of man, is now a skeletal ruin, reclaimed by a rambling wilderness of trees and ivies that wind through every crevice. The visitors there are few at this hour, more trailing out than going in. He finds Mary easily, for she is where they have often sat, a drawing book on her lap, her unguarded expression haggard.

Shelley sits by her without a word and watches the steady motion of her pencil add darkness to the shadows on a mono-chrome sketch of the view before them. They exist side by side in perfect quiet as the hour grows late and the other visitors dwindle, until it is at last only the two Shelleys remaining to watch the dying rays of the sun slink between the ribs and rags of the building.

As the last glimpse of fire sinks, the air grows cool and dusky, for the moon is already visible, and claims the sky for her own at once.

Into the half-night Mary speaks.

"Do you remember William Frankenstein?" she asks. Her voice gladdens him, despite its sad tone.

"The little boy? Of course."

"I wrote him when our Will was just a baby." She does not look sidelong at him, but continues to weigh the scene for her page. "But I wrote him as a child, so exactly like the child our Will became. Do you ever think of that?"

Shelley nods slowly, more to show that he is following than to express agreement. He is not sure of her point yet. For a while she sketches on in silence, glancing between her paper and the night.

"I made my monster kill him," she says, her voice almost too steady. "I wrote my own son into my novel and then had him mur-dered. What kind of person would write such a thing?"

Ah. Now he sees it, and he moves closer, draws his arm around her waist.

"A good writer, Mary, that is all."

"Hmm."

The pencil is still. He watches her with more attention than he has ever given anything. His compassion and his longing to share her pain are so great in him that he feels them press against his chest as if they would surge right out of him. For the first time, he sees an unsteadiness in her face, and when she raises her eyes to the pale moon it reflects in the tears that have gathered there, painting her ghost-white.

"Shelley..." His phantom-Mary shudders a sigh. "Did I do this?"

And he can keep his love in no more but clutches at her tightly, holding her so close that he might melt into her and be one with her.

"No, Mary, my love, no!" The words tumble from him. "You have done nothing. This is not your fault." He whispers any reassurance his mouth can make. Her head bows a little towards him, and a tear or two escapes her eyes, though she does not succumb to sobbing.

"Harriet was, though," she says, her voice stretched thin. "Harriet was. She begged me not to take you from her. She told me it would be ruin for us all."

"Oh heavens, Mary! No, no, no! Do not say such a thing!" And he takes her limp hands in his own, and kisses them rapidly. Poor Mary, are these the cruel thoughts she is whispering to her own soul? Gently he turns her chin so that she must look at him, must see his earnestness.

"Harriet made her choice," he says firmly. "She once ran away from home, just as you did. She had no place to ask that of you. Do not think that if you had turned me away she and I would have lived together as husband and wife. Because that could never have been. There was no future for us. I promise you that. It was a childish delusion that led us to marry, and whatever love there may have been, it was long gone. Besides, without you I would be dead. You well know how little I could live without you. Then Harriet would have been no better, no worse than she was. I told her she could have come with us. There were other options for her. She made her choice."

Mary nods, her mouth drawn down at the corners in an expression of misery.

"Yes, she did," she murmurs. A moment later, she turns her large, ghostly eyes upon him. "Just as Fanny made a choice."

"Poor Fanny," he murmurs, and a spasm of pain twists in his side. "Yes," he says, finding his breath strangely short. "Yes. I do wish we—I wish I had done more for her."

"We could have done so many things differently," Mary whispers. "We could have..." The thought remains unfinished. "And now two children. Three children. I do not forget the first. It is far too much like a curse, Shelley." Her lower lip quivers in a grimace as she hauls in a breath. "Every year there seems to be a new tragedy waiting for us. I fear ours is a life of death. I can't help but wonder... if things had been different... a stable home in a stable environment... a quiet life... If you and I had met differently..."

"There are plenty secure homes in England that suffer just as much tragedy as we have," he says earnestly, cutting off her regret.

"Perhaps Byron was right," she says bitterly. He tilts his head, unsure which of Byron's many creeds instructs her. Mary gives him a smile that looks like it might be intended to reassure. "That life was never for us."

Shelley is not reassured. His heart is so heavy with her grief, he cannot find a reply. Turning his eyes down, he regards the drawing upon her lap. There is more darkness than light in it. The deep leafy vines devour the ancient ruins of unparalleled greatness with a pernicious greed, and above, the vivid light of a Roman moon watches still and silent. But down in the depths of the atrium, where the light falls most, there is a human figure, and here her imagination has departed from life, for he glances around and confirms that there is no one else present at this cold hour. But there in her drawing is a man, gazing up at the moon.

"Who is this?" he asks.

"I am not sure," she replies, and the movement of her jaw drops a tear down onto the drawing. She wipes her face with her hand. "It seemed someone ought to be there to witness the scene."

"An ancient spirit of the past, perhaps?"

"Yes. A mourner, come to visit the tomb of his civilisation."

"What an idea for a story," he says, and the idea begins to twine about his thoughts as he sits quietly by his wife.

"You should write it," he murmurs. She almost manages an empty laugh.

"I am not sure what I would write," she says.

"Then you'll have to help me write it. I am going to write about your ancient visitor here in the Colosseum. How ought I to begin?"

She falls silent a while, and he watches the flicker of her eyes—half looking out, half looking in.

"Imagine there is a man," she says, "who has lost everything, his entire world. What would such a man be? Would that pain be writ upon his face? And who is there to see it? Someone a world away from him. One in the midst of life and love," she whispers.

"A child and a parent," he replies, his tone a hushed echo of her own.

"That will do well." She nods. "And this man, everything he has loved is worn away. He is the only one left from his race."

"That sounds incredibly lonely."

"It is."

"Couldn't there be one other?" Shelley asks.

"No." The word falls heavy as a stone. "He must be absolutely alone. That kind of suffering can't be shared."

"I think it could. Perhaps this child, this child who watches him, she could befriend him, and ultimately, she could help him with his burden?"

Mary turns her face to him in the moonlight and gives him a kind, sad smile, before resting her head upon his shoulder.

"I don't think there is anyone who could help. He is utterly, completely alone."

As she says this, Shelley watches her, and sees her loneliness, and takes her hand in his, hoping the touch will show her that she, at least, is not alone.

Chapter Five: The Dark Journey
Livorno, 30th August 1819

*T*he waves rush towards Mary with a furious clamour, before whispering backwards, apologetic. The headlong fervour, the regretful retreat, is ceaseless. With eyes closed, she listens, trying to discern meaning in the ocean's strange language.

They have come to hide in Livorno for the autumn, completing their slow circle of Italy. Of course they could not stay in Rome. Here the fishing town provides the sense of company, and the wide sea shore provides solitude. She has chosen a spot sufficiently far from the town that no one will pass too close, but not so far as to lose sight of it all together. The Italians may spy her here, and might recognise the English lady who goes about in full mourning with veil, but they have never spoken to her, and will not speak now. The veil excludes them, and they respect it. Shelley and Claire do not.

When Shelley looked in this morning, Mary counterfeited sleep, for company and communication have become difficult.

By the time she rose both Shelley and Claire were out, so Mary took her manuscript down to the sea.

Shelley is always pressing work upon her, urging her to write the story of Beatrice Cenci's revenge on her brutal father, but she cannot stir herself to it. The half-written novel in her bag presses against her. It is raw and angry, something she cannot yet share. She misses the easy work of copying, and thinks of writing again to Byron to see if he has something else for her to do. A nice slow exchange with a hundred miles between correspondents has a pleasant appeal, far more than the nagging of Shelley and Claire.

She has nothing to say to them. How lucky, and how strange, they were both out this morning. But of course, she thinks, as she sits upon her rock and gazes out with empty eyes, there was some talk of taking Shelley again to the medico for the peculiar pain in his side. But this thought leads on to another recollection: Shelley's voice saying, 'It is the only date that he can give us for this week—but a shame it should fall upon Mary's birthday... We shall do something nice in the afternoon...'

So today is her birthday, is it? She raises her eyes to the spotless skies and tries to count the days. The wind dashes her veil about her face and a wave stronger than its predecessors crashes and hurls water through the air and onto her hand and skirt. How cool the water is. The day is already becoming too warm.

In her novel it is always cold. She is writing something quite different from *Frankenstein*, and different too from the novel on Castruccio she has been considering. It is unplanned, and utterly passionate. The young heroine, Matilda, writes from the moment of her death, recalling the awful things that have happened to her, the cruellest betrayal by a father who loved her as a father ought not to love his child, and her final months in which she abandons hope.

Mary spies another large wave coming, but she neither shifts nor flinches. The water crashes, splashes upon her. A foot slips a little and the toe of her shoe falls into a rock pool. So, she shall have wet feet. It is no matter. The day is warm enough that she shall dry soon. But she does not even raise her foot. It occurs to her that she could quite contently sit here all day and simply let the tide come in around her. The rock on which she sits is raised higher than all those around, and a retreat to land would soon be cut off. No matter. She could just sit. She has nowhere to go. And if the tide rose higher? It would not come nearly high enough. Half her shoe is now filled with water, and the heaviness of it is so pleasant that she extends her leg to submerge the whole foot. The hems of her dress now touch the water and glide across the surface where they rest a moment before sinking. The ocean, having gotten this hold upon her, begins to creep upwards through the fabrics of her skirt—and how nice it would be to let it clasp her bosom, her throat, her hair...

A wave races in and crashes upon her leg, splashing her from her knees right up to her face, and only then does she reach protectively across to the bag by her side, shielding the manuscript inside with her own body. She withdraws her foot in a sudden motion, and thinks how foolish it is to sit here and risk her work. She clambers up, and shakes out her wet skirts as she retreats, the bag and novel clutched to her chest.

Her birthday. She is twenty-two. There is another child growing within her, she knows. Is there any chance this child will grow up? And what sort of life can she offer it? A year ago, her birthday was spent packing up the Tuscan house to join Shelley in Venice, setting off with William and Clara in the coach with no idea how close they all were to tragedy. Three children, all dead. She does not need to open the book to remember the last line she wrote.

Do I not look forward to a miserable future? My child, if after this life I am permitted to see you again, if pain can purify the heart, mine will be pure; if remorse can expiate guilt, I shall be guiltless.

This is Matilda's father. Begging her forgiveness. Mary wonders, momentarily, if she can save him. But of course, she can't. He must die.

The heat grows oppressive as the sun gets high and Mary lowers her veil for some respite. Beneath the veil there is a soft, private space. The world beyond is removed, and when her eyes lose focus it seems cross-hatched like a drawing. She sighs, for she must go home to rest, and at home will be the sad enquiring eyes of Claire and Shelley who will bestow birthday wishes upon her and will ask happiness of her when she has none to give.

When she arrives back at the house they are waiting for her, Claire watching by the door and Shelley pacing and tearing at his hair so it shoots off at odd angles.

"There she is," Claire says, as Mary draws closer. She is sloped against the doorframe, scowling through curtains of thick black hair.

Shelley swirls away from his latest turn, his body following a second behind his head, his face a startled, hopeful agitation.

Their attention appals her. Everything in Mary wants to retreat into herself, as a tortoise might. If she can just pass them without having to speak, their intrusion can be forgiven.

"Where have you been?" Claire yells. It is the full-body, full-fire shout of the kind they used to hurl at each other in furious wild-cat fights back home. But now there is no return fire.

"I've been for a walk," Mary says meekly.

Shelley is striding towards her, his arms out as if to embrace her, but his hands fall limp at his sides.

"We were so worried," he says.

"I went for a walk."

"But you didn't tell us!"

"You were out."

"We've been back a long time. You could have left a note. Mary, we were so worried."

"You do not need to worry about me." Mary is aware of her voice pitching upwards but doesn't have the power to control it. "I am, I think, allowed to go out for a walk by myself."

"Of course, of course my Mary, but—"

"You can kindly give me a bit of space and not nanny me every moment. Now if you will excuse me..." She stalks past him and at the doorway pushes into Claire who does not move out of her way. But Shelley's voice, weak and pathetic, follows her inside.

"Mary, please don't shut us out."

"Just let her go, Shelley," Claire says. From her position at the door she can shout to both of them while they are divided. "She's being selfish; princess Mary is the only person who matters, never mind all the worry she's caused."

Mary has crossed the entrance hall, and her foot is upon the bottom stair to take her up to the study and away from them, but Claire's accusing tone causes her to stop, stock still, and she replies without looking back at them.

"I do not want you to worry about me. There is no need for you to worry about me. I am capable of looking after myself on a short walk."

"We know, Mary," Shelley says, and his voice is close behind her, but still she cannot look. She takes the first step, and the second.

"We love you," he goes on, "and you're in such a delicate state."

"Delicate?" She pivots. He is three steps below, giving her an unusual height over him. He sighs.

"Mary, you are obviously upset, just let us—"

"Upset?" Mary all but screams the word, and sees the scream hit his face. "And if I am upset, why do you think that is? I am upset because of you! Because of your worrying and pestering and, and everything! Why do you teaze me so? I was at peace before you came, Shelley! At peace! I wish with all my heart you would just leave me!"

The words echo out into the house, silencing even Claire's captious spirit. Mary hears their echo, but in that moment is not sure what she has said, except that it is draining the life out of Shelley's face and he recedes from her, giving her her freedom to go to the study and shut the door tight, giving her the solitude she so greatly desires. She is aware her curse may have wounded, but she cannot bear to think on it. It is wiser not to speak sometimes. In the study her hasty, trembling hands open the manuscript, and she empties herself out into it.

Matilda, devastated by her father's death, by the sin she is implicated in, despite her innocence, retreats from the world. But she has met a friend, a sweet and romantic poet called Woodville, who is burdened also by his own grief; cannot a friend help her, raise her from her depths? It seems not, for as Mary writes, all she can let Matilda ask of Woodville is that he die with her.

Now the time is come when I may quit life. I have a friend who will not refuse to accompany me in this dark journey; such is my request: earnestly do I entreat and implore you to die with me.

But Woodville will not die. He holds her hand and urges her to live on, and though he sets aside her poison for a while, he must, at last, leave her, quite alone in her wildness.

Only as her writing fervour subsides and she lifts her attention from her story does she notice the new inkwell sitting on her desk, gold in colour and delicately carved with vines and fruit: a birthday present.

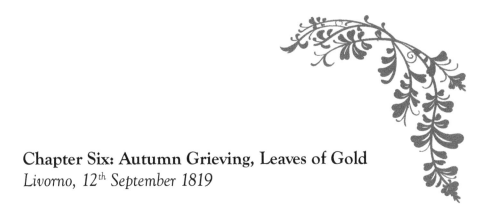

Chapter Six: Autumn Grieving, Leaves of Gold
Livorno, 12ᵗʰ September 1819

*S*helley writes at speed, ink pouring from his pen with passion, splattering across his page and pooling in the crevices of the paper. His sleeves become stained, his hair wild from his agitated tearing at it. Man's cruelty to his fellows exceeds even imagination's fears. News from England of bloodshed and dishonour has thrown him into a writing whirlwind. The words possess him and burst into life.

> *Rise like lions after slumber*
> *In unvanquishable number,*
> *Shake your chains to earth like dew*
> *Which in sleep had fallen on you—*
> *Ye are many – they are few.*

Thousands had gathered on St Peter's Fields in Manchester in peaceful protest against a government that did not represent them. Rather than listen, rather than act accordingly, the local yeomanry charged into the unarmed crowds, leaving hundreds—men, women and children alike—dead or wounded.

And Shelley fears the submission of his people, their acquiesce to aggression. This is the moment they must be roused! As his blood boils, so must theirs.

He draws the lords who rule his England—the detested Eldon, Sidmouth, Castlereagh, the men whose laws create poverty and want, the men who ordered the attacks—and calls them by their true names: *Fraud, Hypocrisy, Murder*. These fiends trample in pageant behind a skeleton robed in black, *Anarchy*, the God, the King, the Law of all, desolating the land around them, slaughtering, and carousing.

Anarchy's bone fingers draw tight the thick black reins of his white steed, the bit in her mouth dragging up her head as she spits foam flecked with red. All her sinuous body is dappled with minute wounds, bare flesh exposed and oozing blood. And yet at speed she runs, colossal hooves trampling any poor souls caught in her path.

Murderers, lawyers, and priests all bow before the anarchic king; none may stand in his way, none except the maniac maid *Hope*. Only Hope can stir the hearts of men to defiance, only Hope can overwhelm the surging forces. Upon the ground she flings herself, her once-golden hair running along crevices of dry earth with rivers of poor-man's blood.

A moment of glorious transformation must come, Hope rejuvenated, Hope with strength to overcome Anarchy.

Shelley's breath is short, his head dizzy as he rises from his writing station and staggers out of his mind's enthusiasm to find himself in the glass-panelled study at the top of the house.

It is hot.

The sun pours in and is caught, keeping the air close.

He drinks up a glass of water that someone must have brought him, and pulls one of the windows open, leaning gratefully against the frame. The study is at the top of the house, an aerial terrace roofed all around with glass, to which a grand vista of the Italian coast is laid out. The wind on his face refreshes him as he gazes out across the fertile fields, the tree-lined lanes, and rooftops of Livorno, down to the glistening sea. He watches a white sail drift across the horizon, so tiny to his vantage, and wonders of the people on that boat.

He is gripped with a desire to be with Mary, and talk with her. But the cold that has settled on her continually shuts him out.

He finds her at her desk, as expected.

"Hello, my love," he says, quietly, so as not to disturb her if she is too engrossed in her work. The subtleties of her working patterns have revealed themselves to him over the years, so he can quickly see she is not writing, nor even distracted by thought or plan. She is exquisitely still, as if carved from marble.

"Mary?" he tries again, but still no response. Her stillness is not the natural stillness of inaction, but a tension that has a grip on all her body and pins her there, suspending even breath.

"Are you alright?"

"Yes." A whisper of an answer. The body remains unmoved.

Her hair is in one loose, irregular plait. There is a suggestion of softness there. One strand is thinner than the other: a reminder of the human hands that must have carelessly braided it this morning.

Yearning for the touch of life, he reaches out to stroke the plait but the touch is too much. A jolt in her body, a tightening of her neck muscles, a heightening of the tendons in her hand. He steps back hastily.

"I wanted to see if you'd like to go out," he says.

"I would far rather not."

"Isn't there anything you *would* like?" he asks, and at once fears the question may be as counterproductive as the touch.

Silence.

"Is there anything I can do for you?"

"Shelley, I really just want to be left to my work."

There is a sharp crackle to her frostiness. A dangerous energy.

"Alright, I'll leave you in peace." He slinks out. He would like to kiss her before he goes, even just the top of her head, but he does not dare.

Claire is waiting for him in the passageway.

"One day you'll learn you've just got to let her alone."

"How can I leave her when she's like that?"

"Because she's asking you to."

He leans on the banister, looking down from two steps up.

"I don't believe she knows what's best for her," he says.

Claire purses her lips and rolls her eyes in an expression he often sees, but can never quite read. She shrugs sharply and shakes her hair back.

"Anyway," she announces, "I've a letter." She produces a small envelope marked by a meticulous hand. "From Godwin. Addressed specifically to Mary."

Shelley snatches it from her hands, ignoring her 'tsk, tsk,' and tears it open as he strides towards the window for better light, scanning the words in a greedy search for their meaning.

"How solicitous you are," Claire mutters from the foot of the stairs. "Reading your wife's letters for her."

"I won't have her further upset," he says through gritted teeth. Only half his mind is on Claire, the other half is processing Godwin commanding Mary to, *'refrain from immoderate grief,'* and providing awful cautions: *'nearest connections might see you fixed in this selfishness and ill humour, regardless of the happiness of anyone else, and they will find they must endure you and finally cease to love you.'*

Shelley shudders at the coldness of the words and closes his eyes.

"Damn him," he mutters.

"Oh, are we allowed to do that now?" Claire saunters over and attempts to read the letter over his shoulder. "Good. Damn the old fool."

Shelley folds the letter abruptly, entraps it back in its envelope, and shuts it up in a drawer.

"Are you really not going to give it to her?"

"Not at once. When she is stronger."

Claire sucks her teeth, seeming to consider something, and then sighs.

"Nothing to be done," she says, almost cheerfully. "What say you and I go out for a bit?"

"I don't see that helping."

"Come, Shelley, don't you be miserable, too. Mary can't be helped here, but that's no reason for you to mope like Scythrop Glowry. Let us go out." With one hand she catches his arm and with the other she sweeps up her bonnet. "Come on! It's a beautiful day. I want to go for a swim. Come with me!"

There is a little cove along the coast that is often secluded, and there Shelley finds a comfortable spot on a large, high rock; the regrets that Mary would not join him drift away from him in the warm, clear air. He wraps his arms around his knees as Claire begins to undress.

"The thing about Mary is that she's a Wollstonecraft," Claire says as she carefully assorts her gloves and lesser garments.

Shelley glances down and she hands up the neatly folded pile of accessories.

"Look after these please," she says, then goes on. "And I know it is absolute *heresy* to ever say anything against Wollstonecraft women, especially Mary *senior*, but it is a thing worth saying. They all have this depressive disposition. Fanny had it, Mary has it, their mother had it. It's just the way they are. You can't change them."

"It's not that I want to change her; I want to help her," Shelley says with a frown. Claire carries on, regardless.

"What I'm saying is, there's no point in you trying to help," she says, unbuttoning her dress. "You're only going to tax yourself. She will be miserable. It's in her blood. You have to wait."

"You aren't exactly reassuring me." He picks up a stray shell and turns it over in his hands absent-mindedly. "Their mother attempted suicide twice. Fanny succeeded the first time. I am genuinely frightened of the path Mary's walking down."

"Mary's made of stronger stuff than that." With her dress fully unbuttoned, Claire wriggles it off, revealing the calf-length weighted bathing gown underneath.

"Do I look elegant?" She poses with a gleeful irony.

"You look like a mermaid that's been caught in a fisherman's net. Or thrown into a sack."

She snorts with laughter.

"I don't like to leave her alone like that, Claire," he says, unable to leave the subject. Claire, gathering up her dress, shakes off the sand.

"Perhaps you just have to respect her wishes."

"Respecting her wishes is difficult when I don't feel she's herself. I miss *my* Mary. I'll tell you what I know." He takes the dress she hands him. "What I know is that I've been leaving her to her grief—at her request—believing that it was the right thing to do for months now. And in all that time I've only seen her sink deeper. I know the wounds of the heart take a long time to heal, but at this point the melancholy has become her. I do not believe she is healing. Do you know when she was a little brighter? The day we finally got her out of the house to go to the theatre. She even laughed at the play. She talked about it on the way home. She was animated. It was like having her back again. And—" He takes a deep breath and finds there are tears threatening. "Claire, I want the woman I loved returned to me. I miss her."

Claire doesn't reply at first, but frowns, and looks out to sea.

"She'll come around," she says at last. "You'll see. Just give her time."

He tosses the shell in his hands away from him, and tries to nod, though the reassurance is transparently false.

"Right," Claire says. "I'm heading in there. Wish me luck!" She scampers down to the water with childish enthusiasm, leaving Shelley marooned on his little island with his spirits quite wrecked.

"You should come in, Shelley!" she cries, as she takes her first few steps into the water.

"No." He folds his arms and legs even tighter. "I am not built for floating. I only sink."

"But you'd like it."

"I don't think I would."

"It's very healthy."

"I'm not a very healthy person."

She scoops some water and hurls it vigorously in his direction, but he is too far away.

After much tentative edging, and a good deal of the sort of enthusiastic cursing Mary would never allow, Claire submerges herself, rising a moment later and settling into a confident if imperfect stroke.

Shelley watches her distantly; she has none of Byron's remarkable athleticism, but there is certainty in her strokes, and he envies her easy command of water. Her black hair, always curling and usually set, now drifts slick behind her, and her face is rosy against the green sea. His gaze shifts to a hazy horizon where a boat shimmers in and out of focus.

He can almost imagine Mary is beside him, that if he rested his head it would meet her shoulder. If he could speak, frankly to her, what would he say?

He fishes his notebook out his pocket.

My dearest Mary, he writes.
If he could speak, with honesty, what would he say?
My dearest Mary
Wherefore hast thou gone,
And left me in this dreary world alone?
Thy form is here indeed – a lovely one –
But thou art fled, gone down the dreary road,
That leads to Sorrow's most obscure abode
Thou sittest on a hearth of pale despair
Where for thine own sake, I cannot follow thee.

After Claire's swim they return, and routine dictates Shelley and Mary and Claire gather in the parlour to read together. They are once again reading *Paradise Lost* and Claire volunteers to read. Though Shelley listens earnestly, his head bent and his legs folded under him in the generous armchair, he finds himself gazing at Mary and taking little in. Her face is passive, and perfectly still. He wonders if even all of Pygmalion's prayers could bring her back to life.

At length, he returns to his study and stretches out in his chair. *The Mask of Anarchy* is done. His Prometheus is not yet clear. He will send the *Mask* to Leigh Hunt and eagerly awaits the responses. It shall certainly garner some hatred from more conservative members of society; its radicalism, however, may awaken many minds, may even stir some to action.

Through the wide window, high banks of thick black cloud stretch out towards them, while, to the west, the evening sun shines uninhibited, flecking the waters of the Mediterranean with light.

It is the weather for tragedy.

With his elbows on the desk, he lays his face into his hands, palms pressing hard into his eye, bringing a universe of ephemeral stars into his darkness.

He wants to write passion, to write misery, to feel the greatest depths of human suffering and shape them onto the page. He wants Beatrice Cenci's fury, the horror of it. A daughter raped by her father. Such agony, such desire for revenge—and yet revenge bringing only further damnation.

Perhaps Mary is right, and he should be the one to write it.

But it must be a tragedy, and after years of the poetic, the lyrical, and the metaphysical, what does he know of stagecraft?

He presses harder against his eyelids, feeling the soft eyeball behind until a pain ricochets through his head. He slams his hands down onto the table and recoils from the surge of light behind his lids. His eyes open, but for a few seconds still see the interior world fizzling above the corporeal.

How to turn this feeling that he knows so well into a specific form? He leans over to the bookshelf and slips out Mary's *Frankenstein*; he sits and turns its pages, as if the structure might reveal itself from a cursory glance. *Frankenstein* is certainly dramatic. It would make a wonderful play. And what are the ingredients that make it so? Its art eludes him.

Then, he tells himself, ask Mary. Mary knows.

Without further meditation, he throws himself from the room, rattles down stairs and slides on fleet footing.

"Mary!" he cries, his voice hurrying on before him. "Mary!"

He rounds the turn of the stairwell, crosses the hallway, and comes abruptly to the open door of the silent room where Mary is at her desk, staring at nothing once more. The air carries the quiet suspension of a newly extinguished candle, and it checks his enthusiasm. But something within urges him to stay, to speak.

"Mary?" he asks, and his voice softly penetrates the room, though he remains at its edge.

Slowly, her head turns towards him, but like a blind woman, she does not look at him.

"I hope I am not interrupting you?"

No reply.

"I wanted to ask for your help with something." The threshold forms an almost tangible barrier. He leans on the door frame, folding his long arms close to his body, watching the distance that stretches between them with deceptive passivity. "I think I shall try to write that drama on Beatrice Cenci, after all."

He pauses. The silence echoes. At last, Mary says, "Mmhmm?"

He takes encouragement.

"I do believe it is just the subject for a tragedy, and you are quite right to say that I must be the one to work on it. But as you well know, I am destitute of the necessary skill for conducting such a piece."

She stares at him across an ocean of floor, and he wonders if she is taking in what he says.

"I wondered," he goes on, "if you aren't too busy, perhaps you might like to help me arrange the scenes."

Her gaze, so distant and nonchalant, engages at last, and Mary rises to the surface.

"You know me," he tries to laugh. "I long to fly into the passion of the piece, and would follow that passion wherever it leads me. But for a play, I feel that isn't wise."

A frown creeps across Mary's face, and then gradually her head shakes. "No," she says. "It isn't."

He takes courage from the concurrence.

"Then how ought I to do it?

The question drifts across the space between, as sound travels slowly through water, and takes a moment to reach Mary. But once it does, she pulls another chair over beside her desk and draws a stray leaf of paper to the middle of the desk. This must be an invitation, but he is nervous to enter. His foot hovers a moment before stepping across the doorway into her territory. He lands, and nothing shatters. Delicately, he walks to her side and perches on the chair she has set for him.

"You will use a five-act structure?" she asks, wetting the pen. He assents. Of course.

"And who is your story about? The father or the daughter?"

"The daughter."

"Yes," she whispers, and looks up at him, the grey clouds in her eyes shifting. He draws his chair closer.

Mary turns abruptly to him. "You asked earlier if there was anything I wanted."

"Yes?"

"I have been thinking so much about my mother lately. In my father's letter he said that there's a woman in Pisa who was once a pupil of my mother's, Mrs Mason. If we had an opportunity, I suppose I should like to talk to her."

It is a request, Mary's voice as he has missed it, and it is like the first sign of water after a long drought.

"Good. Yes, let us get in touch with her. Shall we write? Shall we write to her now?"

"Perhaps later. Tell me more about your idea for this play."

"Are you sure?" He feels such delicate happiness, he does not want to damage it.

"Yes, go on."

"I think the circumstances must be touched very delicately."

"Yes."

"Of course, there would be no attempt to depict a crime so heinous."

"Of course not."

"I desire to show *him* as what one might call a principled man," Shelley says, a little nervous, but very excited. "A *good Christian*. A man who believes he fulfils God's will. And she, Beatrice, she will be lovely and good, and I think a scene where she begs the nobles of the town to help release her from her father's cruelty—even before the deed is done—and none of them will risk making him their enemy, though they whisper that they'd second anyone. And she looks everywhere but sees no help, and then, once he has raped her, she realises no one will save her, so she must kill him. The hired assassins grow frightened, but, ah, yes, but, once he is dead, once the whole family is arrested for his murder, these two hired assassins..."

He is aware he is babbling, but she is listening, so he must go on. "They at first feel guilty, until they see her, her fervour, because she should have just the same conviction as her father that her crime is God's will. They become convinced that they and she have acted justly, and they refuse to confess."

He pauses, licks his lips, and swallows. He has talked too much, perhaps. But a gentle glow suffuses her countenance, a mien of contentment he has missed.

"You underestimate your powers in this area, Shelley," she says. "I don't believe you really need my help as you think you do."

The loveliness of the kind lilt in her voice, the first fond human emotion she has shown for days, gives his heart the lightness of a hummingbird, bright and fluttering, suspended in a moment it dare not break.

"But I would like your help," he says.

She adjusts the paper, and bends to write.

"Tell me the scenes you have considered," she says. "Slowly."

He leans close, and unfolds each idea, which she marks in cryptic notes. She guides him, always following Beatrice's character, steering him from excess to gradual development. They talk it through as the light drains from the sky, and then Shelley begins to write frantically in his book, and she sits beside him, tacitly blessing his endeavour.

Chapter Seven: Mrs Mason
Pisa, 1ˢᵗ October 1819

*T*heir passage through Pisa is slow—the day is hot and dry, as so many days here are. Mary is eight months pregnant and every step takes Herculean effort. Claire is by her side, patiently offering herself as support while her eyes wander off after some fancy, but Shelley walks behind them, followed every step by a crowd of urchin children as he were some kind of pied piper. They are going to see Mrs Mason at last, and Mary, who seems to be the only one paying attention to where they are going, does not know the address.

"Which street do we want?" she asks Claire.

Claire shrugs as if it did not matter, and vaguely suggests that Shelley has it. Mary tries to call out, but he isn't listening. He is so close, but the distance is immense and all she wants is to sit down. She spies a small fountain with a step where she can sit, and, extricating herself from Claire, makes for it, calling back, "Go get Shelley, and find out which street we're looking for."

She drops her weight down with relief, and clasps the sandy stone of the fountain base. An ant scuttles away from the enormity of her human hand. Splashes from the fountain lightly fleck the back of her wrist, a delicate, reassuring cool. Oh, to immerse oneself in the fountain!

Pisa lacks grandeur. The streets are not quite as broad as they should be; the houses of ochre, dusk pink, and brown are a little taller than is pleasant, but without the dignity of the Venetian Palazzo. At this time of day the Italians, wiser to the sun, are mostly inside behind dark-painted shutters. And these streets smell awful to her.

She sees Claire hanging back from Shelley, who is now in earnest conversation with the children. He seems to have found a favourite in a scrawny boy with black hair. Mary sighs. She remembers when he became enchanted with a mountain girl in Switzerland and wanted to take her home as one of their family. There had been the devil dissuading him then, and she doesn't have the strength for that kind of fight now.

"He's coming," the returning Claire informs her. "They're very sweet." Claire's smile dips. "It makes my heart ache," she says.

Mary turns her gaze to the children and briefly wonders what will become of them. But it is too great an enormity to consider. There is nothing she herself can do, and the contemplation of their fate will only pain her, so she shuts it out.

"It's been six months since I've had news of Allegra," Claire says. Mary grits her teeth. She finds it hard to respond to Claire's frequent laments on her lack of contact with the child she chose to give up, especially when she and Shelley have lost so absolutely.

"I must have sent him five letters," Claire goes on, "and not a word back! It isn't too much for a mother to ask word of her own child, is it? He probably thinks it egregious."

Claire casts Mary a challenging look, a look that demands outrage on her behalf. Her Mama was always ready to oblige, and, annoyingly, Shelley often steps into that role, but Mary will not play. She returns the stare.

"Well, fine!" Claire huffs. "I shall write to him again. And I certainly shan't hesitate to tell him exactly what I think of him."

"Just be civil," Mary says. She casts an eye over to where Shelley is talking with the urchin children. "Really you should leave this correspondence to Shelley; you don't help your case at all by firing off angry missives and insulting Albe with every breath."

"Don't call him that," Claire interrupts. "He is a scoundrel, a profligate, an unprincipled, despicable fiend. There is no better word for him. But you still call him 'Albe' and flutter at the mention of his name just because he smiled at you once and flattered your vanity. He knows how to play a foolish girl, Mary, and someone as smart as you ought to recognize that." Her face is a Medusa-sneer of disdain.

But Shelley is wandering over to them now, his merry band at his heels, and Claire assumes the prettiest attitude for him.

He gives them the address, pointing towards the street they need, and continues talking to the child. This one is a boy of perhaps eight years, pretty bovine-eyes and ragged long dark hair. It is more than Mary can bear. She hauls herself to her feet with some effort and starts along the way, keen to get this all over.

The others follow, and as they walk Mary picks up the conversation between Shelley and the child.

"Da dove pensi che vengo?" *Where do you think I came from?* Shelley is asking.

"Dal mondo sotterraneo, signore," *From the underworld, sir,* the child replies in earnestness.

"I think you must be right," Shelley chuckles to himself. "Sì, il mondo sotterraneo. Ho visto Dante," *Yes, the underworld. I saw Dante there.* "Conosci Dante?" *Do you know who Dante is?*

Many of the children have fallen back, preferring their own game to the pale stranger's peculiar talk. Mary walks on, her hands gripping her stomach, her eyes firm set ahead.

"É morto, lui?" *Is he dead?* the child asks.

Shelley's high-pitched laugh fills the air, and his answer comes full of glee and mischief.

"Sì. Ma anche no." *Yes, but also no.* "Questa vita è solo un velo; una volta il velo è rimosso, possiamo vedere più chiaramente." *This life is only a veil; once we remove that veil we see more clearly.*

"You should slow down, Mary," Claire says. The touch on her arm is one of genuine concern and Mary hates her all the more for it.

"Well, I feel somewhat unwell!" she says, louder than intended. Shelley hurries over to her, dropping the hand he was holding.

"Do you need to rest?" he asks, anxiously, putting an arm around her waist. "Here, sit down." With both of them touching her there is even less air in the Pisan street.

"No!" She pulls away from them both. "But I am anxious to get out of the sun. Can we hurry please?" And again she is leading them, dragging them onwards like a cart-horse, when she herself has so little strength.

"La signora," the child says, "Lei è la tua moglie?" *Is she your wife?*

"Sì."

Their voices dawdle behind her.

"È incinta?" *Is she with child?*

"Sì," Shelley says, "Mio figlio." *My son.*

"Shelley!" she cries out, her voice even tighter than before. "Will you please come?! Your wife is unwell, and we shall soon have our own child to look after. Help me!" There are almost tears in her words but anger overwhelms them. Whatever sharpness her words carry, it works, for soon he is by her side, holding her arm. He does not speak, but he is beside her, and Claire follows.

The Italian boy falls behind, and when Shelley looks back he is standing in the street, watching them go. They have an empty house, and that boy has no home. But Mary is right, they will soon have another child. He looks back once more, and the boy has turned his dark head away.

They walk in silence, Shelley supporting Mary as best he can.

"Here, this one," he says, as they come to the street they are looking for.

Peering along they see a striking woman in a doorway, apparently waiting for someone. She is quite as tall as Shelley, and broad shouldered. Splendid greying hair is pinned up high and cascades down her back, flowing with the folds of a classical Grecian-style dress that exposes her strong arms. But it is her face that captivates: a broad forehead and wide-set eyebrows, strong cheekbones and a prominent jaw all frame two lively sparkling eyes. Even the brief first glance assures Shelley that here is a sharp intelligence.

The woman shifts her weight as she sees them.

"Now that must be the daughter of Mary Wollstonecraft!" she says. Her voice fills the street; it is loud, clear and touched by a hint of an Irish accent.

"Mrs Mason?" Mary asks, as if there were doubt. The answer is given not in words; Mrs Mason only holds out her bare arms, and there is a lightness in the way Mary leaves him and goes to her, at almost a run.

"So here you are. Mary Wollstonecraft Shelley," Mrs Mason says. "I am very glad to meet you at long last, and I am sure there is no need for me to tell you what your mother meant to me." Keeping Mary held close, Mrs Mason looks up to Shelley, and takes him in head to toe with a critical, perspicacious gaze.

"And this must be the young poet, Mr Shelley." He bows his head and she makes an ambiguous noise in her throat. "Yes, I've heard all about you from the Godwins. They say it is a pity your face is an angel's, for your heart is the devil's, which I must say *exceedingly* predisposes me to like you."

Shelley laughs.

"Did Godwin say that of me?"

"He did. And you must be Miss Clairmont. Very good. Come in, my children. Come inside."

She sweeps them along in her wake, through a large door with peeling paint, into a beautiful house. They rise through the floors, past dull mirrors and chipped sculptures into a pleasant parlour where Mary is ushered into the most comfortable seat in the room ("And do elevate your feet if you like, my dear, there is no need for ceremony").

She is caring and brusque. She calls in her auburn-headed daughters, Laurette and Nerina, who each bob nice curtseys to the visitors and help with the tea. Following them is their sweet and sheepish father, Mr Tighe.

"Or Mr Mason," Mrs Mason corrects herself, "as you must call him. For we are *quite* proper here." She pours tea for them all, and Shelley accepts a cake from the solicitous children. "I suppose you know we aren't Masons at all," their hostess says, grinning at Tighe, "but one needs a name, and I've taken a fancy to that one."

"I know from my father that you used to be Lady Mount Cashell," Mary replies, setting down her cup.

"I certainly did. I suppose your father told you also that Lord Mount Cashell and I parted ways some years ago? There is only so much a woman can take. But let us not talk of the past. What I wanted to ask is if you knew where the name comes from?"

Mary lowers her eyes and seems to think. But she has told Shelley exactly where she thinks the name comes from, from her mother's writing, and he watches her pretence with surprise.

"I wondered if perhaps it was from *Original Stories*." She answers like a school child, and Mrs Mason nods encouragingly.

"That's right. By your mother. She was perhaps the most important woman in my life. And although I had grown up and travelled on by the time she died, her loss affected me very deeply. I had no picture of her, no miniature, but I had that book, the edition illustrated by Blake—I suppose you know it well. There is a picture of the good governess, Mrs Mason, standing between two adoring children, her hands raised above them," Mrs Mason stands, demonstrating the pose, "as she says 'Look what a fine morning it is; insects, birds and animals, are all enjoying existence.' She was my governess, and no child could have looked upon a teacher with more reverence, with more *love* than I did upon her."

Her fine voice resounds in Shelley's head; he wishes not only for the tutelage of which she speaks, but of her own instruction. He looks to Mary, expecting joy, but sees there a sullenness to her mouth, and a strange flush of pink high in her cheek. Does she hate this wonderful woman, for having the love of the mother she was denied?

"You were very lucky to know her," he says simply, pointedly.

"Of course, my mother didn't like her," Mrs Mason goes on. "My mother didn't like anything that disturbed her world of order."

They chatter the afternoon away, talking of the politics back home, of the massacre in Manchester which Mrs Mason calls "Viscount Castlereagh's barbarism," and of life in Italy (to which she laments that "it is so difficult to get good tea"). Emboldened, Mary joins in, saying that "they shall have to name England Castlereaghland and admit the loss of all liberty" and then, "We have a friend in Hampstead who sends ours."

Mary is more alive today than she has been for weeks, but still she is restrained, her hands clasped about her belly, her back formally erect. It is a vibrancy in her attention that gives Shelley such hope. This woman is important to Mary, he knows, and this parlour talk is hampering them both. When Tighe mentions that Laure plays the piano, Shelley sees an opening.

"Claire plays excellently. And she's a magnificent singer. Do you have a piano here?" This he addresses to Laure who beams and nods vigorously.

"Would you show us? Would you play for us?" Seeing the shyness emerge in the girl, he offers her his hand. "Claire may play too. And if you would like to hear the worst piano playing you've ever heard *I* may play! I am genuinely awful. You might be able to teach me something." And catching her timid hand, he holds out the other for Nerina, and Claire is at his shoulder. "Come along, Mr Tighe, you must be the judge of skills!"

As he had hoped, Mary and Mrs Mason do not stir, and he bundles out the jolly family to give them their privacy.

As Shelley, Claire, Tighe and children sweep out, they take the afternoon's chatter with them, leaving Mary and Mrs Mason in a new quiet.

"I am very glad you decided to write to me," Mrs Mason says after a while.

"I am as well." Mary smiles at her over the teacup.

"It is good to make your acquaintance."

Although the line is often a formality, Mary feels its sincerity.

"I suppose you know that I have been in touch with your father, a little, over the years. He told me something of your novel, and praised it very highly. He is not a man to be biased. I wonder if you would have a copy I could read?"

"Did he?" Mary cannot conceal the surprise. The thought that her father has praised her rushes through her with unexpected warmth. "I would be glad to provide you with one. It is somewhat ghastly, I ought to warn you."

"I am not easily frightened. Do you still write?"

"Daily. I have written a short novel called *Matilda* that I have lately sent to my father in hopes he will find a publisher. I am currently working on a historical piece about the fourteenth-century prince Castruccio Castracani. But I also wanted to write of a woman in the apogee of power, of a woman's choice between her heart and her own sense of right. I know of no historical figure who would be appropriate."

"Of course you don't, because history would not have recorded her story. You must invent that which history has forgotten." Mrs Mason's eyes crinkle at their edges in approval. "Your mother would certainly approve of such a venture."

She sets down her cup and looks directly at Mary. "You must forgive my bluntness. I have heard," she pauses, "mixed reports of Shelley. I don't quite think I have the full story yet."

"Shelley is an exceptional poet," Mary says. "Despite his accomplishment he cannot find the audience he desires, and that burdens him. His health is often poor these days. The more you know him, the more you will realise the excellence of his spirit."

"And he was married when you met him?"

"He was." Mary maintains a confident eye contact, for here is a woman who lives with another man while her husband still lives. "Most unhappily."

"And this will be your first child?"

Mary swallows and composes a smile.

"No. My fourth. The first only lived a few days. But, the others, we only lost lately." She would like to give this kind woman some account of her precious William, of pretty baby Clara, but a lump forms in her throat that words cannot pass.

"Ah." Mrs Mason's simple lament. "You poor thing. Yes, that explains it."

Every fibre of Mary concentrates on maintaining calm. The tempest is always close, and keeping it subdued is enough to prevent a reply, but she makes a curt little nod, diverting her attention to the ragged edge of the sofa. The pink thread has frayed and a strand falls loose. Looking over each string, one by one, is somehow calming.

Mrs Mason seats herself closer, so close that Mary must look at her, however much it hurts. "Believe me," she says, "I can see how you are suffering."

A hot, angry tear rushes out, only for Mary to bolt the door all the tighter behind it.

Mrs Mason leans back, giving Mary a privacy in the slight distance, and slips into thoughtfulness.

"You are very like your mother, Mary."

Mary swallows hard, banishing the tearfulness. It is her favourite compliment, and she will not waste it.

"Thank you."

"Yes," Mrs Mason says, in reply to some internal question to which Mary is not privy. "I tell you it as a warning. I believe you have inherited much of her genius, much of her wisdom, but also her temperament. I am sure you have at the very least read the biography of her your father wrote and know all the details of her early life?"

Mary nods.

"Then you know of her depressive tendencies also, of her suicide attempts. These things are also hereditary."

Mary senses Fanny at the edge of her memory, but will not allow her in.

"My sister..." she starts, but falters.

"Do you speak of Fanny?"

Mary nods.

"I'd love to meet her. I confess I'm surprised to find you travelling with Miss Clairmont and not with your own blood."

"Fanny is dead," Mary says, with some difficulty, and the generous smile that occupied Mrs Mason's face a moment ago dissipates. "She—she was very miserable—at home." Mary speaks quite slowly.

"No!" Mrs Mason whispers and she grasps Mary's hand. "When?"

"About two years ago. Please—we would ask for your discretion. It was her last wish." Even as she says it through gritted teeth, she knows she speaks her father's words, "My father has taken great pains for concealment of the situation."

Mrs Mason closes her eyes and does not let go of Mary's hand.

"You poor, poor girl," she says at length, and at last her eyes open to look fully on Mary. "No one deserves that."

Upstairs the tinkling of the piano; it is something jaunty that can't be Claire. Mary laughs ruefully at the inappropriateness of its cheerfulness. Mrs Mason nods.

"You need to grieve, don't you?"

Mary's mouth trembles as words begin to form in her, words she has hardly considered.

"I have shut fast the door to my heart," she says, and her voice seems to rattle within her. "All I want is solitude, and perhaps, with time... But Shelley doesn't like that door closed, and he will pound upon it with all his strength, and I am inclined to add another bolt, another defence, each time that he does."

"You need to talk to your husband. Women like you and I, Mary, we lose the world with the life we choose. I had to leave my children. Do you know that? I suppose you might not have heard; one doesn't generally discuss such things. When I chose to live with Mr Tighe, I had to leave the children of my first marriage behind me. I doubt I will see them again." She holds her head high, defiant. "There will be sacrifices; we must bear them. But we must remember what we have given all that safety and security up for. For our principles, and for our love." Her fierce green eyes stare back at Mary. "You must talk to this Shelley boy of yours. Don't let grief drive itself between you, for that is a wedge that deepens steeply. And I'll tell you something else," she begins to refill the tea cups, "having Miss Clairmont with you shan't help anything."

Mary cannot restrain a snort.

Mrs Mason smiles.

"I thought so. An inappropriate situation I would say. She has no marriage prospects, I take it?"

Mary shakes her head ruefully. "She has not."

"As I feared."

Mrs Mason stirs her tea a moment, her eyes distant, her lips pursed in her contemplation. "I can probably find a governess position for her. I know a family who would be glad of a musician and a French speaker for their girls."

The thought stuns Mary and takes a moment for her to process. To be rid of Claire, for life to be just her and Shelley once more, ready for their new baby...

"She won't accept it," she says, unwilling to let hope take root.

"They're a fine family and I'm a very persuasive woman. Leave all to me. That's her playing now?"

Mary turns her head; indeed, the tune floating down is familiar.

"Then let's go up and indulge her vanity a little."

Mary watches Mrs Mason manage Claire easily. This is what it would be like to have a mother, she thinks, and is surprised by a rush of nostalgia, not for the great Mary Wollstonecraft of the portrait, but the little kindnesses of the second Mrs Godwin, who, although she always favoured her own daughter, could manage Claire wonderfully when the mood took her.

By the end of the afternoon Claire is talking animatedly about being a free woman who can earn her own way, quite as if it were her idea, and Mary is so grateful to Mrs Mason she would stay in Pisa just to be near her. But the great tour rolls on, and Shelley has heard of a good physician in Florence who can deliver their child; they will take no chances with this child. Still, as they leave, Mary clasps Mrs Mason's hands, and promises they will return soon.

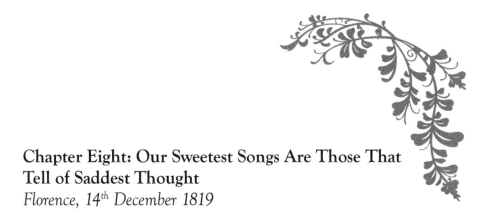

Chapter Eight: Our Sweetest Songs Are Those That Tell of Saddest Thought
Florence, 14ᵗʰ December 1819

Somehow this city of white domes and blue mists opens Shelley's mind. These days he writes. For the first time in his life he feels himself a poet.

Words flow freely—for so many years he has watered and cultivated his works, tended them every moment, and has had only meagre shoots to cherish, but now, at last, they bloom. Although he scarcely pauses to revise, he knows the quality of the leaves that fall. His Cenci play is finished. Lyrics and odes on life and revolution and love and thought all come to fruition in the leaves of his writing book, and always his Prometheus develops—a drama for the theatre of the mind, and all his soul poured into it.

Simply walking the *Ponte Vecchio* with Claire, lines of poetry form in his mind as irresistibly as the ice upon the stones.

> *... the wild west wind, the breath of autumn's being*
> *... make me thy lyre, even as the forest is,*
> *... my leaves are falling like its own...*

He repeats them to himself, gazing inattentively out onto the Arno. *What if my leaves are falling like its own...* He has been turning the phrases of this one around his mind some days now. Satisfied he will remember it, he turns to Claire. They walk out when they can now, for Claire will leave them in the new year to be a governess for a family in Florence, and Mary, Shelley, and their new baby, Percy Florence, will go on toward Pisa. A strange uncertainty hangs over them all, full of the knowledge that things must now change.

Claire dawdles on the *Ponte Vecchio*, her eyes caught by the gems and trinkets. She never buys, Shelley notes, watching her pause by a stall, and speak coyly to the vendor, lightly plucking at her white scarf. There is a poise to her in her purple bonnet and blue coat that suggests she is quite pleased with her appearance just now. Her laugh rings out, and she politely declines whatever he has offered, turning away from his outstretched hands that implore *un altro sguardo, per favore signora*. She will not be won, and joins Shelley with her sweetest smile.

"You'll have to buy something from him one day," Shelley says with a chuckle as she takes his arm. "That, or marry the poor fellow."

"I'm perusing his wares," Claire protests without the least sincerity.

Their boots crunch into snow, with each step Shelley feels the damp creep a little further along his stockings. They turn left along the *Lung Arno*, heading, slowly, for home.

Each one of the statues that clutters the Florentine streets wears the thin blanket of the night's snow, though the sun streams through the cloudless sky to warm their chilled hearts. The air is astonishingly crisp, and everything is seen in relief. High above the slumbering houses rises the snow-capped *duomo* of *Santa Maria del Fiore*. Florence has a beauty in this winter that surpasses anywhere Shelley has ever been.

"Can we go to the bookshop, Shelley?" Claire asks suddenly, clutching his arm, and giving him her little-girl-pleading eyes. "After what we were reading the other night, I'm desperate to get hold of some more Tasso in the *actual* Italian."

"I'm sure we have more Tasso."

"No, we don't. You borrowed it in Venice, but like a little fool you gave it back."

"And you'd have stolen it, would you?"

"Not as a rule, but from the Hoppners, yes. You can't imagine it's *ever* going to get opened in their house, do you?"

Just as he is about to reply Shelley senses something hurtling towards him and instinctively pulls himself back out of the way, with the effect that the missile intended for him lands squarely upon Claire's shoulder where it bursts into a flurry of snow.

"You!" she squeals, "how dare you!" But though her eyebrows are high in shock, her lips are creeping back, and Shelley pivots to see two boys laughing at them. They know them well—for they have made the acquaintance of these boys around the markets, and have before engaged in the deadly combat of the snowball fight. It takes him but a second to sweep a fist of snow from the balustrade and the boys are off running ahead of them.

"Catch them, Shelley!" Claire cries gleefully, though she is already running after the culprits.

They arrive back at their apartment breathless with laughter. Claire's cheeks are flushed a joyful pink, and Shelley has to tell her to hush as they take off their wet things, for they mustn't wake the baby.

He goes to the study, where Mary, sitting at one of the two desks, turns to him at once.

"Shelley, may I ask you something?" Seeing him with his coat she laughs. "I am sorry, you've just come in, I can wait!"

She frets, but there is an animation to her nervousness he cannot resist. He wriggles his coat off and throws it on the floor, sitting himself neatly before her, chin in hands, demonstrably all attention.

"It's nothing really."

"I want to hear it," he says amiably.

"I have something that might suit you. It was just a thought, and you might be busy enough."

On the window sill a small potted plant is gleefully blooming a riot of pink in gay defiance of the winter; Mary's fingers are toying with its stems, and she lifts a bloom with her finger, and seems pleased. Is it the colour of the flower reflected in her cheek? Or is that a touch of warmth?

"I am writing a play for Mrs Mason's girls," she says. "I may write a few, I think. The Roman myths. I suppose if it goes well we could look at publishing a collection..." She shakes her head. "But for now, just a little something for them to play at. I want to start with Proserpine."

"Proserpine? How lovely."

"I always thought of it as Proserpine's story, the way she is stolen by Jupiter while gathering flowers, taken below to be the queen of hell; but reading it now—I found my heart with her mother. It is Ceres we actually see most, grieving the loss of her daughter, taking her case before Jupiter and demanding justice. I suppose, given what has passed, it isn't surprising that my reading should change."

"No," he says quietly.

"I thought it might be nice to have some songs. The girls will like them, and, well, when we were working on your Cenci play I thought how interesting the two of us working together would be. And I'm very confident with the action of the drama, but I haven't anything like your skill at poetry, and I thought it could be nice to combine the two. Would you like to write them?"

She turns her enquiring grey eyes upon him, and something long forgotten flutters and settles upon his heart. He reaches out for her hand; she gives it willingly. This is his wife. This is the brilliant sixteen-year-old he fell in love with, this the author of *Frankenstein*, this the prodigy of the nineteenth century.

"I would love that," he replies. "What would you like?"

"I thought a piece on the story of Arethusa. Or a song for Proserpine while she is gathering flowers?"

Her calm, certain presence acts as strong upon him as the power that draws the compass needle. He must follow and do as she bids, and he cannot do so more gladly.

"Of course."

"Thank you, Shelley. It will be the loveliest addition."

"I hope this doesn't mean that you are abandoning your Castruccio novel."

"Not at all," she says, "I am only taking some time away from it, letting my ideas settle."

He scrambles up, and curls himself up in the adjacent chair.

"Will you tell me about it?" he asks.

"About *Castruccio*? I could." She swivels in her chair, and tucks up her knees so she sits just as he does, as if they were matching bookends. "After working with you on *The Cenci*, I was thinking of what you said about Beatrice Cenci, of how her religion misleads her, and I thought how good Euthanasia is, and how she suffers at the hands of Castruccio's tyranny. Wouldn't it be interesting to have a counterpoint to her, someone not ideal but passionate, deluded by religion and the certainty that God commends her actions? So, and I hope you do not mind, I have created a Beatrice of my own."

"How could I mind?" He is so thrilled to hear her inspiration that he pulls her from her chair to sit on his lap. She comes without resistance, and even nuzzles into him.

"So," she says with a lingering smile, "how is your *Prometheus*, then?"

"I have worked out how to free him," Shelley reports. Her eyebrows raise, enough to ask how. "He has to retract the curse he laid upon Jupiter."

Mary nods. "Ah, I see. That is wise."

"Yes. He must forgive. But... he must also overthrow Jupiter and that I don't know how to do so without violence. I want him to unleash the Demogorgon, that I know for sure, but how to do it, without it being a direct attack..."

"You'll work it out," she says confidently. "I think this will be your greatest work, Shelley."

"It is certainly the one I have fretted over longest," he says with half a laugh. "But it is dispiriting to write knowing no one will publish."

"Now," she brushes back his hair. "You don't know that."

"I really thought a publisher would want *The Cenci*. I did not anticipate printing it at my own expense. I just hope no copies get sent back to me. I really can't bear it. But better that than them sitting moulding on bookshop shelves, I suppose. I just—with Hunt doing so much for me in *The Examiner*, I expected things to have improved."

"Oh, Shelley. Do not preach gradualism and expect landslides. Growing a forest takes autumns as well as springs. The tattered copy that leans even now forgotten in a back corner of a bookshop shelf, dust-heavy, may one day come by chance to the attention of some

young and open-minded prophet, and may be the path to their en-
lightenment. Once rooted in another mind the vine may spread,
and grow strong."

He sighs and leans his head on the chair back, staring at her
in wonder.

"You are very wise, my Mary."

She kisses him fully upon the lips, and then, hovering her
mouth a moment above his, says with an amused smile, "I am para-
phrasing you."

"Then I must have caught some of your wisdom."

She fondly brushes his cheek, and rises to leave. As she moves
away from him he feels the cold creep back in around him, and
wants very strongly to pull her back, to keep her close, and devote
the afternoon to warmth and kisses.

"Mary?" he says, and she pauses.

"Yes?"

"I don't think I would be half what I am without you."

She laughs softly, as if he were a boy at a party making fine
phrases for a young lady.

"You won't ever go away from me, will you, Mary?"

For a moment she looks back at him, the stillness uncertain,
and then she comes back, runs a hand through his hair.

"Of course not. I need you. I will always be here."

"Mary?"

"Yes?"

"Where are you going now?"

"To get my book."

"Are you coming back?"

"Yes."

"Will you sit beside me?"

"Yes, I will."

He lets her go and turns his mind to his *Prometheus*.

It begins where Aeschylus's play ends, with Prometheus lashed
to a rock for all eternity for his disobedience. Shelley can see him in
his fury, his wild defiance, the curse that he has called upon Jupiter
running through him with the blood in his veins.

What he learned from writing *The Cenci* was the righteousness with which people can feel hatred, and he lets Prometheus exhibit that fury.

Defiance is certainly noble; it takes a great mind to resist the dictates of the powerful. Every soul brave enough to stand up in resistance to a corrupt authority ought to be commended. And yet, again and again these times have witnessed the wronged standing up for what they believe in, and again and again the worst violence has resulted.

Hatred is pernicious. Shelley knows he must make his Prometheus forgive those who have wronged him, but how to bring it about? There is no doubt in Shelley's mind that forgiveness is the key. There Christ was right. The sufferer must forgive his persecutor—must retract the curse that he has uttered and repent the hatred he has nursed. But such bitterness, such deep grief is hard to shift.

"Mary," he says, as she comes back in. "Euthanasia you say is the counterpoint to your misguided Beatrice?"

"Yes."

"She does not hate?"

Mary thinks for a moment. "She is not vengeful. She is kind. A good ruler. Because she is principally a counterpoint to Castruccio."

"Who is a tyrant," he says, putting together the pieces of her story in his mind, aligning them with those of his.

"Precisely."

"And... does Euthanasia succeed?" he asks.

"No."

"No."

"No. Castruccio wins with his brute force. Euthanasia will die."

Shelley nods, and lets Mary settle into her book. He must not push her.

He has identified the difference between them. He lays his book open and picks up his pen with his right hand, and wraps his left arm around her shoulder.

She, like Byron, perceives the power in immoral violence, and while advocating good, yet acknowledges that the good will suffer. Their pessimism is a commitment to show the world as it is, while he feels a commitment to show the world as it could be.

He leans his head on her shoulder and the whisper of her pen on paper soon reaches him.

He must show Prometheus triumphant. But what can make him change, desolate and chained to a rock as he is? If he had Mary to lean his head on, that would be different. He laughs to himself and leans into her warmth.

She is his greatest comfort. She is his stabilising force, the mind that completes his own. Without her is uncertainty, nervous energy, a quest without a resolution. Today, for the first time in months, she is really with him again. Perhaps this is the thaw of her winter. The thought brings him such relief that contrast teaches him his recent misery. But, he cautions himself, he must not expect her restoration to be immediate and absolute. There may still be dips. Indeed, her melancholy may return.

The pain of a possible solitude strikes into him a revelation. Prometheus must have a lover. He must have a counterpoint who is not merely his support, but a strength in herself, another who shows him his weakness and completes him.

He moves slowly, breath held for fear of disturbing the vision that is clear in his mind, drawing close the paper, inking the pen. She will be his counterpoint. She will demand justice. She will descend to the depths of the earth and face the Demogorgon.

And at the end of all, when the earth renews itself, she will stand by his side.

Chapter Nine: Drifting
Pisa, 4th January 1820

*W*hen their tour of Italy is complete, they have no desire to return to England, and when thinking of where to settle, Pisa calls them. There they are not far from Claire in Livorno, and they are near Mrs Mason and the friends she recommends.

Mary is delighted to have Pisa's archives at her disposal, and spends long days researching the history of the Guelphs and Ghibellines for her Castruccio novel. She is aware of Shelley loitering, wanting attention, and she spares it when she can, but sometimes the task of simply passing the day is sufficient challenge for her, and she finds she has no energy to give to him.

He misses Claire, she knows.

A fire is raging between Claire and Byron, and every time Mary comes into contact with it she comes away exhausted.

"How can she cause this much drama from so far away?" Mary exclaims, when Shelley complains of yet another furious letter from Byron while they walk along the *Lung Arno* in the late morning. A haze of cloud makes the sky and the broad river a matching lilac grey, but the warm colours of the Palazzos along the bank make the day brighter than England could ever be on such a day.

"He isn't behaving well," Shelley admits. "He's sent her off to a convent."

"*He* isn't behaving well?"

"From what she says it started with her making a polite request to see Allegra."

"I'm sure it was polite." Mary cannot restrain her sarcasm, and now that Claire is gone there is no one to bat it back to her, no one to dispute. This does mean sometimes she issues cutting epithets about her step-sister and they simply fall into the quiet between her and Shelley, and she fears he takes them too seriously. She knows how he loves Claire, and suspects he is missing her company more than he lets on, perhaps more than he even realises.

"I don't think we should be shocked," Mary says, trying to mollify him. "It seems a common course of action in this country to send young girls to convents for their education. And as Albe said, his lifestyle is hardly agreeable to child rearing. In his house she'd only be raised by some servant."

"We don't know what she's writing, of course," Shelley says, more in his own thoughts than Mary's words. "But the letters Byron is writing—to me, by the way, not to her—they've tipped over into cruelty. He says he will not send Allegra to stay with us, for fear of her safety."

"What does he mean by that?" Mary's heart quickens. The guilt she has done so much to rid herself of, the blame she has told herself she does not deserve, is she to discover now that her friend, her Albe, nurses it too? For that would make it real, not simply a mother's grief, but a worldly fact.

"No, no," Shelley says hastily, and rubs her arm. "Nothing like that. I think, I think it is the atheism, quite frankly, it sounds like he is becoming more Christian of late, more conservative in his ideas, you know. Nothing like that." He is trying to reassure her, but he speaks so swiftly, and with a haste that is almost panicky, she does not entirely believe him.

He does not show her the letter, and she stops asking.

She stops asking about a lot of things.

Shelley calls often on a pretty English girl called Sophia and her chaperone Miss Corbet Parry-Jones, both of whom, it seems clear to Mary when she accompanies him, are in love with him.

If he sighs more and shows her less of what he writes, she guesses an infatuation; unthreatened, she leaves him to it, and keeps herself busy with her work and dear little Percy Florence.

Months pass and Sophia leaves for Rome. Shelley writes a lot of letters to people far away.

They make the acquaintance of a beautiful young Italian woman of nineteen called Emilia Viviani, who has been placed in a convent by her father and commanded to marry a man she does not love. Mary knows before it happens that Shelley will pick up his idolisation and apply it to this new subject, and true enough, he does.

She finds the whole thing somewhat embarrassing and tries not to engage with any of it.

Her novel *Castruccio* takes shape, and she thrills to see something wonderful emerging.

Mary,
Come, walk with me in forests once again.
Oh, let our minds and hands entwine beneath
The canopy of fresh forgiving green.
Please, come.

                    Alas, I cannot walk this day.
           You should go forth in pastures as before
           While I remain here, safe within these doors.
              My head is weary and my heart is sore.
              Let me rest, and let me rest alone.

Why, Mary, do you weep, and not accept
The comfort which I long to offer you?

This fragile bark we sail is all but wrecked,
So tempest-tossed, these past few years have been,
As if some demon cursed our voyages.
Were there any crew but I and you
We would have sunk beneath the waves, I know.
But while my Mae beside me stands I yet
Have strength to persevere unto our end.

Oh, Mary mine, let not your subtle grief
So steal your radiant heart away from him
Who loves you, and relies upon that light
Which you alone can shine...
The stream which flows unaided through harsh crags
Knows not the sufferance it overcomes
Until some other joins, not tributary,
But fellow; mingling their strength and might they forge
A path through caverns and sharp rocks, together,
Shielded from violence of a falling tree
Simply by sharing in sweet company.
Until the twain are rent apart at last.

Thus once, when all alone, I fought my way;
Since having known companionship I can't
Now reconcile myself to move with half
My power, half my riches, and half my love.

The words that for so long granted to me
An outlet for my grief all fail me now.
I scarcely write; I scarcely even speak.

If I could speak to him my grief would pour
Upon his poet's heart such fierce deluge
That it would sweep away his fragile bark.
For once undammed my sorrow's flow may be
A deluge that his love might not withstand.
So, ask me not for joyful words, my love;
Let silence reign over this home of grief.

Part Six

Chapter One: A Pisan Garden
Pisa, 12th February 1822

*L*ife is sometimes a dense, ponderous dream in which one anticipates with discomforting confidence a certain end. But, as is
the way in dreams, one cannot grasp its details, nor do anything to
change the outcome. Simply, one must continue, and when the end
is reached we shall all nod and say, 'Ah, yes, of course, it was always
to be thus.' So Shelley, stretched out supine upon the crisp white
linen, senses an oncoming disaster.

Within the quiet bedroom, shadow-light lies limp, its sullen
beams tainted pale by white-washed walls. It drenches Shelley with
its bone-cold chill, and turns his skin ash-white. He sighs. Lying
on the bed fully dressed, he watches his thoughts chase each other
across the walls.

The nature of the oncoming catastrophe evades him. Is it to
be the end of all things? The end of opportunity, of possibility, of
choice? A life sacrificed for an eternity of nothingness?

He tells himself it is just the anxiety of waiting, that within
months his life will undergo a marvellous change, for great plans
are afoot.

Byron, after a long spat across letters that got ugly more than
once, suddenly invited Shelley alone to see him last August. After
the emptiness his life in Pisa had become, and at a time when he
was grieving the loss of a lovely young Emilia Viviani to her promised husband, the long lazy days of rising late and talking literature
late into the night were very welcome.

In one of their discussions Shelley had lamented the state of publishing in England, to which Byron concurred and idly said they should take advantage of the laxer laws here in Italy, and what a shame it was there were no decent English language publishing ventures here. That was the spark, and ever since Shelley has been fanning it into flame.

He wrote to Leigh Hunt with a plan:

My dearest friend,

Since I last wrote to you, I have been on a visit to Lord Byron at Ravenna. The result of this visit was a determination, on his part, to come and live at Pisa; and I have taken the finest palace on the Lung' Arno for him. But the material part of my visit consists in a message which he desires me to give to you, and which I think, ought to add to your determination – for such a one I hope you have formed – of restoring your shattered health and spirits by a migration to these 'regions mild of calm and serene air.'

He proposes that you should come and go shares with him and me in a periodical work, to be conducted here; in which each of the contracting parties should publish all their original compositions, and share the profits. There can be no doubt that profits of any scheme in which you and Lord Byron engage, must from various, yet co-operating reasons, be very great.

Lord Byron is reformed, as far as gallantry goes, and lives with a beautiful and sentimental Italian Lady, who is as much attached to him as may be. I trust greatly to his intercourse with you for his creed to become as pure as he thinks his conduct is. He has many generous and exalted qualities, but the canker of aristocracy wants to be cut out, and something, God knows, wants to be cut out of us all – except perhaps you!

And dear Hunt had written back with enthusiasm, saying that after a year of debts and illness for his family, Pisa might now be just the right thing after all.

He will come in June, Byron a little before, and the three of them shall work on something the world will read, and at last life will actually be happening!

But for now, Shelley must wait.

At the small desk across the room, Mary writes determinedly, glancing every now and then to the couch where their child lies sleeping. He ought to be in the nursery, being watched by the paid nurse, but Mary keeps him close. Shelley observes her, notes her strained inhalation, the careful scrape of shifting pen, the pause for replenishment of ink, the scrape resumed, and then, the glance. Only when she looks at little Percy does Shelley see her face. The contorted brow, the narrowed eyes; all tension and pain.

Beyond his wife is the room's only window, a resolute square depicting the abstract shapes of undistinguished houses: a slanted roof, a lined wall, the side profile of a palazzo; sienna, terracotta and burnt umber. Why don't the colours come inside, Shelley wonders, why can't this still room be infiltrated with their warmth? Why indeed are he and Mary and their child inside on such a day?

"Mary!" he says with urgency, sitting up in a swift movement that brings a tinge to the old ache in his side.

"Hush."

She points to Percy, his blond curls just visible beneath his favourite blue blanket, and does not look up to Shelley.

"Mary," he says again, more quietly, "let's go for a walk."

"Percy's asleep."

He clambers off the bed, more carefully now, and puts his hands on Mary's shoulders.

"We have a nurse for precisely this reason. We'll tell her we're going out and she can come sit with him. Or we'll take him. I can carry him."

"No, Shelley."

It is that dismissal, that tone that says he is reckless and foolish and that only she knows what is right, which makes him lift his hands from her. For a moment he regards the back of her head. There used to be someone there. *Dearest Mary, wherefore hast thou gone, and left me in this dreary world alone.* The line echoes in his head.

"I'm going out anyway," he says to her silence.

She does not reply.

He descends the stairwell with a heavy tread. Surely one day she will look at him again, won't she? On the second storey he pauses by the door where their new friends Ned and Jane live, and almost knocks for their company. But his is a melancholy mood, and their youthful ebullience might draw from him some secrets he would rather keep.

If Claire were here she'd cajole him out of his ill humour, and as he steps out of the house and into the golden afternoon, he wishes she were here, for arm-in-arm they would join the chatter of human and aviary voices enjoying this first warmth after winter.

Their house sits at the very east extremity of the *Lung Arno*, and turning the corner to tuck back behind the houses he enters the public gardens through a gate in a high wall. Within is an Italian paradise. Long flat lawns are interspersed by easy pathways, and vast trees at regular intervals tower upwards and spread their generous shade. The low sun coaxes deep warm hues from the stones; trees and flowers are still in their leafy shadows, for no wind creeps in. Whatever may be beyond these walls—the boats on the Arno, the busy people running about their busy lives, Mary with her stern coldness—none of it enters here. The warmth washes over him, and he shivers off his sadness, dropping it behind him like an unwanted coat.

Shelley strolls through the gardens, pushing away his own troubles and filling his mind with what he sees, ascending a short flight of steps to gain better vantage. In one corner children draw words, or their own mysterious symbols, in the dusty ground with sticks; by a wall a young woman with fine black hair and a lilac dress reads alone; along the path three boys almost at full height walk side by side, pretending they are men. And there, beneath a trellised bower, two lovers sit, hands much involved in examining and caressing. But this is no fleeting infatuation, for at their feet are two children, the first tall enough to rest his head upon his mother's lap, the second scarcely walking. Shelley smiles at the sight. It is his friends, Ned and Jane. Now the sense of approaching spring is thawing his cold, and he ambles towards them.

The scene they make is blissful. And though there are plenty cloistered minds who would condemn them if they knew the *sin* these lovers live in, there is nothing of their illegitimacy on view. Indeed, Shelley feels privileged knowing it; he has been trusted with their secret.

Some sense that human minds have not yet articulated causes

Jane to look up, as if she feels his presence, and she welcomes him with a wave. Jane is tall and beautiful, with slinking hair that shifts from dark blond to chestnut with the shifting of the sun; her long face is raised to him with a sympathetic, knowing kindness, while Ned, who still holds his lover's hand to his chest, has only his open, easy, honest smile.

"A good afternoon to you, Shelley!" Ned cries.

"Hello Ned! Hello Janey! How are you both?" Shelley asks, and receives a happy response. On the next bench is their nurse, keeping a small distance though her eyes are fixed on the infants. Rosalind, the six-months babe, has spotted her uncle Bysshe and is making a steady crawl in his direction. "And, how are you?" he asks, dropping to the ground before her.

"I think she's been looking for you, Shelley. You're her absolute favourite," Jane says indulgently.

"I am, am I?" he asks Rosalind, and receives a toothless grin in reply.

"I'm glad you're here, Shelley," Ned says, leaning back into the recesses of the alcove. "I've news! But perhaps it ought to wait for Mary."

"And where is Mary today?" Jane sighs, with the head-tilt of a tutor asking after a naughty child. Where is Mary indeed! Shelley picks up Rosalind and lifts her into the air, eliciting a squeal of delight.

"That, my dear child," he returns her to the ground, "is what the world looks like from all the way up here." He chuckles at the parents, and returns, reluctantly, to the question. "Where is Mary? She is indoors. Writing, I think. No, translating." He contemplates sending Rosalind to the sky once more, but she is already astonished by the world at foot-height as a ladybird lands on her toes. "This new thing from Greece, the declaration. She's sending it back to England for publication in *The Examiner*."

"I didn't know she spoke Greek," Ned says.

"She didn't until recently. She's been learning from this Greek Prince, Mavrocordato."

"Quite a splendid fellow. Ever so charming." Ned grins. "I do like him."

"So does our Mary." Jane says archly, "I've seen the two of them wandering along the *Lung Arno* talking politics hour in and hour out. It's remarkable she can have so much to say to him when she says so little to the rest of us: she seems almost animated with him."

Shelley hears this and refrains from remark.

The conversation is halted abruptly by the wail of the toddler Medwin fallen over, and at once the nurse is up at a scuttling run, fussing and cooing, and Ned, seeing that there is no real harm done, saunters after her to reassure the casualty that no bones are broken.

Shelley watches a moment, then looks back. Jane Williams is an image lovelier than truth. Her slender face has an equine elegance and her pristine ringlets are a rich brown in this light. The flowers on her lace neckline echo those that bloom in the alcove around her in coy lilac. Warmth radiates from her skin and Shelley feels the desire that has haunted him since he met her, to take that flesh in his hands and merge himself with her, devouring the life that shines from her.

She must feel his gaze, but she makes no sign of it.

"We were talking about Mary," Jane says after a moment.

Shelley nods, and takes a seat on the dusty earth where the grass is thin. It is deliberately a seat by Rosalind who sits on the bare earth and stares, fascinated, after her brother, but it is also close to her mother, just a few inches from touch.

"I'd rather not," he replies.

Above him Jane tuts.

"She treats you badly, Shelley," she says. She leans forward, so that her skirts crinkle against his arm, and with a plump white hand she turns his chin so that he must look fully at her, must look at the blue eyes so bright and clear. "I hate to see you unhappy," she says.

As she holds him there, those blue eyes take on the pinkish whisper of the flowers that curl around the trellis.

"I'm not unhappy now." He shakes his head. "And Mary doesn't treat me badly. She has a melancholic disposition. She cannot help the way she is, and goodness knows it causes her enough pain."

"You are miserable. You must tell her."

"It would hurt her; that is something I won't do."

"Honestly, Shelley." Her voice is louder in his head than his own. "Your loyalty is admirable. But I don't see why you adhere so tirelessly to the principle you don't believe in. When love died I left my husband. When I found love again I grasped it, and now that I have Ned I am happier than I've ever been." He looks at her again; she holds herself high, defiant. "You know," she sighs and gazes over at Ned, releasing Shelley from her grip, "Neddy and I were talking about you the other day. We call you Ariel."

He smiles to himself.

"Do you really?"

"Yes. A poor imprisoned spirit, unable to be free, unappreciated in the bonds cruel fate has bound him with."

He returns her frank stare, scrutinising her look, her kindness. Here is a beauty to make a man mad.

"And, you and Ned, I suppose," he holds her gaze, "are Miranda and Ferdinand, weeping at your own love. It is a pleasing analogy."

"Hm. Look. Ned has found your Mary."

Shelley turns around, and indeed, Ned is walking back across the gardens with Mary, little Medwin stumbling along beside Percy of whom Mary keeps a tight hold.

Jane extends her elegant arm in greeting, and though she smiles at them, she speaks softly to Shelley.

"Just don't let your *Prospera* keep you imprisoned."

She rises before he has an opportunity to respond, the circumference of her skirts rustling against him and disturbing the summer perfumes of the flowers as she goes to embrace Mary. Shelley does not get up. Rosalind looks at him questioningly and he offers a finger for her to hold. Something troubles him. Jane is wrong about him. About Mary. And yet... not entirely so. As he watches Mary greet Jane with that slow, peculiar way she has now, her head high and her eyes low, with pale greedy hands that clutch at Jane's soft wrist, there is something uneasy stirring within him, and he cannot dismiss Jane's words.

Percy toddles over to Medwin and the two meet with a delighted embrace that makes the adults laugh.

"Now we're all here let me tell you, I've realised the Carnival is coming up and there's a fancy-dress ball—*Veglinoe*, I believe the natives call it—so I want promises that we're all going and we're all dressing up! And the theme, the theme—" He has to talk louder, for Jane has incited excitement in the children, who know nothing of the cause but are easily infected by her happiness. "The theme," Edward goes on, "is the Orient! We must all dress as Turks! What fun, eh?"

"It sounds magnificent!" Shelley agrees.

Only Mary is quiet, and she is looking at Shelley's hands, clasped about his knees, with strange intensity.

"I thought you didn't like parties," she says. Her voice is low and flat, but its rarity slices through all their laughter, demanding silence. Even Medwin and Percy fall quiet, watching her curiously.

"I wanted to hold a party last summer, and you wouldn't. You said you couldn't bear it," she goes on. "You said you don't like parties."

Shelley finds a hot blush creeping into his cheeks, and is surprised to recognise anger stirring. Why will she not look at him? Even in this moment of direct accusation she does not look at him. He remembers the incident well. The whole thing was strange—how she had gotten a sudden odd plan to become some kind of socialite and hold soirees in their house, inviting all the finest people. And how mad the idea had driven him.

"It's a different sort of thing," he says, weakly. There is no flicker upon her to suggest that she has heard. "Quite different. The thought of people we hardly knew coming into our house, and laughing and judging us, it upset me." He doesn't want to talk like this here, before Ned and Jane and all their happiness.

"It *is* a different thing, Mary," Jane chimes in, and Ned nods his agreement. "To have guests in one's own house is entirely different from visiting elsewhere, for one thing! You can't blame Shelley!"

Mary makes a single curt nod, and Jane pats her hand reassuringly.

"Good."

The Williamses are at once on the talk of parties, and what they shall all wear.

"And Shelley must take the guise of one of his characters!" Ned cries. It is a kind thing to say, for they have read so many of his poems since they met him, and they both say the nicest things about them, good friends as they are. "And if Byron does come back to Pisa, as he said he might, won't he have the most wonderful clothes from his oriental travels."

"He does," Shelley says, and wants to tell them of the Turkish military dress Byron owns, the rich orange fabrics, the opulence of it all, but he feels dampened by Mary's gloom.

He has tried a thousand times to draw her into the light, but she will not laugh with him, will not sing and talk and read and live as they once lived. And yet, he cannot disconnect himself from her. He cannot be happy when she is sad.

And why must she revel in melancholy? If she was so very upset not to have her party before, why can't she be happy there is now a party to go to? Would she have been happy if they had held that party? He knows she wouldn't, because it has been so long since anything in her stirred, that he has finally stopped hoping, stopped looking for ways to brighten her life.

Even as the thoughts sear through him he is ashamed of their ungenerousness. His poor Mary, she has suffered, he tells himself once more. She has suffered and is suffering still. Perhaps this party will be recompense for the party she missed, and she will come out of her shell and be her old self once more.

Chapter Two: Carnival
Pisa, 18th February 1822

*T*he *Veglione* is beautiful. The ballroom is draped with lush pinks and oranges, young and old alike dressed in the shades of Araby, and one could almost imagine they had stepped out onto the sands of Turkey. *Almost,* Mary thinks, but as she walks, arm-in-arm with Jane Williams, she feels disappointed at the pale imitation. The skin too pale, the dresses too European, even if they are paired with turbans and capes.

"What a funny game," she murmurs.

"What game?" Jane asks brightly. "Who is playing a game? Shall we play?"

Mary can't reply. The game is merely something to do, and they are all playing with their silly costumes. Perhaps one day she will go to Constantinople and see the East. Surely they don't have silly parties there where they all dress up as Italians and English visitors.

Jane, although in no way Arabic, is utterly beautiful. Hers is the kind of beauty that makes Mary understand how the maids of Lesbos fell in love with Sappho. The abundant jewellery she wears highlights her slender hands and neck, the apricot silk of her turban offsets her warm skin and sun-blonde ringlets.

"Come, Mary," Jane says. "Let us find Captain Trelawney. He was looking for you earlier, and I promised you'd dance with him."

Mary assents silently and lets herself be led through the ballroom. She feels a small, surprising pride in the elegance she has achieved in her own costume, very much aided by an afternoon of dressing with Jane. The white muslin dress she wears is unexceptional, but she has bound it at the waist by a fringed red scarf, and drawn it up to show a deep purple underskirt, borrowed from Jane. Over these flashes of colour she wears a long sapphire-blue coat with swirling silver embroidery. Her hair is braided, her eyes lined in black.

"Where did Shelley and Ned go?" Mary asks, aware they had lately been nearby.

"Oh, off with some of those Greeks." Jane waves dismissively, but Mary glances about, because she would very much like to talk politics with the Greeks, especially as she is feeling a little brighter than usual today.

"Is Prince Mavrocordato here?"

"I haven't seen him but I suppose he might be. But I shan't have you sitting talking politics on a night like this! As your friend I command you to enjoy yourself! In your condition you can't expect too many more excursions of this sort."

"In my condition," Mary smiles weakly. "Indeed."

"Don't look so doleful." Jane stops abruptly and puts a soft hand to Mary's cheek, and Mary has to set her face still to hide the spark the contact gives her. "Confinement is a bore, but think how wonderful it'll be. Think how happy Percy will be to become a big brother!" She glitters with all of her gems, and in the lantern light her skin is softly luminous.

"Yes, he is. But... Jane." Mary turns her hand over so that her palm embraces Jane's, and feels there the thin lines of the chains between them. Yes, there is an energy in her tonight and she can speak. "I'm probably being quite foolish, but I have such an ill omen about this pregnancy."

She can't quite bring herself to look into her friend's eyes, and traces instead the lines of the thin chains that run from Jane's bracelet to each of her rings.

"I have a foreboding that this will end terribly. That there is some great misery coming, though what could be greater than what I have already suffered I do not know."

Jane's fingers interlace with hers, and Mary's knuckles strain white against the friendship they offer.

"Such fears are common," Jane murmurs. Her green-blue eyes are full and kind. "I was so worried my first time... Four children later I know what I am doing. And a woman of your experience has nothing to fear. It is natural you would worry. I know you grieve your lost children. But you must look to the future. To Shelley, and to Percy. Trust me, all will be well." She gives her a loving smile, and then squeezes and releases her. "No more fears. Look, here comes Trelawny. You must dance with him and enjoy yourself."

"Perhaps later you and I could dance?" Mary says hastily, impulsively.

"Oh, no need for that, there are plenty of gentlemen here!"

"So there are," Mary says quietly to herself. "Never mind."

"Mary, come, you know Trelawny, don't you?" Jane says loudly, as a tall dark man approaches. His broad bearing demands not a ballroom but a ship deck, though he has made every effort for the evening, his loose ragged hair resisting the ties he has attempted to hold it back with. He looks upon Mary with deep, fierce eyes.

"Indeed I do," she says. "Captain Trelawny. How nice to see you again."

He gathers up her hand and presses it to his mouth; and she feels the thick bristles of his beard and a strange, intimate wetness to his lips. The floor-length coat he wears is deepest green with violet embroidery around golden buttons, and if she is not mistaken he has combed his moustache and curled it up at the ends. The impression is almost comical, but still impressive.

"A great pleasure it is, Mary Wollstonecraft Shelley; a great pleasure."

"He means it, Mary," Jane giggles. "I don't think he's said a word but about how he's hoping to dance with you this evening."

"I'm afraid I am not an accomplished dancer," Mary insists.

"Oh Mary, you can't! You wicked thing!" Jane protests at once, though Trelawny merely looks crestfallen, and turns his hat in his hands. "Then you must practise now, Mary," Jane pleads, almost bursting in the enjoyment of her role. "Look at the poor fellow, you'll ruin him."

Trelawny lightly raises his downcast eyes to her and she cannot but relent.

His tall, straight form guides her onto the dance floor with more grace than she expects. The song is struck and he leads with confidence—just as well, for Mary has only a faint understanding of where she is meant to be at any moment. Every part of her seems to be more than it ever is—her eyes more open, her mind clearer, her feet swifter, her whole body lighter.

"Where is your beardless boy today, Mrs Shelley?" he asks, as he sails her round the hall.

"Shelley's here somewhere. Off with the wind, perhaps."

"Who knows the ways of poets?" He laughs, and turns her about. "When I met him I couldn't believe such a willow of a man was this hell-fire demon I'd heard so much of; the very child of Satan from the way they speak of him in England."

"He has never been well understood."

"He's lucky to have such a wife." As they draw close Trelawny's voice is deep and resonant, with the vibration of horse hair upon cello string, ancient as the forests, deep as the ocean, seeming to sing of an ancient tale.

"I hope so," she replies.

"You hope so?"

But Mary dismisses the subject with a shake of her head, and besides the music is changing into something fierier: a waltz.

"They still think the waltz immoral in England," Trelawny says, rolling the world 'immoral' around his mouth with some pleasure. "But I don't imagine you hold with such prudishness. Will you accompany me once more?"

She glances back towards Jane with some longing, but Jane has found a ginger-whiskered man to accompany her. Ned and Shelley have emerged and found themselves a table where they talk animatedly with bowed heads.

"Very well."

She dances the waltz with Trelawny, and then another with an Italian gentleman. A new dance is called she does not know, and she has lost sight of all her acquaintances but she joins three women to make a four. At last, exhausted, she tears herself away. Her bosom heaves with excited breath as she presses through the house in search of a little fresh air, a lift in her step, despite the pinch in the pointed toes of her Turkish slippers.

Away from the hall the party dissolves into dark corridors inhabited by murmuring strangers in their private conversations. She walks through as demurely as her skipping heart will allow, the hallway echoing with distant footsteps. From the corridor she turns into an empty smoking room, and from there, through French windows into the mild night.

Here is a long, empty veranda that looks out upon the garden. At its edges are large tubs of flowers, and on the eaves little paper lanterns hang. The evening flowers emit a powerful aroma that is almost sickly and shake their heads in a breeze that swings the lanterns on their strings. Out here the air is cooler than within and Mary gulps it in, wriggling her shoulders out of the Arabian jacket so she may enjoy the breeze on her bare arms.

Into this little moment of peace intrudes a well-heeled step, and glancing back towards the house she sees a shadowy figure—a sultan of some sort perhaps, for his silhouette shows a high turban and long robes. The stranger stops, and though she can make out no detail within the outline, she is certain he is staring at her. She swallows, and is suddenly aware of her naked shoulders and her isolation from her companions. Rolling up the jacket in her hands, she starts confidently back towards the door, hoping to pass the stranger at some pace and return to the corridors and protective company, but just as she reaches the doorway, he speaks.

"You don't look at all pleased to see me."

The voice from the shadows is Byron's and Mary's relief floods into a laugh.

"Albe! I didn't recognise you!"

She embraces him, meeting a strong smell of alcohol from his breath, and brings him to the lantern light to see him better. He is magnificently dressed, as of course he must be, in full Turkish military uniform with a jewelled scabbard at his side. But his eyelids are lazy, his eyes unfocused.

"Look at you, Mary," he says, his words drifting lazily. "Look at your eyes! I've never seen you at a ball... you look years younger."

Mary takes the compliment with agreement. "I rather feel like I'm borrowing someone else's life tonight. I've never been to a ball before."

"You've never been to a ball?"

"Never."

"What on earth did you do with your youth? Read books I suppose. And wrote them. How dull to be a Godwin."

"I fear so." She pulls a stray hair back off her forehead, and pats the labyrinthine sinews of her braids to check all is in place. The sweat on her back makes her dress cling.

"Come, walk with me." He offers her his arm, and together they walk slowly along the veranda, breathing in the scent of the flowers.

"And Shiloh's here?"

"Yes, Shelley's inside listening to the music."

"And your troubling step-sister?"

"Claire is in Florence. She has a position there. Believe me she will not step in Pisa as long as she knows you may be in it." Mary tuts at Byron's expression of relief. "I must say I think your animosity has reached a foolish extremity when you cannot share a city for fear of walking past each other on the street."

"I hear we shall be seeing more of each other soon. This plan of Shelley's to start a magazine."

"Yes. He thought to call it *The Liberal*." Mary knows how dear it is to Shelley's heart, and how important Byron is to the plan. "It will be a very good thing for all parties," she says.

"And Hunt is still planning to come over to edit it?"

"That is my understanding."

"It may actually happen then. Very well. I'll talk to Shelley about that. Now, I believe you are planning to stay in Pisa a while?"

"We are."

"Good. I am thinking of having a bit of fun soon," he says.

"I didn't know you ever did anything else, Albe."

"I try not to." His voice is rich with a smile. "I want to put on a play. I'm very much hoping you'll get involved." Having reached the end of the veranda, they stop, and lean against the trellis. Mary admires the purple flowers, and lightly touches their blooms with her fingers. "You know Trelawny, don't you?" Byron asks.

"I do," she says. "I believe he is a good man."

"I agree, though I don't believe a word he says about anything."

"Yes, he's rather playing the role," Mary says, wistfully. "Like someone else I know." She casts a look at Byron then, but he either misses her point, or ignores it.

"Well, he and I have spoken about putting on *Othello*."

"*Othello*?" Mary echoes.

"He wants to be Othello. I want to be Iago."

Mary laughs softly. The flowers here are tangled, and it is soothing to draw one strand away from its clutter and let it lie singly. Their trumpet-like petals are unusually large, and she feels their heads must be heavy on such light stems.

"And you, Miss Mary," Byron separates himself from her so he may better see her face, "we want you for our Desdemona."

"Desdemona! You think I am a heroine?"

"A beautiful and tragic one, certainly."

She laughs happily. The way she feels right now she would love to act in such a play, and to spend evenings of conversation and merriment with such friends, but an echo reverberates inside her that the person she was an hour prior would not agree. She makes no promise, but does not refuse.

"Perhaps I cannot act," she says pointedly.

"I have seen you act plenty of times," Byron whispers at her ear. She shivers and he steps back. "Besides," he goes on, louder, "I have heard you recite poetry, your voice is strong and your passion is clear. You'd be wonderful. And I do think Trelawny wants a kiss from you into the bargain."

"He has already come calling to me asking for that."

"And you wouldn't give him one?"

"I would not."

"Though he is such a gallant, romantic figure?"

"Even though."

"It is hard to win the heart of Mary Wollstonecraft Shelley."

"Only one has ever achieved it," she says, and takes her hands from the flowers.

Byron sways a moment and steps closer to her, too close. "I must talk to you about Shelley," he says. There is a new seriousness about him.

"About Shelley?"

He swallows and blinks rapidly, and she can see him trying to clear his head. He briefly puts his hands upon her bare shoulders and then, frowning, makes his way to a long garden seat overhung with potted flowers and collapses heavily onto it.

"I have been hearing things, Mary. Regarding that sister of yours. And Shelley." He looks up at her. "The word is that Claire is Shelley's mistress."

Her heart sinks to hear such words. It is nothing new, she has heard it before, from all sorts of strange places, she knows directly from Shelley of occasions he and Claire have indulged themselves, but all with the agreement they made so long ago, to liberty and to love. And when the thought of them began to grieve her, she told him so, and he swore he would not cause her misery. Above all things she trusts him.

The pain comes not from the fact itself but from its repetition.

Byron leans back, stretching his arms over the back of the chair and lets his fingers play amidst the nodding heads of the evening blooms.

"This has been said before, Albe," she says with an even tone. "And it has only been said by idle gossips. No one who ought to command your attention."

His eyebrows are coolly raised, and he idly caresses the flowers that grow around him. Mary can only stare at him in silence, her heart clenched. She is angry with him for listening to such gossip and for bringing it before her.

"It is said by the British Consul in Venice, and by a great many respected guests. It is confirmed by your own servant, Elise. And more than that, it is said that Claire was with child by Shelley. That upon discovering this they procured a means of an abortion, all the while keeping the matter from you. That Claire went away for this reason, but that the abortion only brought the child early. He hid it from you, took the child to a foundling hospital and left it there. The report from Elise is that they two have kept you in the dark a couple of years now, gallivanting whenever your back is turned." He crushes a flower between forefinger and thumb.

"How can you say this?" she says, her voice now trembling with fury. "You who know him? How can you think it of him?"

Byron turns a nonchalant expression upon her.

"I have plenty reason to think the worst of the best of men," he says.

Mary shakes her head. He has sobered himself remarkably, and this is worse, to meet his gaze, to have him look at her in seriousness and pity.

"Are you not our friend, Albe?"

"Do not be angry with me, Mary." He rises from his seat to approach her but she steps back. Suddenly the man before her has transformed from the man that she loves to the fickle beast she has heard stories about. How can one ever claim to know anyone?

"I am angry," she says, "because I must defend him with whom I have the happiness to be united, whom I love and esteem beyond all living creatures, from the foulest calumnies! I might expect strangers to believe such things. But you? Not you, Albe. I thought you loved us better than that."

He makes to speak but she will not let him, not yet.

"That my beloved Shelley should stand slandered in your mind!" she says, and there is an emotion in her voice that threatens to overwhelm. "He, the gentlest and most humane of creatures... That is more painful to me, far more painful than words can express."

He sighs deeply, and holds up his hands in a defeat that speaks more of regret at disturbing her than of a change in conviction.

"It is not true," Mary says, low and clear once more. "Those who know me well believe my simple word. My father once said that he had never known me utter a falsehood, but you, easy as you have been to credit evil, who may be more deaf to truth, to you I swear by all that I hold sacred upon heaven and earth, by a vow which I should die to write if I affirmed a falsehood, I swear by the life of my child, that I know the accusations to be false."

The wind drops and silence fills the space around them. Inside the house a dance starts, a light merry melody accompanied by cheers and laughter. Across the veranda Byron stands solemn, his arms useless at his side. The warm light of the lamps glinting gold upon his silks.

"If I am wrong, forgive me," he says at last. "I only speak so because I care for you and do not wish to see you ill-used."

The fire in Mary is stoked and she cannot extinguish it, but she makes a stiff nod.

She turns to face Byron, and in doing so, sees coming towards them from the open French windows his latest lover, Theresa. She is a dark-haired and pretty girl, who is open in her love of the great lord, and her husband is quiet enough about it. Byron takes her by her slim waist, looking more besotted than Mary has ever seen him. She makes her excuses and leaves the evening to the lovers.

Back inside, the party still sparkles. Everywhere the colours of fuchsia, orange, and turquoise blue meet and mingle without coalescence. Masks and feathers and pearls dance to erratic music. None of it touches Mary. Her eyes recognise nothing, gazing instead at everything beyond.

Her life seems to weigh itself, and everything she has ever felt rises in stark juxtaposition with everything she ever dreamt. Between the swirling skirts of the dancers scuttle children who have long slept underground, behind the masks of comedy and tragedy hide the faces of the dearly departed. Time has wound up his mechanical figures, and they cannot be stopped. Mary alone, in the midst of everything, is still, and not only still, but powerless.

There is nothing now, nothing she can do to change what is gone. A stranger sweeps her into the dance, and, feeling she has no alternative but to accompany him, she joins his steps forward and back and going nowhere, and she laughs at the absurdity of it all. She looks at nothing, sees nothing, but joins in the ridiculous game.

Pisa, 25th April, 1822

When she looks back on the ball, perhaps a week later, Mary cannot reconcile her memories of dancing, laughter, and giddiness with any understanding of herself. It is as if somehow they are the memories of another person that have lodged in her mind. Still, when one is sick with a cold, one's temperature runs hot.

Here, in her little colourless bedroom with its white walls and egg-blue furnishings, dancing seems impossible. To move with lightness, to release the grip she holds upon herself enough to let her body soar, might bring about a cataclysm.

The change troubles her, so she tries not to look at it.

She lay late today, as most days, and is scarcely dressed, a robe pulled around her nightshirt, her hair lank and loose around her neck. She sits back in the chair before her desk, one hand resting lifeless upon her lap, the other holding a delicate china cup. She notices the cup with mild surprise, having somewhat forgotten it. It is still full of weak, greyish tea. She lifts it to her lips, blows softly upon its surface, sending a neat furrow of ripples across the surface, and takes a cautious sip.

It is utterly cold. She stares down at it. Has she really left it so long? And did she really dance with Trelawny and laugh so loudly that heads turned? Is she confusing what she did for what she witnessed? Surely that was some other girl who danced—a young and happy thing at her first ball, delighted to be wearing her new dress at last, giddy upon her first taste of punch.

From below comes a sweet song of Jane's guitar, speaking of an easy love and a wistful sigh. Her voice dances in a moment later, too soft for Mary to make out all the words, but clear enough for the sentiment of the melody to be expressed. The song breaks into a laugh, though the guitar plays on, and a muffled male voice says something. Is it Shelley? No, it must be Ned. Or perhaps not. Another pretty laugh, a flirtatious chide from Jane, and the rhythm of the guitar slows.

In her silent bedroom Mary listens. There, the gentle sound of kisses, soft as rainwater dripping from the trees. Mary runs a finger around the edge of her cup, and tilts her head; she notes that although the guitar slows, its player never quite lets the melody stop, and she cannot but admire Jane's skill. It is just the sort of tune that a pretty young girl ought to dance to. Surely, Mary will never dance again.

The door opens, and Mary is so startled by the intrusion of life into her sanctuary she drops her cup; it rattles into its saucer with great clink and clatter, a sluice of cold tea falling from safety onto Mary's robe, where it slowly bleeds out into an ambiguous shape.

"I am sorry," Shelley says from the door, "I didn't mean to make you jump."

Mary places cup and saucer upon the desk, and lays her hand

over the stain, feeling dampness beneath her fingers. The mark is somewhat like a rose in bloom.

Downstairs, another playful laugh from Jane, a last, singular kiss, and the guitar begins a new song with gusto. Ned says something distant and indistinct and his footsteps creak across the house.

Shelley leaves the doorway and comes to stand beside her desk. He is too tall there, looming over her.

"Mary," he says.

She looks up to him, his face is pained, his eyes anxious, needing.

"What is it?" she asks.

He stands there, turning an envelope in his hands, seeming to search for a way to say what he must.

"We've had a letter," he says.

How insufficient his voice is; it hardly overcomes the distant music.

"What letter?" she asks after some silence, to show that she is listening.

"From Byron." He turns the letter over, offers it out to her, and then, when she does not take it, folds his hands around it and attempts to smile. "Allegra has died."

Mary closes her eyes. In the safe darkness behind she puts the news off a moment more. It is words, only words. She waits for sadness, but finds only weariness. Another child, another casualty. God. Claire. She opens her eyes to Shelley. There are tears spilling down his cheeks. Were they there before?

"Has Claire been told?" she asks.

He shakes his head, and his shoulders shake. He swallows, composes himself.

"Not yet," he says through his emotion. "Byron thought the news would come better from us than in a letter from him."

Byron. He rises in Mary's mind. He has lost a child, too. And did he weep? Did he tear at his dark hair and strike out in anger at inanimate objects in need for vengeance? What sort of man is he really?

"What happened to her?" she asks.

"Apparently she took a fever. They thought she would recover but she declined quite suddenly."

"Just like Clara," she says.

"Mary!" Shelley drops to his knees and clasps at her hands.

She cannot summon the energy to return the pressure. She ought, she knows, to exhibit sadness, as he does, but she has lost the ability to act. Her heart commands stillness.

"Poor Clara," she says.

"Yes," Shelley nods. "Poor, poor Claire. I think," he says, "that we should go to the coast, just like Ned wanted, and ask Claire to come with us. We can find a large house for the five of us out there fairly cheaply. We tell her once we're there. This shouldn't be something we tell her and then leave her alone. She's going to need us."

"She will be miserable," Mary says, "but she will be furious too. At least I had my children while they were alive, poor things."

Shelley clears his throat, and lightly touches the stain on her robe. "She will be furious," he nods, "and I think," he wipes away the last of his tears, "we will need to be careful."

As he says this, Mary realises how, despite all his emotion, he is already being clever.

"You want to take her to the coast rather than bring her here so that she can't reach Byron."

"Can you imagine anything good coming from their meeting?" he replies placidly.

"No."

"And she'll be with those who love her best."

"Yes."

"But what about the Hunts?" Mary asks. "Don't you want to be in Pisa when they arrive?"

"That is still a few months away. Either we shall return when they arrive, or bring them up to us. It would be wise for Hunt and I to be close, and perhaps have Byron a slightly greater distance. I can't imagine he will be as involved with the minutiae as we shall both be. We will still see him often, of course." There shall be no play then.

"Of course," she echoes him. He has thought of everything, hasn't he?

"Mary, you have spilt your tea."

"I have."

"You should change."

"I'll get dressed soon."

"I think sea air might do us all good."

"Very well."

He is still looking at her with peculiar longing, but she cannot meet that look for long. She does not know how to return it, nor how to act beneath its gaze. He presses her hands once more. The letter is now crumpled in his hand, and Mary recognises Byron's writing.

"Should I leave you now?" Shelley whispers.

"Yes," she replies. "I shall get dressed soon and come through."

"Very well. I'll go talk to Ned and Jane, tell them what we know."

He gets to his feet. His shoulders bow, his head seems heavy. He looks exhausted, exhausted by this cruel life. Why do they persevere?

Chapter Three: Shut Out
San Terenzo, 10th June 1822

Shelley fixes on the bay of Spezia, although there is only one house to be found, one house not only for himself, Mary, Percy, and Claire, but for Ned, Jane, Medwin, and Rosalind too, not to mention the clutter of servants between the two families.

The house is *La Casa Magni*, a magnificent old building so close upon the shore that the sea laps at its feet, and indeed, they soon learn, creeps up over the doorstep and lets itself in, leaving when it goes a floor soft with sand, driftwood and, occasionally, small crabs. They live in the upper levels, and behind a high wall that protects their garden from the invasive sea. There are no other houses nearby. The nearest town is across the bay, and that has no English, no casino or play theatre, only peasants who dress roughly and speak a dialect alien to their learned Italian. Behind them, to the north and east, the mountains loom; away across the bay before them the distant tip of *Porto Venere* is outlined; to the south, simply open water stretching eternally.

At night, when the sea creeps into the house, Shelley imagines himself on a ship, and sometimes into his half-dreaming mind comes the conviction that the tide will never turn, but only rise, and rise, and swallow them all.

The house creaks dreadfully as the waves whisper ever closer, and Mary, who maintains her Pisan silence, haunts the white-washed corridors with mute introspection.

Shelley cannot stand it. But he doesn't have to. He and Ned

have a boat, one of their own design, and it is in this boat, more than in the echoing house, that Shelley lives.

Out in the open the sun's furious heat burns and there is no shade other than a broad-brimmed hat. Even the gulls retire in the height of the day, so that the ocean is a desert, an empty page on which Shelley draws wide arcs that linger before they turn for land. Just one more hour, he says to himself, ever postponing the moment when he must return and call out to Mary with dry, cracked voice, and she, more likely than not, will fail to return the call.

He wishes that Claire would sail with them. The fury at her loss of Allegra was passionate, but brief, and she has returned to them much more a woman than when she left. She works at her writing and sits often with Mary, scowling at Shelley and the Williamses. Shelley hardly knows her now.

Ned comes with him most days, though he only learns his madness from Shelley. They lend each other books, and Shelley reads Ned passages of particular importance, and tells him stories of the devil and demons of this world.

And often Ned brings Jane, and Jane brings the guitar that Shelley bought her in Pisa and weaves her melodious tunes upon the deck.

"You will like this, Shelley," she says, as the tips of her fingers step *en pointe* across the strings.

"Will I?"

They are drift easily away from shore, the land and the house only half-remembered by the horizon.

"I have written some music, a simple song." She talks as she plays, her ear tilted towards the instrument. "Although the words are not mine, but another's." The expression she raises to him is as warming as the sun's rays, and so full of encouragement and care, he knows that she is about to sing one of his poems to him, though he does not know which.

> *The fountains mingle with the river,*
> *And the rivers with the ocean;*
> *The winds of heaven mix forever*
> *With a sweet emotion;*

Nothing in the world is single;
All things by a law divine
In another's being mingle –
Why not I with thine?

A musical laugh brings him back to the present movement, drifting through the waves, and he looks over to see Ned emerging from the kiss he has laid on Jane's neck with an unrestrained grin. What bliss is theirs!

And then he begins to write, addressing Ned Williams with a poem that says that which he cannot speak: that he is the serpent cast out of paradise, that he is the widowed dove, that he who once knew love is left now forlorn.

Therefore, if now I see you seldomer,
Dear friends, dear friend! know that I only fly
Your looks, because they stir
Griefs that should sleep, and hopes that cannot die:
The very comfort that they minister
I scarce can bear, yet I,
So deeply is the arrow gone,
Should quickly perish if it were withdrawn.

When I return to my cold home, you ask
Why I am not as I have ever been.
YOU spoil me for the task
Of acting a forced part in life's dull scene, –
Of wearing on my brow the idle mask
Of author, great or mean,
In the world's carnival. I sought
Peace thus, and, but in you, I found it not.

He snaps the book shut.
Mary must not see this one.

Mary does not sleep these days. She approaches the sixth month of her pregnancy, and cannot shake the feeling that this one is wrong. It cannot end well; surely she will die.

Nights are strange here. While the moon is high her eyes must be wide, so she walks around the house at Livorno. Room after room her bare feet tread. And every turn she takes, every doorway she steps through, she is certain that there was *something* she was looking for, although she never remembers what it was. Still, she feels that if she continues searching, her purpose will return to her. The house enables her nocturnal wanderings with a forgiving silence. No floorboard nor hinge creaks to betray her. All the house is asleep.

Shelley created a witch, a mad, ethereal thing, for a poem. *This lady never slept*–his line torments her. Shelley's line dances round her head as she rises from the curtained bed. His Witch. She lay in fountains and viewed the world through waterfalls. Perhaps that is all Mary is doing. Existing in some half-waking world, for at night time she does see clearer. She is untroubled by her friends, their irritations and requests.

Even the nights here are warm, so she wears nothing but her nightdress, a simple long white gown, and enjoys the cool air upon her arms and ankles. It is strange, but she feels freer here in the empty night than she does in the long days that drag her down with their weighty hours.

Her steps lead her to the study, which she enters without intent, slowly scanning the night scene with a gaze only remotely curious. The moonlight is so bright she scarcely needs the candle she carries. Poor Shelley's eyes are beginning to fade, and he has left the shutters open to admit all the light he can get. He complains to her often of his failing eyes and the pain in his side, and talks nothing of poetry.

Coming to Shelley's desk, she draws the candle down to spread its light upon the pages. She does not recognise any of the lines there, and even the subjects are unfamiliar to her. Once they would talk of such things. How long has it been? They have not spoken of writing all the time they have been here. Aware that she ought to feel some guilt at prying, but finding none in her own heart, she sifts through the pages.

A *dramatis personae*; an act one, scene one; King Charles; Queen Henrietta; Bastwick; Laud, the Archbishop...

So he is writing the tragedy on Charles I, the one he so long ago encouraged her to write. Why had she not written it at the time? No doubt something else was occupying her. It had been her father's idea, hadn't it... well, her father's idea for a subject, Shelley's idea to make it a drama. And now at last Shelley was writing it— another historical play after *The Cenci*! But this time he has not asked her help, her advice on plotting, her guidance in research. He broaches it alone.

'*I am not averse / From the assembling of a parliament*,' the archbishop says, '*are these not a bubble fashioned by a monarch's mouth*.' The argument falls heavily from governor to governor. Ah, but here a Shakespearean fool to lighten the scene. He is part-way there.

A sudden heat sears her hand as a drop from the angled candle misses its saucer and lands upon her skin. Biting her lip, she puts the paper back, anxious not to mark Shelley's papers with testament of her trespass.

She withdraws from the desks, troubled by the discovery. Of course Shelley is working on something. He almost always is. And often he keeps the work private until finished. All this is perfectly reasonable. And yet.

And yet she is saddened.

In the window pane her face reflects back at her, lunar pale, and she fixes upon the image of her own eyes. How large and glassy they seem, like crystal balls that show nothing whatever question is put to them. Her eyes clouding while his darken. Is this how they are to live their evening years?

Evening years! They are neither of them yet passed the age of thirty.

The thought enters her mind sharp and clear to lodge in her quiet consciousness. If he should slip away entirely? Would she have the strength to reach out for him, to hold him fast?

But what if she should be taken from him by the coming child? Others would take care of him, would love him and protect him as his age blinds him. But must she leave him as a stranger?

Beyond her reflection the ocean sighs, upon its surface a thousand fragments of moonlight shift and shimmer, but beneath, an eternity of inky blackness. A thin edge of fear grows within Mary as she stares out, for it suddenly seems to her that all the horror of her life is concealed beneath that thin beautiful layer of brightness in the dark fathoms of the ocean. Some deep, irrational part of her wants to run to the sea, to scream into the water, to draw out her suffering from its depths... but she knows the water would fall through her frantic fingers, and she would be left cold and useless on the shore in her nightdress.

She pushes open the window and the loveliness of the night ushers in around her. A soft throb of night insects in the trees, the steady breath of the ocean, and the sweet call of a lone aziola owl.

All of a sudden she spies something that shuts everything else from her mind, a lone figure she did not see before—and surely, surely, it is Shelley. But perhaps it is the darkness playing tricks? There is certainly *someone*—a slim phantasmal figure trailing its feet in the wave-wash, neither quite on the land nor in the sea. It must be Shelley. She leans closer, but her breath fogs the glass and she wipes it hastily with her bare palm. He is looking up, whoever he is, but with the moon directly behind him his face is lost to the shadows. Still, there is something darkly cavernous about the sallow cheeks and the hollows where the eyes must be. Whoever it is, they are staring right at her.

Mary holds up a hand in an uncertain wave. Does he see her? The head lowers, and he walks on along the sea's edge. She shudders—the night is growing cold after all. He walks slowly through the surf, his slender shoulders undulating.

No, he must not have seen her. His mind is set on higher things, as if she were not even there. As if she were a ghost. As she watches him slink away into the night Mary hugs herself tight, seeking reassurance from the comfort of her own flesh.

Chapter Four: Rivalling the Sun
San Terenzo, 11th June 1822

"*H*ave you had any sleep?" Claire asks the next day.

Mary, sitting at her desk, is mid-yawn. She shakes her head. All she has managed this morning is to read the page over and over, and no new words have come.

Such is the heat even the words on the page waver before Mary's eyes. Letting her lids fall the second she lays her fingers to her temples. Mary arches her back and the bones in her neck click.

She has tried to sleep, but cannot; she has splashed cold water upon herself, but the murk upon her mind will not stir. Writing waits on the page, looped and slanted, neater for the effort it has cost her. It is only a short story, something for *The Liberal*, drawing on all the research she undertook for *Castruccio*, a delineation of human passions in a time of war, uncertainty, fear. The brave Despina has just revealed herself from her male disguise before Lostendardo. Though he loved her with all his heart, Mary is coming to the conclusion that he will have to kill her.

"I'm getting nowhere with this today," she says.

Looking out the window she sees the boat is still on the shore, its sailors playing upon the land. Ned and the boy manoeuvre the coracle they have been making to trail behind the *Ariel*, and near them Shelley sits beside Jane, talking animatedly to her. It is odd to see him on land in the day. He is like a child with this new toy. And an unquiet child too, one that runs wind-maddened out of doors when it ought to be still.

"How is your work?" Mary turns her attention to Claire. "Are you still working on your Goethe translation?"

"Yes," Claire replies, sitting back in her chair. "Thought I'd better have something to do. It distracts the mind."

It certainly does, Mary knows.

"And does it progress?" Mary asks. "It's really worth working on. I was very impressed by what you sent us in Pisa."

"Hmm," is Claire's only response. The compliment goes unheeded. "It goes on well enough. Are you going down to the beach?"

"The beach? I wasn't planning to."

"Well you should. Before it gets too hot. We could go see what Shelley is up to."

"I suppose we could," Mary replies vaguely. Claire is being opaque, as ever, and Mary is always wary of being entangled in her schemes.

"Good. We'll go now." And with that Goethe is snapped shut, his elegancies forgotten. She is at once on her feet, and chivvying Mary.

Claire looks striking in a white dress, her black hair only half tied up. As she throws a shawl imperfectly around her shoulders, trapping the loose curls, Mary intervenes to lay the ringlets over the white cotton.

"Thank you, Mary," Claire says, with unusual gentleness. "Now come along, let's see if we can tear our Shelley away from Jane Williams for half an hour."

The brusqueness returns and Claire marches on ahead. Mary shakes her head fondly but follows all the same.

"Doesn't it worry you?" Claire says as they pass through the hall. Claire strides ahead and turns sharply at the top of the stairs to fire back an accusatory look. "How much time he spends with her?"

"No," Mary replies, simply, and lets herself be scrutinised.

The owlish intensity in Claire's face softens. "Why not?" The question carries neither surprise nor exasperation, but a tone of bewilderment.

"I thought you were the first subscriber to all that talk of free love and liberty?"

"We're not sixteen anymore," Claire says.

"I didn't realise it was a child's game," Mary replies calmly. "I am aware when Shelley's head is turned. But the thing that never changes is that he will always be mine, as I will always be his. And it's sweet that you worry about me, but you needn't." She slips past Claire and begins to make her slow way down the stairs. "Besides," she calls back, "my skin is tough."

"Jane says you're too cold towards him." Claire's voice rushes down after Mary, making her stop, look back. Claire is as still as the bust at the banister head. "I know you're not. I know she just doesn't know you both. But... sometimes... just occasionally... you could be more... warmer." She ends with a shrug and an anxious glance.

"Jane says..." Mary chuckles. "You were Jane once." Claire's face is impassive. "I appreciate your concern, but Shelley knows I love him. And Shelley is an exceptional man. People will always love him, as well they ought. And he has such an enormous capacity for love, he will always want to love them back. It is his nature. I assure you there is nothing I can do that will stop either of those things from happening. Jane worships him, and you know as well as I that she is not the first to do so. Do you want me to worship him like that?"

Claire wrinkles her nose but says nothing, slowly beginning her descent.

"I can't," Mary goes on, "because I know him. He is not a God, he is a man, albeit an extraordinary man. And I love him. Worship is not love. It is an evanescent thing. I will not debase myself to be what I am not. Or would you rather I chased them from him? Forbade his childish whims and made myself his enemy? He granted me a lover once, confident that I would always love him above all others. Now it is for me to do the same."

Side by side now they cross the sand-swept lower floor in silence. Claire is absorbed in her own thoughts, and Mary feels a rare kinship, a gratitude to her sister, for a kindness, if an unnecessary one. As they pass into the outside a wave of heat washes over them. She raises a hand to shield herself from the brightness and changes the subject.

"I'm glad you're continuing to work on that translation. You

ought to dedicate yourself quite seriously to it. You have a real apti-
tude, Claire."

"I am working seriously," Claire says, but somewhat dutifully,
uninterestedly.

"I mean it. You really write very nicely, you have more talent
than you know."

Claire puts her hand to her chest as if flattered. "Why, *thank
you* Mrs Shelley! Thank you, Oh-author-of-*Frankenstein*, for your
boon! I blush at your kind words."

Mary shoots her a withering glance.

"Serves me right for being nice to you. If you're going to
mock—"

"No, Mary. You say I have more talent than I know. It is possible I am not the one who is underestimating my abilities. I certainly
have more talent than Byron knows, and everyone takes what Byron
says as gospel, despite his barbarous nature, his lack of care, his
inability to love even his own child." Claire stops abruptly, seeming
to gather herself.

The pebble stones slide beneath their feet as they proceed
towards the distant boat.

"Byron knocked me down a long time ago, but don't think I'm
still that sensitive." Claire shakes back her hair. "But I should rather
like to show him. Shelley thinks if I finish it I ought to publish
it anonymously, but that simply wouldn't do. It's going to Byron,
and it's going to Byron with my name on it and if he wants to read
Goethe and feel some kindred of genius he's going to have to do so
through me."

There is a glorious defiance in Claire's voice, and Mary sees
that familiar passion set to purpose, and feels it is finally formidable.

As they approach the beach, the scene has changed; Jane is
now sat in the finished coracle, and Ned and Vivian are pulling
the little boat along the sand at a run. Shelley has wandered away
by himself a little toward the shade of the garden wall, where he is
inspecting some stray lichen that trails along the rocks.

Claire strides towards Jane and the others but casts a glance
back at Mary and tilts her head to Shelley. Mary nods back, and
slowly makes her way towards her husband.

He is absorbed, apparently, in the minutia before him, but no doubt in truth by his internal visions. Mary scuffs the ground to make her tread audible as she approaches, and at once he drops his ponderous attitude and adopts a welcoming demeanour in her direction.

"Now," she says to him, "what ails my elfin knight, thus wandering the sands, alone and palely loitering?"

He holds out his arm to her.

"What can ail him indeed?" he echoes, and she slides nicely against him, looping her arm through his.

"Will you walk with me?" she asks. "If I'm not keeping you from your loitering."

"I'm sure I can return to it later. But you mustn't be too much out in the heat."

"As if there were anything but heat here now! Come, we can wander around the garden wall. There's a nice path through the trees."

They walk arm in arm, quietly at first, along the rough grass that borders the pebbled beach. When they reach the end of the garden wall, Mary guides them around its corner, away from the sea, and up a gentle slope where trees of olive, ilex and cypress grow intermittently, providing occasional, dappled shade. The weight of the forming baby slows her; it is heavier than any before, but not in a way that suggests strength and good fortune. Like a stone. A great stone inside her that will pull her down, drag her into darkness.

Shelley matches her pace.

"I'm glad to have you to myself for a moment," Shelley says, his thumb stroking the back of her hand firmly and repeatedly. "I actually do need to talk to you about your father."

"My father? Oh dear." Mary sighs heavily. To walk without words was nice; it is too hot and she is too tired for serious conversation. Nonetheless she asks, "Is there news?"

"Yes, via Mrs Mason. If I'm completely honest, we had a letter some weeks ago, while you were not very well. I didn't want to add to your worry at that moment." He speaks with caution. "His financial situation is somewhat worse."

Such Mary anticipated. "How much worse?"

"He has lost a lawsuit." Shelley's nervous glance moves from the ground before them to Mary's face and back again. "They have had to leave the house on Skinner Street. I am unsure what their new living arrangements will be; he has given a false name at a temporary address to write to. I believe his creditors are after him."

"My poor father." The memory of the bailiffs at that awful little apartment comes back to Mary now. It was horrible then, but she was young and so confident of a different future, as the young always are. To be in that situation now would be dreadful, and for her father... she can imagine his indignation, his wounded pride.

"What can we do?" She asks the question though struck by her own impotence. From this distance she is wretched; even were she closer, could she do anything? The only person they know with money is Byron, and they have already asked a lot of him for this magazine.

"Has he sold my manuscripts?" she asks.

"I believe not."

"Neither of them? He should have the novel of *Castruccio* by now, and he still has *Matilda*."

Shelley shakes his head. "He did not mention them."

Despite her distress on her father's behalf, she feels a flush of irritation with him.

"Why does he not sell them?" she mutters. "I have written two perfectly good novels, and I have granted him permission to publish, even to edit, them—and to take all the money himself, that is my filial duty unto him. And yet he does nothing, helping neither himself nor me. But, quite honestly, I didn't send them to him so that they could be locked away in his desk drawer. If he won't sell them he should at least return them to me."

Shelley does not break his ponderous stride, but murmurs an assent. Still his thumb rubs against her hand in a way that has long stopped being pleasant. His physical presence is all that is here of him, and even that seems somehow uncertain to Mary.

It is as if they are both walking this path at different times, centuries apart, and only by hallucination do they appear to be together. She lays her other hand upon the weight in her stomach. Perhaps it has already claimed her, and this is the dream of the dying, the haunting before death.

She shakes her head. "When you write to him," she says, "tell him he *must* sell them. That is why I sent them to him. I realise that he—" she handles the word delicately, "objects to *Matilda*. But there is nothing objectionable in *Castruccio*. It will sell." She has spoken frankly in the agitation about her father, but realises at once she has hit a sore spot. Shelley smiles sympathetically.

"It would of course sell if the public had any taste. You know I think it's wonderful."

He is attempting to prepare her for the disappointment he has faced; she accepts his sympathy and does not push the point. But she knows what will sell, and she knows—and has tried to tell him—why his poems do not sell, that it has nothing to do with his genius, and that with just a little pandering he could have quite the audience. But she knows from experience he will not comprehend. By the sounds of it, *Frankenstein* is doing well back in England.

"I did write back," he says, "reiterating exactly what you said about *Castruccio* before, and that he may edit it. Although, and you must forgive me here, I applied my own caveat." He has become at once coy, like a child confessing to the stealing of a sweet. "That in whatever edits he should make he must do nothing to the scenes with your Beatrice in them." He turns upon her his boyish grin, and, as they have come to the place where the trees grow too thick and the path fades into the grass, he turns about and offers his other arm. "She is such a magnificent character," he goes on. "You know how I love *Frankenstein*, but it has nothing like Beatrice. You have made me love her, and that is quite a feat."

Ah! Now here they are at last in the same place, the same moment in time once again!

"It is not that much of a feat, you are very open-hearted, Shelley," Mary says, in a tone that is half reproach, half appreciation. He loves all things, all people, all nature, and that is why she loves him.

He looks about.

"I have not been here before. I did not know there was such a wood so close." It is indeed a lovely woodland. The shade allows a thick green moss to grow around the roots of the trees, and the insects that flutter beneath the leaves buzz softly.

"How did we get here?" Shelley asks. "I haven't been paying attention."

Mary smiles, because he makes her think of Dante wandering from the path, and as they slowly make their way back, she recites.

Io non so ben ridir com' i' v'intrai,
tant' era pien di sonno a quel punto
che la verace via abbandonai.

"One must be careful where one wanders," he says, his eyes now heavenwards to the canopy. Mary looks ahead for roots that might trip him, and silently guides them.

The cicadas hum out of sight, and in the high boughs the little owl calls to its mate. The lovely softness of the woodland reassures her.

"Listen," she says. "Do you hear the aziola's cry?"

Shelley flinches and looks around him. "Who? I don't think I could take company today."

"No," she says, very gently, and draws him near to her. "The aziola. It's the local name for the little owl."

He half laughs at himself, and raises his head to listen. Obligingly the owl calls out her plaintive call once more.

"Isn't that beautiful?" Mary says.

They both look to the branches, but can see no sign of the creature.

"I've heard it before," he says. "An aziola?"

"Yes."

"She sounds sad."

"Yes."

He presses her hand, and they walk on. Up ahead, another owl calls its answers.

Perhaps, Mary thinks, they could be as once they were.

"What are you writing now?" she asks.

"Me?" He returns to the earth. "Nothing. I think I have lived too long near Lord Byron and the sun has extinguished the glow worm."

"You mustn't feel so."

"And yet I do. It is no matter."

"You must have something for our magazine. Hunt will be here soon, and then we must all have something."

"There will be something lying around, I'm sure. These days... the words don't always come as they once did. It's strange."

They come once more to the edge of the woods, to the unsheltered beach where their friends are laughing in the sands. There is more to say, more to tell Shelley, to confess she has seen his play, to encourage its improvement. Evening should be closing in, but the sun, though, is still bright. Mary recoils from the shadeless sands, from the wavering heat, from the pain inside her.

"I'm going to go inside and lie down a while," she says. He frees her arm, and stays where he is while she walks away. When she glances back over her shoulder he is still there, standing straight, watching her go. She gives a little wave and he heads down to the beach and to the boats.

Chapter Five: Ariel
San Terenzo, 14th June 1822

Sometimes Shelley sails alone, though everyone says the boat needs at least two to man it. He can manage. He sails alone, and he sails late into the evening. There is a particular blissful quiet out on the water as the light dims, and the loveliest lull comes upon the motion of the boat.

There are moments of clarity upon the waves, and moments of despair upon the earth. Perhaps he was born in the wrong form. To draw the boat up on the shore and, alighting, land on the pertinacious stones after the sweet suppleness of the water sends displeasure ricocheting through him. The hour is late, and he must go home at last. His steps are slow as the stones beneath him shudder and shift, drawing him down amongst them.

Light slips from the high dome of the sky, and the sea grows dark. Across the heavens a thin sigh of gold cloud drifts, a last beauty as the sun sinks into the sea, a brief testament that it has been which shall likewise be lost unto the shades of night.

Up ahead the house is a cavity on the beach where the shadows gather to murmur out their grief. A faint light glimmers from a window. Shelley stops and, turning his back upon the house, looks longingly at the sea, at the faint light on the far horizon. If only all this led somewhere, he would follow.

His eye is caught by a tall, thin fellow out along the shoreline, standing still and appearing to watch him. Shelley lowers his gaze to avoid any connection, for that gaze, he feels without knowing why, is hostile. Desire to escape this stranger's scrutiny sets him on again towards the house, but the stones are less obliging even than before and slide beneath his feet so that one long step ushers him back further from the house, and he struggles to gain any progress.

The rocks here are worn smooth by a hundred years in the ocean and a hundred more clamouring amongst their fellows on the shore. In one step his foot sinks into their masses, and he feels their reassuring weight press down upon it. Would it not be nice to lie down on such a beach and rest the heavy stones upon one's body.

Glancing up he sees the stranger suddenly quite close and drawing nearer, stepping with light untroubled step, and always, though his face is hidden from Shelley by the shade that drapes across it, keeping him firmly in sight.

As Shelley looks up, a slow, terrible certainty creeps over him, and he longs with all his heart to look away, yet knows there is no power on this earth that can keep him from what he must see.

The coat and shirt he knows well, even the tear upon the cuff is intimately familiar; the slender hands have acted at his behest a thousand times; the pointed chin, the long nose, the large, hooded eyes that glare right back at him... all these are his own. His breath stops for a second and then floods, rattling through his throat as if he would cry, would weep here, at last, face to face with himself.

But the other is sombre and serious, looking at him with something a little like pity, but more like regret.

"Come, Bysshe," he says, in just his very own voice. "How long do you intend to be content?"

It is far, far too much, and Shelley collapses to his knees with an anguished cry, a sudden wound torn upon his heart. The sound pouring out of him is wild; it keens out into the air where it claims every mite of dust and drifting debris and storms them all back down upon him. He bows further to the ground, the sobs rasping from within him, as the pale double stands tall and erect by him. Shelley lays his face upon the smooth stones, finds his hands pushing deeper into their midst.

Content? How could he be content with this? With this house and all it holds... To be caught every day between the love of Jane

Williams and the success of Byron and to have none of it himself. To have only Mary's coldness. To have written piles of poems and plays that no one will ever read. He and all that is his could burn and who would lament him?

He curls tighter, deeper into the stones as his sobbing subsides, and the cool quiet air returns to drape its evening hush around him. He draws breath in. He swallows deeply. His forehead still rests upon the ground, and as he heaves himself up he shamefully wipes away the tears and spittle that have dampened his face and the earth.

The other is gone.

Bysshe is entirely alone, a crying child upon the shore.

He drags himself up once more, and still sobbing, staggers towards the house.

Out across the sea the last ember of light within the cloud glows and dies, leaving behind a colourless dusk.

16th June, 1822

The heart can only speak its desire so many times before, regretful of the boon it receives not, it hides away its longing. He asks Mary once, and twice, and thrice again, to sail with him, but always her brow clouds and her countenance turns pale.

"Not today, Shelley."

But one morning, already hot with the sun's fury, while readying the boat and all upon it, he looks up and sees across the sands with white parasols and white-gloved hands, Claire and Mary heading his way.

They lift a small kite of delight within him.

"Are you coming with us?" he asks.

"Yes, please!" Claire calls back. They pick their way slowly, Mary holding her sister's arm, and Claire, half watching her slipping feet, half grinning up at him.

"Ned, Jane!" he calls out. "We have two more sailors!"

As they board, the atmosphere on deck changes.

As ever Jane sits sweetly in the prow, picking a melody from the guitar upon her lap. Ned mans the rudder, but he has his book with him too.

"Perhaps we can make music together, Claire," Jane says. "I hear you are a remarkable singer."

"Well, I shall sing and you may play along if you like to."

But Claire does not sing, and neither does Jane, she only picks the notes gently and idly.

Shelley opens his notebook and lets his gaze soften across the open sea. It drifts lightly over the waves, each briefly crested for a single moment with a perfect pearl of sunlight; it roves back to the distant sands where the house stands white and mute, certain in the knowledge of their return. Mary sits with face raised to the clear sky and eyes closed, one raised hand holds her hat in place. A phrase he wrote long ago winnows through his mind.

Listen, listen, Mary mine, to the whisper of the Apennine.

"Oh, listen, listen, Mary mine," he murmurs beneath his breath. If it is an incantation, it works, for though she is too far to hear, her heavy eyelids open.

"How are you feeling?" he asks. "Not too sickly?"

She does not shake her head but twists her mouth demurely, a gesture he has come to know well.

"Come sit with me."

He holds out his hand as she approaches, and he steadies her. But rather than sit beside him on the bench she sinks to the deck, sweeps off her hat and lays her head upon his knees.

He lets his hand lay upon her head. The parasol she brought is now left with Claire, and the gauzy strands beneath his hand are already hot. Her weight against his leg is warm and comforting like a newborn baby. They will have a new baby soon. Another life. Perhaps a little girl. Perhaps they will become something of a family again.

She is neither talking, nor looking at him, but he feels close to her once more.

It was just like this, with her curled up against his legs, that they crossed the Channel in 1814. How magnificent that liberty had felt, but how frightening too, her slim shoulders clenched, her head held low in a vicious sickness so foul she could not speak. The sea had been so wild he had reconciled himself to death, to death by her side. And she was sixteen, running away from home. How frightened she must have been, and how brave.

On a stray impulse he unclasps her hair and teases it out of its coils with his fingertips.

"What are you doing?" she asks, but softly, with a smile in her voice.

"Your neck's getting sun-burnt," he replies and draws her hair out and around her like a curtain.

She makes a small noise—a 'hmm' that says she does not believe him, but also that she doesn't mind so much—and he bends to kiss the top of her head. He lets his hand slip beneath that cascade, gently strokes her hot skin. Against his knee he feels her gently nestle.

By his side his notebook still lies open, and lazily he lets his thoughts peruse the fragments he has jotted for his poem. It is to be a descent into the underworld of sorts, with Rousseau for his guide where Dante had Virgil. It is to be called *The Triumph of Life* he decides, and as he starts to sketch some lines out, his free hand weaves through Mary's hair, and her arm winds around his leg.

He envisions the multitudes of men, as numerous as leaves clinging to the sky-concealing canopy within the forest. All scurry, some fleeing what they fear the most, some hastening towards an-other's fear. And amidst them all, himself, watching, aghast, at the madness of humanity.

Sitting curled up at his feet, Mary feels his fingers through her hair, senses from the patter of fingertips against her skull how pleased he is to have her near.

But the weight within her is vast and cold.

This child will kill her. She knows it with absolute certainty. And poor Shelley will be left alone. It is kind, she thinks, to give him these moments of comfort. He will remember them when she is gone.

Chapter Six: Blood
La Spezzia, 16th June 1822

Shelley's dreams that night are wild and terrible, full of strange phantasms and haunted by an awful screaming. From these nightmares he is woken by Claire shaking him.

"Shelley," she says, an urgency in her haste. "Shelley! Wake up!"

He tries to orient himself. It is dark. Claire is a white ghost before him, eyes glittering in the half-light, strange dark marks streaked across her nightdress, and the agonised groaning of his dreams has crept into the waking air.

"What is it? What's happened?" he asks, afraid to know the answer.

"It's Mary," Claire whispers.

He forces himself out of his sleep haze.

"Mary? What has happened to Mary?"

He scrambles from the sofa where he had fallen asleep. The blanket he had pulled around himself for comfort tries to ensnare him now and he kicks violently at it, all the while hearing Claire's hushed, frightened explanation—*the baby—bleeding—in so much pain.* Shelley lurches clear and staggers across the threshold, down the corridor, to Mary's room, where lights are burning, and Jane, wrapped in her rose-embroidered dressing gown, is standing hesitantly beside the bed. There is a large dark stain of blood upon the disordered bedclothes. In the middle of the blood lies Mary, shuddering, her eyes fixed upon the ceiling, her face set in the resolute agony reserved for the Christ.

Shelley falls to his knees by the bed, takes her hand in his, strokes back the damp hair from her face. She turns her grey eyes upon him with the effort of Sisyphus, her dry lips tremble wordlessly, but she squeezes his hand.

"The doctor?" he asks in a hoarse whisper.

"Already sent for," Claire replies from the doorway.

The doctor does not come.

The servants gather in the doorway, peering in anxiously. Shelley hears them whisper.

"*La Signora Shelley sta morendo.*
Poveretta. Pace alla sua anima."

Ned brings Shelley and Claire dressing gowns to keep them warm, and at Shelley's request brings brandy for Mary to stop her slipping out of consciousness. She is exhausted and pained. She does not speak, but utters awful, strangled shrieks.

After an hour she delivers a still-born babe.

The foetus is not quite as long as Shelley's hand. Its head is bizarrely big for its body, the un-opening eyes ghastly bulbous, the thin eyelids bluish in hue. Shelley takes it away quietly, wraps it up in a blood-soaked towel; it will be quietly buried in the morning.

He returns to the labour room, to Mary's half-weeping groans. Blood is pouring from her, and as fast as they can bring a cloth to stem the flow that cloth is drenched. Her skin is paler than any Shelley has seen on a living soul. Why will the doctor not come?

There is ice. It is the only thing he can think of, and at once he is running, shouting on the servants, to follow him, to fetch a bathtub, to break up the ice, to hurry, hurry!

Jane's tearful voice breaks through the commotion.

"I think we should wait for the doctor."

But what the hell does Jane know? He moves swiftly, and always Claire is beside him, acting to his instruction, though tears may be rolling down her face.

"Mary mine, my Mae." He comes to the bed, and as gently as he can slides his arms beneath her. "I'm going to lift you now, my love, we're going to put you in the ice, to stop the bleeding. Do you understand?"

She does not reply. She cannot reply. Her head lolls against his shoulder as he lifts her.

Everyone scuttles about them as he carries her over, their hands hovering where they might be of use; towels, not fresh, but now rinsed, are held at the ready. As he lowers her into the ice Mary gasps from a new pain, but her teeth shut down hard as her shaking hands reach out for the edges of the tub. He leaves one arm around her, so that her head can lean back on him.

"There now, my good Mary, my clever girl, you can come through this. How much you've suffered, how much strength you have!"

Her eyes, open once more, rove slowly round and fix on him. There is a request there he can read as plain as it were writ upon her face in ink: *Shelley,* she is saying, *Let me go.*

His breath catches as he takes it in, and he brushes back her hair, as tenderly as if they were sailing out on the boat once more.

"No," he whispers. "I am not ready to let you go yet," he says, subduing the tremor in his voice. "Stay strong, my Mary, for me. I still need you."

Her eyes close, her brow contracted in pain.

She drifts in and out of consciousness, and within an hour the bleeding stops, and he is able to lift her out, take her to a clean bed. She curls round with shuddering groan, drawing her legs up to her stomach. He lies down beside her, his body a shadow around hers, and he watches her as she slips into fitful sleep.

It is almost dawn by the time the doctor arrives. He looks over the scene, examines Mary, talks to them all. He commends Shelley for his actions. There is very little to do now. The worst has passed.

Chapter Seven: Shadows Upon Glass
La Spezzia, 22nd June 1822

*M*ary lies in bed, lifting her lashes very rarely and seeing the room gauzy-veiled, passing through different lights, different shades, different worried faces. Time loses shape.

"What day is it?" she asks, not knowing who is there to answer.

"Saturday," says Claire.

"Saturday," Mary repeats. What day *was* it? She can't recall. "Where is Percy?"

"In the nursery with the nurse, where he should be. He is well."

As she tries to move, pain sears through her, and she groans out loud.

"This will be the death of me," she grumbles as she finds a position where the pain is lessened.

"You'll be better in no time."

Claire comes into focus, her white dress, her dark hair, the linens held in her arms.

"I don't know." Mary slides herself up, just a little, and pushes back the quilt. "There's something mysterious about this place, and I really feel I shall never get away from it, that this bay will hold me here."

"That's foolish talk," Claire says brusquely, tugging at the counterpane around Mary.

"I was about to escape," Mary says, pained at the realisation. "We're supposed to be going to Pisa in a few days. I'm hardly going now, am I?"

"No, you're certainly not."

Beneath them the southeast wind, the *scirocco* rushes through the ruined half of the house.

"I hate this place," Mary murmurs, and closes her eyes against it all. In the darkness behind her eyelids is a dark world that she can almost, *almost* drift away into. To sleep, to sleep away all the ache, would be nice. A kiss upon her forehead, light, sweet, brings her back to the world of light, and her opened eyes look with surprise upon her sister. Claire is looking down, patient, concerned, and sits then upon the bed, taking Mary's hand in her own.

"You've to get better, d'you hear me? Get better and not sink into gloom. You've got the whole world. Alright, you hate this place, and you're sick now, but you'll get better and you and Shelley will move on. The whole world, Mary. Where will you go?"

"I don't know."

"Where would you want to go? To Greece?"

"Oh Greece! I should love to go to Greece. To Constantinople... Beyond..." The world seems impossibly far away to her. "Do you think we'll go, Claire? Do you think we will ever manage to leave this house?"

"Of course you will. You two never stay in one place long. Talk to Shelley, plant the seeds now and they'll be ready for harvest in the spring, you know what he's like." Claire's smile slips. "But I'm not sure I'll be going with you. I think I'm to go back to Florence for a while."

Mary frowns, she wants to say something, to assure Claire that she is always welcome, that she will always be with them... but it isn't quite true. It has never been quite true.

"You must always be strong for me, Mary," Claire says. "We won't always be together, but I'd hate to lose you. We've both lost too much."

For a moment they say nothing, for only silence can acknowledge what is lost.

"You never talk about Allegra," Mary murmurs.

Claire sticks out her jaw, thoughtful, but not sad. "I have lost my only daughter," she says. "The only one I ever had and perhaps the only one I will ever have. I was not much of a mother to her.

You would never have let any of yours leave you. In an awful way I think it for the best. Is that very wicked of me? I am absolved now. But you... You are a good mother. Percy will be your comfort, right into your old age."

Mary shakes her head, fearful that such a sentiment will tempt the cruelty of fate. Claire continues.

"And that's why you have to cling to Shelley, you see. The man you love loves you back, don't underestimate that. I've never had such luxury." Her voice is dry, level, but there is a firm set to her jaw that suggests her speech is difficult to her, so Mary stays quiet. "I never told you," Claire goes on, "that in Florence I heard about an old acquaintance of ours. Do you remember Polidori?"

"I do," Mary says, alarmed by the turn of subject.

"Apparently there was some unpleasantness with the vampire story he wrote; someone published it under Byron's name. There was a lot of arguing and a lawsuit, and of course Albe said some pretty disparaging things about him. He had a lot of debts, took to gambling as I understand it. It's all such a damn shame. Anyway, he shot himself in the end."

Mary's mouth falls open but before she can speak a timid knock interrupts, and the door sneaks open, the young maid Editta peering around.

"*Scusi, i letti Signora?*"

"No thank you!" Claire says, louder than necessary, and the girl bows her way out.

Mary eases herself up. "Is that true, about poor Polidori?" she asks, knowing full well it is not the matter for a lie. Claire shrugs.

"He was a nice young man as I recall," she says. "Had a bit of a soft spot for you, though they all do, don't they?"

Polidori's face insists itself upon Mary's mind, his black eyes and dark hair, and in her memory he is waving from a high window, about to fly. Tears well up behind her eyes, but they are not enough to fall. He is too far in her past, though it was only a few years. Poor Polidori. That's another one.

"I sometimes wonder if it is worse to die or to be left behind?"

Shelley has a bedroom of his own across the house, where he does not disturb Mary's recuperation. He has not yet left the bedroom, but sits disconsolately at the dressing table, gazing out the window to where the *Ariel* ought to be. The boat is sent away for minor repairs, leaving him land-locked and chastened. It is a penance, he feels, as if his wings had been clipped.

Instead of sailing he must stay earthbound, and stare at the works that will not do what he wants.

His *Triumph of Life* is troubling him. He argues with Rousseau in it, asking for the great Monarchs of time gone by to be discarded and forgotten.

'The world and its mysterious doom
Is not so much more glorious than it was,
That I desire to worship those who drew
New figures on its false and fragile glass
As the old faded.'

But easily Rousseau replies:

'Figures ever new
Rise on the bubble, paint them as you may;
We have but thrown, as those before us threw,
Our shadows on it as it passed away.

'Much I grieved to think how power and will
In opposition rule our mortal day,
And why God made irreconcilable
Good and the means of good.'

In this argument he finds his own falsehoods, his own fears looming large. Has he too not been trampled by life? In his short years he has reached, as Prometheus reached, and has dared to hope that the world could be better, but what has that given him? Nothing. He is an exile from his homeland. No one shall ever read his words. He will die alone in the dark depths of a night like this. He will be easily forgotten.

The door opens timidly, and a maid peers round.

"*Scusi, Signore. Doppo?*"

"*Bongiorno, Editta.*" He waves her in, "*Bongiorno, prega entra.*" Though no sooner has he said so than he realises he'd have been as well to send her away. There's nothing that can't wait. He gathers up his book to leave her to her work.

"*Signore,*" she says hesitantly, "*Madame Maria, lei é sveglia.*"

"She's awake? Thank you! *Grazie, grazie, Editta.*"

The past months Mary has been like a ghost to him, but now that she has skimmed her fingers upon the surface of death he finds her alive, here and real and astonishingly alive.

He walks through the house towards her, unsure if he should run or dawdle. He is frightened of her. Frightened to talk near her, to enforce his troubling self upon her quiet.

Shelley approaches the bedroom door on silent feet and tilts his ear; he pushes open the door only slightly and with the greatest care so it should not creak.

Peering round he sees Mary reclining on the pillows, and Claire sat beside her.

Her face is still ghastly pale, and the whiteness of her lips is disconcerting.

"I heard you were awake," Shelley says.

"She's tired now," Claire responds, very quietly. "I was just telling her she needs to get some sleep."

He creeps across the floor. "Then I won't disturb you, I just wanted to see how you were." He lays a kiss upon Mary's forehead and she smiles. "How are you feeling?"

Mary sways her head a little. "Not feeling spry. But better than I was."

He kisses her again, lets his hand cup her cheek. There is a stale, unpleasant smell to her. She has been bedridden for days and is insufficiently washed. But beneath that is the lovely Mary smell that has become part of his life.

Claire stands, and draws the shutters, encasing the patient in a tranquil half-light.

"Get better," he whispers to Mary and she presses his hand reassuringly as she closes her eyes.

Claire ushers him out.

"She's recovering well enough," she says as she draws the door closed behind her.

"You've been a good nurse," Shelley replies meekly, and falls into a slow saunter down the corridor beside her.

"You haven't."

Her tone isn't cruel, but sharp. He doesn't argue.

"I'm not going to be here long, Shelley," Claire says. "I will of course stay as long as I'm useful to Mary, but then I shall set off on my own."

"You want to go back to Florence?"

"Perhaps that, perhaps somewhere else. But I'm not staying."

So, this really is to be the end of Claire in their lives.

"I'll miss you," he says simply.

For a few seconds Claire does not answer. She turns into the empty parlour and walks to the window only to stop abruptly.

"I will miss you, Shelley. I have missed you terribly. I missed Mary. But when I was working I was in control of my own life, and that was right. I have a little money of my own now. My mother travelled by herself, as did Mary and Fanny's mother, and they both had children in tow. I am unencumbered. I am free. I ought to make use of that."

He follows after her, and takes her plump hands in his own.

"If that is what you desire, then that is what you must do. But, Claire, know that you will always have a home with us when you need it."

"Yes." She clears her throat. "I'm going to go for a walk now. By myself. I think I need some air."

She coughs, retrieves her hands, but still does not quite leave. "I used to wish it was me that you loved," she says, half a laugh in her voice. "Yes. How silly that was." Shaking her head, she leaves him.

He returns to the bedroom, the sheets now crisply turned out by Editta, and falls upon them, crumpling them at once. How long has Claire loved him? When she was sixteen, all those years ago, yes, he knew it then. In Italy, when they became closer than before, he saw something hopeful in her eyes. But he had always taken her love as the love of a friend, and if sometimes kisses were exchanged, the extent was in full accordance with the desires of all concerned, and no heart was left yearning. But it was surely Byron who broke her heart, surely Byron who has been her one great love.

The afternoon fades, he drifts to sleep, and wakes but does not rise, only lies still and unhappy as darkness creeps around him.

Lying on his back he watches the cold beams of sea-reflected moonlight slip in the open window and swirl across the ceiling. His mind wanders with them, as if he is full fathom five beneath the waves.

The pearlescent echoes of the waves trace ambiguous patterns in the air, and he squints and tries to read them, but his ageing eyes are failing. And the images will not keep still, for they ever drift and sway until the very walls are brought alive, swaying and creaking like trees in ancient forests.

The *scirocco* rushes through the house, carrying a pained, hollow wailing. Only slowly does he realise that is the sound of human agony, and everything within him recoils from it. He does not want to ask, does not want to discover what new misfortune has befallen them. Somewhere, someone is calling his name.

He rises slowly, dread weighing him down, slowing his motions. If he could only reach the door! Even that seems impossible.

But now he sees in the doorway Ned and Jane, who he has loved so well, and all across their skin are open wounds, long gashes through which the while of bone is visible. Blisters boil up and burst before his very eyes, flesh peels back to show all the dark web of muscle that make these flimsy creatures. The cruel moonlight shows their falling blood slick and black.

The first, awful instinct is to retch at the sight of them, these half-corpses, who yet stand staring at him with beseeching eyes.

"Get up Shelley," Ned rasps, "the sea is flooding the house." He falls, and Jane crumples with him.

Quite suddenly Shelley realises that the wind is coming in, that sound of the sea is louder and nearer than it has ever been. "It is all coming down, Shelley," Ned groans, and Jane sobs upon his shoulder.

"The sea is flooding the house!" It is Shelley's own voice now that bellows, and he is propelled into motion at last, pushing past Jane and Ned, his heavy feet drawing angry creaks from the floorboards as he staggers through the house—to Mary! He must get her out!

But as he rounds her bedroom door he sees a dark figure bent over the bed where Mary lies sleeping and the waves below them crash with fury. A figure of awful familiarity, the brown hair streaked with grey, the tan coat, and the long white fingers wrapped around Mary's throat. He wants to cry out, to move, to attack, but he is frozen in his horror. Slowly, silently, the other turns his face, his mirror face, to look back at Shelley.

A howl, a loud, terrible, unearthly howl breaks out all around them, shattering the glass, rending the silence and the very air. It wakes Mary and she runs to Shelley, calling his name, but still he can say nothing, his eyes locked upon that other Shelley, and his ears ringing with that awful screaming. He wants to hold fast to her and she, rather than cling to him, runs from him, and stumbles—Oh, she must not go out into the flooded house! She must be warned of the tragedy! Why can he not warn her? He shakes his head, twisting his neck in search of his own voice, and only then realises it is he who has been screaming. His breath is scarcely coming, and before he knows it Ned is before him, clutching his shoulders, dear Ned, unbloodied and unspoiled. Shelley grasps his arms, touches his face.

"Ned?" Shelley gasps.

"Yes, it's me. Be calm." Ned is in his nightshirt. Behind him is Mary's bed, the covers disturbed; no one else is present.

"Who has been here?" Shelley asks.

"Just breathe, breathe, Shelley, it's fine. Everything is fine."

"Who has been here?" Hysteria is rising in him.

"Here? No one. Only Mary. She's on the landing. You scared her. You scared us all, you've been screaming."

Slowly stillness and silence re-enter. Shelley takes in the room. He feels the warmth radiating from Ned's body.

"I saw..." he begins, but will not say it. "Is Mary hurt?"

In the moonlight Ned's face is tinted blue, but his broad face smiles softly.

"I think you frightened her," he says. "She did fall in the hallway, but she seems to be fine. Jane's with her."

Shelley wipes his eyes. They are stinging.

"I didn't hurt her?"

"No, no, I don't believe you did."

"No. Good. Take me to her, Ned?"

She is in the hallway in her white night dress. Jane and Claire are there too, talking in whispers, but Mary is looking in at him. Anxious, but unafraid. He releases his hold on Ned, and lurches towards her, wrapping her in his arms. But she is strong, now she is the rock, and he the drowning sailor.

She sends the others away, assuring them all is well, and leads him back to her bed.

He keeps his arms around her, hides his face in her nightgown.

"Mary," he murmurs, "I've had such terrible dreams lately."

"I know," she whispers.

"I have watched them, unable to interfere, unable to change what was happening. I am afraid, Mary."

"Hush! Sleep now, my poor Shelley."

And she lies down beside him, closes her eyes. He does not sleep at once, but lies there, his hand holding hers, watching her sleep, guarding her from his nightmares.

Chapter Eight: Reverdie
La Spezzia, 1st July 1822

*L*ying on a low couch in the morning room, Mary torments herself by imagining entertaining scenes she will not witness. The morning has dawned bright and fair. Today Shelley will sail for Pisa.

Hunt has arrived from England with his family, and Byron is in Pisa, patient for now; all the pieces of the grand scheme are in place and it only remains for Shelley to go, to introduce the great men and start the project, and a magazine will be born, a magazine that cannot fail to bring a liberal readership and success.

"Alright, Mary," Shelley says as he comes in. "Ned and I are ready to leave." He kneels by the couch and kisses her. "You rest, now. I shall be back in perhaps a week. I'll write and keep you updated. Will you be better by then?"

He asks fondly, teasingly, but the depressed, languorous mood has recaptured her this morning.

"I might be dead," she mutters.

"Don't talk like that," he says, and looks away from her with an unhappy glower.

"No. I've been cheated of my death. And cheated of my life! Go on, go, enjoy life. See Byron, see Hunt, write your magazine."

"Mary!" his tone is reprimanding. "Don't. You know I wanted you to come. The Hunts will be very disappointed to miss you. But you'll be better soon, and you can come to Pisa the next time. Won't you, Mary? You do have to want to get better, you know."

"It doesn't make much difference what I want. A new tragedy

shall befall us every year. I wonder if the miscarriage of an unborn child is enough to satisfy whatever mischief has cursed us. Go on, go."

Shelley hesitates, opens his mouth but closes it again, and, standing, puts on his hat.

Only at the door he pauses, and says, "Don't be melancholy, Mary. It helps no one, and hurts most of all, I believe, yourself."

Alone, she closes her eyes and draws the shawl around her. She bites her lip and tries not to feel hatred, not for Shelley, not for herself.

Shouts reach her from the beach, Jane's "Cheerio!" and laughter cutting above the sailor's back and forth. A seagull yells, setting off a chain of cries from its fellows. The relentless sigh of the sea.

Mary breathes.

Her eyes flutter open.

Sunlight pours through the open doorway, casting a living, ever-shifting mosaic of sea-reflections.

An orb of light races across the room, the reflection from something shining outside. It speeds across the walls, and then disappears abruptly.

In the vivid sunlight tiny flecks of dust drift regretfully, their minute bodies vividly outlined. Watching them, Mary becomes aware even of her eyelashes at the periphery of her vision, painted like golden flame by the gorgeous sun.

A shadow blocks the light, passes through it, returns, and Mary looks up to see the silhouette of Shelley in the doorway. With the light behind him Mary cannot make out his features.

"I really don't want to leave you, Mary," he says.

She could cry. The moment of peace repents her of her words.

"I don't want you to go," she replies.

"I suppose I must, though."

"I suppose so."

Yet still he hesitates, something unsaid anchoring him. Mary tries to make out his expression, but he is half consumed by the sunlight. Only the edges of him are clear, the strands of his hair, the creases at the elbow of his coat.

"I am sorry," he says at length. "Things aren't as I wanted them to be for us." The orb of light returns, crosses the room, and disappears once more. In this quiet of sunlight, Mary can hear his heartbeat. "I have always acted as best I could," he says. "I never intended you the least unhappiness, but that seems to be all I've caused you."

She wants to rise, to embrace him, but cannot stir from her couch. She is leaden, forced to witness and not act.

"You were extraordinary, Mary," he says. "You were sixteen and brilliant, more intelligent than anyone I had ever met. You were such a magnificent creature to behold... but perhaps I did wrong to take you from your home. There was probably a happier life designed for you."

With great effort Mary summons her voice.

"Do you think I had no choice?" Mary replies. "You do not get to take credit for all that has happened in my life." She speaks softly, for she can feel the vulnerability, the fragility of him. "I made my choice, and it was you, Shelley. It is a choice I have made over and over again these past seven years. And it is a choice I will continue to make." As she reaches for him a stab of pain makes her wince, but he has turned his head away, looking back out to the sea.

"I cannot stay, my love," he says. "But rest, and take the comfort that you can. I will be with you again."

And he must have left for the sunlight floods full in once more, and all Mary can see is the drifting dust and her own eyelashes, wet with tears.

"I will always choose you, Shelley," she murmurs to the place where the shadow so lately was, but Shelley is gone, borne away on the waves.

Chapter Nine: The Sea
Bay of Spezia, 8ᵗʰ July 1822

*T*his storm will end all storms.

This ocean, born of an eternity of weeping, rises sharp as the fell peaks of mountains come alive and plunge into ever-shifting valleys.

Even the air is ocean, for the rain flows thick and Shelley—alone at the end of all—feels the water pour down his arms, his chest, his body, and in rivulets carries away all that he has been.

It is a storm that will end all storms.

Ned is already gone. Swept away on the wave that broke the mast. The boy Vivien who assisted them lasted a moment longer, shouting and kicking off his boots, ready to swim, but when the wave that drenched the deck-top in its suffocating rush had drained, Vivien too was gone. And Shelley is the last, alone.

Amid the tempest's turbulence he is thrown about so that his feet and head know no more of up nor down. The sea rears ahead and behind, above and below. The boat forgets its purpose and cradles a shock of rocking water upon its deck.

Although Shelley's body is battered about, although his limbs shake at their impermanence, in the very kernel of himself he is calm, and recognises only regret.

From Pisa he had dashed off a note to Mary that said nothing at all, fool that he is. But she will know, won't she? She will know, after everything, what he would say in this moment.

And Claire, Claire will be well; she must make her own way at last.

But Byron, Hunt, and Trelawny are all left in Pisa, their great project ready at last. And now Shelley must leave this world, just as *The Liberal* is ready to grow, to deliver his words to a waiting world. Perhaps it is best he will not be around to witness the world's indifference.

The wind whips up, dragging its weight about him in close, insistent circles, as if he were the heart of its centrifugal motion.

Upon the gusts dance leaves—leaves even here on the open ocean—leaves ancient and skeletal, leaves crinkled and discoloured, leaves red and streaked with autumn gold. There are words upon the leaves, words like seeds full of potency. Even in this moment of crisis he can ask what brings leaves here, to swarm around him, fast and free. They seem to whisper, to offer promise of the world that will not die, of the ages that will live on, though he is gone.

Water runs down his face, his arms, his entire body. Sometimes the water fills even his eyes, and gives him a glimpse once more of another world, a world he glimpsed before, and will now know fully.

Beneath his feet the deck tilts, and he instinctively shifts his weight to accommodate it, to stay standing to the last. This is the draw back before the release, and he knows the moments are finite.

Mary! If he could but clasp her to his breast now he would leave without regret. In leaving, he will make her suffer. Oh Mary! Do not sink into the waves. Trust to Percy, for only Percy will keep you from the sea.

As the water runs in rivulets down his arms he feels the burden of earthly chains falling away, and tears fall from his eyes, as if the water in himself is reaching out for the water all around, beginning the metamorphosis.

Larger, larger the wave looms behind him, and he can feel it drawing high a wall between himself and everything that he has ever had, has ever loved.

But no, are there not shapes in the water? Do the waves not beckon with familiar faces, with the voices of the great and good, with the cries of his beloved children?

Do not the leaves that fly through the air, so swift they slip between the rain, sing now songs of all that will be, do they not amongst them form a shape, so like Shelley, so like the child that he has been, slim and wild-haired and bright-eyed, so full of love.

All at once an extraordinary streak of brilliant light pierces the clouds, the rain, even the ocean, illuminating the waves with the most gorgeous cerulean blue and clouded heavens with an ethereal silver that sings.

He feels the breath of the wave now, tearing against the wind, and raising his eyes to that light he sees the moon large and gloriously bright and his heart aches for the pained beauty he must leave behind. Suffering is for the living.

An extraordinary weight slams against him, crushing every thought, every breath. The boards of the deck shatter with his bones, and he is borne deep, further and further down through the fathoms of the ocean and into the Elysian fields beyond.

Ah! he is gone – and I alone;
How dark and dreary seems the time!
'Tis Thus, when the glad sun is flown,
Night rushes o'er the Indian clime.
Is there no star to cheer this night,
No soothing twilight for the breast?
Yes, Memory sheds her fairy light,
Pleasing as sunset's golden west.
And hope of dawn – Oh! brighter far
Than clouds that in the orient burn;
More welcome than the morning star
Is the dear thought – he will return!

Mary W. Shelley

Epilogue: Mary After Shelley
Kentish Town, 30th November 1823

November brings a bleak, pale winter to London. A murky fog lies low in the city streets with no breath of wind to disturb it. The intermittent sounds of trundling carts and whispering pedestrians are dampened in the still air, and echo peculiarly around the two young widows who walk together, arm-in-arm.

Mary Wollstonecraft Shelley still wears black. She has no intention of shedding her mourning though a full year has turned; grief has become her disposition. But this winter Jane Williams has chosen a muted purple for her jacket, and the roses in her cheeks cannot help but bloom. It is pleasant, Mary thinks, to have such a companion, in the absence of that other and she presses Jane's hand through their gloves.

"Did you hear that?" Jane says, grinning at her.

Having been very much in her own mind, Mary had heard nothing, and she shakes her head, looking about her for the matter referred to.

"The two gentlemen who just passed us," Jane continues. "They were discussing *Frankenstein*."

"Were they?" Mary says, quite bewildered. The street is fairly quiet, only a few people in sight about their private business, and she easily picks out the gentlemen in question, walking away at a leisurely pace. "What did they say?"

"They said the play had nothing of the novel's brilliance. *Brilliance* was the word used." Jane looks pleased with herself. "I quite fancy running after them and telling them the author of that brilliance is right here. Should I?"

She makes a step away, as if to go, but looks back at Mary.

"Oh, don't! Jane, for goodness sake!"

And Jane laughs, taking her arm once more. "You ought to be proud."

"Pride has nothing to do with it. Come along, the boys will be finished with their tutor soon."

"It is marvellous though, we should go to the theatre and see it again."

"Don't be silly, Jane."

"I'm not. We deserve some amusement, and what better? We should do something nice with the children tomorrow, perhaps we could all have a picnic?"

"Yes, let's do that instead."

They turn for home as the daylight seeps from the sky, though it is still only afternoon. Jane is placated by the idea of a picnic, and makes plans for it as they walk, to all of which Mary mildly agrees.

Her thoughts are taken up with other picnics, times that seem so long ago. Shelley setting fire to paper boats on Hampstead Heath, his slender profile illuminated by the flames, his irrepressible smile, and big, curious eyes that shine with fire of their own. There will never more be nights like those.

There is a new life now, a life with Jane, of passions she had not considered, and comfort in their children. From the tutor's house they collect Percy Florence and Medwin, and Mary ensures that Percy is wrapped up as they walk home. He relates his lessons to her with care but not imagination. At four years old he has the round blue eyes and slim face, but does not look as much like his father as William did. He is a good boy and a hard worker. If sometimes he does not think for himself, but thinks instead like other people, Mary is quietly relieved.

The sky has entirely darkened by the time they get home, and Mary sees her son to bed and takes herself to her study. Despite the chill, she opens the window, but it is eerily silent. The cry of the aziola, the hum of cicada, the soft sigh of the wind through the ilex are all left behind in Italy.

On the desk a letter from Claire lies unanswered. This latest epistle is from Vienna, and speaks of plans to go to Moscow. The letter from Byron that is propped up on her shelves is months old now, is replied and long due a successor, but he is in Greece to support the uprising, and ready to go to war. She fears for his safety.

Beside the desk are boxes.

Boxes of Shelley.

His letters. His notebooks. His poems. His drawings. His smallest scribblings. They mean more to her than the oak box in which his heart, rescued from the flames that consumed his ocean-bloated body, is preserved for her. This last remnant of his flesh says nothing, when the piles pages will speak quite suddenly in his own beautiful voice.

From one box she takes a notebook, and selects some paper for fair-copying. This is her nightly task, transcribing the words he wrote, winnowing through the notes, accounts, and drawings of boats to the poetry. All these words, unread, would be a grief to him who thought that poetry unread was wasted ink. So, she works, tirelessly, preparing them for publication, omitting the fiery phrases that might dissuade a publisher.

A breath of air slips in and touches, gently, her cheek and hair. It stirs around the papers on her desk, shifting Shelley's words beneath her fingers.

Evening becomes night. After several hours of work, she lays Shelley's poetry aside and takes up instead the novel she is working on. It is a vast piece, a plague narrative of suffering and loss, and most particularly of the pain of being the only one left behind. She will call it *The Last Man.* If she is honest with herself, she has some hopes for it. She must, after all, think of the future. She has Percy Florence to raise, and hopes to brook a truce with Sir Timothy Shelley, enough for him to fund his grandson's education. She has her own father to care for. She has Jane, and a new kind of love. She has hopes to soon meet, for the first time as an adult, the great poet Coleridge, and speak with him as a peer. Yes, she thinks to herself, she has much work to do for the future.

The End

Author's Note

This novel grew from a desire to read a book that did not exist. In 2008, I began my undergraduate degree with a love of Percy Bysshe Shelley, and shortly afterward was introduced to the works of Mary Shelley. The realisation that works such as *Frankenstein* and the famous Mont Blanc poem "Lines Written in the Vale of Chamount" were written at the same time and in the same household prompted a multitude of questions. I wanted to know the level of discussion and collaboration that existed between the two Shelleys and immediately began looking for a book that could enlighten me. But it was not easy to find. At the time there was little critical material comparing the works of the two Shelleys, and even the biographical studies that necessarily had to include both leant towards their singular subject with such bias as to provide very little study of the other.

Where I did find the Shelleys juxtaposed was in dramatic retellings of their lives, in film, on stage, and in biographical novels. I was frustrated to see there too depictions often 'sided' with one Shelley or the other, and as I began to do independent research on the Shelleys' lives, I realised that the majority of these depictions were not merely inaccurate but insufficient tellings of an extraordinary story.

I attended a talk by Shelley biographer Richard Holmes, and took an opportunity afterwards to ask if he had any recommendations to better learn about this illustrious relationship. He replied that there wasn't a good book about the pair of them, but that someone really ought to write one, and kindly added, "perhaps you should do it."

I started an English Literature PhD in which I tracked the collaborative element of the Shelleys' writing process. Principally looking at manuscripts, letters, and journals, I analysed the many times the Shelleys had collaborated, and sought patterns in their work that could suggest their off-page conversations.

Part way through the process I realised, prompted by a fellow post-graduate student, that I had the wrong final goal for my study. My first love has always been fiction, and I was treating the thesis I was writing as a stepping-stone to the novel I wished to write. After some discussion with my supervisory team I was able to transfer the focus of my research: everything I had learned so far would be expressed in a novel, alongside an essay presenting a theory of historical fiction.

I studied a huge amount of biographical fiction, observing what I did and did not want to emulate. Biographical fiction, I maintained in my essay, should observe the same ethical duty as history. Authors become educators, and if they are to diverge from the historical record, they should make clear where they are doing so.

For my own novel, I'd started it with the desire to tell a story, and had no interest in diverging from the facts. While for a long time the approach to biographical fiction has been to take historical fact as a starting point but to answer foremost to the demands of fiction, I have sought to present a novel that respects absolutely the historical record. Of course, historical record is not a stable and certain thing, and I have had to consider my sources carefully, returning to primary material wherever possible to construct my own understanding of past events. Some sources, such as Claire Clairmont's late recollections, I have largely dismissed as unreliable. Once I had satisfied myself with an outline of historical facts, I had to consider my selection and interpretation of said facts.

My primary sources have been the letters and journals of the Shelleys and their friends, with frequent recourse to the many excellent biographies and academic studies. Whenever I have quoted letters or poems, I have tried to use the original documents verbatim, only editing to remove elements not pertinent to the narrative. Where no letter remains I have adapted from other texts; for instance, Fanny Godwin's final letter to the Shelleys is no longer extant, so I have adapted from the letter she sent to the Godwins at the same time. The poetic dialogues between each part are entirely my own.

Of course, there are gaps and details I've needed to use invention to fill; the historical novelist must speculate on dialogue and gesture and a thousand minute details the historian never touches on. I have spent enough time in academia, enough hours reading countless biographies, to know that no two interpretations of the historical record are ever the same. In telling the Shelleys' story there has inevitably been selection and interpretation, and I know the version of the story I put forward will bear traces of my own view point. While many recent interpretations of the Shelleys have shown them as antagonistic towards each other, I am fascinated by the collaborative element of their relationship, and see their pairing as a complex one with many joys and pains.

I wanted to write the story of two incredible people involved in a remarkable relationship, so I have strictly limited my story to the years Mary and Shelley spent together. My next project is *Mary After Shelley*, a novel of Mary's most unusual life after her husband's death, a story of false identities, forbidden loves, and a woman alone doing whatever it takes to protect her son.

Acknowledgments

No creative exists in isolation, and I have been helped by a great many kind influences.

This work builds on two hundred years of Shelley scholarship, and I am grateful to all those scholars and biographers who have shared their research on Percy Bysshe Shelley, Mary Wollstonecraft Shelley, and their circle. I wish to thank Dr. Bruce Barker-Benfield and the Bodleian Library for granting me access to manuscripts of the Shelleys during my research.

I owe much to my PhD supervisors and examiners, and everyone within the English and Creative Writing departments at St Mary's University during my research who provided support.

Two special thanks are due to Dr. Russell Schechter and Dr. Peter Howell for their unwavering support, insightful guidance, and generous kindness to me.

Also, I am very grateful to Michael Rossington for acting as my external supervisor and staying with my project as it changed shape.

I have been lucky enough to share my work with writers groups and creative forums, and am grateful to everyone who has provided feedback, suggestions, or guidance in the writing and publishing of this novel, especially Joel Bradley, Christine Demack, Anne Fontaine, Nick Gifford, Katie Haworth, Sarah Kirwan, Lena Moser, Sarah Nelson, Kieran Rayner, Clare Rees, Stephanie Smith, and Robbie Westacott.

Particular thanks to Colin Mustful of History Through Fiction for believing in this book and being an excellent editor.

Full of gratitude to my devoted friends Hannah Morey and Cameron Touchard for their support.

And of course, my Evelyn, thank you for everything.

About the Author

Born in Scotland and now living in London, Dr. Ezra Harker Shaw is a non-binary writer who loves all things Gothic. While earning their PhD, Harker Shaw explored the collaborative writing of Percy Byssche Shelley and Mary Shelley, a project that led them to write *The Aziola's Cry*. A celebrated performance poet, Harker Shaw regularly hosts poetry nights in London and was nominated for the Outspoken Prize for Poetry. Harker Shaw has also showcased their talent as a playwright with works such as *Tolstoy Tried to Kill My Partner* and *The Grouchy Octopus Story*, both of which were performed in London by the esteemed Pajoda Theatre Co. Possessing a profound passion for teaching, Harker Shaw often conducts university lectures and workshops with aspiring young writers. To further inspire and educate others, Harker Shaw hosts the *Meliorist Writes Podcast*, where they provide valuable writing tips and engage in insightful interviews with fellow creatives.

Other Books by History Through Fiction

South of Sepharad: The 1492 Jewish Expulsion from Spain
By Eric Z. Weintraub

Reclaiming Mni Sota: An Alternate History of the U.S. – Dakota War of 1862
By Colin Mustful

A Noble Cunning: The Countess and the Tower
By Patricia Bernstein

The Education of Delhomme: Chopin, Sand, & La France
By Nancy Burkhalter

The Sky Worshipers: A Novel of Mongol Conquests
By FM Deemyad

The King's Anatomist: The Journey of Andreas Vesalius
By Ron Blumenfeld

My Mother's Secret: A Novel of the Jewish Autonomous Region
By Alina Adams

If you enjoyed this novel please consider leaving a review. You'll be supporting a small, independent press, and you'll be helping other readers discover this great story.
Thank you!

www.HistoryThroughFiction.com

Milton Keynes UK
Ingram Content Group UK Ltd.
UKHW012205190124
436354UK00003B/38